Beneath
the
Surface

Jo Spain has worked as a journalist and a party advisor on the economy in the Irish parliament. Her first novel, *With Our Blessing*, was shortlisted for the Richard and Judy 'Search for a Bestseller' competition and became a top-ten bestseller in Ireland. Jo lives in Dublin with her husband and their four young children.

Beneath the Surface

AN INSPECTOR TOM REYNOLDS MYSTERY

JO SPAIN

Quercus

First published in Great Britain in 2016 by

Quercus Editions Ltd
Carmelite House
50 Victoria Embankment
London EC4Y 0DZ

An Hachette UK company

A CIP catalogue record for this book is available
from the British Library

TPB ISBN 978 1 78429 927 9
EBOOK ISBN 978 1 78429 318 5

10 9 8 7 6 5 4 3 2

Typeset by Jouve (UK), Milton Keynes

Printed and bound in Great Britain by Clays Ltd, St Ives plc

For Isobel, Liam, Sophia and Dominic

GLOSSARY

Glossary of Irish language (Gaeilge) terms

Dáil Éireann – The lower (main) house of the Irish parliament
Seanad Éireann – The Irish parliament's upper house
Oireachtas – The combined houses of the Irish parliament
An Taoiseach – The Prime Minister
Teachta(í) Dála – Member(s) of Parliament
A Chara – Dear Friend

AUTHOR'S NOTE

This book is fictional. The story is an invention of my imagination and not intended to resemble any real-life people or places.

PROLOGUE

The Death

I am going to die.

I know this as surely as I know I don't want to.

I can't bear it. I cannot stand the thought of leaving my girls, of not seeing them again.

Kathryn will never recover. We have defied the odds of so many married couples and are as much in love as the day we met. Sweet, beautiful, funny Kathryn.

And Beth. Oh, my little baby girl. The newness and perfection of her skin. The smell of her soft hair. Her little pudgy hand clasping my finger like she'll never let go. She's part of me, but she'll never know me. People will tell her I loved her but she will never understand how much. She won't know the almost physical pain I felt when she was born, so overwhelming was my love for her. I couldn't speak when I held Beth for the first time, the lump in my throat was so large. Kathryn laughed. She'd never seen me cry before and it was because I was so happy.

I'm crying now.

Did I know it would come to this? Why didn't I realise that I was playing Russian roulette not just with my own future, but with my family's too?

I fall forward into the cold arms of the angel. The images fall from my hands, scattering across the floor.

My leverage and my downfall.

How little they mean now.

I would give anything to turn back time and be with my girls, to take them in my arms and squeeze them tight, my heart exploding with love.

Because too late, I know that's all that matters.

My body writhes in agony as I try to turn my head.

I want to look my executioner in the eye. Who is this person who will steal everything from me?

My punishment is cruel. My threat was to a career, not a life. This is not fair.

I will beg. I will wail and I will plead and maybe God will intervene. He will forgive my naivety, my arrogance. This angel will carry me not to Heaven but to help, and I will fight to live. I will fight for them, Kathryn and Beth.

But all hope of salvation evaporates as I behold my attacker.

My mouth struggles to form the word.

It's not 'Please'. It's not 'Stop'.

It's . . . 'Why?'

And then I see it, but I don't see it. The end.

There's no shot at redemption.

I am going to die.

The gun is in my eyeline as the second bullet is fired.

That's the one that kills me.

The Deal

'Is it done?'

'We've been over this. I will deliver my end of the deal.'

A magnificent old grandfather clock chimes imperiously from the corner of the room, marking the late evening hour. All else is quiet. Other parts of the sprawling building are still busy, people going about their business, unaware of the presence of the two men and the nature of their conversation.

The atmosphere between them is tense, oppressive even.

The businessman stands and pours himself a second brandy from a crystal decanter. The drink has little effect on him. He is used to consuming everything to excess.

He wasn't always this way. As a child he was neither the eldest – chastised and disciplined as the first always is – nor the youngest – coddled and worshipped, forever basking in the love of multiple older family members. The businessman had been a quiet middle child, generally ignored. Some would say he went on to achieve so much because he craved attention. They would be wrong. He discovered early that he enjoyed the rewards of success, not its spotlight.

He holds the decanter's stopper up to the low-hanging chandelier. The light casts brilliant illuminations through the prism of the perfectly cut glass, multicoloured diamonds that dance over bookshelves heaving with a gloriously eclectic mix of modern and dated texts. He drops the stopper carelessly on the mahogany drinks cabinet and brings the brandy glass to his lips, inhaling as the spirit wets his mouth and hits the back of his throat. A Hennessy Cognac Paradis. Excellent, but far from the best. Presumably the taxpayers' euro can stretch to mid-range luxury, but not premium.

'I asked you, is it done?' The businessman's tone is crisp, sharp, insistent.

The seated man smiles coolly and tries to appear at ease, though the slight trembling of his right hand says otherwise.

'Look. Have I given you any cause for concern so far? Everything is in hand. I foresee no issues, but don't underestimate what I am trying to do here. Do you know what would happen if this was leaked and spun in a certain way? If people knew what you and I were doing and I lost control of the story? We're not just talking about the fall of a ministry. This could bring down the government.'

The businessman doesn't respond immediately. He tilts the

liquid in the glass, observing its colour with interest. A mellow, honey-golden hue.

'Don't be so dramatic,' he says dismissively. 'Governments come and go. Business carries on regardless.'

'I don't think it is being dramatic to point out that you stand to lose millions if this doesn't go to plan. Another government might not be so . . . sympathetic.'

'I've yet to see the proof of your sympathies. Your administration has been in office for nine months, but still my company is the subject of negative publicity. I was promised that our operations would be allowed to run smoothly. Why is it taking so long?'

The man he addresses tries to suppress an eye tic that is threatening to manifest itself. A symptom of fatigue, it will betray weakness. No doubt the tremor in his hand has already been noted with concern.

The shaking isn't, in fact, related to any stress.

He had let the businessman pour him a glass of the brandy. Five years, three months and twelve days dry. This is a test. He won't drink the alcohol, but oh, the temptation! It's always there, tap, tap, tapping – a neverending battle of will versus desire. And at times like this, when he's at his lowest, the struggle is tremendous.

'In a week or so, the new law will be brought before the House and passed quickly,' he says. 'Everything is going to plan and if any unexpected *minor* issues arise, they will be dealt with. Immediately.'

In that moment, the urge to down the whole decanter of brandy almost conquers the seated man.

Because there is a complication – one so unexpected, he was taken completely unawares when it was dumped in his lap just days ago.

He could do without the crisis, this meeting. His personal life is imploding. He could be about to lose the one person who means everything in the world to him and the businessman and his demands just don't seem as important as they once did.

The man buries a sigh. He is being forced to neglect his own affairs for the moment. This new obstacle to the businessman's plans will be overcome. No matter what it takes. He hasn't worked so hard for so long and neglected all else for nothing.

Of that much, he is sure.

The other man is studying him with frightening intensity. It makes the seated man feel naked. No, worse. Transparent.

'I hope so,' the businessman says at last. 'Because if you can't ensure I get what I want, I will use somebody who can. Am I making myself clear?'

The seated man looks into his glass of golden liquor, its heady, sweet scent filling his nostrils, enticing him. He picks it up. His hand is sweating and his palm almost slips on the ornate indentations.

'Crystal,' he replies.

The clock continues to tick, counting down the seconds to murder.

The Hunt

60, 59, 58, 57 . . .

The man marks the passing minute, his fingers drumming the desk, body tense, breathing fast. The printer whirrs behind him, disgorging the images he needs at a snail's pace. When it pauses to calibrate, his heart almost stops too, with the sudden realisation that a ridiculous, unplanned technical glitch could put everything on hold.

50, 49, 48, 47 . . .

He's almost there. An empty cardboard folder lies open, waiting for its bounty. The last image of the collection is still on the computer screen and it catches the man's eye. He feels ashamed, embarrassed, his stomach knotting with revulsion at his plan.

He starts downloading the images onto the USB stick in the side of the machine.

35, 34, 33, 32 . . .

The penultimate page slides onto the printer tray. Just a few seconds more and he'll have the complete set.

That's when he hears it. The unmistakable hum of the elevator at the end of the hall. He freezes as the drone ceases. The lift has reached its destination and the door is opening. On this floor.

There's no time to lose. He doesn't want to be discovered and he senses danger. He rushes to stand, knocking a precariously balanced pile of papers to the floor.

'Shit!'

The word escapes him involuntarily and – thankfully – quietly. The man grabs the material from the printer and shoves it into the folder. Every inch of his body is taut with stress.

There it is – the soft click of a door being opened in the distance. A few moments pass, then the sound of another door opening, a little closer. He doesn't know how it came to pass, but he knows in his gut that this person is looking for him.

Each office along the hallway is being checked systematically. That gives him a chance to think.

He tries to plan his escape. This is the second-to-last room. The double doors at his end of the corridor are locked; he can't use the stairs that way. He has to exit the way he came in and that is towards whoever is in the hallway now.

The solution is so simple and yet it almost doesn't occur to him. This office has a connecting door to the neighbouring office, which, presumably, the searcher will reach first. As the person moves towards this office, the man can slip into the adjacent room and, from there, out to the hall. If he is indeed being pursued, he can make a run for it. Hopefully his weak leg won't betray him. He hasn't done any serious exercise since the accident, but adrenaline will surely carry him for the next few minutes. He can already feel it pumping through his veins.

He clutches the folder to his chest as the door to the neighbouring office is opened. He waits a few seconds until he gauges the other person is satisfied the room next door is empty, then launches his evasive manoeuvre.

He misjudges it by a hair's breadth. The hunter is moving faster than he had estimated. The door to the man's office opens just as he is moving into the adjoining room.

A blurred figure rushes at him, bearing nothing but ill will and threat. Panicking, the man slams the shared office door into his pursuer and flees. He barrels out into the carpeted hall, hurtling down its length as fast as his weakened body will allow, grasping the folder so tightly his fingers have turned white.

He reaches the lifts. One is out of order; he'd seen that when he came up. The second must have waited momentarily before returning to its station on the ground floor. It will take too long to summon back.

The man makes a snap decision. He crashes through the fire doors to the stairwell and descends, two steps at a time.

That haste on the stairs is his second mistake. A couple of flights down, his bad leg buckles and he tumbles six steps. He lies on the landing between floors, winded but intact. He's cut his hand on a splinter from the banister, but he can barely feel the sting. He is there just long enough to hear the fire doors open again two floors above.

He has to move.

He pulls himself up painfully and continues running. He doesn't look back, doesn't want to see what is behind him.

The man emerges into the building's open-plan coffee dock. Nearly there. He has his swipe card for the underground tunnel at the ready. Once through those doors, he only has to run a couple of hundred metres and he will be back in the populated part of the building. Or should he go up – to the main level? He doesn't have to return the way he came. Are the doors upstairs locked yet? Might there be an usher present?

He can't think straight.

In fact, what had he been thinking? Why had he taken the risk? Because he hadn't understood the danger.

Now, the consequences of his actions are terrifyingly clear.

The tunnel doors are open, held in place by two fire extinguishers that weren't there earlier. He doesn't stop to think what that means but keeps running as fast as his feeble, treacherous body will allow.

The statue looms large in front of him – the beautiful stone angel that always seems curiously out of place in this lonely, functional corridor.

The man knows his hunter has gained on him. The hairs on the back of his neck are standing on end.

If asked earlier, he would have brazenly declared that the folder of pictures would only be relinquished if it were prised from his cold, dead hands. He would carry his plan through, no matter what. Now, he wants to fling the images away, screaming: 'Here, take them, leave me in peace!'

The man is in front of the statue when he hears a muted popping sound and feels a searing white heat. The pain tears through his body, paralyzing his legs, his back, his arms.

But not his mind. He is aware of everything. In this instant, the man knows exactly how much he has left to chance and what he is about to lose.

He is pitched forward into the outstretched arms of the seated angel. The folder falls from his splayed fingers, its incriminating contents spilling onto the floor.

In his agony, the man twists his body to see his assailant.

His eyes widen, his mouth opening and closing soundlessly as he tries to speak.

'Why?'

This is the sole word he manages to utter before his killer raises the weapon and fires the second bullet, this time aimed at the head.

Blood explodes across the green stone angel and the red wall behind it. The man's body slumps. He is dead in that instant.

The hunter lowers the gun. There is a moment's reflection. Then, stepping around the blood seeping onto the granite-coloured tiles, the murderer approaches the body, leans down and gathers up the fallen pages.

Job done, the killer turns and runs back to the lift, returning to the office and the computer with the abandoned USB stick.

The only sound in the hall is the slow, steady drip-drip of blood forming a pool on the floor, reflected in the dead man's remaining eye.

Trapped between his body and the sculpture is one of the pictures that set the events of the last few minutes in motion.

An image that landed beneath the victim as he fell.

A page the killer has missed.

CHAPTER 1

The Investigation
Friday, 11.30 p.m., Dublin

Well, that had been a total and utter disaster.

Detective Sergeant Ray Lennon closed his eyes and raised his face to the hot shower, letting the spray wash away the stress of the evening. The warmth surged through his stiff joints, chilled on the walk home in the fine autumn rain.

He lathered soap onto his chest and stomach, conscious of his changing body. He'd lost weight recently. He was exercising too much and eating too little but the physical activity served as a distraction from the anxiety he'd carried for the last year.

Ray hadn't wanted to go on the date in the first place but Michael Geoghegan had forced his hand. Motivated by his own domestic bliss, his detective colleague was on some sort of mission to rid the world of singletons. Ray was his latest victim. Michael and his wife Anne were meant to have made up a foursome with Ray and a single friend of Anne's, but at the last minute they had begged off.

Emotional blackmail and a sense of duty saw Ray standing alone outside the restaurant at 7.55 p.m., waiting for his 'blind' date.

She had offered little apology for arriving a full half-hour late, was rude to the waitress taking their coats (unforgivable), and then clicked her fingers for the wine list before ordering the most expensive bottle on the menu. Ray wasn't usually a food snob, but by the time she'd demanded that her thirty-five euro prime fillet steak be 'cremated if possible, I don't want it mooing at me', he was ready to join forces with the beleagured waiting staff, should they decide to turf her out. She was an attractive woman, but brought nothing, literally, to the table – not manners, not humour, not even an offer to share the bill.

He'd give Michael an earful in the morning. Regardless of Ray's lonely heart status, that girl was single for a reason. And no, he was not too fussy. Or still hung up on . . . well, he didn't want to go there.

Fair enough, he knew he was struggling to get back on the dating scene. But he just hadn't met a woman recently who appealed to him, on any level.

An unbidden image of DS Laura Brennan, one of his colleagues, surfaced. She always made him smile and he could relax in her company.

But, no. She was a workmate. He wouldn't be going there again.

Not after what had happened last year.

He reached for the shampoo. Pointless, really. It slid off his dark buzz cut as soon as it was applied. As he shook water from his ears he realised the phone was ringing in his bedroom.

Ray felt his heart sink. It was nearly midnight. That shrill repetition could only mean one thing. Work.

He flicked off the shower and grabbed a towel.

Everything had been relatively quiet for the past couple of days and the team had been grateful for it. Detective Inspector Tom Reynolds, Ray's boss, was on a well-earned and much-needed break with his wife and had told them, under pain of death, not to contact him for the long weekend. They were only twenty-four hours in.

Ray entered the bedroom, acknowledging mournfully the lonely, unruffled double bed. He didn't want to think about how long it had been since anybody had shared it with him.

His night was about to get worse. Flashing on the screen was the personal mobile number of Detective Chief Superintendent Sean McGuinness, head of the National Bureau of Criminal Investigation. The Bureau contained numerous specialist teams dedicated to investigating serious crime, among them the murder squad, led by Tom Reynolds.

Ray composed himself before greeting the chief in a tone that made it sound like he was still at his desk, a busy Friday-night martyr, as opposed to standing in his bedroom, dripping wet and naked bar a towel.

'Ah. There you are. I suspected when you didn't answer immediately that you might have a lady friend with you. It being the weekend.'

McGuinness's thick County Kerry accent voice boomed down the phone.

'Well, eh, I'm actually just . . .' Ray started.

'Don't try to convince me you've company, son – I've a car sitting outside your apartment the last ten minutes. You should consider getting drapes. Willie Callaghan can see right in.'

Ray's jaw dropped as he peered through the Venetian blinds of his ground-floor apartment, blinds he'd neglected to close. On the other side of the green patch that faced the apartment block, he could see the car. He tightened the towel at the waist, blushing furiously. Bloody perverts.

'What can I do you for, sir?'

'Right, all joking aside. This is serious, lad. I need you to get hold of Tom for me.'

'But he's . . .'

'I know. And his phone is off. I want you to go to the hotel he's staying in and fetch him. I'd go myself, but I'm afraid of his wife.'

'Can I not deal with whatever it is myself?' he pleaded, in vain hope.

McGuinness paused before answering, his voice low and grave.

'No. Get Tom, then both of you go to Leinster House. I'm on my way there now. Pick two presentable members of your team and send them over to meet me.'

Ray drew a sharp breath.

Leinster House was the seat of the national parliament, *Dáil Éireann*.

'Couldn't we just ring the hotel?'

'I tried that, Detective. They wouldn't put me through. Even after I used the "do you know who I am" line. I don't know what this country is coming to. You need to go there and flash your badge.'

'Okay. Can I ask . . . ?'

'Best wait until you get to Leinster House. Tell Tom I'm sorry, but this is unprecedented. He has to come in.'

McGuinness hung up.

Ray still had the phone to his ear, his head spinning.

Had somebody just been murdered in the Irish parliament?

CHAPTER 2

Saturday, 12.30 a.m., Wicklow

This is the life.

Detective Inspector Tom Reynolds was sitting on his hotel room balcony, admiring the stunning Wicklow landscape. Bathed only in moonlight, the rolling woods and fields were still delivering beautifully on their county's moniker – 'The Garden of Ireland'.

He zipped his fleece jacket up to the neck to ward off the cold nip of the breeze and took another pull on his cigar. He wouldn't stay out much longer. It had been an unusually mild autumn so far, but the temperature was starting to dip as the evenings drew in and it had rained most of today. At forty-nine, Tom was still relatively hale and hearty, but in recent years he'd noticed a sneaking creak in his joints, the hint of weakness in his knees. He had become more susceptible to colds and bugs and hated leaving his warm bed in the morning more than ever.

It wasn't lost on him that his body had begun to betray him at precisely the same time his jet-black hair had turned salt and pepper. Maybe it was nature's way of telling him everything reverted to dust and ash in the end. Even the green in his eyes seemed duller with each birthday. Given how far away he had to hold a newspaper in order to peruse it these days, no doubt he'd soon be wearing reading glasses as well.

Tom hadn't wanted to come to Wicklow to begin with. He had suggested to his wife that they go abroad for their long weekend: Paris, maybe, or Rome. Louise, however, was determined to be within driving distance of their daughter, Maria, and their infant grandchild, Cáit.

Tom hadn't fought her, biting his tongue when she suggested a neighbouring county for their break. Really, it didn't matter where they went as long as they were together and he could get a full night's sleep.

Cáit was five months old now but still woke several times a night. Maria, just turned twenty, still lived with them. While Tom relished being a grandfather, he was not enjoying the pseudo-parental role Louise kept inflicting on them both. Of course he agreed they should help Maria. The baby's father, a fellow college student, had so far proved to be an utter disappointment and their daughter was, to all intents and purposes, a single parent. He suspected, though, that Louise was doing a bit too much of the heavy lifting. She'd even taken a sabbatical from her English literature PhD, which she had resumed before Maria became pregnant.

He shook his head. He wouldn't let negativity creep in. They'd had a terrific day, starting with a stroll through the captivating gardens of the old aristocratic Powerscourt Estate in the foothills of the Wicklow Mountains. As the afternoon drew to a close, they'd checked into their hotel in the Glen of the Downs and retired to the residents' restaurant for a delicious five-course dinner.

Tom smiled. Paris or Rome! Sure, they couldn't hold a candle to the Irish countryside, when you thought about it.

He placed his cigar in the ashtray to burn out and stood up, inhaling the night air, infused with the smell of wet October foliage. Heavenly. But now it was time to warm up with his wife.

He shut the sliding door gently and crept over to the suite's king-size bed. Louise had left the lamp on and fallen asleep with her book in her hands. It was a rip-roaring American thriller, full of action and sweeping generalisations about world politics, which she seemed to be reading just so she could give out about it. Her long brown hair fanned out on the pillow behind her, her dark lashes resting on soft, creamy cheeks. The Sleeping Beauty image was only slightly tarnished by her trumpeting snores, caused by the half-sitting position she'd been in when she dropped off, her chin resting awkwardly on her chest.

Tom was carefully extricating the book when the bedside phone trilled angrily.

He jumped, as did she, and the novel clattered to the floor.

'Bloody hell, Tom!' she barked, before realising what had disturbed her slumber.

Tom hesitated. The phone was still ringing.

'It could be Maria?' Louise suggested.

'She'd try your mobile first.'

They both knew what the call meant. Unless it was reception ringing to tell them there was some emergency in the hotel (and Tom fervently hoped one of the floors was ablaze), the call meant work.

He wasn't happy. He'd specifically asked the reception clerk to ensure no external calls were put through to the room and his mobile was switched off.

He lifted the receiver.

'I apologise sincerely for disturbing you, sir, but there's a gentleman down here who is quite insistent. He says he's a colleague of yours. He threatened to arrest me if I didn't ring your room.'

Tom sighed wearily.

'That's all right. Put him on.'

He gave Louise an apologetic look. She frowned in return.

'Boss, it's Ray. I'm really sorry about this.'

'Ray, unless you are about to tell me the Taoiseach has been murdered, I suggest you get back on the road to Dublin,' the inspector snapped.

There was a brief pause.

'Well, that's the thing . . .'

'What?' Tom's heart skipped a beat. 'You're joking . . .'

'I don't know the ID of the victim, but I'm under strict instructions to pick you up and bring you to Leinster House. The chief sends his heartfelt apologies to Louise.'

Tom covered the mouthpiece with his hand.

'Leinster House,' he whispered.

His wife's eyebrows shot up.

'Give me ten minutes,' Tom said into the receiver.

'Who's dead?' Louise asked immediately.

'No idea. But the national parliament . . . McGuinness wouldn't have sent for me for anything less. I'm so sorry about this, love.'

She sighed, exasperated.

'And there I was thinking you'd woken me because you wanted to ravish me.'

'I did. I do. I'm starting to think there's an alarm bell that goes off somewhere whenever I'm feeling amorous.'

He cupped her face, still warm from sleep, in his cold hands.

'Our lovely weekend . . .'

'Your lovely weekend. I'm staying. There's a spa downstairs.'

He smiled ruefully. 'I'll call you in the morning. You never know, I might get back out tomorrow evening.'

She snorted. 'Do me a favour? Call by the house and check on the girls. If you get a chance.'

He swallowed.

'What?' She squinted. It was a challenge.

There was nothing to lose. The weekend was already ruined.

'Maria has a team of people helping her this weekend, Louise. She's the child's mother; she has to learn to cope on her own.'

He moved to retrieve his clothes from the chair where they'd been discarded. Mentally, he ducked.

'She's twenty years of age and a single mother trying to manage full-time education,' Louise growled. 'She needs all the help she can get.'

He never would have dared rolling his eyes if he'd been facing her. He grunted, concentrating on dressing. She began to say something else, then stopped. Maybe she had taken his silence as a sign of agreement. He turned round.

Nope. That was not the face of a woman satisfied she had won the point.

'You're right,' he said, in a last-ditch attempt to keep the peace. He never learned.

She pursed her lips.

'I suppose I'll have to drive your dodgy Citroën on my own this weekend. Why did you replace one crap car with another?'

He sighed. He thought he'd defused the situation, but she'd just paused to reload. It never ceased to amaze Tom how his wife – no, scratch that, every woman he knew – could skip from one subject to another in an argument without pausing for breath. He'd known for months the new Citroën, with its insistent, inexplicable flashing warning lights, was driving Louise nuts, but she'd been biding her time to throw it at him in the midst of a spat about something else. She stored nuggets like that.

He also knew it wasn't the car she was unhappy with. Louise's patience with Tom's job was almost bottomless, but they'd been away so rarely over the last couple of years it was no wonder she was feeling irritable.

'I'll get my mechanic to have a look.'

Tom made to plant a kiss on her lips, but got a cheek instead.

'Hmm,' she said, her expression firmly set in long-suffering mode.

From talk of ravishing to rejection. The holiday was over.

CHAPTER 3

'If you had your own wife, Ray, you might appreciate what a man means when he says he and the missus aren't to be disturbed. Three days. That's all I asked. Three bloody days.'

Willie Callaghan, Tom's garda driver, chortled from the front of the car.

'Leave the poor lad alone. While he's single, we can live vicariously through him. Why should he sign up for a marital life sentence just because we were duped?'

Tom grunted and gazed out the window, watching regretfully as the thick Wicklow woods disappeared, to be replaced with civilisation in the form of housing estates on either side of the main road back to Dublin. The aftermath of the couple of glasses of wine with dinner had manifested as a headache, the cherry on top of his bad mood.

'Don't mind the boss,' Willie said to Ray, who was seated beside him, pointedly ignoring Tom. 'He was probably on a promise. It's rare for us married folk to strike it lucky like that. You wouldn't understand that sort of drought.'

Willie, a tall, thin man in his late fifties, was one of life's gentlemen. A prim and proper appearance belied his easy-come, easy-go attitude. His uniform was always starched, the corporal-like moustache neatly trimmed, his thin hair groomed tight and Old Spice judiciously applied. He was one of Tom's favourite people in the world, as much for his relaxed demeanour as for his dry wit and extensive collection of useful (and often useless) facts.

Ray, pondering his romantic failings as a single man, took his turn to stare glumly out the window.

It was almost 1 a.m. and the roads were deserted. It took them just half an hour to reach their destination.

Dublin city centre was still busy. The country had been in the grip of a nasty recession for the past couple of years, so bad that the Troika of the International Monetary Fund, the European Commission and the European Central Bank had descended on the government's financial institutions. A strict programme of cutbacks and tax hikes had been imposed but it was a Friday night and Dubliners – those who had a few quid to spare – were trying to be their usual sociable selves. Most of the pubs, clubs and restaurants, the ones that had so far survived austerity's depredations, had adapted to their customers' demands for more competitively priced bills of fare.

Ray observed the last of the night's revellers being expelled from the city's drinking joints. Beautiful girls tottered past the car in ridiculously high heels and short skirts, their scanty clothes the last vestiges of a long-passed summer. One young woman blew a kiss at the car window, then shrieked with laughter at her bravery.

'We're going in the Merrion Street gate,' Willie said. 'An attempt to keep things quiet. For now.'

Merrion Street was the rear entrance to the Leinster House and Government Buildings complex, but the inspector didn't imagine for one moment they'd be able to keep tonight's events hushed up for any length of time.

Two uniformed guards met them at the gate. The barrier was raised and the car rolled onto the tarmac that provided parking along Merrion Lawn, the green area behind Leinster House.

Tom had been in the complex several times and it never ceased to amaze him how this collection of buildings, in the heart of a crowded city centre, could be at such a remove – physically and metaphorically.

A former ducal palace, Leinster House had been built in the mid-eighteenth century by the Fitzgeralds, Earls of Kildare and Dukes of Leinster. It had become home to the Irish parliament in 1922 after the War of Independence and the departure of the British administration.

The complex consisted of more than just the main House. The adjacent Government Buildings housed the Taoiseach and his ministers.

As they progressed along the driveway they could see the side profiles of the Natural History Museum and the National Gallery through railings to either side of the lawn.

'The cavalry,' Ray said, pointing up ahead.

Tom saw the two canvas-covered trucks. Army vehicles. The complex had a permanent military and garda presence. But if somebody had been murdered in the precinct, a protocol for a security threat of the highest order would have been triggered.

In the inspector's memory, Leinster House had never been subject to a terrorist threat and Ireland wasn't exactly top of the list of target countries in current world crises. There was a first for everything, though.

Willie brought the car past the main door and parked across from a small gate in a curved wall that ran along the side of the building. A stranger stood ready to greet them. The dark-haired man had a military bearing not unlike Willie's and was dressed in a distinguished naval-type uniform. He was well-built, bulkier than the inspector's sinewy driver. The Chief of Security, Tom assumed.

Leinster House had its own security staff, responsible for the safe operation of the complex. The Chief of Security was assisted by the Head Usher and the Captain of the Guard in managing both internal security and the general running of the House. They, in turn, were supplemented by a full-time cadre of gardaí and armed members of the defence forces.

The man stepped forward and offered the inspector a firm handshake, his countenance grim. He seemed like somebody who was rarely rattled, but tonight was proving the exception to the rule.

'Shane Morrison, Inspector, Chief of Security. Your Superintendent asked me to escort you. He's with your colleagues at the scene.'

The man's voice was deep and gravelly. It suited his authoritative air.

'Thank you,' Tom replied. 'Should I use your official title?'

'Mister is fine.'

'Good. Did the incident occur in the main building, Mr Morrison?'

The other man shook his head. 'Not quite. None of us are sure what he was doing where we found him. Shall we?'

So, the victim was male.

Morrison was eager to move their little group inside, away from any long-lensed prying eyes.

He led Tom and Ray through the gate and up a set of stone stairs. At the top, they found themselves outside a modern building, part of the complex not visible from the front or back vistas of Leinster House.

'This is LH2000,' Morrison said, slipping into what sounded like tour-guide mode. 'It was opened, as you may have guessed, in the year 2000, to provide extra office accommodation for elected members and their staff. There are six floors and a basement containing rooms for committee meetings.'

The chief of security rapped on the glass door. An usher swiftly appeared to unlock it.

Morrison nodded at the man and maintained the fast pace as they made their way to a descending set of stairs beyond the building's reception desk. He continued to narrate LH2000's history and describe its layout as they walked.

'These stairs lead down to the coffee dock, but also to an underground tunnel that connects this building to Leinster House proper. There are several rooms along the tunnel, but its main function is to provide speedy access for members, the *Teachtaí Dála*, to the chamber when debates or votes are called. The tunnel is where we found him.'

'Were there people in this building when the body was discovered?' Tom asked.

Morrison hesitated.

'No. But you should know something. Normally, the military police are based in an office off the tunnel. They moved into temporary alternative accommodation last week. We are in the process of enhancing our security provisions and repairing some essential infrastructure. Their base is in a part of the building that is being upgraded with new technological systems and water and heating facilities. It was decided the work could proceed quicker if the offices were empty.'

The inspector swallowed. There was eating and drinking in this for the media.

'Who found the body?' Ray asked, as they arrived at the foot of the stairs.

'One of our ushers. The door we just came through was locked at 9 p.m. this evening and the floors upstairs had been checked beforehand to ensure they were all empty. Jim, the usher, had left his bag behind the reception desk and came over from the main House to retrieve it. He used the underground passage and that's when he found the body. This was at 10.45 p.m.'

A bellow brought their conversation to an abrupt close.

'Tom! Thanks for coming in.'

Chief Superintendent McGuinness loomed large over the people gathered around him. The small group parted like water as he made his way over to shake the inspector's hand vigorously with his vice-like grip.

'I write with that hand,' Tom winced, as usual unprepared for the sheer strength of the man. McGuinness ignored him. He was nearing retirement, but the Kerry native hadn't lost any of his imposing physicality. Tom was barely shy of six foot himself and still McGuinness had three inches on him.

McGuinness regularly used his height and booming deep voice to his advantage. Those who didn't like the man often remarked that he'd be more at home with his arm stuck up the backside of a calfing cow than running one of the most important garda divisions in the State. It was a serious underestimation. Tom and the chief went back a long time and were good friends. The inspector knew the other side of his boss, the sharp-witted aesthete who enjoyed fine wine and concertos, a man who read the *Guardian* daily and could quote the Bible and many other tomes, chapter and verse.

McGuinness could run rings around anybody who had him pegged as a loud-mouthed, thick culchie.

'I wasn't aware I'd a choice whether to come or not,' Tom snapped irritably.

'Hmm, sorry about that. I don't need to tell you how serious this is, though. The assistant commissioner was just on the phone. This is going to explode when news gets out. The Taoiseach is climbing the walls.'

'I get it,' the inspector sighed. A murder investigation was challenging and wearisome enough without all the bells and whistles this one would come with.

'Good. Right, to start you off, I want you to meet Darragh McNally. He's the chair of the Reform Party. Speak to him while we're waiting for forensics to finish sweeping the scene.'

Wonderful. The Reform Party was the governing party. Tom hadn't even seen the body yet and already politics were a feature of the investigation.

McGuinness stood aside to introduce the man he'd beckoned over. The diminutive man had the look of someone who rarely slept – sunken eyes underlaid with deep bags. His colouring, naturally pasty excepting an unfortunately placed birthmark on his right cheek, made his face appear particularly gaunt in the low lighting. His brown hair was receding rapidly and greying at the roots – most likely further evidence of the stress that accompanied his job.

'Inspector Reynolds, I'm glad you're here. Your reputation precedes you.'

McNally was hoarse, his body language jittery.

Tom shook his hand, noting the clammy palm.

'Do you know the victim, Mr McNally?'

The other man nodded.

'Yes. I can't tell you how shocked I am. He's only back in work. He was in a car crash six months ago and nearly died. He's literally just back a few days. I'm struggling to get my head around this. '

'Who is he?'

'Ryan Finnegan.'

Tom stared at McNally, waiting for more. It took the other man a moment to realise the name meant nothing to the inspector.

'Oh, I'm sorry. Forgive me. I'm working here so long, sometimes I forget there's a world outside. Ryan Finnegan is the political advisor to Aidan Blake. He is – was – one of the most senior advisors to the government.'

Blake. That was a name Tom knew. The Minister for State Resources and Energy Efficiency was the man of the moment – the most popular government figure and one of the youngest members of the cabinet. He had been elected in the Reform Party's landslide victory earlier in the year when the former governing party had been dumped out of office, a consequence of their mismanagement of the economy and the arrival of the Troika. Blake, handsome, confident, assured and energetic, was tipped to be a contender for the party leadership. Even Louise, who generally greeted political coverage on the news with a long sigh, had mentioned during the election that she found Blake *fascinating* – his wife's code for I *fancy him*.

'You can see our dilemma, Inspector,' McNally said. 'A man of Finnegan's standing, murdered here, of all places. This is sensational.'

Tom noted the use of the word 'dilemma'. Surely it would be more apt to describe this as an unqualified disaster? And 'sensational' – it was a word a PR handler would use.

He weighed up his reply. He wanted to say the victim's standing meant nothing to him, nor the location of his murder, but he was conscious that McGuinness was eyeballing him. Putting McNally in his place would cause more of a headache than the fleeting satisfaction it would bring.

'I need to take a look at the body,' he said, instead. 'I'll want to speak to you again in the morning. Does the victim have immediate family?'

'Yes. His wife, Kathryn. They've a small baby.'

Tom felt the familiar knot in his stomach. Before the night was out, he'd have to break the heart of a young mother and wife.

'Excuse me,' he said, making his way over to the plastic police tape tied at either side of the doors to the tunnel Morrison had mentioned. Beyond it, several officers, suited and booted in their white gear, laboured to secure the scene and gather evidence.

Amongst them, Tom could see one of his detectives, Laura Brennan.

She joined the inspector and Ray at the tape, removing her hood and letting long chestnut curls spill out. At twenty-nine, she was the squad's youngest member and one of Tom's most diligent and intelligent officers. To compensate for her age, Laura wore smart, tailored suits and a studied look of concentration. She was so classy that she somehow managed to make even the white forensics getup look sharp.

'It's definitely murder then?' Tom asked, already knowing the answer.

Laura nodded. 'Without a doubt. The forensics team isn't finished yet, but Emmet is letting us in with protective clothing.'

Tom was relieved to know that Emmet McDonagh had personally taken charge of the scene. The head of the Garda Technical Bureau, the unit that dealt with crime scene forensics, McDonagh was thorough and, more importantly, had a good relationship with Tom. Luckily for the inspector and his team, because Emmet was an egotistical, smart-arsed git who acted the maggot with everybody else.

Tom and Ray stepped into the outfits provided and dipped under the tape.

A few metres ahead, the inspector could see the top of a stone sculpture sitting in an alcove. Even at this distance, he could see the splashes of blood on the cream ceiling above, the frenzied spray incongruous in the functional space.

As they approached, the forensic scientists – one of them the artificially dark-haired, extremely broad McDonagh – stood up and away from the body so the two detectives could see the victim.

Ray cursed and looked away. He'd never become inured to gore, no matter how often he was faced with it.

The inspector would later learn that the greenish-hued sculpture carved in a sitting position was called 'Fame' and had originally sat at the front of Leinster House, beneath a larger statue of Queen Victoria. The lady herself had been lent to Australia for its centenary celebrations in 1988.

The large angel-type figure held a trumpet of some sort across its lap in outstretched arms.

It also held the limp body of Ryan Finnegan.

Finnegan's one remaining eye was wide open, its glassy surface caught in a petrified moment. Where his other eye should have been was a bloody cavity. His mouth was contorted in agony.

'Hellish, eh, Tom?' Emmet McDonagh said to the inspector. 'Give me a good old-fashioned strangling any day of the week. The pathologist is going to move him shortly before rigor mortis sets in. Otherwise, it might be a tad difficult to get him off that sculpture. He has nothing on him, no ID, no phone, but I gather the people who work here know him.'

'What happened, Emmet?' Tom asked, slightly dazed.

The other man threw out his arms as he spoke, his mop of brown hair bouncing unnaturally (the inspector was starting to wonder if it wasn't so much a dye-job as a wig-job), glasses slipping lower on his nose the more animated he became. Ten years older than Tom, Emmet was still renowned for having an eye for the ladies, hence the vanity. None of it, sadly, was for his wife.

'Call me poetic, but it looks to me like the victim was fleeing something and fell into the arms of one of God's angels. What he was running from, I don't know, but it may have something to do with this. We found it between the body and the statue. Not sure if it has anything to do with him, but it seems like an odd thing to be lying about.'

He produced a plastic evidence bag and held it up for Tom to examine.

The background noise of the various police officers, security personnel and medical and science professionals died away as the inspector examined the image.

It depicted two young men performing a sexual act. It wasn't the intimacy of the act that disturbed Tom. It was the knowing eyes one of the men was casting over his shoulder at the photographer. Experienced, old eyes, that screamed 'sex for sale' and carried the haunted look of someone who had witnessed too much. Only the back of the other man's head was visible.

Tom looked back to the victim, cradled in the arms of that which symbolised purity and innocence.

Ryan Finnegan was wearing a light blue striped shirt and black trousers. Office wear. Professional dress in a professional setting, which made the blood-spattered crime scene all the more disturbing.

The inspector turned to Ray.

'We're in the basement of Leinster House,' he declared, incredulous.

'I know,' Ray replied, having found the courage to look back at the body. 'I had to see it before I could believe it. The shit has well and truly hit the fan.'

*

Kathryn Finnegan wasn't sure if the baby was crying in her dreams or was actually awake and yelling in her ear.

It took her a few more moments to come to properly. She was so exhausted, she felt almost hungover. Her head ached with tiredness and her limbs felt like she had the flu.

The young mother raised herself from the pillow and looked down at Beth. The baby was headbutting her breast, trying to get at the milk through Kathryn's vest top.

'Oh, my God,' she whispered, drowsily. 'How can you be hungry again? This isn't on. You're six months old and feeding like a newborn.'

She pulled herself up into a sitting position, plumping the pillows to get comfortable. She'd feed her daughter this time, but – and Kathryn promised herself she meant it – if Beth woke again tonight Ryan would have to give her a bottle. She needed a break. Beth must be going through a growth surge as well as teething. The only thing that seemed to bring the child any comfort was being fed and walked.

She cradled the baby and adjusted her clothing to let the infant latch on. As she did this, Kathryn looked across at the empty side of the bed where her husband normally lay.

Her brain was only now starting to fully engage.

Where was Ryan? It was Friday night – wasn't it? Or was it Thursday? No. It was definitely Friday. What time was it, anyway?

Kathryn reached across to her phone with her free hand and tapped the screen. One a.m.

She felt her heart beat a little faster. There were no missed calls on the phone. If Ryan was working late, he'd have rung or texted, surely? He knew how much she worried, ever since the car accident – and also that she was dead on her feet, with Beth being so cranky and wakeful lately.

Why hadn't he sent her a message?

A feeling of unease began to creep into her stomach, but she held it at bay.

It was probably nothing. He'd got caught up in something or maybe he'd gone out for a drink to end his first week back at work. He'd forgotten to ring her or his phone was dead. She'd read him the riot act but there was no need to get herself worked up. The chances of him having been in another accident were surely minuscule.

With no hands free, Kathryn had to blow away the hair that had fallen onto her face and was tickling her cheek. Despite all the advice from her friends and her hairdresser, she'd made the rash decision when she was pregnant to cut her hair short. Now it was bob-length. Long enough to be annoying, too short to tie back. Ryan had told her she'd still be beautiful even if she shaved it all off; right now Kathryn was feeling sorely tempted.

She dialled his number and listened as it rang out, willing him to pick up.

'Ryan,' she snapped when it went to voicemail, but quietly, because of the baby. 'Where the hell are you? Ring me as soon as you get this.'

She flung the phone angrily onto the bed covers and stared at it, hoping to see the screen light up with her husband's picture as he returned the call.

Beth pulled off the breast and looked up at her mother, sensing something wasn't right.

Kathryn looked down at the baby.

'Where's your silly daddy, eh? Mammy's going to kill him when she sees him.'

CHAPTER 4

Tom knelt beside Ryan Finnegan for a short time before the body was moved from its awkward position, half on, half off the lap of the sculpture. He studied the deceased man, trying not to dwell on the crater where his right eye had once been.

Who could have done this? Who hated the man enough to shoot him in the face? The state pathologist had indicated already that the victim had been shot twice – the other bullet most likely to the back. The inspector surmised that Ryan might have been running from his attacker when the first shot was fired. Perhaps he had turned to see his killer before sustaining the fatal wound. Emmet's team was already suggesting that the murder weapon had been fitted with a silencer. Otherwise, the reverberations of the gunshots would have echoed throughout the tunnel and beyond, possibly drawing attention.

Had Ryan's killer known the military police weren't in their usual accommodation? Had they been there, would the murderer have dared to strike, even with a silencer, within spitting distance of the security services?

Finnegan was youngish, his skin relatively unlined. Nearing forty, maybe. He had a pale, sun-starved ring around his remaining eye, indicating he probably wore spectacles often. Where were they now? Or had he recently taken to wearing contacts?

Tom tried to imagine the man alive, animated. He thought he would look intelligent. Sincere. Quite pleasant, in fact. So what had he done to die so brutally? Was he the other man in the photo they'd found, the man only visible from the back?

When he eventually stood up, the inspector felt dizzy. He stretched his knees. It was time to begin.

Emmet closed the tunnel doors as the body was prepared for removal.

McGuinness was pacing, talking on his phone as he waited for Tom back out in the coffee dock.

'Bronwyn Maher,' he said, as he hung up, naming the assistant chief commissioner. 'She says the Taoiseach has been on to the commissioner. He's at that conference in Canada. It will be all hands on deck for this, Tom. You're going to have to conduct interviews with a lot of important people. And I want you to bring Linda McCarn in.'

'Linda McCarn,' Tom parroted, nodding his head back in the direction of Emmet McDonagh. 'Are you sure that's wise?'

Linda was the State's leading criminal psychologist, a woman Tom respected and feared in equal measure. She and Emmet had a history and the inspector liked to avoid creating situations where they might encounter each other. There wasn't enough room in Dublin for their large personalities, let alone for the brief illicit fling they'd conducted. The relationship had ended acrimoniously and the two main players refused to divulge why – but they liked to make everybody aware of how much they detested each other now.

'I don't care about their feelings on the matter,' McGuinness barked. 'We will be seen to be using our brightest and our best on this investigation. The man was a minister's PA and he's been gunned down in Leinster House, for God's sake. What's your plan now?'

The 'seen to be' wasn't lost on Tom. The resources war continued.

He sighed.

'I'll go inform the victim's widow. We'll let forensics gather their evidence here then get the team in first thing and go over what we have. I presume the victim had an office in the building. I'll send Ray over to check it out before he finishes up.'

'Good. Let me know how you get on. I suggest you start your interviews in the morning with Shane Morrison. He'll give you a rundown on the building, who was here tonight, and so forth. McNally can fill you in on Ryan's work record and you'll have to talk to Aidan Blake, the minister he worked for. Statements have already been collected from those who were still in the complex when the body was found.'

'Right. Sean, how much independence will I have in this investigation? I only ask because you're already talking about the commissioner checking in from Canada and Maher's on the phone to you . . .'

'Listen, they're going to be breathing down our necks, but neither of them want to be seen with cabinet members – they won't want any photos leaking out to accompany headlines of "Guards interview government ministers in Leinster House murder". You question whoever you need to; the investigation will be under your control. I'll make sure you have the full cooperation of the security services in here.'

McGuinness took a deep breath.

'Don't let politics interfere, Tom. This is a murder case like any other. But do everything by the book and be discreet, okay? Bronwyn and I will take care of the media circus. Hopefully this is down to some deranged member of the public who managed to get in here as a visitor.'

'Unlikely,' Tom remarked. 'Do you really think Ryan Finnegan was just in the wrong place at the wrong time and somebody blew his head off? Did you see the picture forensics found?'

McGuinness sucked in his cheeks.

'Unfortunately, yes. Perhaps it was something in the man's personal life that resulted in his murder?'

'It was hardly just sitting on the floor of Leinster House and Ryan Finnegan happened to fall on it when he was being murdered. Which then begs the question: what was he doing with a pornographic image of two young men on his person?'

'Is he one of the men?'

'I can't tell,' Tom replied. 'Not yet. We'll examine it.'

'Hmm. There's another issue you should be aware of.'

'Uh-huh?'

'The Taoiseach was in Leinster House tonight. As head of the investigation team, you should interview him formally. He'll want you to.'

The inspector clenched his jaw.

'Marvellous. Bloody marvellous. I presume we're shutting the building down?'

'For now, anyway. But government has to resume business at some stage. Sorry, I need to get this.' McGuinness walked away, his phone glued to his ear once more.

Tom summoned Laura.

'I'm going to inform next of kin,' he told her. 'I want you to come with me. I'm leaving Ray in charge of closing down here.'

Laura grimaced.

'Sure. I'll just get out of this suit.'

She knew that the victim's family could have important information pertaining to their investigation. She also knew that Tom didn't like to delegate the breaking of such bad news. When possible, he took on the responsibility himself. And Laura was also aware that he was choosing her to come with him both because he wanted it to be a male and female arriving at Mrs Finnegan's door, and also because she could do with the experience.

But knowing all of that did little to stop Laura's heart sinking. There was no end to this day.

*

Willie drove them to the quiet North Dublin suburban village of Raheny where Ryan Finnegan had lived. Tom made a couple of calls during the ride, but aside from that, nobody in the car spoke.

A brand new silver saloon was parked in the Finnegans' drive-way. The family must have had to purchase a new car after the crash that Darragh McNally, the party chair, had mentioned. The garden was well tended, a red rose in late bloom scenting the air. A couple of adult-sized bikes rested against the wall in the narrow walkway through to the side gate. A man's cycling helmet hung on one of the handlebars.

Tom's steps were heavy with apprehension as they approached the door, his stomach knotting. He willed every second to last longer. He wanted to give this woman every last drop of blissful ignorance before he knocked and shattered her life with his news. He'd done this often enough to know that even in the unhappiest, the most strained of relationships, the sudden knowledge that a loved one was dead was an arrow of grief to the soul.

A light sensor was triggered just as Tom raised a reluctant fist to hammer on the wood.

It never made contact. The light had alerted the homeowner and the door swung open. A young woman stood there, baby in arms. Her raven, bobbed hair was dishevelled, her grey-coloured eyes bloodshot with fatigue. She was still pretty, even in that state.

'Where have you been?' she started, her face furious.

The anger died as she looked from Tom to Laura and realised they weren't who she was expecting.

Their faces must have given it away.

'Oh, my God.'

She crumpled and they both rushed to catch her. The baby, shocked from a fragile sleep, opened its mouth and screamed.

'I'm sorry,' Tom whispered, to Kathryn Finnegan and to the infant. 'I'm so sorry.'

*

Laura stood with her back to her boss and Kathryn Finnegan, stirring unasked for sugar into unrequested tea. She'd slipped into comfort mode. In her career, she'd only broken this news three times – twice to the families of traffic accident victims and once to the wife of an elderly man accidentally murdered in a bungled bank robbery. There hadn't been any young children involved and she'd never had to tell a thirty-year-old new mother that she was now a widow.

Kathryn sat clutching the baby in her lap like a life raft. The six-month-old was taking the visit surprisingly well, after the initial shock of being so rudely awoken. The mother bounced the infant softly up and down on her knees, eyes wide and unfocused, talking nineteen to the dozen. She was in shock.

'Beth's teething. Just when I thought I had her in a routine. She's started waking up every couple of hours, wailing. Nothing works. I've tried all the gum gels, homeopathic remedies, everything. It was okay when Ryan was off work. We could take turns, once his leg had started to heal. She's like the Antichrist some nights.'

Tom looked down at Beth, who was giving him the baby stare and drooling vast quantities of spit onto fingers that were rammed into her mouth. She smiled at him and gooed, thrilled to be the centre of attention. They were wont to do that, he thought, looking at the contented baby. Make liars out of their parents. No one would ever guess this little angel was giving her mother sleepless nights.

'Ryan only went back on Monday. I didn't want him to. The last few months – I know it's terrible to say – but they've been brilliant. Once I got over the shock of the crash I was so happy to have my husband home. His job is so stressful and just before the accident he was under even more pressure than usual and we'd just had the baby. Oh . . .'

Kathryn looked down at the top of Beth's head and let out a loud, shocked sob.

'She'll have no daddy. How do I tell her? Will she even remember him?'

Great big tears spilled down the mother's face and onto her daughter's hair.

Tom felt a lump in his throat.

At the kitchen counter, Laura's shoulders stiffened as she gathered the strength to turn around with the tea. She placed the cup in front of Kathryn, but out of reach of the baby, who eyed this other new person with equal wonder.

'Beth will always have her father because she'll always have you,' the inspector said gently, holding his hand out to the baby and letting her take his finger in her tight, sopping grasp.

Kathryn looked up. 'Oh, I'm sorry, I don't drink tea,' she said to Laura.

'Just take a few sips. It's for the shock. Is there anyone we can call to come over?'

'Um . . . My brother and his wife? But, no, they've two children; I can't wake them at this hour.'

The inspector shook his head. 'That's not going to matter. Just give Laura his number.'

'Who'll tell Ryan's parents? Should I ring them? And his sisters . . .'

A fresh wave of tears sprang forth and Tom waited patiently for the moment to pass.

'Let's get your brother over here and he can take care of the calls,' Tom said, passing over Laura's notepad and pen for the number.

'I can't remember it. I have to check my mobile.'

Laura fetched the phone from the counter and gave it to Kathryn, who tapped at the device, fingers shaking as she retrieved the information. The detective took the notepad and made her way out to the hall to place the call.

Kathryn reached out and took a sip of the tea, her face contorting as she swallowed the sugary drink. She was happy to take orders. In Tom's experience, the people who dealt with grief best were those who let it wash over them immediately and didn't try to stay strong, the ones who let others take charge and do the thinking for them. Kathryn was holding up okay so far, talking and answering questions. That lucidity, he knew, was a temporary symptom of shock. It would pass, so he had to make the most of the opportunity.

'God, the irony,' she said. 'I went through all this only a few months ago, when we thought Ryan wasn't going to make it after the accident. What was that? A practice run? You'd think that would have prepared me.'

'There is no preparing for this,' Tom said. 'Not if it's a long illness, not if it's a sudden heart attack.'

'But murder?' Kathryn shook her head. 'It doesn't make sense. He was in work. How could someone shoot him in Leinster House? How did someone get a gun into Leinster House?'

'We're working to find out what happened,' the inspector reassured her. 'Please, let us worry about those questions. That's our job. But I do want to ask you a couple of things that might help with the investigation.'

He waited until she nodded, but he could see the faraway look already glazing over her eyes. She was going through the 'ifs' in her head. If her husband hadn't gone back to work this week. If he had come home early. If she had rung him at a certain time or said something different to him as he left the house.

'Was there anything going on with Ryan lately that was out of the ordinary? Did he talk to you about any disagreements he might have had, anything he was worried about? Was he different in any way?'

Kathryn bit her bottom lip, worrying away at some chapped skin until a little bubble of blood appeared. She brushed it away with her fingers and shifted the baby, who was becoming unsettled, around to face her.

'Ryan was out of sorts these last few weeks,' she said, 'as it got closer to him going back to work. There was a period when he seemed content to be away from that place and his job. He was so enamoured with Beth, she took up all his time. And I guess, because the accident was so bad, people just left him alone. No one rang or emailed. Believe me, that was unusual. We were on holidays last year and one evening I actually sent him a text to remind him I was sitting beside him, he was so busy on his phone.'

She smiled at the memory. Then the pained expression returned, the realisation that she would happily have that little argument every day of the week rather than have to endure this.

'In the last week or so before he returned to Leinster House, he started to get tense, just like he was before the car crash.'

'Tense because his job is tough, or for some other reason?' Tom asked.

'It was different from his normal stressing about work. Yes, I sensed that.'

'How did he get on with the people he worked with?'

She cocked her head to one side, weighing up an answer.

'I don't know . . . if you'd asked me that question a couple of years ago, I would have said they were his friends, not just colleagues. But in recent times he seemed to keep clashing with other party members, especially Aidan. You know he worked for Minister Aidan Blake?'

'Yes. That must have been exciting. He's quite the star, isn't he?'

Tom was speaking as gently as he could, coaxing Kathryn along. She looked dazed, but was still eager to talk.

'Nowadays, sure. I suppose he was always destined for that, he's very ambitious. He and Ryan used to get on great but in the last year or so . . . I guess you could say they diverged on policies. My husband is very principled. He always has been.

'One night, he came in late and I was still awake. I was nearly due with Beth and finding it impossible to sleep. It was just after the election. He was really angry, so I made us both some hot chocolate and we sat up in bed together. He said that being in government was going to ruin Aidan, that he was too weak for power. What it boiled down to was that Ryan believed the Reform Party should deliver what it had promised during the campaign. He'd suddenly realised that Aidan's philosophy was more cynical – that you said what was necessary to get into power and once there, you evaluated what could actually be delivered.'

'I can see how that would make for strained relations,' Tom agreed.

'Aidan's department was working on something and Ryan wasn't happy about it. Some law. But I'm just rambling. I mean, Ryan wasn't killed because he disagreed with something political,' she said. 'Jesus, that's not what happened, is it?'

'We don't know what happened yet,' he said, though privately he was thinking people had been murdered for less. 'Did he mention anybody he specifically wasn't getting on with? What about his relationship with the Reform Party chair, Darragh McNally?'

Kathryn shook her head.

'Ryan has never got on with Darragh. Thinks he's an egomaniac.'

With every mention of her husband's name, the woman flinched. She was still using the present tense. It was time to wrap things up, Tom decided. She'd given them enough for tonight.

'I mean nothing by this question, Kathryn, and I don't want you to think I do. I just have to ask. Was everything okay between you and Ryan? Were you happy?'

He was thinking of the image that had been found with Ryan. There was nothing about this young woman's response so far that indicated their relationship had been anything but good. But then, he'd encountered many situations before where grieving spouses, faced with the finality of death, felt they had to present a rose-coloured view of their partners.

She looked at him blankly.

'Yes,' she finally choked. 'We're together seven years. We have a good marriage.' She started to weep. 'We *had* a good marriage . . . He's gone, isn't he? He's really gone. I need to see him. I have to . . .'

Her voice rose as the panic set in.

Laura, back from phoning Kathryn's brother, crossed the kitchen and put her arm around the other woman.

'Your brother's on his way,' she said. 'It's okay. Everything will be taken care of. It's okay.'

She looked over at Tom to check she was doing the right thing.

He nodded. There was really very little they could do for Kathryn now except find her husband's killer.

And that wouldn't bring him back.

CHAPTER 5

Saturday

Leinster House had been effectively shut down, but the presence of a large number of gardaí and onsite security staff meant the complex was busier than normal for a weekend.

Tom met with Shane Morrison and Darragh McNally in the LH2000 coffee dock area. The inspector wanted to see the building in the daylight and get a feel for the layout of the entire complex.

They sat in black leather armchairs at the far side of the café area. Tom relaxed into his, the other two men perched nervously on the edge of theirs. There was still a small forensics crew in the tunnel where Ryan had been found, though the body had been moved and most of the blood cleaned away. Soon, it would be like nothing had ever happened at the spot.

'Why would Ryan Finnegan have been in that tunnel last night?' Tom asked, sipping gingerly at a scalding hot coffee. 'Didn't you say, Mr Morrison, that this building was empty when it was last checked yesterday evening?'

Shane Morrison still wore the worried look of a man used to order and routine who had just witnessed the detonation of a metaphorical bomb. Tom could tell he was distressed by, but not upset at, Ryan's death. He suspected the man's main concern was what impact the murder would have on the running of the complex.

Darragh McNally sat wringing his hands. There was constant

movement in the other man's eyes. He was planning. McNally appeared to be treating the murder of Ryan Finnegan like any unexpected political event – an incident that needed to be managed. But Tom saw something else in the party chair's demeanour. He was nervous, distracted, even.

'I don't know, is the honest answer,' Morrison replied. 'Ryan's office is over in Government Buildings, beside Minister Blake's. This building was closed earlier on Friday evening and on the last check by my ushers, there was no one on any of the floors. The offices aren't locked at night and while the tunnel doors are closed, anybody with an internal swipe card can pass through them. The usher who found Ryan said the doors at this end were held open with fire extinguishers. That wouldn't be usual.

'The main House was still operating and busy enough. We're trying to compile for you as complete a list as possible of people who were here. We had some visitors in – we'll have a full log of who they were and when they arrived and departed. The Dáil bar was open until 11 p.m. or thereabouts and was quite full, I'm told. Some political staffers were working in the building, as well as the usual *Oireachtas* employees – civil servants, ushers, etc.'

'It seems like a lot of people for so late on a Friday,' Tom observed.

'Unfortunately, there were many more people than normal because of the event that was taking place across the road. There's also a good deal of legislation going through the House at the moment and that entails a lot of people working unusual hours. I'm afraid it's going to make your job more difficult. If it had been a regular, quiet Friday night, my ushers would no doubt be able to account for the movements of everyone in the House, but with so many people here . . .'

'You said an event was taking place across the road? What does that have to do with anything?'

McNally piped in. 'Minister Blake's wife was hosting a charity ball in the Grand Hotel on Merrion Square. Most of the cabinet were in attendance.'

'Okay,' Tom said, trying not to show alarm. Exactly how many ministers, he wondered, had been floating around Leinster House last night?

'Talk to me about the security arrangements,' he said. 'Are there any cameras in these buildings?'

'No.' Morrison shook his head in response to the last question. 'I'm afraid not. We've tried to install some on numerous occasions, but the TDs always complain about invasion of privacy. There are cameras at the perimeter gates.' He furrowed his eyebrows to show how unsatisfactory he found this state of affairs.

'Do we know how many people had left the complex by the time the body was discovered?'

Morrison shrugged and shifted in his seat, evidently uncomfortable.

'Most people had left before the alarm was sounded. Anybody still in the complex gave initial statements to the on-site guards and to those who came later. We have their details for you to follow up.

'That said, we have another problem in addition to the lack of camera footage. There's no electronic check-in system for political staff. There are over one thousand valid passcards for Leinster House and their holders don't have to swipe them at the main entrances. The cards are just flashed to the ushers at the entrance gates. Staff come and go as they please. We'll try to establish who was here, but it won't be easy. Unfortunately, this incident took place just as we are in the process of reviewing all our security procedures.'

Tom felt his shoulders tense. He, probably like most members of the public, had been labouring under the delusion that Leinster House was a secure building. It was starting to sound like anyone could get into the place, and that was before they considered just how many people had been in the complex legitimately last night.

'How was it possible for somebody to bring a weapon in?' he asked. 'Aren't there metal detectors?'

Morrison sighed.

'We can do a body search and bag examination if given cause for suspicion, but the only detectors in place are for visitors entering Government Buildings further along Merrion Street. There are no sensors in the complex, either. Anybody could walk around one of the locked buildings undetected. We've never had an incident like this. Ever. But, like I said, we were already considering updating our security procedures. More in light of recent international terror events than because of any possible domestic threat, but now we have fresh impetus.'

The chief of security couldn't disguise how pleased this made him, despite the circumstances.

Tom nodded at Ray, who'd just joined them. He could tell from the look on the younger detective's face that he had news.

He introduced Ray to the two other men before continuing.

'How long had Ryan worked for Minister Blake?' Tom asked, turning to McNally. 'Was he going to this ball? You said it was Aidan Blake's wife's charity?'

'Silent Voices,' McNally said. 'She's the CEO. You must have heard of it?'

Now the pieces were falling into place. The inspector had read about the high-flying patrons' ball for the children's charity, to be held in a luxury hotel across from Leinster House. He remembered thinking that a great deal of money would be made for the charity if a seat at the dinner cost one thousand euro a pop. That, and if he was paying that price for a ticket he'd be expecting pan-fried Dodo.

'Ryan wasn't attending the ball, no,' McNally continued. 'And for the life of me, I also can't figure out what he was doing in this part of the complex last night. I've thought about it: if he wanted to talk to somebody, he would have phoned ahead to check they were in – he was still limping. His leg was badly broken in the car accident.'

'What was he like?' the inspector asked.

'He was just an ordinary staff member,' Morrison said, his countenance filled with regret. 'Smart. Polite. Maybe a little radical for my liking, but then I'm an old conservative. Such a waste.'

'Was he the sort to make enemies?' he probed.

Morrison looked taken aback, while McNally frowned.

'You fall out with people in politics all the time,' the party chair explained. 'It's the nature of it. If every row in this place resulted in a shooting, there'd be regular bloodbaths in the Dáil chamber.'

A door leading to the lifts behind the coffee service area opened and DS Laura Brennan emerged. She was wearing a fitted grey trouser suit and had her hair swept back in a neat ponytail. She had to be as tired as the inspector and yet she'd turned up earlier than him this morning, doing her best to look as fresh as a daisy.

Laura glanced around, spotted Tom and Ray, and signalled she wanted to speak to them.

The detectives excused themselves and joined her over at a glass safety barrier, beyond which a set of stairs led down to what Tom guessed were the committee rooms Morrison had mentioned last night. Laura was accompanied by a uniformed garda, who introduced himself as Eoin Coyle.

'What have you got?' the inspector asked.

'Eoin here has discovered something significant. Hopefully, we've figured out the last known movements of our victim.'

'It might be nothing,' Garda Coyle insisted, almost apologetically, 'but Detective Brennan thought you'd be interested.'

Ray noticed the sideways look the guard gave Laura. And she'd used his first name with a degree of fluency. There was a familiarity there that wasn't usual between a detective and a uniformed guard. Did Laura know him? Ray hadn't noticed him before.

'We've been over the offices upstairs,' Eoin said. 'I took the sixth floor, the top. Each office appeared undisturbed, until I got to the last couple. One in particular caught my attention. It was untidy, but not dirty, if you know what I mean. Sort of organised chaos, isn't that what they say? So I almost missed it, but then I noticed papers scattered on the floor that just seemed out of place. Also, the internal door to the neighbouring office was open, whereas the corresponding doors in the other offices with similar layouts were closed. On the off chance, I put on my gloves, touched the computer keyboard and the screen came to life.

'I went back and checked the other offices' computers, but they were all shut down. Apparently, a diktat has been in operation for a year now ordering computers be powered off at night to save on energy costs.'

He hesitated and received a nod from Laura, urging him to go on. This time, Ray noticed the tiniest sparkle in Laura's eyes. He wasn't imagining things. Her face seemed different. She was . . . glowing. Ray refocused on Eoin.

Surely not . . .

'I think the victim may have been in that office, was discovered there by his killer and chased downstairs,' the officer concluded.

Tom narrowed his eyes. He was happy to encourage some detective work in the young lad, but that was a hell of a conclusion to jump to. How to say that, though, without making Eoin Coyle think twice about showing initiative to his superiors again?

Laura guessed at her boss's thoughts.

'It wasn't just the office, sir. Eoin?'

The guard looked to her and back to Tom. He was embarrassed to be thrust into the spotlight. He stood a head over Laura and was roughly the same age, perhaps early thirties, but his tight dark curls, full lips and wide blue eyes made him look younger, especially when his porcelain-skinned cheeks flushed red, as they were now.

He was like a big baby – far too pretty-looking for a man, Ray decided, then wondered why such a churlish and childish notion had floated into his head.

'The office just got me thinking,' Eoin said. 'I wondered how the victim might have reacted to being confronted. I figured if it was me I'd have made a run for it through the adjoining office if an attacker was blocking the hall door. At the end of the corridor there are two lifts, but one is out of service and the other tends to wait on the ground floor unless summoned. There'd be no time for that. There is a stairwell, though. I took the stairs and on the bannisters two floors down I found bloodstains. I've checked and the cleaners come in at 6 p.m. on a Friday. If they were any way thorough, they'd have wiped those bannisters, which means the blood could be from our victim or maybe his attacker. Forensics are on it.'

Tom nodded. That was better. There was more to go on there.

'Very good work, Garda Coyle. Did you notice any blood on the office door?'

'None visible to the naked eye.'

'Right, Laura, summon whoever normally works in that office to confirm whether or not the room was disturbed and if the computer had been left on. If Garda Coyle's theory is correct, Ryan may have used that room to print out the image he was found with and there might be something on the machine.'

The inspector hoped this was the case. The photograph was the only solid clue they had right now.

*

Tom returned to the leather chairs.

'Mr Morrison, would you be so kind as to help identify the occupant of an office upstairs? Detective Brennan will give you the details.'

'Of course.' Morrison nodded and stood up to leave.

The inspector turned to McNally, who was checking his watch distractedly.

'Mr McNally, I want to speak to Minister Blake. If he worked closest with Ryan Finnegan, he may have been the last person to see him yesterday evening. And I'd like to take a walk around this place. Could you ask him to come in to Leinster House?'

'He's en route, Inspector. I spoke to him earlier and informed him you'd be here. I can give you the concise tour on the way across to his office – Government Buildings are at the far side of the complex. Give me a moment to call him and see where he's at now.'

McNally moved away from them, phone in hand.

Tom turned to Ray to ask him what was on his mind, remembering his deputy had looked like he had new information when he'd joined the inspector at the couches.

'Is there something going on between Laura and that guard?' Ray blurted, before the inspector could open his mouth.

Tom creased his forehead, puzzled.

'What? Who?'

'That Coyle bloke. Didn't you notice anything?'

'I'm a little busy directing my powers of detection towards figuring out who shot Ryan Finnegan, Ray.'

He was about to irritably point out that his deputy had a habit of picking the most inappropriate moments to notice women, but stopped himself. He remembered only too vividly the timing of Ray's last love interest and how the whole sorry affair had ended.

The younger man read something in his boss's expression and his own darkened.

This was different, Ray's inner voice reasoned. He didn't have a thing for Laura. She was a work colleague. Nothing more. He was just being nosy.

McNally had returned, meaning Tom had no chance to ask Ray what he'd discovered.

They took the stairs back up to the front door of LH2000 and quickly covered the short distance outside to the main entrance of the parliament building. The early rain of the morning had drifted on, but the day was still overcast, the clouds low and grey. The inspector had always thought Leinster House was a beautiful building, but in this light it appeared rather bleak and imposing. Perhaps he was biased. His first visit inside, after all, had been to see a dead body.

'Visitors sign in over there when they're coming into Leinster House,' McNally said, pointing to a hatch on one side of the impressive lobby they'd just entered. Tom glanced across, then quickly tried to take in the rest of his surroundings.

A rare original copy of the 1916 Proclamation of Independence hung on the wall facing the revolving entrance door. A portrait of Cathal Brugha also caught the inspector's eye. The oil painting of the revolutionary who had taken the anti-Treaty side in the Irish Civil War faced a portrait of Michael Collins, the leader of the pro-Treaty side. Neither had survived the conflict.

The building was steeped in history but it seemed to all go – quite literally – over McNally's head as the short man steamed ahead, eyes down. The party chair obviously saw the complex as his workplace.

'How long have you worked here?' Tom asked, stopping beside a tall pillar and forcing McNally to grind to a halt. 'Do you know much about the main building – its history and that? It must feel like a privilege working here.'

'It does.' The other man looked around him, taking a moment. 'I'm here decades. I tend to forget where I am – most of us who work here do. You just see it as the office. You know, it was only meant to be a temporary location for the parliament when Michael Collins requisitioned it in 1922, but the State subsequently bought it from the Royal Dublin Society.'

'The RDS? I didn't know that.'

'Yes. The parliament was nearly going to be in Kilmainham Hospital, or in the Bank of Ireland on College Green. But nobody wanted to go near Kilmainham after the 1916 Rising leaders were executed in the Gaol there and the Bank of Ireland wanted too much money for its premises. Half of Dublin was living in slum tenements at the time, so overspending wouldn't have gone down too well for the newly formed government.'

'What's through there?' Tom asked, indicating an arch to their left.

'The library and research room, and there are also stairs leading up to the *Seanad* Chamber, where the Upper House of parliament meets, or down to the tunnel we just came from. Have you seen the Seanad before?'

'I haven't seen any of the building,' Tom replied. 'So that's the tunnel entrance on this side?'

'Yes. That's actually the older part of the original house. I think the Seanad used to be the picture gallery. There's a portrait of Countess Markievicz on the landing. She's my mother's idol, not least for insisting that the term "Irish women" be inserted into the Proclamation. Mother has always been ahead of her time, a bit like the Countess.' McNally smiled fondly.

'I must get a full tour at some stage,' Tom said, indicating they could move on. 'Tell me, Mr McNally, did you see Ryan yesterday evening at all? Or Minister Blake?'

'I didn't see Ryan. I saw the minister. And his wife, Sara.'

'Were you at that ball she was hosting?'

'No. I met them in Leinster House. She was chivvying some of the cabinet members over to the event. A few had started their evening in the Dáil bar and weren't showing any signs of moving across to the Grand Hotel.' The party chair lowered his voice. 'There were a lot of journalists at the ball; it would have been a disaster to have ministers turning up barely able to stand. Poor Sara was tearing her hair out.'

'So was Blake here to help his wife? Surely it didn't need two of them?'

There was barely a pause before McNally replied, but Tom's gut told him the other man was now on his guard.

'Minister Blake had a meeting scheduled at 9 p.m. with a very important guest. Carl Madsen. The vice-president of Udforske.'

'Udforske.' Tom rolled the foreign word around in his mouth. 'You mean the drilling giant?'

McNally nodded.

'The very same. One of the largest exploration companies in the world.'

The party chair fell silent.

'And?' Tom said. 'Why was Madsen here?'

McNally glanced up at him as they walked, as though he was trying to figure out whether the inspector really had no idea as to why Carl Madsen would have been in Leinster House. Tom's face revealed that he didn't.

'There's a significant piece of new legislation being introduced by the government that would revolutionise the country's tax treatment of our natural resources. The Bill is being handled by Minister Blake's department. It's been mentioned on the news several times. That's the chamber, by the way.'

McNally pointed through double glass doors. They'd arrived at the main landing of an ornate staircase that continued up on either side to two balconies, lined with formal portraits of former prime ministers, the *Taoisigh*. Tom peered through the glass doors into the debating chamber, its rows of seats descending like a Roman amphitheatre.

'We're leaving the main Leinster House building now and entering Government Buildings,' their guide continued. 'There's a suspended bridge that connects the two buildings.'

'So there's an uninterrupted flow within the complex,' Ray

observed. 'You don't need to leave any building by the main entrance to go to the next one?'

'Not if you've the right security pass.' McNally pointed to the one that hung around his neck.

Tom was still thinking about the piece of legislation McNally had mentioned. He had a vague recollection of hearing something about it but sadly, like his wife and most others, when certain political items hit the headlines he had a remarkable ability to filter them out.

'Sorry, just go back a minute. You say there's a Bill coming to revolutionise Ireland's tax treatment of our natural resources, by which you mean oil and gas, right? So why exactly was the vice-president of a Danish oil and gas drilling company, which just happens to be operating off the northwest coast of Ireland' – this much he did know – 'meeting the minister in charge of drafting the Bill?'

McNally smiled thinly. 'Don't worry, Inspector. There wasn't anything untoward about the meeting. This government was elected on a promise of transparency and accountability. Mr Madsen's appointment last night was recorded in the visitors' logbook. He was here to consult on the legislation. We're meeting all the industry leaders, as well as public groups, on the issue. And Carl Madsen is not some murky, greedy business figure. He's a long-time philanthropist and friend to this country.'

Ray shot Tom a look over McNally's head, eyebrows raised.

McNally caught it.

'You're sceptical, Detective. That's understandable, considering how corrupt the last government was. But the Reform Party made a promise in opposition. We need the jobs their industry brings, but we also need more revenue from their discoveries. This legislation significantly increases our share of royalties and charges for the issuance of new drilling licences.

'Udforske already holds a drilling licence for areas off the western coast and the legislation is not retrospective, so it doesn't affect the company in that regard. Future finds will mean more royalties for Ireland, but the likes of Udforske have such large profits that the increased tax is of little concern to them. What we all want is for Ireland to benefit from whatever is extracted while maintaining good working relationships with the companies willing to front the exploration costs. The minister is just concluding his consultations now. It's all above board, I assure you.'

Tom wasn't convinced, but said nothing. He didn't know enough about drilling licences or the pending legislation to comment. What he did know was that the presence of the vice-president of a billion-euro company in Government Buildings, last night of all nights, would probably send Sean McGuinness's blood pressure off the scale.

They crossed the bridge and passed through a set of double doors to another, far plusher, hallway.

A thick red carpet ran down the centre of a chequered marble floor. Delicate chandeliers hung from the high ceilings and gold-framed artwork adorned the walls.

They'd entered Government Buildings.

'Austerity, eh?' Ray quipped, letting out a low whistle. 'Not for everyone.'

McNally flashed him a sharp look.

'Considering how little selling off the carpet would contribute to reducing the State's deficit, Detective, I'm not sure it would be worth it.'

Ray didn't respond, but in his head he retorted that the nation's least well off might disagree.

They came to an abrupt halt outside one of the hallway's cream-panelled doors.

Tom stared down the corridor. He'd seen movement – a figure had been approaching but had abruptly ducked out of sight.

McNally rapped on the door and opened it.

'Sorry, I thought he'd be here by now. I'll just run downstairs and check if his car has arrived. Would you like to wait inside?'

'Sure,' Tom replied. 'One thing before you go, Mr McNally. I need you to give one of my officers a formal statement about your own movements last night. We have guards here all day – any of them can take it. What were you doing yourself for most of the evening?'

'I met with Madsen after the minister,' McNally replied. 'Then I returned to my office to work until I was summoned by Shane Morrison. I will give a statement, of course; it's just – I'm in a rush to get somewhere today. My mother . . . she's very ill. I was meant to leave for Clare last night.'

'There's no panic, but please stay in touch.'

The party chair nodded and scurried away, shoulders hunched forward, head low.

His mother's condition might explain why McNally seemed so on edge, the inspector mused.

Ray made to walk into the Minister's office but Tom stayed where he was. He was sure he'd seen something further down the hall. McNally had just disappeared from view when, suddenly, Linda McCarn materialised from behind a large potted plant.

'Have I started hallucinating or is that who I think it is?' the inspector muttered.

'Tom, darling!' The criminal psychologist's husky drawl was unmistakeable. 'Fancy seeing you here!'

A vision in multiple shades of green approached them.

Linda's unmistakable shock of brown corkscrew curls shot out at various angles, but today they looked almost tame compared to her garish head-to-toe dress. She looked more like a psychic than a psychologist. Her tall, thin frame covered the short length of the hall in a few strides and then she was upon them, planting sloppy wet kisses on Ray's cheeks, while air-kissing either side of Tom's.

'How come he gets proper kisses and I get pretend ones?' the inspector asked, not in the least offended, but slightly curious.

'Oh, Tom,' she purred, her voice dripping with mock disdain. 'He's fifteen years younger than you and has the body of a Calvin Klein model. Do you have to ask? Hmm, though you do seem to be thinning out a little, sweetie.' Linda poked at Ray's ribs while he flushed bright red.

Tom tutted in disapproval.

'I take it McGuinness was on to you. I was going to ring you myself this morning. What on earth were you doing behind that plant?'

'Must I state the blindingly obvious? I was hiding. I saw you with that hobgoblin McNally and was waiting until he'd departed. Have you seen his tiny little feet? Proof that the Devil walks among us. He'd have launched into an interrogation about my presence. That man could give you a few tips on interview technique. You and the KGB.'

'McNally? What's your beef with him? No, hold on.' Tom took a breath. 'Tell me first, how did you get into Government Buildings without coming in with us?'

'Oh, is that where I am? I hadn't noticed.' Linda planted her hands on her hips. 'Honestly, this isn't my first time, Tom. Don't make me say it. You surely know who my father was?'

The realisation hit the inspector like a smack to the forehead. Fionn McCarn, Linda's father, a previous minister for justice.

'There it is,' Linda said, observing his evolving expression. 'History for slow learners. I've kept in with most of the ushers over the years. The family members of former ministers get to keep a few privileges and, anyway, they know I'm one of your sort. Right, let's pop in here and wait for our man. So, spill the goss – did Blake do it?'

Ray's jaw dropped. Tom just raised an eyebrow and held the office door open for the psychologist.

He never felt entirely comfortable around Linda. She was

absolutely brilliant, of that he was certain. But her eccentric manner, her bizarre dress sense, the upper-class dismissiveness of her tone, was all extremely off-putting.

'Are you sure we're allowed in here?' Linda wondered aloud, as she strode in. 'If not, this is the first time I've engaged in a spot of breaking and entering with the police.'

The minister's desk dominated one end of the office – an expensive-looking oak affair, flanked by comfortable leather-upholstered chairs, studded with gold. There was a meeting table just inside the door, varnished until it shone. The inspector pulled out a chair for Linda and sat down himself.

A door to the left of the desk looked like it led into an adjoining office.

Ray followed his eyeline.

'Finnegan's office. I'll fill you in on last night's finds afterwards,' he said. 'Actually, if you have Linda here, I might pop in and give it another once-over.'

'Go on, then,' Tom said. They didn't need a panel interviewing Minister Blake.

'The usher who found Finnegan last night – Jim,' Linda said, as Ray left. 'I've known him for donkey's years. He was one of the staff who gave families of the newly elected TDs their introductory tour of the House. Always keep in with the little people, Tom. They're a mine of information. The poor man was horrified by what he found. Naturally. Some of them in here would leap over the corpse in their rush to get to a television camera.'

It never ceased to amaze Tom how much Linda could talk. He couldn't begin to imagine how fast her brain worked. Twice the speed of his, at any rate. She would lend great insight into some of those they would be investigating in this case, but he was nervous about letting her loose on ordinary folk.

'Linda, let's backtrack. Why don't you like McNally? And why hide, rather than greet him with your usual acerbic wit?'

Linda mock-shivered.

'Darragh McNally makes my skin crawl. He's an inoffensive-looking evil little mastermind. I can't handle his type of cut-throat, Tom, so I just steer clear. The sensible option. I bet he's already told you all about the wonderful new legislation that's coming. His brainchild, the law that will save Ireland's economic future and provide us with limitless jobs and energy into the future. Even in the middle of a murder investigation, he'll have found time to tell you. Never stops spinning, that one.'

'He mentioned that Bill on the way over,' Tom said. 'Not quite in those terms and not that it was his idea. He said the initiative comes from Minister Blake's department.'

'Pfft. He has his grubby little hands all over it. Anyway, no harm your being aware of it. It's already causing tensions in the Reform Party and your victim was working for the minister directly responsible.'

'How do you know so much about it?' Tom asked, running a hand over the bristles on his chin. He'd forgotten to shave.

'You know my father was in cabinet with Paddy Shelton? One of our pal Aidan's forerunners? No? He was the Minister for State Resources in the early '70s. Now you're getting it. Anyway, Shelton was a great man. He and my father were brilliant ministers. Not like this shower of . . .'

'Jesus wept! The point, Linda.' Tom was mildy interested in the Bill because they'd discovered that Carl Madsen was in the building last night, but he couldn't quite see the relevance of some tax law to their murder investigation. The photo found with Ryan was far and away the most interesting piece of evidence in their case.

'I'm getting there. Stop interrupting. Shelton knew there were potentially vast supplies of oil and gas reserves off the west coast of Ireland. He knew it and most of Europe knew it too. So he wrote laws to ensure that whenever anyone tapped into our natural resources, we'd get the lion's share of the profits. Are you still with me?'

'I don't know if anyone is ever fully with you, but I'm vaguely familiar with what you're talking about.'

'Good boy. So, the government that followed Shelton's crowd, it championed businessmen. It abolished the notion of reserving oil and gas for the Irish people. Then it got rid of royalties on finds. Now the companies are taxed virtually nothing.'

'Okay, that's the history, Linda, but this government is remedying that now. Isn't it?'

'No, no, no. Tom, you must understand – the only reason the government is doing anything is because of the huge pressure its representatives are under in the west of the country. The Reform Party is not strong in the capital – it only has a few TDs here. Its real strength lies in the rural counties, especially along the western seaboard. The people in those counties are up in arms about the activities of oil and gas companies and they are the Taoiseach's and half the cabinet's voters. But this Bill, what they've done . . .'

Linda stopped short. The door had opened and the owner of the office filled its frame.

'Linda McCarn. I didn't realise you'd be here. Sorry – Aidan Blake, Inspector. I apologise for delaying you. Now, what's this about a Bill?'

*

Tom stood to shake the minister's hand.

It was a cliché, but the inspector couldn't help but think how the man had always appeared taller on television, whereas in real life the top of his head hovered at Tom's chest level.

Blake was just as handsome in the flesh, though, even if he did look haggard this morning. There was certainly something charismatic about the man – magnetic, even. Thick and floppy red-gold hair bounced above vivid blue eyes and the minister wore an expertly tailored designer suit that looked like it cost a few months' worth of Tom's pay packet.

Just to rub it in, Aidan Blake also seemed to be a pleasant fellow. He appeared sombre now, but normally his smile was genuine and warm. Blake, in fact, was everything the leader of the country wasn't. Taoiseach Cormac O'Shea, the head of the Reform Party, was an aging, balding, ruddy-faced, stout countryman, who had all the facial markings – the broken-veined cheeks and bulbous nose – of a man who enjoyed his liquor. Aidan Blake, just turned forty, was the fresh-faced poster boy for Irish politics and for the country.

Tom glanced from Linda to Blake, wondering what she had been about to tell them and what the minister would make of it. The psychologist looked uncertain about continuing with her exposition, even a little on edge. A rarity for her.

'I just mentioned to Tom how busy you must be with the Bill you're writing,' Linda said, and averted her eyes as the colour rose in her cheeks. She was a master of analysing when somebody else was lying, but terrible at it herself.

'I see,' Blake said, and gave her an odd look. He turned to the inspector. 'I apologise, again, for your having to wait. I had to have a cigarette before I came up. My nerves are frayed.'

'Understandably. So, you know each other?' Tom asked, surprised. He hadn't missed the coolness in the minister's tone and body language towards the psychologist.

'Yes,' Linda replied. 'I'm a patron of Silent Voices. I was meant to attend the ball last night but got stuck at something else. How is Sara coping with the news?' She directed this to Blake.

He shrugged and slumped down in a chair in front of Tom, rubbing tired eyes with manicured hands.

'Neither of us can believe what's happened. It's surreal. A nightmare. Ryan, dead. I'd told him to go home early yesterday. I don't even know why he was still here. Are you absolutely certain he was murdered? Could it have been an accident? And poor Kathryn. How is she?'

'As can be expected, Minister,' Tom replied.

'Call me Aidan, please.'

'Aidan, then. Look, Ryan's death was no accident. He was shot twice, once in the head.'

Blake recoiled, his hands falling away from his face, along with any remaining colour.

'Are you serious? In the head? I was just told he'd been shot . . . I didn't . . . I guess I thought he'd been shot in the chest or something. Are there any witnesses?'

'That's what we're trying to establish. How long did you know Ryan?'

'Years. He's worked with me for years.'

'And you got on well?'

'Of course. I mean . . . he was a friend and a work colleague. A decent chap. Why would somebody kill him?'

Tom sat back in his chair. Why, indeed?

'We've established that Ryan was attacked in the tunnel connecting the LH2000 annex to the main House some time after 9 p.m., when the building was last checked, and before 10:45 p.m., when his body was found. Aidan, I have to ask everybody who was in the complex during that period what they were doing here and if they saw Ryan. You were clearly with him at some point; can you tell me what time? You may have been one of the last people to see him.'

Blake ran his hands through the hair at his temples, his forehead creased in concentration.

'It must have been about 8. I was just leaving to go to Sara's ball. I told him again to go home. It was Friday night and he'd only started back in work this week. He had been on sick leave. Ryan was determined, though, to pick up where he left off. I popped back over just after 9 p.m. for a meeting. I didn't see him then, but I didn't check his office. I was back at the ball by 10:30.'

'You came back over for your appointment with Carl Madsen?'

'Yes, how . . . ? Oh, McNally told you. Well, it's not a secret. It was an unusual time for a meeting, but he had flown in late that afternoon. He was en route to the opening of a new Udforske facility in the west. I agreed to meet with all the stakeholder drilling companies out of courtesy before I sign off on a new Bill my department is drafting. Mr Madsen is as busy as I am. He diverted his flight to Dublin to accommodate our brief session. It was pointless in the end. He didn't have anything new to suggest, but still, better he come here than I go to his holiday home. Aesthetics.'

'Madsen has a holiday home in Ireland?' Linda asked.

'Yes. In Donegal. I say holiday home but it's more like a palatial retreat. Built into a cliff, like something from a spy movie.'

'So you met Madsen at what time, exactly?' Tom continued.

Blake hesitated for a moment. He seemed to consider something fleetingly, then change his mind.

'We were finished by about 9.30. As I said, it was a short exchange. Then I went looking for my wife. I found her in the bar at about a quarter to ten. She was trying to get the remnants of the cabinet and . . . eh, other important guests, over to the ball for a group shot. We were busy. I didn't think of Ryan . . . then I heard the news this morning . . .'

The minister trailed off. Tom studied him closely. Blake appeared genuinely devastated by the death of his PA. The inspector wondered what Linda thought of his reaction. The psychologist was peering intensely at Blake but saying very little. Her quiet behaviour was not what Tom had expected.

'The tunnel where Ryan was found – do you have any idea what he would have been doing there?' he continued. 'Nobody seems to know.'

Blake shook his head.

'I can't think of a single reason. There are equipment supply offices down there, but my secretary, not my PA, would be more familiar with them. Unless he needed something for himself?'

Tom paused before asking the next question. The minister seemed to be ruled out as a potential suspect. The fifteen-minute period between 9.30 and 9.45, if Blake's alibi was valid, could hardly be enough time to cross to LH2000 from here, find and murder Ryan Finnegan and return to the main Leinster House building. It was an approximate eight-minute walk at a brisk pace to the minister's office from the site of the murder.

And yet, he had to keep Aidan Blake under consideration. It felt absurd, yet the chances of Ryan having been attacked by a random stranger were slim, especially when the location was taken into account.

'Minister – Aidan – I won't keep you much longer, but tell me this: were you aware of any particular . . . proclivities on Ryan's part? Was he a consumer of pornographic material?'

Blake's eyes widened and angry red blotches erupted on his cheeks.

'What do you mean, pornographic? He was a regular man. I'm sure he looked at, you know . . . stuff. How is this relevant?'

'It may not be. One more thing: do you own a gun? Have you any experience with firearms?'

The minister looked puzzled, then taken aback.

'Oh. Jesus, you're serious. No, I don't own a gun. I don't own any weapons.'

Tom held his gaze. Blake didn't blink.

'I think we'll leave it there,' the inspector said.

The minister nodded curtly and stood. He shook Tom's hand vigorously.

'Ryan was an honourable man,' he said.

Tom scrutinised the other man's face. What emotion lay there? Was it grief, shock or guilt?

'Honourable'. It was an unusual way to describe someone. Old-fashioned. Was that the best eulogy Blake had for his former PA?

It was always the same. There was nothing like a murder investigation to bring to light the truth of people's dealings with and feelings about the victim. Ryan was dead, but a spotlight was about to be shone on every detail of his life.

Tom informed the minister before they left that they would need to talk to his wife, who had also been in the building.

When they were back in the corridor, the inspector turned to Linda.

'You were tight-lipped in there,' he said, keeping his voice low as they walked.

She chewed her lip. He could almost see the cogs in her brain turning.

'I don't like Aidan Blake,' she responded, finally.

Tom was surprised.

'Everybody else seems to,' he said.

'From afar,' she pointed out. 'That said, it's not like we're bosom pals. I really only know him through his wife. There's just something . . . I can't put my finger on it. I just wanted to watch him and listen. Did you notice it?'

'What?'

'When you asked him whether he owned a gun, you also asked if he had any experience with them. Blake answered the first question, but not the second.'

Tom frowned. She was right.

Had Blake been so thrown by the query he hadn't answered it fully? Or was it a deliberate omission?

'Why did you ask how Sara was?' he probed.

'I've heard her mention Ryan once or twice as being a lovely fellow. I suspect, knowing her, she'd be much more sincere in her devastation about the man's death.'

Tom was curious about Linda's read of the minister. He'd found the other man's apparent distress about his PA's death convincing enough.

Ray emerged from Ryan Finnegan's office back down the corridor and they waited for him.

'Any joy with the minister?' his deputy asked.

'None.'

'I must leave you now,' Linda said. 'I've an engagement this afternoon. You give me a shout when you need me, Tom. I'm excited about this one. Politics, intrigue, murder – our very own *House of Cards*. Do let me sit in on the meetings with other ministers. I get a disproportionate amount of joy from watching powerful men sweat.'

'Eh . . . okay,' Tom replied, bemused. 'If you could sit in on some of the interviews with mere mortals, that would help also.'

'Bleh.' She stuck her tongue out. 'Boring plebs. If needs must.'

'I'll keep in touch,' the inspector called, as she glided in the opposite direction. 'Now, Junior, what have you got under your hat? I know you've been itching to tell me something all morning.'

'Am I that transparent?' Ray lamented, as they picked up the pace.

'You're virtually translucent. And actually, Linda's right. You do appear to be fading away. Are you eating these days?'

Ray chewed the inside of one of his hollow cheeks and said nothing.

The inspector had watched his deputy with concern over the last year. The change in the younger man stemmed from a traumatic case nearly twelve months ago, when Ray had become emotionally involved with somebody who later died horribly. The young man had become more introverted since then, more intense. Maybe his detective sergeant had needed to grow up a little, Tom often speculated, but he would have preferred if it had happened naturally and in happier circumstances.

'He'd left everything in his office, by the way,' Ray said, deftly ignoring the inspector's question about his eating habits. 'Ryan, that is. His phone, wallet, coat, even his reading glasses. When he went over to LH2000 he clearly intended to come back here. There were ten missed calls from his wife.'

Tom shook his head to dispel the image of poor Kathryn Finnegan desperately trying to get hold of her husband.

'And what's your big discovery?'

'I think I know why Ryan was over in LH2000. And I might know how his killer found him.'

CHAPTER 6

Laura's phone buzzed as the text message came in.

'Important?' Eoin asked.

'Notice of the first team meeting. You should try to get assigned – it would be good experience for you.'

Laura looked up at Eoin. She could tell he was itching to reach over and take her hand, but she gave her head the smallest of shakes. Not here.

Inwardly, she beamed. They'd only been seeing each other for two months, but she still couldn't believe her luck. Bridget, her housemate and colleague, had introduced them on a night out. He was Bridget's second cousin and Laura still wasn't sure if it had been entirely accidental, bumping into Eoin that night in the bar in town. If it was planned, her friend knew her well, because they made a good match. Eoin might only be a rank-and-file garda, but he wouldn't be staying there for long. He was smart and showed initiative. Were it not for the fact Eoin had entered the force in his late twenties, he would probably already be working his way up to detective. He'd started out as a fireman, which still made Laura swoon at the thought.

'Come over to mine tonight,' he said quietly. 'It doesn't matter how late you finish, I'll leave the door on the latch. One of my other women might get there ahead of you, but feel free to just jump in.'

Laura noticed Emmet McDonagh approaching and discreetly moved a step away from Eoin.

'Detective Brennan. Will you be rejoining your boss any time soon?'

'Yes. Shortly, as it happens. We're setting up an incident room in the Park.'

Garda headquarters was situated near the city centre end of Phoenix Park. The Dublin park was one of the largest walled green areas in Europe and a favourite recreation spot for Dubliners. It also contained many important public buildings and places of interest, including the President's home, the American Ambassador's residence and the Zoo. The inspector, who lived at the far end of the Park, near Castleknock, generally liked to situate his team in Blanchardstown, away from what he liked to think of as the actual zoo – headquarters. But McGuinness had insisted.

'Lovely,' said Emmet. 'You'll be upstairs from us. Well, tell the inspector we've confirmed there were just two shots fired. We've retrieved one of the bullets; the other is most likely still in the victim. The State Pathologist is conducting the post-mortem this morning and he'll send over a report this afternoon.'

'The boss will be pleased. I don't think we've ever had such a fast turnaround from pathology. It seems like Leinster House is a good place to be murdered if you want the investigation into your killer expedited.'

'A couple of members of my team have been over that office on the sixth floor looking for traces of the victim. I'll get the report on that over to you, too. I believe the office's regular occupant confirmed the room had been disturbed.'

'She did,' Laura replied. She turned to Eoin. 'Can you make sure the computer from upstairs gets to the Garda IT specialists? Tell them I'm sending Detective Michael Geoghegan over to sit on them until they give us something and remind them that every other department is operating at top speed.'

'Yes, ma'am.' Eoin gave her a cheeky wink as he left and she had to bite her lip to prevent a grin spreading.

'Oh, give it up,' Emmet snorted. 'Do you think we're all blind? It's sickening. Pah!' The Tech Bureau chief stomped off. Laura stared at his huge retreating back, stunned.

What had she been expecting? That the people around her, who unearthed secrets for a living, wouldn't figure out she was seeing one of her colleagues?

Michael Geoghegan, one of her teammates, sauntered over. He was wearing his usual plain-clothes uniform of tracksuit hoodie and blue denims. He stood beside Laura, in her smart Zara suit, looking like she'd just hauled him in for dealing drugs. He was a good-looking man with short, spiky brown hair, blue eyes and an olive complexion – but his idea of dressing up for the job was wearing a plain-knit sweater over a shirt. She'd never seen him in a suit. It was hard to believe he was a settled-down husband and father, let alone a senior detective.

'You look like you're trying out for a part in a silent movie over here. What's with the pained facial expressions? And did I hear you mention my name?'

'Have you noticed anything different about me?' Laura asked.

'Different? Like what? Do you mean that glow of somebody who's shagging a handsome young guard?'

'Jesus. Does everyone know?'

Michael laughed.

'No. Bridget let it slip last week. Don't worry, I haven't had time to spread it around. I'm waiting for the next big night out when the whole team is there and I've a loudspeaker.'

'Git. I'm going to have words with her. Listen, could you keep on top of IT when we send that computer over?'

'No bother. I'm looking for tasks that help me avoid Ray. We set him up on a date with one of Anne's friends. I always thought she was a bit of a cow, but he does need somebody. Anyway, Anne got a full half hour of ranting on the phone last night from her. It seems the evening didn't go well.'

Laura kept her smile rigid. She'd buried any feelings she had for Ray months ago, when he'd so obviously fallen for somebody else. Only her closest confidantes had known she was holding a torch for him back then and nobody else needed to know now. And yet she still felt a pang in her stomach at the thought of him seeing other women. She didn't know why. What did it matter if he was back on the dating scene? He hadn't noticed her before, so why would he notice her now? And, anyway, wasn't she seeing someone herself these days and blissfully happy?

Michael saw somebody he wanted to speak to at the top of the stairs and excused himself.

Laura waved him off, then gave her head a quick shake. What was happening to her? Here she was, yards from where a man had been brutally murdered, contemplating her love life. Was she that desensitised?

But it was what Tom always said, wasn't it? Life went on. Cruelly and inexplicably, the world kept turning.

The only person for whom it had stopped was Ryan Finnegan.

*

'He'd received an email earlier in the day.'

Ray and Tom were making their way back through Leinster House. The inspector had noted that they hadn't needed a pass card to get from Government Buildings to the main House. The security swipe was only required for the doors on the Leinster House side. But the doors to the tunnel where Ryan was shot apparently did need a pass card. Did that mean the killer worked here and had one? Or had a swipe card been stolen?

'An email about what?' Tom asked.

'I'll tell you, but first there's another thing: Finnegan's isn't the only desk in that office. There's another.'

'Who owns the other one?'

'The minister's secretary, Grace Brady. Morrison filled me in. He also scanned the preliminary list of people who were about the building this evening. Ms Brady was in until around 8 p.m. An usher has confirmed seeing her leaving. So she was gone, apparently, by the time the body was discovered.'

'I can't wait to see how many people are on this list of Morrison's – all potential suspects. A list, by the way, that includes the Taoiseach himself.'

'The Taoiseach? You're joking!' Ray spluttered.

'I wish I was. Go on, the email.'

'Right. So, we know Ryan returned to work this week. Well, I looked through his emails last night, which was easy, because his computer was only in sleep mode and he hadn't set up a security password. Again, he obviously assumed he would be returning to his office. The screen came to life as soon as I tapped a key and this email I'm about to tell you about was open on the desktop.

'I spoke to Morrison and the head of Oireachtas IT. It turns out that while Ryan was off recuperating, his original computer was taken by the Oireachtas IT team for updating.'

'They just took it away when he wasn't there? Are we going the right way for the car park? It's through here, isn't it?'

'Yes, yes and yes. While the computers are allocated for personal use, they still belong to the Oireachtas. When the techies came to collect Grace Brady's computer for updating, she told them they could take Ryan's as well.

'So, he got back this week and discovered that the computer on his desk was not the computer he had six months ago. He sent an email, followed by a phone call, to the IT department on Monday and they emailed him back early on Friday apologising for the error. They confirmed that the original computer had been accidentally transferred to LH2000, floor six, room six point eight. The mix-up was to be sorted out next week – as in, his machine returned to him – once the person currently using it was given notice. Tom, I just hit a button on Ryan's computer and that email was open on the screen. Anyone could have walked into his office, seen it, and known exactly where he'd gone.'

'Yes, if they knew the layout of this complex and also had access to Government Buildings. We can't rule out the idea that somebody might have just followed him from the main house. That aside, why was Ryan so impatient to access the computer that he went over there? Something to do with that picture, do you think?'

'I'd imagine so,' Ray agreed. 'Where are you off to now?'

'Press. McGuinness is making me.'

'Is he . . . okay?'

'What do you mean?'

'Is there stuff going on with his wife, June?'

Tom sighed. It wasn't that he had forgotten the family crisis Sean was dealing with. He just didn't like to think about it. June was the chief's wife and had been recently diagnosed with early onset Alzheimer's. Sean doted on his wife and had been looking forward to their retirement together. Her diagnosis was overwhelming and heartbreaking.

'He's . . . managing,' Tom said, and left it at that.

*

Inspector Reynolds sat at the far end of the top table at the press conference, becoming steadily more depressed as journalists fired questions at Assistant Commissioner Bronwyn Maher, McGuinness and the Minister for Justice. Was this a terrorist attack? Had any suspects been identified? What was the motive for the murder? Who had been in the parliament complex last night? Was the Garda Commissioner cutting short his visit to Canada to come home and take charge?

The chief superintendent didn't expect Tom to speak. He was there as a show of force, allegedly. In reality, the inspector knew his boss wanted him to see the pressure that he, as the head of the Bureau, would be under in the time ahead. Maher had given him a swift nod when he'd come in. Her blond hair was in its usual immaculately coiffed style, not a strand out of place, her make-up casually elegant. She wore a trouser uniform but still looked feminine. Tom had always admired her. She'd made the choice not to sacrifice her style or personality to get ahead in what was still a male-dominated workplace, and nothing was standing in her way.

McGuinness and Maher talked at length and gave away nothing, while the minister spoke convincingly about directing mass Garda resources to the case and increasing security at government and other high profile buildings, though everybody believed the attack to be an isolated incident. The commissioner had made an overnight decision (after a phone call from the Minister for Justice, though that was left unsaid) to leave the Quebec conference and come home to be at the media's disposal.

Tom had to suppress a wry smile when the minister mentioned resources – only last month he had sent a memo to the commissioner banning all paid overtime and extending the moratorium on recruitment for the force.

The inspector encountered Ray again in the corridor on the way to the incident room in Phoenix Park headquarters. The detective had a large cup of coffee in one hand and was balancing a roast chicken and stuffing sandwich on a folder in the other.

'If I wasn't married already . . .' Tom said, reaching out gratefully.

Ray watched, irritated and amused, as his boss stole his lunch. The same man who had been concerned he wasn't eating enough just over an hour ago.

'Who have we got?' Tom mumbled, through a mouthful of food.

'The usual suspects. Ourselves, Laura, Michael. Bridget Duffy and Brian Cullinane are here. Hairy Kelly has transferred from Blanchardstown so I asked for him. We've been allocated a squad of about twenty rank and file for interviews, supplemented by Leinster House security.'

'Mass resources, my eye.'

'What?'

'Nothing. Don't get me started. Okay, let's get this show on the road.'

The noise and bustle in the room died down when they entered. Laura muted the television in the corner, which showed a reporter in blustery weather outside Leinster House, a tracker story feed running at the bottom of the screen: 'Gardaí hunt gunman following shock shooting in Dáil.' To the uninformed, the headline might imply that an irate citizen had stormed the parliament when it was in session and taken out an elected member.

Tom surveyed the case board, on which various sheets and established facts had been pinned. He took in the highlights, then faced the room.

'It's not that I don't like spending my weekends with you lovely people, but seriously, seventy-two hours was all I asked for. Credit where it's due, though. It's a spectacular way to get me back to work.'

There were grim smiles and apologetic shrugs. The team members knew how hard the inspector worked and the weight of responsibility that being in charge carried. They also knew that he always ensured each of them got time away when it was needed. It was one of the characteristics that made them grateful to be on his squad and fostered their loyalty to him.

'So, folks, we have a man shot in the back and face, most likely while attempting to flee an attacker within the parliament complex. The incident took place inside a locked office building that could only be accessed through an underground tunnel, which originates in Leinster House. We have – how many people do we know for certain were in the complex last night?'

Brian Cullinane lifted a sheet of paper and held it at arm's length as he squinted at it through narrowed eyes. He needed reading glasses but was fighting it. The poor sod was already sporting a Benedictine bald patch and he hadn't yet turned forty. The last thing he wanted was a pair of spectacles. It was hard enough being a gay policeman. Receding hair and glasses would be the nail in the coffin of his love life.

'Thirty-five employees, consisting of twenty ushers, six bar and canteen staff, five members of the "Bills Office", and four civil servants working in the one-stop shop, an information go-to point for TDs. And a partridge in a pear tree.'

He turned the page. 'There were ten guards at various positions throughout the complex. I have seventy names of people who were definitely in the buildings in and around the time period we're looking at, ranging from political staff to ministerial secretaries, TDs, ministers and the Taoiseach himself. Twenty-three people were signed in as visitors in that 9 p.m. to 10.30 p.m period, according to the log. Those signed in earlier in the day had returned their visitor passes before 9. All bar two of the late visitors were guests of TDs and were brought to the Dáil bar. The other two were a relative of a staff secretary, collecting her from work, and a Mr Carl Madsen. We can check this list against the CCTV footage of people entering and leaving the complex.'

'Jesus H Christ! How many is that in total?' Tom felt the back of his head start to throb.

'One hundred and thirty-eight. That we know of. From the sounds of things, we're lucky. There could have been a thousand on an evening when the Dáil was in session.'

'I don't know,' Laura mused. 'We have enough people to make the investigation cumbersome but not so many that somebody was bound to have seen something. If they'd all been in, it would have been next to impossible for the killer to strike.'

'Boss?' Michael was reading a text on his phone.

'What is it?'

'The IT lads. I'd better run down to them. I've been on their case all morning and it sounds like they've found something.'

'Something that will shed light on that photo we found, hopefully,' Tom remarked, casting a glance over his shoulder at the case board and the copy of the picture pinned to it. 'Go ahead, Michael. Okay, we've one hundred and thirty-eight people – how many gave initial statements?'

'Seventy, including the ten gardaí. And you spoke to two more this morning – Aidan Blake and Darragh McNally. The rest had left the complex by the time the body was found and the alert was sounded.'

'We need to organise formal statements from McNally and Blake,' Tom said. 'And that's still a lot of people not interviewed. Who were these guests in the bar?'

'Constituents, mainly. They were in small groups and the TDs hosting their attendance are swearing to them all being in the bar for the duration, excusing toilet trips. All told, it looks like there were about sixty people in the bar between 9 and 10.'

'We're talking about a bar,' Ray said. 'Was everybody sober and keeping an eye on each other?'

Brian shrugged. 'Your guess . . .' he trailed off.

'Did anything come out of the initial statements?' Tom asked.

'Bridget and I are going through them. Nothing yet. One usher reckoned he saw Ryan making his way through the main building around 9. Alone.'

The inspector sighed.

'Right. We need to organise initial interviews for those who had left the complex before the body was discovered and talk again to those questioned last night. Now they know how serious it is, they'll all be wracking their brains trying to recall if they saw Finnegan or anyone else acting suspiciously. I'll be talking to the Taoiseach, obviously, and I'll take Carl Madsen too. Anything from forensics or pathology?'

Laura stood up.

'Initial reports from both departments are in.'

She paused as half the room clapped.

'Why, thank you. I'll take full credit for their speedy turn-around.' Laura smiled wryly. 'So, Ryan was shot twice. In the back, then the face. Ballistics say the weapon fired was most likely a Glock .38, 9mm. Both bullets have been retrieved, one at the scene, the other from the victim. Ryan was in good health, bar the injuries he sustained in the car crash. He suffered bruises and minor injuries consistent with a tumble down stairs and falling after he was shot. That fits with Garda Coyle's theory about Ryan fleeing his attacker from the sixth floor. They're estimating time of death between 9.30 p.m. and 9.45 p.m. That's the tightest they'll give us.

'There was tonnes of DNA at the scene and it will be extremely difficult to eliminate it all – the tunnel is open to everyone in the complex. There wasn't anything unusual on Ryan except a little cartridge ink on his fingertips, which he could have picked up handling pages hot off a printer.'

Tom stroked his jaw. The bristles were getting longer. Louise would ring him later to tell him he had looked a right state on the news. McGuinness would be thrilled, though – his lead detective working so hard he'd no time for bathroom breaks or personal hygiene.

'So he was shot with a Glock,' he said. 'Well, there's another lead. Who in Leinster House last night could have had a Glock in their possession? Let's run a check and see if anyone has a firearms licence or training certificate, though we can't rule out somebody getting their hands on an illegal weapon.'

'Could it be a professional hit?' Laura asked.

It was Tom's turn to shrug.

'Easily. Though if it wasn't somebody who worked in the place, they would have had to be signed in. Make sure to look closely at new employees, just in case.'

The inspector felt hopeful. It was extremely difficult for an ordinary civilian to get their hands on a gun in Ireland. They might be able to trace where these bullets and the weapon they belonged to had come from.

Tom filled them in on his visit with Kathryn Finnegan and the meeting with Blake.

'Ryan Finnegan seems to have been a fairly ordinary man,' he concluded. 'The only striking evidence so far is that dodgy picture we found.'

Tom turned and stared at it again. Amongst photos of the victim's bloodied corpse, it still stood out on the board. He peered at the back of the man's head in the foreground of the image. Was it Ryan himself? Their victim's hair had been lighter than the black hair of this man, but it could have been dyed. Or was it somebody Ryan knew?

It could, of course, just be an image of two random men taken from the internet, though why Ryan had it on him was beyond Tom.

'Moving on from how he was killed – the real question is why?' The inspector faced the room again. 'He doesn't seem the sort to have been involved with criminal elements. Maybe he was cheating on his wife, but there was nothing in her demeanour or reaction to make me consider her as an avenging spouse. We'll verify her statement about being home with the baby all night, though. That photo is the only anomaly about Ryan Finnegan that's jumping out. Is it possible he was being blackmailed or bribed, or was he doing the blackmailing and bribing?'

'Did Linda McCarn have anything useful to say when you interviewed Blake?' Ray asked.

Tom hesitated. Could he describe the psychologist's behaviour as strange, when she was always a bit odd?

'She started telling me about some piece of legislation Minister Blake is working on that's not kosher,' he replied, and shrugged.

Ian Kelly snorted, running a hand over his shiny egg-shaped head. He'd carried his ironic nickname 'Hairy' from his role as station sergeant in Blanchardstown to his new post in headquarters. Tom preferred to call him Ian, fearing his crown might also go in that direction and not wanting to be a hostage to fortune.

'That's hardly news, is it? A politician doing something dodgy. It's government. Bought and paid for.'

Bridget Duffy, Laura's flatmate, shook her head in disagreement, her dark ponytail whipping back and forth, her little snub nose indignant.

'That's a terrible, sweeping generalisation. Aidan Blake is a decent politician. Everybody knows that. One of the only ones, I grant you. I like him.'

'You and every other woman in the country,' Ian retorted.

'St Aidan, Minister of the God-like Resources and boundless Energy,' Brian quipped.

Bridget made an un-ladylike gesture with her middle finger.

Tom held up his hand.

'Children! I'll follow up with Linda. She still hasn't seen the photo. Maybe she'll be able to deduce something from it that we can't.'

On cue, the door opened.

Michael was back. He was holding a brown envelope, his face as grey as his Adidas hoodie.

'What is it?' Tom asked.

Michael swallowed.

He handed the envelope to Tom, holding it between his finger and thumb as if it was contaminated.

'You'd better look for yourself.'

CHAPTER 7

'Jesus, you look like I felt when I woke up in the honeymoon suite of the Gresham and realised I'd married the girlfriend.'

Willie stood beside the car, stroking his neat grey moustache, his garda uniform, as ever, starched and ironed with precision by his much-maligned wife. Leaves blew through the Park, October gusts battering the ancient trees. Tom pulled open the passenger door, leaving Ray and Michael to jump in the back. When they travelled in this manner, the inspector always felt like they were a parody of a family out for a jaunt, he and Willie playing the parents, his two detective colleagues their teenage charges.

Not today. His thoughts were elsewhere.

Tom slipped into the seat and turned to Willie.

'You know the fastest way to Sean McGuinness's house?'

'As it happens.'

Willie Callaghan was a font of all knowledge when it came to Dublin geography, no surprise given his years behind the wheel. The man was never happier than when he was in the car, especially when he had a captive audience listening to him whine about his wife. Tom knew that his driver was very happily married but he enjoyed the exaggerated tales of homelife woe and the humour Willie brought to them. Louise, in a moment of psychological insight, had suggested that perhaps Tom kept buying unreliable cars because he liked driving around with Willie. Butch Cassidy and the Sundance Kid. In their heads.

Tom had phoned Sean McGuinness to let him know they were

coming. The chief had gone home directly after the press conference to mind June, telling Tom he was on the other end of the
phone if he was needed.

And now he was.

The inspector spun round in his seat. He was holding the
envelope on his lap, afraid if he let it go it would fall – into the
wrong hands.

'Tell me again, from the top.'

Michael was sweating. He'd nearly had a heart attack when the
head of the IT department had pulled him into a small office and
shown him what they'd discovered.

'Right. So, we've confirmed the computer in the office on the
sixth floor was originally Ryan Finnegan's. The Oireachtas IT
team had updated the system and security features, but they left
the browser history and personal files untouched. Luckily. Or
they'd have seen what we've found.

'Each Oireachtas employee is given an account for the intranet
in Leinster House. That's the internal server. They're set up on
this system called Parliament Notes, which gives them an email
address – so and so at oireachtas dot com. Seven months ago, Ryan
logged into Blake's account and saw an email containing the pictures you currently hold in your hand. After forwarding them to
himself, he saved all of them deep in the hard drive of his computer and deleted the email from his account – most likely
because he feared they would be too easily hacked into there. He
thought they'd be safe where he'd hidden them.

'Last night, Ryan went over to the office where his computer
had been mistakenly transferred and accessed the images, print-
ing them off. He also saved them to an external device, most likely
a USB stick.'

'Which wasn't found,' Tom said.

'No.'

'Hold on,' Ray said, confused. 'Just go through this again. If

Garda Coyle was right last night and Finnegan was discovered in that office and then pursued, we can make the leap that the killer took the USB stick from Ryan or from the computer itself. Presumably, having taken the offending images from the scene, our murderer would want to ensure there were no other copies. So, why leave them on the hard drive? And can the IT guys tell what time the USB stick was taken out of the machine?'

'Yes, to your last question. The USB was removed at 9.46 p.m. So, unless Ryan flung it somewhere, we can speculate that the killer took it. IT said Ryan had successfully downloaded the images onto the external device. He then either closed the hard drive or the computer automatically locked after a period of inactivity. The killer probably did want to examine the machine to find and delete the image files, but without Ryan's username and password, he wouldn't have been able to log in. This wasn't like the computer you brought to life in Ryan's office by just touching the keyboard – the computer on the sixth floor had all the security walls enabled. And even if the killer could have gained access, he would have struggled to find the images – they were buried in an obscure file.

'Our man just had to hope that no one found the images on the computer. Granted, he could have taken the machine itself, but it's large and presumably he didn't want to draw notice by wandering around Leinster House with a stolen desktop under his arm. He could have smashed it, but that would've definitely drawn our attention and he'd no way of knowing if the images could still be recovered by an IT expert. He took a risk that we wouldn't chance upon the office and recognise the significance of the computer. Remember, too, that the picture we found was hidden beneath Ryan's body. The killer must have assumed he'd taken all the images and the USB stick, so there'd be no trail or reason to search a computer other than the one in Ryan's office.'

'You said the original account the email was sent to was Blake's. Did Ryan hack it?'

'No,' Michael replied. 'He actually had access to that account in his position as PA. The IT guys were able to track his computer activity on the night the emails were sent.'

Tom turned to look out the windscreen as Michael ran through the IT department's explanation. They had crossed the River Liffey and were now driving past the heavy police presence on Merrion Square to the rear of Leinster House. They turned left onto a bustling Baggot Street, heading for Sandyford. They'd soon enter the affluent leafy suburbs near the national soccer and rugby stadium.

The envelope and its contents burned on his lap.

What in God's name had they stumbled upon?

*

'Come in, come in. Michael and your driver are not planning to stay out there, are they?'

'June, what did I say about answering the door? Oh, it's you, Tom.'

Superintendent McGuinness rounded the stairs just as his wife was ushering the inspector and Ray in. His look of concern was replaced with one of embarrassment, when he realised his colleagues had witnessed him barking at his spouse.

'Really, Sean, I'm not completely doolally. Not yet.' June glared at her husband. 'It's Saturday afternoon, I thought it might be one of the kids.'

Tom couldn't see anything different about the chief's wife. June was a couple of years older than Sean but her complexion was still youthful. She kept her greying hair neatly bobbed, complementing exquisite cheekbones and full lips. She had been attractive in her prime and still was, in a schoolmarm-ish way. And of course, that had been her chosen career, teaching. She wasn't long retired.

There was nothing to give away the deterioration of her brain, no sign it had already embarked on its regressive journey to a child-like state. There wasn't a single clue to indicate the heart-break to come, the devastation of lost memories and personality, of everything that made June herself.

Tom kissed her warmly on the cheek, inhaling the scent he and Louise had gifted her last Christmas. Her favourite, he recalled, though he couldn't even begin to remember the brand.

'Michael's on the phone and Willie is having a cigarette,' he said, answering her question.

The chief's residence was not quite as salubrious as some of his neighbours' and was quite dated in its furnishings, but it was welcoming and pleasant. Every room was carpeted or lino-ed, no polished wooden floors here. The walls were papered, not painted. The kitchen contained an old-fashioned crockery dresser, the television in the sitting room had been manufactured when LED was still something found in pencils. It reminded the inspector of his parents' home.

'Sorry, dear,' McGuinness said, patting his wife on the shoulder by way of apology for his outburst. He moved aside so everybody could enter the large hallway properly. 'Perhaps you could make us a pot of tea, while I talk to the lads?'

June's features softened and she smiled.

'Oh, all right then. See that, gentlemen? He doesn't trust me to not wander off or invite some lunatic into the house every time I open the door, but he's quite all right with me being alone in the kitchen with boiling hot water, knives, scissors, matches, and an oven. As long as it's housework, eh?'

McGuinness looked alarmed, even as his wife winked at him and retreated to the back of the house. Tom felt relief in the very depths of his soul. Whatever the doctors diagnosed, for all he could see, June was still the same sharp woman he'd known and loved for decades.

The chief directed them into the sitting room, pausing at the stereo to turn down Mozart's clarinet concerto adagio. Although the inspector liked to think that he too was a classical music aficionado, he couldn't hold a candle to his boss. In modern vernacular, Tom knew the popular pieces – McGuinness knew the B-sides.

'What's happened?' McGuinness asked, reclining in a deep red fabric armchair as Tom and Ray arranged themselves on the red- and beige-striped sofa that also graced the room. The *Guardian* was still on the arm of the chair, folded to the crossword page.

Tom handed him the envelope.

McGuinness raised one eyebrow as he withdrew its contents, fanning them out on the glass coffee table to get a better look.

'What are these?'

It took a moment.

'Oh! Bugger me!'

The chief's jaw dropped as he beheld the full complement of photos from Ryan Finnegan's computer. Ray covered his mouth so he wouldn't be caught smiling at McGuinness's rather inappropriate choice of words.

'Is that— ?'

'Yes,' Tom replied. 'Minister Aidan Blake, in flagrante. There are four men in total pictured. The photo we found with Ryan showed two of them but it wasn't until we saw this complete set that we discovered Blake.'

The picture nearest to his boss showed an image of the minister reclining on black satin sheets, propped up by pillows. His head was cast back, eyes half closed in ecstasy, in what appeared to be a drug-induced high. His sandy red hair was damp with sweat, as was his exposed chest. The bedside table visible in the photo was littered with a mixture of beer bottles, glasses and ashtrays.

In one hand, Blake held what looked like a half-smoked joint.

His other hand was resting on the back of the head of the young man between his legs.

McGuinness's eyes bulged out of their sockets as he sifted through the pictures, withdrawing the ones with Blake in them. Naked, semi-dressed. Having sex, watching others screwing. Drink in hand, snorting a line of cocaine.

'He's younger looking,' Tom said. 'These shots were taken a good few years ago. He could have been in his early twenties. He probably wasn't in parliament then. Maybe a county councillor, though.'

McGuinness sat back in the chair, hand on his chest, his face pale.

'If I have a heart attack, make sure you remove these pictures before anyone arrives,' he said, at last. 'This must be how Pandora felt after opening that box.'

Tom's face was creased with worry, a mirror of the chief's.

'Who's seen these?' McGuinness asked.

'Two officers in the IT department. My team. And you.'

'Good. Let's keep it to as few as possible. So, what's your theory? Was Finnegan blackmailing Blake?'

'I don't know who was doing the blackmailing, but it certainly looks like someone was, or intended to. Blake is the government's leading light; I'm sure he wouldn't want those pictures getting out.'

'But why would Ryan, his PA and possibly his closest work colleague, blackmail him?'

'That I'm not sure about. I'm toying with a theory. Linda McCarn mentioned that Blake has an important piece of legislation going through the Dáil and she was hinting at it being a bit dubious, but I've yet to get the full story. And Kathryn Finnegan said that her husband and Blake had diverged politically in recent years and there was some law Ryan wasn't happy with. Maybe he came back to work, discovered what his boss was up to, and was using the pictures to try to persuade Blake to back down on this Bill. Or maybe others were using the pictures against Blake to get him to do what they wanted. Ryan could have been planning to expose them and was shot for it. Again, I don't know. He had those images for a while, though.'

'Does Blake have an alibi?' McGuinness asked.

'He says he does. He claims he was with Carl Madsen . . . yes, that Madsen, the vice-president of Udforske, until 9.30 p.m. I'll be doing that interview when we get hold of him. Blake says he then joined his wife at 9.45 p.m. in the Dáil bar. I still have to talk to her. Our IT guys say Ryan's USB stick was taken out of the computer in LH2000 at 9.46 p.m., so that puts Blake in the clear, if his alibi holds.'

'How did Ryan get these pictures?'

Ray took up the explanation. 'As the minister's PA, Ryan had access to Blake's email account,' the detective explained. 'The images were originally sent to the minister from an account outside of Leinster House. We're tracking it now. Ryan went into Blake's emails earlier in the year and forwarded them to his own email address. He did all this on his own computer about a month before the car accident that took him out of work.'

'The secretary, Grace Brady, she didn't have access to Blake's accounts as well, did she?' Tom asked, the thought suddenly occurring to him.

'No, not to that account. Morrison told Ray that Grace would have mostly handled his phone, written correspondence and diary. General organisational stuff.'

McGuinness picked up one of the photos and threw it down, his features contorted with concern.

'There's nothing wrong with the sex,' he said. 'It's 2011 – no one cares if the man is gay. It would have been just as stupid being photographed in that state with women. But the drugs! And are those men even the age of consent? They look young. We don't know who they are, do we?'

Tom shook his head. 'No clue. I'd guess they're of Asian origin. And those are Chang beer bottles, that's a Thai brand.'

'Let's presume his alibi holds, but if it doesn't, is it conceivable that Blake could have killed his PA?' McGuinness asked, his voice incredulous.

Tom shrugged.

'We have to confront him with the images. He's involved in this now.'

'Tom.' McGuinness's voice was low, careful. 'This is explosive. Murder in Leinster House and now this. The media are in overdrive, rightly so. You've got to tread carefully. I know I don't need to say it, but Blake is tipped to be the next leader of the Reform Party. They may be riding high in the polls but O'Shea is floundering as Taoiseach. I like him personally, but anybody can see he's not cut out for the job. That means Blake is being lined up as the next leader of the country. If the man has done nothing wrong – apart from making some incredibly stupid decisions in his youth – I don't want us to be responsible for his career being hung out to dry.'

The Inspector sighed as he listened to his boss, the weight of responsibility resting heavily on his shoulders. McGuinness was being very fair to the minister. Tom knew there were many others who'd love to see such a powerful man exposed and deposed. He also knew that Blake faced an uphill struggle, as it would be next to impossible to keep a lid on these pictures now they were evidence in a major crime. The inspector's team was tight . . . could they really keep this one quiet, though?

The sitting room door opened and June popped her head in.

'Can one of you young men lend me a hand?'

Ray, nearest the door, stood up to carry in the tray she'd rested on the hall table. McGuinness and Tom hurriedly bundled up the images.

The chief reclined in his chair, rubbing his hands nervously, as his wife poured the tea.

'You're still milk and no sugar, Tom dear?'

'You know me, June. Sweet enough.'

She laughed.

'Did you notice I'm wearing the perfume you got me last Christmas?' she asked. 'I say "you". I mean your lovely wife.'

'I did, actually,' he said, feeling comforted once more that June wasn't as bad as he had first imagined when he'd heard about the Alzheimer's.

'Ha!' she said, stirring in the milk. 'I'm amazed. I assumed it was Mary who picked it out for me. Unless you make a habit of buying ladies' toiletries? How is she anyway – still beavering away to get that law degree?'

'You mean Lou . . .' Tom started to say, then froze. His wife had finished her law studies over twenty years ago, just before Maria was born. And Mary was June and Sean's daughter.

June looked up, confused eyes meeting his. The moment passed, realisation dawning. She cupped her mouth with her hand.

'Oh,' she said simply, tears glistening.

McGuinness leapt up and placed his hand tenderly on her elbow.

'That's all right, pet. Here, let me finish that tea. Why don't you get us some of that delicious cake you bought yesterday? The boys will love it.'

June gazed searchingly at her husband. He smiled at her gently, reassuringly.

'Of course,' she said. 'Something sweet to go with the tea. Where are my manners?'

She turned to leave the room. McGuinness watched her, his face tortured. Tom felt overwhelmed. He was so used to seeing the big man in charge of difficult situations, being sarcastic, abrupt, strong. Now he was helpless and trying his best not to show it.

McGuinness cleared his throat.

'Sorry about that,' he said, gruffly. 'Right. Let's prepare a plan of action for questioning Blake.'

Tom opened and closed his mouth. Should he say anything? What use were words of compassion in this situation? What would they change?

His boss added milk to Ray's tea without asking his preference and the inspector suddenly had a horrible glimpse of the future. A nightmarish vision of Sean McGuinness making tea for one. Alone, in this house. No June.

It was too sad to bear thinking about.

*

They drove across the city to Howth in North Dublin, stopping at a fish and chip shop in the scenic fishing village before continuing to Aidan Blake's house. They'd dropped Michael home en route, popping in to see Anne and the baby. It was a pleasant distraction from what had happened in McGuinness's house.

The infant Matthew was a chubby thing, quiet with a stern little face. The child wasn't, if Tom was honest, the most attractive baby he'd ever seen. Not that his parents cared. It warmed the inspector's heart, seeing Michael's face melt when he picked up his son and nuzzled the fleshy rolls of his neck. The young couple had tried long enough to have him and deserved every happiness now.

'Are you going to eat that scampi?'

Ray leaned over Tom, eyeing what was left in his boss's cardboard takeout box. They were dining al fresco, sitting on a wall across the road from the chip shop, overlooking Howth's picturesque harbour.

'Not now you've breathed all over it,' Tom said, handing over the remnants of his dinner. He brushed the salt and vinegar from his hands.

The inspector stood up and walked away from his colleagues, phone in hand. He had forgotten to check in with Louise. It was nearly 8 p.m. and it had been a long day.

Out on the marina, leisure yachts were sailing in, joining the fishing boats that had anchored that morning with their early haul. The wind had died down and the lights of the pubs and restaurants along the harbour front twinkled on the calm waters.

His wife answered after a couple of rings.

'I saw the news,' was the first thing she said. 'You could have shaved. I like my men rugged, don't get me wrong, but you just looked like a vagrant.'

He sighed. His long-nursed secret ambition to grow a beard would never be realised if she wouldn't let him get beyond one day's growth.

'I had a lovely day,' she said, filling the silence. 'I spent a few hours in the spa with a hunk called Boris. Russian. He gave me a good seeing to. I mean, massage.'

Tom laughed.

'I'll have his papers checked. Hopefully he's here illegally. What did you have for lunch?'

'Aside from Boris? Porcini and truffle risotto and a half bottle of Moët. I thought it only proper to give your credit card a going over, after you abandoned me.'

'Do you want me to send a car over to pick you up tonight, so you don't have to drive the dodgy Citroën?'

'I'm staying. Pam is coming.'

Louise's friend Pam lived in Bray, a seaside town on the border of Dublin and Wicklow. Tom was happy his wife had found someone to join her at the hotel. It would be a shame to see the short holiday package wasted.

'You two take care,' he said. 'That Russian might try to get you intoxicated so he can traffic you. I hear there's a roaring trade behind the Iron Curtain in attractive middle-aged women.'

'You cheeky git. How's Cáit? And Maria?'

Cáit first, Maria second.

'Your granddaughter sends her regards. Thank God I got home in time to fetch a bottle for her. I've told the assistant commissioner, the chief and the Taoiseach that I'll work this case, but only if I have time off to check on my grandchild every few hours.'

'Sorry, you're breaking up. I just heard moan, moan, moan and something about moaning. Get me a signed photo of Aidan Blake, will you?'

Tom swallowed. If only she knew.

'I'd better go. I love you.'

He blew her a kiss and returned the phone to his pocket.

The inspector returned to Ray and Willie, who were now engaged in a heated debate about the merits of smoked versus fresh cod.

'You can't taste the fish when it's smoked,' Ray said, shaking his head. 'What's the point?'

'The point is, you can't taste cod anyway, it's that bloody bland. And sure it's not even cod we're getting. It's John Dory or pollock, isn't it? All the cod is gone. Nicked by the Spanish and Icelandic fishermen. Robbing bastards.'

Ray guffawed.

'True enough. You win.'

'If you two are finished with your racial profiling, can we get a move on?' Tom asked. 'This envelope is burning a hole in my coat. Ray, will you give Laura a ring and get an update from today's interviews? And tell her to go home. Tomorrow's another day.'

Willie gathered up the empty wrappers and strolled with Tom to the car parked on the other side of the road.

'Nothing has happened between those two yet, huh?' he said, throwing a glance back over his shoulder.

'No,' Tom replied. 'He's still getting over Ellie. He'd just got his head around what happened in Kilcross, but her death knocked him for six.'

They were both silent for a moment, remembering the beautiful crime scene expert for whom Ray had fallen hard.

Tom felt a surge of affection for the younger man sitting on the wall, head bowed, his feet scuffing the ground as he conversed with Laura.

The inspector had noticed Laura had a crush on Ray last year. Then he had witnessed her quiet heartbreak as his oblivious deputy pursued another woman. He used to worry what would happen if two members of his team became involved in a relationship. He'd seen that scenario play out well in the force, and also horribly. Ray and Laura were so well suited, though, Tom reckoned he'd have happily turned a blind eye. But it wasn't to be and he suspected she'd moved on without Ray ever knowing there'd been anything there. The man was an enigma. He could be so insightful in an investigation yet completely obtuse when it came to personal matters.

Ray stood up and hurried over to the car, unaware that his boss and driver had just been dissecting his affairs.

'Anything to report?' Tom asked.

'Yep. They covered most of the interviews this afternoon. Though we're still checking the backgrounds of all the visitors to see if anybody had any relationship or history with Finnegan. Anyway, Laura made a good catch. She printed out as many images as she could of visitors who were in Leinster House last night. Several of those in the bar were elected councillors, so it was easy to get photos of them. Same with Carl Madsen. The photos were then given to the interview teams to assist people in identifying anybody they had seen in various parts of the complex. She figured staff in particular – like the ushers – were most likely to remember seeing people that aren't usually about the place. Guess what?'

'What?'

'One of the ushers saw Madsen walking through the main reception and asked him where he was going. Madsen said that McNally had left him in the Dáil bar to wait for his driver and that he was looking for the toilet.'

'What time was that?'

'9.55 p.m.'

'And is there a toilet around that area? Where's the bar?'

'Further into the building, not near the main reception. The toilets for the bar are a few metres away from it. The male toilets aren't signposted well, though, so maybe Madsen was lost. It's hard to know.'

'Hmm.' Tom considered this. 9.55 p.m in the main reception area fitted exactly with somebody returning in a hurry from LH2000. They knew that Madsen had been in Government Buildings, which meant he could have seen Ryan's emails. But would he have had a reason for killing Ryan? And if he'd been with the minister until 9.30 and then with McNally for a short time afterwards, didn't that put him out of the picture timewise?

Willie was resting on the bonnet, stroking the edges of his moustache, clearly pondering something.

'What are you thinking, Willie?' The inspector looked over.

'I'm thinking that if you're talking about Carl Madsen, the vice-president of that big oil and gas company, he's hardly somebody who has to wait for a driver to turn up. Not if that driver wanted to keep his job.'

'Very true,' Tom agreed.

'There's more,' Ray continued.

'Let me guess. You're going to tell me the Taoiseach was wandering around wearing a holster, brandishing a gun and whistling the tune from *The Good, The Bad and The Ugly*.'

'No. But he was also in the main reception area. Again, only notable because he's not often in that part of the building.'

Tom rested his elbows on top of the car and placed his head in his hands.

'One more thing.'

The inspector groaned.

'Go on.'

'The woman who works with Ryan. Grace Brady. Nobody can find her. She's disappeared.'

CHAPTER 8

Across the city, in a room they'd been designated in Leinster House, Laura stared at the floor plans laid out on the table in front of her. Each showed the layout of the different buildings in the Oireachtas complex. She picked up the one displaying the subterranean floor of the building she was in now and the tunnel that connected LH2000 to the main building.

'Laura?'

The detective looked up. It was Bridget, her colleague and housemate.

'Do you want to come for a drink tonight? Eoin just rang, says he can't get you on the phone but that you were heading over to his anyway and he's on for going out.'

'We have to track down this Brady woman,' Laura replied, still distracted by the map.

They'd been on the verge of wrapping up for the night, doing a final checklist of the interviews they'd got through and what was outstanding, when they discovered that no one had been able to get hold of Grace Brady.

Initially, Laura hadn't been concerned. She had been busy coordinating the interviews and checking the statements they already had against the hours of CCTV footage from the external gates. They wanted to make sure everyone had entered and left the complex when they claimed. Grace had departed well before anything had happened to Ryan. But after failing to get her on her mobile,

Laura had decided to send a car on a fruitless trip to the woman's home. She was starting to worry a little now.

Where was Grace Brady? The minister's secretary could hardly have missed the wall-to-wall coverage of what had happened in her workplace. Ryan's name had been released. His picture was on every news bulletin and in every evening paper edition. Grace might not have been in the building when Ryan was shot, but she worked in the same office as him, so it was imperative they speak with her.

Two of Grace's colleagues, the only pair who seemed to have any knowledge about the woman outside the workplace, mentioned a sister in Meath. A search had turned up Maire Doran, forty-two, living in Ashbourne. Her number kept ringing out as well. Could they be away for the weekend or something?

Bridget was staring at her.

'Earth to Laura. Come in, it's your social life calling. We have to call it a night at some stage.'

Laura blinked. 'Sorry. Yes, let's do that. Tom said I could finish up, but I need to check something first.'

She picked up her phone. She had two missed calls from Eoin. Yet she'd answered Ray the minute he called. Well, that was normal, wasn't it? Ray was a team colleague and they were on a case. Eoin might be on the force, but she knew he was ringing as her boyfriend.

'Is everything okay?'

'Yep, I'm just wondering how I missed Eoin's calls. This thing will take ten minutes. And do you mind if we go home first? I want to freshen up.'

The two women shared an apartment not far from the city centre and near garda headquarters in the Park.

Bridget cocked her head to one side and squinted at her friend. 'Spill.'

'What do you mean?' Laura blushed.

'You look distracted and not in a work way.'

'I am thinking about work. I've just realised something about the Leinster House basement.'

'So it has nothing to do with that phone call you just took, when you were so animated?'

Laura's colour deepened.

'Oh, honey,' Bridget tutted. 'Not again.'

'What? What have I done? Don't go all preachy on me.'

'I'm not going to say anything. Except this. You and Eoin make a lovely couple. He's a good-looking, sweet, smart guy who's besotted with you, and I'm not just saying that because we're related. There's no getting away from it. Ray's not interested in you. He has a penchant for unstable women. You're not his type.'

Laura flinched.

'Don't, Bridget.'

'For God's sake. Okay, he was completely unaware of your poetic unrequited love last year, but you're still entitled to have a bloody vent. More fool him, chasing a woman who turned out to be the mayor of crazy town, when you were there, saving your virginity for him.'

Laura snorted.

'Saving my what, now?'

Bridget's features relaxed and she too laughed.

'Seriously, Bridget, don't worry. I'm not going there. Sure, my mind might drift to "what if" every now and then; it's hard to switch off completely when you've nursed a hope for so long. But, even if he had noticed me, we work on the same team. It's too close. How could it have developed into anything? Don't worry. I like Eoin. He's even found my long-lost virginity. He found it several times the other night.'

'I think I just got sick in my mouth.'

Laura mock-swiped at her friend and got up to leave.

'Do me a favour and try Grace Brady again while I'm gone, will you? If you spent your time more productively, you wouldn't have to obsess about my bedroom activities.'

She found Shane Morrison in the main lobby, speaking to ushers behind the visitors' desk. Despite the long day, he was still the most well-turned-out, proper-looking man Laura had ever seen. Aside from Willie Callaghan, that was. The chief of securities posture was as stiff as his shirts. But there was something a little off about him, in the detective's opinion. He had a strangely intense way of looking at you, like he was drinking you in. She wondered if that was with everybody, or just women.

Laura waited until he finished issuing orders to his staff. The ushers had been extremely helpful to the team all afternoon and she could see how tired they were. No doubt they too were eager to get home.

'Ah, Detective Brennan. I'm told your officers are wrapping up for the evening. Will you be needing the House tomorrow as well?'

She shook her head.

'No, thank you. The bosses are worried we're attracting too much media attention working out of Leinster House. We've arranged for the remaining interviews to be conducted at our headquarters. We'll probably be in and out over the coming days, though. Will Leinster House return to normal business next week, or is it to stay closed?'

'We're generally fully staffed Monday to Friday. The Dáil normally sits from Tuesday afternoon until Thursday evening, but the government has decided to suspend the House for one sitting day, so parliament won't resume until Wednesday. Only essential staff and those with whom you want to speak will be asked to come in on Monday. The media have had their passes for Leinster House suspended until the Dáil comes back. They're not happy.'

'I imagine not. Can I ask for your assistance with one more matter?'

'Of course.'

'The underground tunnel, Mr Morrison – Mr McNally told the inspector this morning that it could be accessed via the Seanad stairway. Over there, am I right?'

Laura pointed to the arch across the lobby.

Morrison nodded.

'Yes, you can take those stairs.'

Laura opened up the floorplan she was holding and pointed at one of the red circles she had drawn.

'That's the correlating point there, isn't it?'

He nodded again.

Laura pointed at a second red circle.

'So what's that, then?'

'Come, I'll show you,' he said.

They made their way past the reception desk, towards the Dáil Chamber. They'd walked a few yards down the hall when Morrison stopped and opened a door to their left.

'The stairwell through here leads to the start of the tunnel from this end,' he said.

Laura chewed at her lip as she contemplated the information.

'Is this door always unlocked?'

'Yes.'

'Can we go down?'

'Sure. After you.'

They took the stairs.

The carpet underfoot felt damp and smelt musty, rarely used. At the bottom was another door. Laura opened it and found herself in the dimly lit tunnel.

'What's in these offices here?' she asked, indicating the doors to either side.

'Storage, mainly,' Morrison replied. 'That room there is where the TDs collect their freepost envelopes. There are file rooms, rooms full of replacement equipment, and so forth. The offices with full-time occupants don't really start until beyond the

Seanad stairs entrance, along that part of the corridor where Ryan was found.'

'So, would there have been anybody in this section of the building after normal working hours?'

'There was nobody in any of the rooms in the tunnel after 9 p.m. last night. But this end is usually deserted anyway. We don't use it for much because we had a little, ahem, problem, a couple of years ago. Rodents. This basement area was originally the servants' quarters, the kitchen, and so on, and it's connected to the old drains and sewers. The infrastructure has required a good deal of updating over the years.'

Laura shivered.

It was cold where they stood and as silent as the grave. She looked down, half expecting to see a rat scurrying along the poorly lit floor. There was no reason to feel frightened. She wasn't alone. But still, the detective was unsettled. The presence of the chief of security was little comfort in this eerie silence. In fact, Laura felt he rather added to her sense of unease.

'Are there any other tunnels in the complex?' she asked.

Morrison considered for a moment.

'Not in use. As I said, this was a functioning part of the original House, but there are old tunnels leading out to coal bunkers and there were some built later as passageways to air raid shelters. Very few people are aware that there's a shelter under Merrion Square Park, beneath the grassy mound at the Fitzwilliam Street corner.'

'Interesting,' she said. 'They can't be accessed now, can they? Nobody could gain access to the House unnoticed through an old tunnel?'

Morrison frowned.

'I wouldn't have thought so, but I'll have the engineers in the Office of Public Works check it out just in case.'

'That would be good, thanks. We can go back up now.'

Bridget was waiting for Laura at ground level and Morrison bade them goodnight as he left to supervise the shutting down of the building.

'What's down there?' her colleague asked, tugging the bobble from her dark hair and shaking her ponytail loose with relief. 'Oh, thank God for that. I've a fierce headache. No luck getting hold of Grace Brady, by the way.'

Laura frowned.

'Everybody we interviewed today was asked if they had seen anybody in the vicinity of the steps through that arch at the main reception, the ones that lead down to the tunnel where Ryan was killed,' she said.

'And?'

'And that door I just came through is another entrance to the same tunnel. If you wanted to go down there unseen, surely that's the one you'd use?'

Bridget's eyes widened.

'Of course it is. The reception area was staffed the whole time on Friday, with a clear view of that archway leading to the Seanad stairwell. But somebody could have slipped through that door behind you completely unseen.'

Laura nodded.

'It's just as well you had the map and asked,' Bridget added. 'Because nobody I spoke to mentioned a second access point.'

'Anyone using that tunnel would have to have been familiar with the building's layout,' Laura remarked. 'The Leinster House tour includes the Seanad chamber – I've a vague recollection of seeing it myself on a school trip – and ushers probably tell visitors nowadays about the tunnel that connects the old building to LH2000. But only people who work here would know that tunnel extends further under Leinster House.'

'Well, you may be on to something then. Why do you look so perplexed?'

'I'm wondering why Mr Morrison didn't mention this entrance before. Or McNally, or anybody we or the inspector talked to up to this point.'

'You think Morrison deliberately didn't say anything?' Bridget asked.

Laura shrugged.

'I don't know. He was happy to show it to me, but only after I'd asked. It just strikes me as strange, that's all. He knew we hadn't had the opportunity to explore the length of the tunnel today because Emmet's team was finishing up down there, but surely he saw the relevance of another access point? Anyway, let's go. I'll send somebody out to check with Grace Brady's neighbours to see if she left word about going away for the weekend. That's the only reason I can think of for her not answering her phone.'

'We hope,' Bridget added, her voice ominous.

CHAPTER 9

Aidan Blake's house wasn't as grand as some of the surrounding properties on the Hill of Howth. No doubt it still cost a fortune, Tom mused. Up here, one paid for the postcode and the panoramic view over Dublin Bay.

They pulled into the driveway after pausing for the electric gates to be opened. They'd phoned ahead and were expected.

The house sat on a half acre of land with woods to the rear. It was a dormer bungalow, built on a slight hill so they ascended as they drove, passing neatly trimmed hedgerows and dainty flowerbeds. The car had rolled a few metres around the first bend when Ray murmured with concern: 'What's that?'

The three men peered at the side of the house.

A woman was gesticulating in their direction, her frantic movements illuminated by the outdoor light.

Willie hit the accelerator and the car sped towards the house.

They were within a few feet of the bungalow when something hit the windscreen.

Willie and Tom flinched and Ray cursed.

'She's not waving, she's throwing things at us,' he exclaimed.

The vehicle skidded to a halt and they all leapt out.

'Hey!' Tom called, his voice urgent.

The woman froze, arm mid-swing, and dropped her next missile, which looked like a small stone. She strolled nonchalantly towards them.

'I'm Detective Inspector Tom Reynolds; we're here to see Aidan Blake.' Tom was unnerved by how relaxed the woman seemed. 'Is everything okay?'

'Of course,' she said, looking puzzled. 'I'm his wife. Sara.' She wiped her hands on the sides of her jeans and offered him one to shake. Tom took it gingerly.

Compared to her handsome husband, Sara Blake was fairly nondescript. The woman's facial features were a little too small, with her eyes too close together and her lips on the thin side. Despite that, she had an approachable countenance. Her smile was shy and engaging and there was gentleness to her handshake that befitted her slight frame. Her blonde hair was pulled back in a plain French knot, bereft of adornments. No, she couldn't be described as pretty, Tom thought. Refined, was the best he could come up with. Which made the manic throwing activity just minutes ago all the more incongruous.

'What are you doing?' he asked, cautiously.

'I'm committing snail genocide,' she said. 'The little pests keep getting in at my gerberas and night-time seems to be their feeding period. The ones I can't kill, I'm lobbing into the neighbour's garden. He deserves it, the cranky old git. I was trying to distract myself from what happened last night and taking it out on the snails seemed like a good idea.'

She was waiting for Tom to reply when the penny dropped.

'Oh, sugar! I'm sorry, did I throw one at you? I turned when I saw the car. My aim is terrible.' She clasped a hand over her mouth, mortified.

Tom was relieved. They weren't dealing with a mad woman, after all.

'Would you not just put a plate of beer out for them?' Willie said, knowledgeable on all things garden-related.

'I wouldn't give them the satisfaction. Let him next door waste his ale and get them tanked up. If you ask me, he threw them in here in the first place. We're engaged in snail air warfare. Come in and I'll get you some refreshments. You must be exhausted after today. Aidan is waiting for you. He's on the phone. Been on it for hours. We just can't believe what's happened. It's . . . well, it's unbelievable.'

She shook her head and led them into the house, kicking off her trainers inside the front door. The minister's wife wore a cream wool hoodie and fitted jeans. She really wasn't at all what Tom had expected, not with her husband being so suave.

'Aidan,' she called out. 'The guards are here.'

She brought them down the hall to a large kitchen and offered them seats at the breakfast table.

'I'm sorry to be meeting you in these circumstances,' Tom said, watching her move efficiently between the kitchen counters and an island workspace.

Sara hesitated mid-task.

'To be honest, I'm finding it hard to process,' she said. 'I've being trying to do normal things all day, you know? Putting the washing on. Hoovering. Gardening. Just keeping busy. And then I remember . . .'

She inhaled, eyes closed, her face desperately sad and angry all at once. 'It's not a normal day.'

'No, it's not. You knew Ryan well, then?' the inspector asked.

Sara's shoulders drooped.

'Very well.' Her voice broke, but she gathered herself quickly. 'Like I have a right to be upset. Like it matters how I feel, compared to what Kathryn and his family are going through.' A small, distraught sob escaped her lips. She wiped her eyes roughly.

'I'm sorry,' she said. 'I imagine this is hard work for you, too. Daddy was on the force; I know the toll it takes.'

'We manage,' Tom said. 'We get to go back to our own lives. The victims' family and friends have to cope with what's happened. Tell me how you knew Ryan.'

'He started working with Aidan over ten years ago, fresh out of college and full of ideas. We were already battle-hardened. Aidan had lost two general elections at that stage but was serving on the city council. Equal parts soul-destroying and character forming, really. Ryan gave Aidan a shake-up. Made him enthusiastic about politics again. God knows he needed it. I love my husband to bits but he's like all politicians. Sometimes he can't see the wood for the trees. Ryan will really be missed, now the Reform Party is in government.'

It was an interesting statement, Tom thought.

'Mrs Blake, I was told you were in the complex last night. What time was that? Did you see Ryan?'

'I didn't,' she answered. 'But I wasn't looking out for him. I was preoccupied. The press wanted a photo opportunity at this event I'd organised, with all the cabinet members in attendance. I had to track down several ministers and em . . . an important guest. I know we left the ball about 9. I found two ministers quickly and a couple more in the bar at about 9.15 p.m. I got stuck there waiting for them to finish their pints for nearly three quarters of an hour but I was afraid to leave without them; they were the most unreliable on my list. People kept offering to buy me drinks. Like there wasn't somewhere I needed to be!'

Tom picked up on something she'd said.

'Who was this important guest you were looking for? Your husband mentioned something similar this morning.'

She hesitated, momentarily.

'It was the Taoiseach. I don't want to imply he was one of the ones drinking all night.'

'Of course not. But you did find him?'

'Yes.'

Tom waited for her to say where, but Mrs Blake didn't expand on her answer.

'What time did your husband join you?'

'I guess about 9.45? I was still in the bar. I'm sorry, I know you need everybody to be exact. I remember glancing at my wristwatch when he found me and thinking we had to speed things up. He'd been in a meeting, but I'd asked him to come help me drag the others out as soon as he was free. Some of the older ministers tend to get a little misogynistic when they've a few jars in them. I figured they would pay attention to Aidan, if not to me.'

'It seems unfair,' Tom remarked. 'Missing your own ball.'

'You make it sound like I'm a debutante. The ball wasn't for me, I merely organised it. I always find at these events it's your job to make sure everybody else has fun and to look like you're having a great time, when really you spend most of the affair in a state of abject panic. It was worth it, though. The charity made a lot of money. My colleague Hugh managed to talk a celebrity chef into catering. Then it was easy to sell it to the Grand. We spent practically nothing organising it but raised plenty because it was such a fancy venue.'

'What does your charity do, exactly?' Ray asked.

'It's a children's foundation. We provide refuge, support and counselling to kids who've been abused, live in poverty, that kind of thing. You'd think, wouldn't you, in a first-world country like Ireland, that there would be few children in such circumstances. But there are more than you think.' A shadow fell over her features and there was no doubting the genuine compassion in her eyes. 'I called the charity Silent Voices because no one hears them. Silly, probably, but the name means a lot to me. Children are so precious and yet, they're rarely listened to. I've firsthand experience of that.'

'It sounds very admirable,' the inspector commented. He wasn't entirely sure if her comment about 'firsthand experience' referred to the children she routinely dealt with, or her own childhood. Should he ask her, he wondered?

He didn't get the chance. The door opened and Blake entered the kitchen.

'Inspector. There was no need to call out to the house; I'd have gone wherever you needed.'

Blake looked tired and despondent. His eyes were red-rimmed and puffy and his usually stylish hair was unkempt. The suit had been replaced with a polo shirt and faded jeans. He didn't look like a man who'd murdered somebody last night. He had all the appearance of a man devastated and in mourning.

'Shall we go to my study?' Blake asked.

'I'll bring tea and coffee through,' Sara offered.

Tom nodded gratefully as he and Ray stood to accompany the minister. Willie remained in the kitchen with an offer to help with the refreshments.

'Mrs Blake, before we leave, will you make a note of those who were in the bar with you last night?' the inspector asked, pausing at the door.

'Certainly. I remember exactly who was there. I was stone cold sober while I waited for everybody to finish their drinks and their interminable yarns.'

Blake's study was a comfortable room, its centrepoint a large oak desk flanked by burgundy leather chairs. It wasn't unlike his office in Government Buildings, bar the absence of a meeting table.

Tom saw the move to the home study for what it was, as the minister took his seat behind the desk. In the kitchen or lounge they would have sat as equals. In here, Blake was in charge. They were positioned like petitioning constituents on the other side of the table. The minister was a man used to being deferred to.

Well, the power dynamic was about to shift.

'Are we any closer to knowing what happened last night?' Blake spoke first. 'I've had reporters trying to get hold of me all day. I can't wrap my head around it at all. Ryan dying is one thing. But to be shot in Leinster House, it's incredible. The audacity!'

He shook his head, half in outrage, half in amazement.

'We're making some progress,' Tom said, cautiously. 'Something significant has come to our attention and we want to talk to you about it.'

The inspector had unbuttoned his dark overcoat when he'd sat down and now he withdrew the envelope from it. The door opened and Sara entered, carrying a tray.

'I'll just leave this here,' she said, glancing at the envelope, obviously curious as to what it contained. She wasn't going to find out from Tom. He'd leave that to her husband.

'Back to last night,' he continued, when the minister's wife had left the room. 'We're trying to establish people's exact movements during the time period Ryan was killed. Nobody is being accused of anything. We just want to paint a picture of where everybody was and try to jog people's memories for anything that might help us. Can you tell me again the exact time you met with Carl Madsen and what else you did during the evening?'

Blake seemed transfixed by the envelope, but now he snapped to attention.

'Sure. I went over it in my head this morning after I talked to you. I want to help, but I don't know if I can.'

'Nonetheless . . .' Tom kept his tone even.

'I finished in my office in Government Buildings at 9.30 or thereabouts. I crossed over to Leinster House to find Sara and found her in the bar at about 9.45 p.m. She had one more minister to grab and he arrived just before 10, as we were encouraging the others out the door. We made certain they were en route to the ball, then we left together to look for . . .'

'The Taoiseach?'

'Yes – how did you . . . ? Ah, my wife told you. We found Cormac and then Sara and I left Leinster House and were back at the ball before 10:30, just in time for dessert. I didn't want you to think the Taoiseach had to be forced to go over to the event. He was just . . . busy.'

'I see.'

Blake's eyes drifted back to the envelope.

'When we met this morning, Minister, I asked you a rather obscure question about whether Ryan had any strange proclivities. Do you remember?'

The other man swallowed nervously. He picked up his coffee and took a sip.

'A picture was found under Ryan's body,' Tom continued. 'It was part of a set. Your former PA printed out the lot minutes before he was murdered. I imagine he had them on his person when he was pursued. As he fell, the pages must have flown from his hands. His killer removed them but missed one. I have all the images here.'

He slid his finger under the lip of the envelope and withdrew the pages. Blake was prominent in the first picture.

The minister dropped his coffee cup. It clattered noisily on the desk before falling to the carpeted floor. Tom hurriedly grabbed the pictures to save them from the liquid spreading across the table. Blake shot up and yelped as the scalding coffee hit his thigh.

'Christ almighty!' he groaned, reaching for tissues on the desk.

Tom pushed the box towards him and he and Ray each grabbed a handful to dry the table as the other man dabbed at his jeans.

'Are you badly burned?' the inspector asked.

Blake shook his head, wincing in discomfort.

'No.'

He checked the chair to make sure it was dry and fell back onto the seat.

Tom lifted the pictures again, but Blake held up his hands.

'Please. Don't. I can't bear it. They're too awful. And if Sara came in and saw them . . .' His expression was pained.

The inspector nodded.

'I understand. Your wife isn't aware of any of this, then?'

'Of course not.' Blake looked horrified. 'Please, don't say anything to her.'

'Aidan, we have a real dilemma here. Someone took the time to remove compromising and potentially damaging pictures of you from the crime scene. This person may have also been responsible for Ryan's death. You have given us your alibi for the time in question but these photographs put you in the middle of our case. Why would Ryan have had them?'

'I don't know.'

'Was he blackmailing you?'

'No.'

'Because, you know, blackmail is an evil thing. It can force people to respond to situations in very desperate ways.'

Blake shook his head agitatedly.

'He wasn't blackmailing me. He wouldn't. You don't understand. He just wasn't the type. Ryan was a principled individual. I don't want his name besmirched like this. Jesus, he couldn't even get to grips with the necessary acts of government, he was that idealistic.'

'What do you mean by that?'

'Just that the whole thing was too damn grubby for him. We argued quite a bit about it. He didn't understand that being in government is very different from the simple black and white of opposition politics. Power involves taking nuanced positions and making compromises to get things done.'

'I see. You seemed to already know what I had brought with me this evening,' the inspector pointed out.

Blake nodded slowly.

'I wondered when you were asking about Ryan having . . .

certain urges. It was such a strange question. I knew those blasted pictures would come back to haunt me.'

The minister buried his head in his hands.

Tom sat back in the chair, motioning to Ray to pick up the questioning.

'When were the photos taken?' his deputy asked.

Blake gulped.

'Over twenty years ago. I was on a gap year, travelling. That was in Thailand. I was in a bad place, in my head. I wasn't sure what I wanted to do with my life and my family had high expectations of me. I was drinking a lot, taking recreational drugs . . . I'm not proud of it. There are no excuses. I was stupid. I barely drink these days, let alone touch drugs. I'm not gay – I mean, I'm not in the closet or anything. I got up to plenty with women, too. I was just experimenting. I didn't realise what I'd done would be used against me.'

'How do you mean?'

'A couple of years ago, one of the men in those photographs discovered what I did for a living. I don't know how. My picture must have been in some international publication or something. He emailed the photos to me, looking for money. I'd erased that night from my mind. I don't even recall there being a camera.'

'Did you pay him?' Ray asked.

'Yes, I had to. You've seen them. Would you want those pictures getting out?'

'Why were you concerned in particular? Were you worried about your wife finding out? The public? Were the men you were with of legal age?'

Blake baulked.

'Jesus, of course they were. You're not suggesting . . . ? I had sex with men, Detective. That doesn't make me a bloody kiddy fiddler. Christ, is that what you think homosexuality is?'

'No,' Ray protested. 'Not at all. I apologise, but I had to ask.'

Blake remained distressed. He roughly massaged the sides of his temples.

'I couldn't let those pictures ruin the career I've worked so hard to build. And yes, I panicked that Sara would find out. She's the love of my life. Look, I know it's hard to believe given the position I hold now, but I had a bit of a wild side. I told Sara I'd been reckless as a kid, but I settled down when I met her and she has no idea, really, of the true extent of what I used to get up to. Then this . . . bloodsucker came along and tried to wreck everything. I paid, Detective, every time he demanded.' The minister's voice was brittle with anger.

'And how many times was that?'

'I don't know. Six? Seven times?'

'Is he still blackmailing you?' Tom asked.

'No. The emails ceased in late spring. Just in time, because he knew I had been promoted to ministerial rank. He thought he could escalate the demands. Then, suddenly, there was nothing.'

'And why was that?'

'He died. I never thought I'd be so happy to hear about a person's death. I made some discreet enquiries and discovered he'd taken an overdose.'

The minister shook his head in wonderment, as if he still couldn't believe his luck.

'We're going to need his name and the last known contact details you had for him,' Tom said. They'd have to make sure the man was actually dead and verify Blake's story.

The minister nodded. He glanced at the envelope again.

Tom examined the man's face, trying to figure out what he was thinking.

'Ryan forwarded the photos to himself from your email account, Aidan. I can't imagine you left them sitting in your inbox, so perhaps he happened upon an unopened email. Why would he have sent them to himself and why did he print them out last night if not to blackmail you?'

Blake's shoulders sank and his voice was hoarse when he replied.

'I've already said, I don't know.'

The minister was lying. Tom was sure of it.

He put his hand on the envelope and its loaded contents.

'You mightn't believe Ryan was planning to blackmail you. But maybe somebody else did. Who would kill to protect you, Aidan?'

Blake wiped his brow and the sheen of sweat that had formed there.

'Nobody,' he replied. 'I don't know anybody who would do such a thing.'

The inspector said nothing. They'd given the minister his chance to tell them what he knew. And he'd refused to take it.

'One more thing before we leave, then.' Tom spoke quietly. 'I'd strongly advise you to tell your wife about these photos. They will feature in this investigation. I can assure you they are safe in the hands of my team, but I can't give you a cast-iron guarantee of confidentiality and the media will be all over this case. I'm sure that isn't how you want her to find out.'

Blake put his head in his hands, the picture of a broken man.

'I'll tell her,' he croaked.

'Do you believe him?'

Tom and Ray were back in the car, being driven by Willie in the direction of the inspector's house. The weather had stayed calm and dry, the clear night sky was dotted with stars.

'No,' Tom answered, mesmerised by the lights of passing cars. 'He's lying.'

'Which part?'

'I think the better question is which part was truthful. What's your take on him?'

Ray arched his eyebrows.

'That thing he said about having a wild side – I'm not con-vinced he was only talking about the past. Which is fascinating, considering how he's lauded by press and public alike as the best politician in the land. And it sounds like he's trying to convince himself, not us, that Finnegan wouldn't have had it in him to resort to blackmail, when it looks like that's exactly what Ryan was planning. Why else would he have sent himself the pictures?'

'I'm starting to form the opinion he had them for security,' Tom said. 'Relations were deteriorating between him and the minister. Maybe Ryan wanted something in his back pocket, even if he didn't intend to use it. Again, interesting, because it doesn't really fit with the notion of Ryan being this principled fellow we keep hearing about, not if he was willing to resort to blackmail. Unless he was fooling himself into thinking he was doing it for the greater good or something. I found what Sara Blake said intriguing.'

'What was that?'

'That Blake – and the Reform Party – will miss Ryan, especially with them being in government.'

'She thought Ryan was good for her husband.'

'Yes,' Tom agreed. 'She's the head of a children's charity and passionate about it. Maybe she was closer to Ryan's alleged ideal-istic view of the world than her husband's. Aidan Blake talked about the nuances of governing. I imagine when you're dealing with kids who've been neglected or hurt, you have fixed opinions about what's right and wrong.'

Ray hesitated.

'You don't think she and Ryan were . . .'

'What?' Tom responded. 'Having an affair?'

'Yes.'

'I don't see it. He's been away for the last six months and has a new baby at home. It seems like all was good with his wife. What are you thinking, that he was going to out Blake to Sara, or blackmail Blake into leaving her?'

Ray shrugged.

'Something like that. Or Blake was going to tell Kathryn Finnegan and Ryan tried to stop him by saying he'd reveal his dirty secret?'

The inspector rubbed the back of his neck. He was exhausted. He closed his eyes and leaned back against the headrest.

'Madsen,' he said, remembering.

'What?'

'I don't believe in coincidences. Madsen was in Leinster House last night to consult on this new law of Blake's. That Bill is a recurring theme. Would somebody as busy and high-flying as Madsen really take time to meet with a minister about a piece of legislation that doesn't have any noticeable impact on his business? According to Darragh McNally, anyway. That's not really how companies work, is it? They usually meet governments in order to lobby.'

'What's your point?'

Tom massaged his jaw as various theories floated around his head. He landed on the one that made the most sense.

'Say Ryan Finnegan comes back to work, falls out with the minister for some reason and decides to blackmail him. Maybe Madsen's company stands to lose out in some way . . . What is Madsen capable of?'

'How would he even know who Ryan was, though?' Ray mused. 'He deals with ministers and governments, not lowly PAs.'

Tom sighed. 'I don't know. But he has been put in the frame, from what we know already – wandering around Leinster House on his own at the right time, in Government Buildings with access to Ryan's office. He needs to be questioned, so let's organise it.

Blake is claiming him as an alibi witness during a crucial time period and it all seems a little off to me.'

'Isn't he in Donegal?'

'If Mohammad won't come to the mountain . . . And let's talk to Linda McCarn before we see him, find out a little more about the minister and his political work. Here is okay, Willie. If you pull up outside the house the baby will hear me coming. She has an in-built granddad alarm.'

Willie brought the car to a halt across the road from the inspector's house on Blackhorse Avenue, alongside the old stone wall that surrounded the Phoenix Park.

'Tomorrow,' Tom said, before getting out of the car, 'I want to speak to McNally again. How long exactly did he spend with Madsen before he deposited him in the Dáil bar? It couldn't have been long if Madsen was in the reception area by 9.55. Get hold of him and see what time we can meet. McGuinness will let us know when we're scheduled to interview the Taoiseach.'

Ray nodded and jumped out of the back to take up residence in the vacated front seat. The inspector gave the roof of the car a tap and Willie pulled away.

Tom entered his house to what sounded like shrieks of laughter from the sitting room. Coat still on, he flung open the door, ready to confront whoever was determined to wake up Cáit. It was close to 10.30 p.m.

Maria's friends from college were there. The three young women and his daughter were gathered around what looked like a giant ladybird on the rug in the centre of the room.

'Oh, Dad, look. Isn't Cáit gorgeous? The girls brought it over. It's her first Hallowe'en costume.'

Tom could just about make out his granddaughter's tiny face under the black hood and pair of antennae.

She looked adorable.

'Shouldn't she be in bed?' he asked, annoyed at how annoyed he sounded. He was turning into his father. Grumpy McGrumpy, Louise called the old man.

'I'm leaving her up,' Maria said, her voice full of authority. 'This business of Mam insisting I put her down at 8 is ridiculous. She's waking four times a night. If I leave her up, she might actually sleep. Look at her, she's perfectly happy.'

Cáit gurgled cooperatively, earning a fresh round of oohs and aahs from her adoring fans.

'I'll leave you to it, so.'

Tom backed out of the oestrogen-filled room. His granddaughter appeared to be in capable hands.

He was pleased at how Maria seemed to be coping on her own. She still looked exhausted – dark circles ringed her eyes, the same deep brown colour as her mother's. Her long auburn hair, a previous pride and joy, was now in a permanent ponytail, out of the way. She'd put on weight with the pregnancy and kept some of the chubbiness, but it suited her, Tom thought. She'd been too skinny before, a teenage girl obsessed with weight and appearance.

He couldn't help but wonder, though, what Louise's reaction would be to the change in routine when she got home. She'd read a book when Maria was pregnant about the importance of an evening routine for babies – bath, massage, story, bed – and she'd been overseeing it rigorously since Cáit was born.

It was all new to Tom, who seemed to remember them taking turns to let Maria fall asleep on them when she was a baby, then carrying her upstairs like she was the Hope Diamond, slipping under the bedcovers without breathing and trying not to move all night for fear of disturbing her.

He had come to doubt the merits of the sleep routine himself since Cáit rarely ended up staying in her own cot. Things could be about to heat up at home, though, if Maria was going to start challenging Granny's dominion at bedtime.

Tom fetched himself a tall glass and a bottle of pale ale from the kitchen, along with a Padron cigar he'd been saving for something special. He was meant to be on his holidays, after all.

He made a beeline for the special sitting room, the one that they never seemed to use for anything, and closed the door tightly. Once he'd opened both windows and moved the armchair as close to the sill as possible, he felt safe to light up. Maria had inspired him by breaking the rules with Cáit and now here he was, sparking up indoors, albeit practically sitting in the garden. If Louise took a fit and decided to come home tonight, there'd be no telling how she'd react. It was anarchy.

He took a long draw on the cigar, savouring the peppery spice on his tongue. He was exhaling, wafting the smoke outside with his hands, when the phone rang. His instinctive reaction was panic. Louise had either fitted the house with a baby-cam in every room and was monitoring them remotely, or her inner smoke detector had gone off. Luckily, he stopped short of throwing the evidence out the window. It was just Ray.

'Bad news and bad news,' Ray said.

'Start with the bad news.'

'We can't see McNally tomorrow, unless you really fancy criss-crossing the country.'

'Why not?'

'He's gone to Clare.'

'What?' Tom cursed through clenched teeth. 'This is a bloody murder investigation; what is he playing at?'

'He told us, remember, that he had to leave the city?'

'I didn't realise he was heading off for a long weekend. He'll just have to come back up.'

'No, boss, listen. He's with his mother and she's not just ill. She's dying. The priest is on the way to give her the Last Rites.'

'Oh,' Tom replied, chastened. 'Well, I suppose there's not much we can do about that. We'll have to wait until he returns to Dublin.'

The inspector did the calculation in his head. It would have been crude to say it aloud. If McNally's mother died tonight, she would be waked either tomorrow or Monday and buried by Tuesday. A typical grieving relative might take at least a week off work, but Tom was sure, after just a couple of encounters with the party chair, that McNally would be back in the office by Wednesday, if not before.

The situation did explain, though, why the man had been so distracted.

'And the other bad news?' he asked Ray.

'We got hold of Carl Madsen's private secretary. She says he's incommunicado when he's at his holiday home in Donegal. If we'd rung this morning, she could have reached him because he was working, but once he goes back to the house he doesn't take calls or check emails. He's due to fly back to Denmark from Belfast International on Monday morning. We won't get him on the phone, but we could send a local patrol car out to tell him to come to Dublin.'

Tom paused and considered.

'No,' he said. 'There's a regional flight from Dublin to Donegal tomorrow at noon. Book us two seats on that. I want to see Madsen face to face and I don't want him to hop on a plane back to Denmark after a visit from a squad car. These top business guys have an awful habit of considering themselves too important for us lowly police folk.'

'Do you just keep airline timetables lying around or are you some kind of flight schedule Rain Man?'

'You should never underestimate me, Junior,' Tom huffed, not disclosing he'd looked up the plane times that morning. He'd had an inkling Madsen would be hard to get hold of. 'Ring Laura and let her know she's in charge tomorrow. They can finish any outstanding interviews and keep going with the background checks. And tell her to make sure she gets hold of the minister's secretary, Grace Brady. When you said you'd bad news, for a minute there I thought you were going to tell me she'd been found dead. Laura texted that she reckoned she might be away for the weekend, but it's still bugging me that we can't find her. '

'Will do. I've been worrying about her myself. G'night, then.'

Tom hung up and turned off his phone. He looked at the blank, lifeless screen. Good. That felt liberating.

He took a long pull on the cigar, bringing it back to life, and poured his ale. He closed his eyes. Relaxed.

Two minutes later Tom sat up and turned the phone back on. Louise might ring. Or Ray. Or McGuinness.

It was more stressful worrying about who he might miss than having to take the calls.

*

Across the city, Ray decided to walk around his apartment complex a few times to stretch his legs before turning in for the night. The worst thing about being involved in a case like this was the lack of time to work out. He needed exercise to stay sane. Being stuck in the car or doing interviews all day drove him nuts.

He'd ring Laura. Hopefully she wasn't in bed yet. It was cheeky, this late on a Saturday night, but Tom had asked him to pass on a message. And they all knew what it was like when a serious investigation was underway. They could chat while he walked.

When Laura picked up, he could hear noise in the background. It sounded like a pub.

'Hello? Can you hear me?' he repeated a couple of times.

'Ray,' she shouted. 'Hold on, I'll go outside.'

He waited impatiently for her to find somewhere quiet.

'Sorry, are you out?' he said. He was surprised at his own

curtness. Now he thought of it, why wouldn't she be out? It was the weekend. She was probably with that Eoin guy.

'Yes. I almost couldn't be bothered, to be honest. I'm so tired.'

'Oh. Right. I was just ringing to pass on a message from Tom. He said you're in charge tomorrow. We're going to Donegal to see this Madsen guy.'

'Donegal? That's quite a trip.'

'We're flying. It's quicker.' Ray's stomach did a little flip. He'd just realised a domestic flight would probably mean a small plane, and he hated being in the air. 'He also wondered if there was any update on Grace Brady?'

'Not yet.'

'Okay. Well, keep working on it.'

There was silence for a few seconds before Laura spoke again.

'Is there anything else? It's just, I'd better get back in.'

Ray tried to think of something to say.

'No, that's everything. Enjoy your night.'

He hung up so abruptly he shocked himself. What was the matter with him? He tried to analyse his behaviour. He was tired, sure. But it was more than that. He was lonely.

Ray had spent the last year going over and over the Kilcross case and the tragic event that followed it. How had he missed so much? To try to put the whole sorry saga behind him, he'd buried himself in work and the gym, keeping himself busy.

The only people he'd really spent time with had been Laura's family.

After they had discovered that Laura's aunt had died in the Kilcross Magdalene Laundry, Ray had tried to help her mother find her sister's unmarked grave. He'd seen quite a bit of Laura over the summer and started to realise she was really good company. She was smart and she was funny. He'd even begun to notice how attractive she was.

But she was a teammate. They had to work together morning,

noon and night. He shouldn't be looking at Laura in that way. So why was he so tetchy with her? It couldn't be because she was seeing somebody, surely?

Unconsciously, Ray had veered in the direction of the main Drumcondra Road. He was going for a pint. Thinking had worn out his brain.

CHAPTER 10

Saturday Night, County Clare

'She's not in pain, is she?'

Darragh McNally reached for his mother's hand and stroked the frail, liver-spotted skin, noticing how cold it was. She'd always had warm hands. Strong hands, always busy – whether it was milking the cows at 5.30 in the morning or, as the day wore on, kneading lumps of dough for fresh bread in their small country kitchen.

Those were the hands that pulled him close to make him feel better when other, taller boys bullied him in school for being so different. The hands that stroked his cheek lovingly when he'd wet the bed and couldn't find sleep. The hands that held his when they visited his father's grave each Sunday, a man he loved by reputation but had never met.

Darragh felt the sting of tears in the back of his eyes, knowing this was the last time he would clasp her fingers in his. She was so thin, almost insubstantial in the hospital bed. Even the hacking cough that had racked her body for months had ceased. The cancer had ravaged her for too long, bout after bout. No matter what treatment she endured, it came back, more aggressive and vicious each time. It was an evil, insidious disease.

The nurse leaned across and softly brushed the few remaining snow-white strands of hair from his mother's forehead. Her lashless eyelids were closed, most of the hair lost after recurrent bouts of chemo. The tubes in her nose had been removed but the white plaster remained. Her lips were so parched; it made no difference how much they dabbed at them with wet sponges.

'She can't feel a thing, pet,' the nurse said to Darragh. 'It will be soon. Just think of the relief she will feel, not suffering any more. She's going to a better place. She'd be so happy, knowing you are here.'

Darragh flinched. He should have come earlier. But how could he have got away from Leinster House with everything going on? Silently, he cursed Ryan Finnegan and the trouble he'd caused. Ryan, the saint. Ryan, who put his own superior opinions above everybody and everything, including his own safety.

The gobsmacking idiocy of the man.

Not that McNally could talk. Wasn't he the biggest fool of all, letting himself be so corrupted? And what had he been thinking last night? Why had he lied and got himself so embroiled in every-thing? He'd entered politics to make his mother proud and look how he'd ended up.

The guards wanted to talk to him again. He had no doubt that he'd be hung out to dry. Nobody would step in to protect Darragh McNally. He'd made too many enemies over the years. He con-sidered himself a straight talker, somebody who got things done. That, ironically, was what made him such a threat. When some-body needed Darragh in their corner, they'd promise anything to get him onside. Once he'd expended his usefulness, that same person would invariably try to marginalise him, knowing just how much influence the party chair was capable of wielding if left unchecked.

He had thought his plan was foolproof. He had moulded a leader, a man capable of achieving the highest position in politics but who would ultimately always defer to Darragh. He would have power through Aidan Blake, without having to seek it out himself.

Now, it was all over.

A movement from the nurse on the other side of the bed drew his attention.

Her name was Rose and she had been his mother's regular carer these last few years. She was a typical country lass, bouncy strawberry blonde curls and flushed red cheeks, wide hips and big, fleshy arms. She was always going to end up as a nurse, you could see it in her eyes – no nonsense, but caring. If only Darragh had been blessed with a different body, a better face, a less ambitious disposition. He might have ended up marrying a girl like Rose and staying at home in Clare.

The nurse's eyes were brimming with tears. She'd loved the woman in the bed. Rose had spent more time with her these last few years than her own son had. The desperately weak rise and fall of his mother's chest had ceased, a final expiration of breath the only sound. She was gone. The one person in the world who had ever cared for Darragh, his sole remaining family. He would never have a Rose. He would never have children. He'd sacrificed everything for a career that was built on sand.

And now he had nothing left to lose.

Sunday, Dublin

'It's a Bloody Mary. Hair of the dog. I lost the run of myself last night, darling. Go on, have one. It's pathetically sad, drinking alone.'

'No, Linda. We've a flight to catch in a couple of hours and this unfortunately isn't a social call.'

Tom was in fantastic humour, but not quite merry enough to be knocking back vodka and tomato juice at 9 a.m. in Linda's kitchen. Maria had pulled it off. She'd kept Cáit up until 11.30 p.m. the night before and the baby had slept through until 7 a.m. The

inspector had awoken to the smell of bacon on the grill and per-
colating coffee. He'd taken his time showering and shaving and
felt like a new man by the time he was done.

Downstairs, Tom had found his daughter feeding his granddaughter in the kitchen, both of them well rested and happy, and
his breakfast ready on the table.

'How much does that hotel cost a night?' Maria had asked. 'We
could put Mam up for another few days. Have Cáit sleeping twelve
hours straight by the time she got home.'

Tom laughed, then immediately felt guilty, like he was betraying Louise.

'You do want us helping you, don't you?' he asked. 'If we're
interfering, you have to tell us.'

'It's fine, Dad. I know Mam only wants the best for me.
Sometimes, though, I'd like to try things my way. I have to
find my own feet. God knows, Cáit's dad is never going to be much
use, not when she's this age, anyhow. He looks at her like she's
some kind of alien that might explode. I'm all she's got. I'll never
be as perfect as Mam, but I'm not going to drop her on her head
either.'

Tom wondered if he should tell his daughter about the time
Louise had actually dropped Maria on her head. Not that it was
intentional. She'd been changing her on the nappy table and
turned away for a moment to get a fresh pack of wet wipes,
unaware Maria had learned how to flip herself over. He'd arrived
home from work that night to find Louise sobbing on the stairs,
declaring that she was an unfit mother and insisting he take the
baby away before she accidentally killed her. Maybe that was why
his wife had taken to reading baby manuals for Cáit.

No, better not share that story. Louise wouldn't thank him
for it.

Linda drained her drink and slammed the glass down on the
table.

'That hit the spot!' she laughed.

Tom had to smile.

The criminal psychologist was channelling an ageing Hollywood starlet this morning. A flimsy silk dressing gown was wrapped loosely around her body, held in place by a belt that kept threatening to unwind. Her wild hair was tucked up in a black headscarf, knotted like a turban with a brooch pinned at its front. She picked up a delicate silver cigarette holder, waving it like the costume accessory it was. When they'd knocked at her door, Linda had answered fresh from a shower, wearing only a towel. She'd told them she was going upstairs to slip into something more comfortable and came down ready for her next scene.

Every time Linda leaned forward, Ray almost broke his neck trying to avoid catching an eyeful. Tom kept his gaze at eye level and prayed there was something under the gown. He knew the psychologist was revelling in Ray's discomfort, but even he found her attire off-putting.

'As I said, I'm sorry to disturb you at home like this. But it's important. How's Geoff, by the way? Is he home?

'My husband? You're joking, right? He's golfing. He's a surgeon and it's the weekend. It's in his contract. No, it's just plain old me.'

'Ah, golf. I should have been doing that this weekend.'

Tom plonked himself on a stool beside the oval kitchen island.

The room was colossal and could easily have featured in a glossy magazine photo shoot. Even so, this house was nothing compared to Linda's family abode. Tom had only ever read about the ancestral pile. Linda's grandfather had made serious money in the States – doing what, nobody knew. The inspector had heard an unsubstantiated rumour about bootlegging. On his return to Ireland, the old man oversaw the construction of a sprawling mansion in South Wicklow.

The Gothic design of that stately home could not have been more different from Linda's modern house and décor. Everything in this southside Dublin home was white or cream, from the marble floors and leather couches in the lounge to the bespoke kitchen they now occupied. It was all strangely at odds with the pyschologist's colourful personality. It might have been her husband's choice of interior and Linda wasn't bothered, but Tom suspected it was yet another quirky layer to her complex personality.

'I need to chat to you a little more about Aidan Blake. You mentioned you don't like him. Why, exactly?'

'Well, to start with, I have an issue with his politics.'

'Nothing personal, then?'

'I come from a family of politicians, Tom. It is personal.'

'Right.' The inspector clenched his jaw. He hated it when the psychologist sparred with him. She was too good at it. 'Look, you started saying something yesterday about some legislation Aidan Blake is working on. Before we were disturbed by his arrival. You seemed nervous when he came in.'

'Surely there's something more exciting behind Ryan Finnegan's death than the Natural Resources Bill?' Linda was playing with him again.

'You're the one who brought it to my attention as a potential issue,' he responded. 'Ryan worked in politics and, as you say, it can get personal. So, humour me.'

The psychologist pursed her lips, then smiled faintly.

'I'm passionate about the whole oil and gas business, you see. Taxing big oil and gas finds was one of daddy's hobby horses. I grew up hearing him talk about it all the time. When you adore a man like that – and I worshipped my father – their view of the world seeps into you. I wish I'd paid better heed to his other opinions . . .'

'Pardon?'

'Never mind. I'm rambling. Anyway, his generation of politicians was so very different. Their parents had taken the State from being a colony to a sovereign entity and they believed we had the potential to be something as a nation. Daddy wasn't even keen on us entering the European Union. Thought it was just swapping one foreign master for another. To be honest, I think he was also a bit of a xenophobe.' Linda laughed. 'The first time he saw a black man on O'Connell Street he nearly passed out.'

'Relevance?' Tom asked, his hands outstretched, pleading.

'All right, keep your panties on. I'm giving you context. You see, it was a period when the body politic thought that Ireland could establish an economy based on its own resources, be they people or energy. We're a small country but our offshore territories are huge. Do you know we're estimated to have access to billions of barrels of oil and gas equivalents beneath our seas? That's a few bob's worth, Tom.'

'I know all this, Linda. The estimates vary, but whatever is there is sizeable and the rights to it were more or less given away in the '80s. We started talking yesterday about how Blake's Bill was set to change that. Allegedly.'

'Indeed. That's the point. Blake might have had good intentions once. Even our esteemed Taoiseach used to make the right sounds about getting more from our natural resources. But cometh the power, cometh the greed. This government has been bought and sold. Their landmark Bill is restricted to future licence issuances, and it has one other significant omission – or inclusion, depending on your pedigree. Licences are time-limited and companies that wish to renew – and all the existing firms will – can do so with the conditions attached to their previous licences.

'So, regardless of what percentages are written into Irish law for future oil and gas finds, big companies like Udforske, Scandioil, and so on can carry on pillaging our natural resources without paying the Irish state a cent more than they already do. And they pretty much have a monopoly on what's there at the moment, so who's going to enter the field with those advantages stacked against them?'

Tom and Ray exchanged a puzzled look.

'Are you serious?' the inspector asked.

'Deadly. I've seen the Bill. It's written into the appendices. Somebody from the opposition benches will spot it and there'll be some uproar but the government will easily marginalise the most vocal opposition as the "loony left". It has the majority needed to pass the legislation, anyway. The debate will be guillotined and the Bill signed into law.'

'Guillotined?' Ray asked.

'Time limited and cut short,' Linda explained, making a chopping motion with her hand. 'Then, the spin machine will go into overdrive. The government will sell the law as a major victory for David against the energy Goliaths and a reversal of previous administration sell-outs. Already, the hype around the legislation is being used as a tool to quash resistance to the activities of the drilling companies off the west coast. Those big protests about the safety of onshore piping are starting to lose numbers. Those who keep demonstrating will be vilified as hardline and subversive because most people will think that these big multinationals are going to be paying big bucks into the public purse.'

Tom's brain was reeling.

'I thought the Bill was still being drafted – how did you get a copy?' Ray asked. 'And if word is out, why hasn't there been a wider reaction?'

'The bulk of the Bill was written over the summer months. Most politicians disappear back to their constituencies for July, August and most of September. The appendices were only recently added and I just saw the Bill in the last couple of weeks. I have my sources. Don't ask me to say any more.'

'The public will go mad, though,' Ray declared.

Linda shrugged.

'Maybe. Maybe not. Most people still think, after years of being conditioned, that we should be grateful these companies are willing to take the financial risk and explore our seas for oil and gas. They think we should be grateful for the jobs when there's a find. They haven't a clue how much the country is sacrificing in potential income. And all this at a time when we're being told we ordinary folk have to pay more taxes because Ireland is broke.'

Tom let the comment pass. Linda was anything but ordinary.

She picked up the cigarette holder and began to tap it on the table.

'You asked me why I don't like Aidan Blake. Well, here's the main reason. He's the man who's going to sell this Bill for the government. He's their ace card. Everybody loves Blake. He's the future of politics, Mr Style-Over-Substance. There's a reason he was put into that department and it was to make the unpalatable, palatable. Darragh McNally knew what he was doing with that one, the dastardly bastard.'

Tom mulled over what she'd told them, all sorts of questions springing to mind.

'So, if what you say is true and Blake's reputation was damaged, the whole Bill could fall.'

'Of course what I'm saying is true, Tom. Don't be so rude. What do you mean – if Blake's reputation was damaged?'

'I think somebody was trying to blackmail him.'

'Like Ryan Finnegan?' Linda probed.

Tom nodded. 'Blake insists he wasn't, but Ryan had damaging photos of Blake. We've been told Ryan disagreed with Aidan increasingly on political issues. Maybe this Bill was a step too far.'

'I see. Very interesting.'

Linda turned to Ray.

'What do you think, handsome? Do you think Blake would have shot Ryan rather than just accede to blackmail and change the Bill – if that's what Ryan wanted him to do?'

'I just can't see it,' Ray answered, blushing under her intense gaze. 'Murder is usually the result of an emotion. Love, hate, revenge. Motives more . . . basic. And we don't know everything about Ryan's life yet.'

'No,' Tom answered. 'But we do know where he was killed and that he had photos linked to Blake. There's only one problem. Blake had already caved to somebody else's blackmail.' He expanded for Linda's benefit. 'The original holder of the photos was hitting him for cash. The minister has admitted to that. So why not give Ryan what he wanted?'

'Personal cash is one thing,' Linda remarked. 'Telling somebody as ambitious as Blake how to do his job is quite another. Maybe it was a tipping point. Maybe he stood to lose a lot more if he acquiesced. I need coffee. Coffee, anybody?'

Tom and Ray nodded gratefully.

'You boys really have your work cut out for you,' Linda said, tossing a handful of coffee beans into a grinder. 'Leinster House is a snake pit and politics breeds contempt.'

She hit the button on the machine and it whirred to life; the noise and aroma of the beans being crushed filled the kitchen.

'It's survival of the fittest in there,' she hollered, over the racket. 'And reputation really is everything. But this in an interesting one, Tom.'

He waited until the noise stopped to reply.

'What do you mean?'

'The way Ryan was killed. It's unusual. It doesn't have the hallmarks of a spurned lover. That's normally something intimate and ferocious, like a stabbing. Or if he'd clashed with Aidan on this Bill business and tried to blackmail the minister, I would have expected strangulation or a punch-up that ended badly. But you've nothing like that. Your victim was targeted for assassination. Which means somebody very unemotionally and very professionally decided to take him out.

'You're dealing with one cool operator. And that's going to make your job that bit harder.'

CHAPTER 11

Donegal

'I can't go up in that thing.'

'Why not?'

'I have a morbid fear of flying, Tom, and that's in normal planes. Look at that. It's a tin can. The wings are stuck on with Sellotape.'

'If it's your time, it's your time.'

'And if it's the pilot's time?'

Tom eventually coaxed Ray onto the aircraft, which, admittedly, was quite small. Now he was humming 'I'm Leaving on a Jet Plane' just to rub it in.

Ray kept his eyes closed for the whole flight from Dublin Airport to Donegal, trying to block out his boss. There was something different about Tom this morning. He was far too happy. Ray had barely slept. Two pints had failed to knock sense into him and he'd ended up lying awake in bed with uncomfortable images of Laura and her new boyfriend still running through his head.

The landing was so bumpy that the detective was green by the time the plane taxied to a halt.

'We're driving home,' he snapped at Tom as he stormed towards the small terminal building.

A patrol car was waiting for them outside, two uniformed guards leaning casually against its side.

'They didn't have to send the entire Donegal division for us,' the inspector greeted them, jocularly. 'I'm DI Tom Reynolds. This is my sidekick, Robin.'

'DS Ray Lennon,' his deputy corrected, still irritable.

The first guard, young enough to be just out of training school, grinned as they shook hands, but his colleague maintained a dour frown. He adjusted the cap on his oversized head and straightened his jacket.

'The sergeant would like you to drop by the station. As a courtesy call, like.'

Tom and Ray exchanged a knowing look.

The specialist murder team was often sent to other parts of the country to assist with investigations. Sometimes the local gardaí were glad to have the extra resources and would happily hand over the reins in a burdensome case. Some areas, though, received them with hostility, suspicious that the team was being sent out because the big boys up in Dublin didn't rate the locals. Not every garda station appreciated the concept behind centralising talent in units like the National Bureau for Criminal Investigation.

'We're not here for any local matter,' Ray barked, his ill humour happy to find another target. 'We're here to interview a witness connected to a Dublin case.'

The grumpy guard just shrugged, while the younger guy had the good grace to look embarrassed.

The inspector sighed and got into the back of the car.

'After this, you can drive us to our witness's house,' he said, exerting some authority.

'Well . . .' Grumpy started.

'No problem,' the young chap interjected, showing some character.

'Thank you. What are your names, by the way?'

'I'm Gary Dillon. My colleague is Stephen McGettigan.'

The other guard grunted.

Grumpy will suffice, Tom thought.

They drove out towards the West Donegal coastal road.

Tom sat back and enjoyed the ride. He loved the northwestern county, a sparsely populated wilderness filled with all the beauty nature could summon. No other place in Ireland could boast such an array of diverse, breathtaking landscapes. A traveller driving the length of Donegal could take in everything from bogs, loughs, forests and cloud-peaked mountains to scenic villages, mighty cliffs and isolated, unspoiled beaches.

The only downside was the capricious weather. It was often said that a visitor could enjoy all four seasons in a single day in Donegal. In a winter storm it could seem like the bleakest spot on earth; on a sunny summer's day the most idyllic.

Tom had been visiting the county since he was a child. Every year, his family had packed the old VW van and braved country roads of varying states of repair to holiday with relatives who lived near Malin Head on the Inishowen Peninsula, Ireland's most northerly point.

The inspector's favourite memory was the annual trip they took to the secluded Kinnagoe Bay. Their vehicle would make the hair-raising descent down to the white sands and lapping blue sea, the resting place of the Armada ship *La Trinidad Valencera*, which sank there in 1588. His mother would throw down an old blanket and distribute sand-infused sandwiches, before yelling at them to be careful as they rushed, screaming with excitement, into the exhilaratingly cold Atlantic Ocean thinking they could hunt for treasure.

Ray stared out the window, blissfully ignorant of his boss's nostalgic meanderings. His colour was only starting to return to normal.

'I love cars,' he said, confirming for Tom that the joyous look on his face had nothing to do with the Donegal scenery.

Houses began to dot the landscape, indicating they were nearing a population hub.

'Better take the inland road,' Grumpy instructed Gary. 'The crusties are out again today.'

'The what?' Tom asked.

'Crusties. Protestors. You'll see them in a minute, but we'll turn off so we don't meet them.'

Sure enough, after a mile or so, they could hear the rising clamour of people chanting in protest. The car left the main road and began its ascent up a hill, giving its passengers a view of the scene below and the people gathered there. The crowd of roughly one hundred held placards and banners aloft outside a set of gates. Beyond the adjoining fencing Tom could see a building site running down to the sea. It was a bruise on the otherwise pristine coastline.

Two squad cars corralled the protestors.

From their vantage point, the inspector could see guards attempting to push the crowd back against the ditch by the hillside so the road would be passable. They were failing. Further up the road, a concrete-mixing truck destined for the site idled, waiting for the path to be cleared.

'What are they protesting?' Ray asked.

'Progress,' the older guard grumbled.

Tom said nothing. He knew why the campaigners were there. And he and Ray would shortly be visiting the man responsible for ruining the view.

They drove on to the nearest village in silence, pulling up in the car park of the small police station. In keeping with the other village houses, the walls were whitewashed and an old-fashioned lantern stood just beside the front door.

Tom and Ray waited outside Sergeant Cathal Gallagher's office for five minutes, watching through venetian blinds as he paced the floor with files, picked up the phone and shouted something into it, then slammed a few drawers. Eventually, he opened the door.

'Sorry about that,' he said, in a tone that expressed no remorse. 'We're having trouble today down at the site.'

He invited them to sit in the two chairs facing the desk.

Gallagher was roughly the same age as Tom. The man was tall and still athletic but would never be described as handsome. His strawberry-blonde thinning hair was combed forward but still failed to hide the pink scalp peeking through. He had a weak chin and a sour downturn of the mouth. A beard would help, Tom mused.

'We saw the protest on the way here,' he said. 'Still no resolution?'

The sergeant shook his head, angrily.

'What do they want?' Ray asked, hoping for more success this time.

'To waste our bloody time and resources, hi,' Gallagher snapped. 'Half the county force are down there, day in, day out, but that doesn't stop the locals whining if we don't have a car immediately to go check out whatever their gripe is at any given time. Supposed to be everywhere at once, we are, hi.'

Ray threw Tom a questioning glance. Did anyone give a straight answer in this place? And why, he wondered, did the sergeant keep saying 'hi'? Not having Tom's experience of the county (his family had holidayed in Butlin's every year), Ray had yet to learn that many Donegal locals stuck 'hi' on the end of random sentences, not as a greeting but as a turn of phrase.

'They're protesting the building of an onshore gas pipeline,' Tom explained. 'You've heard about it.'

Ray scanned his memories. Ah, yes. He had seen it on the news recently. A scenic area in Donegal, gas being piped in from the sea, locals opposed to a pipeline being run under their community by . . .

'Wait, isn't that being built by Udforske?' Ray said, finally getting it.

The inspector nodded.

The sergeant cleared his throat, drawing their attention.

'We saw the squad cars down there,' Tom said. 'I can imagine you're pressed. It must be difficult, though, for the locals to come to terms with that sort of upheaval. And don't they also have concerns about the pipe's safety?'

Gallagher frowned.

'It's not a straightforward situation, Inspector Reynolds. There are fifty men down there working on that initial infrastructure stage. Udforske pays extremely well and there'll be more jobs coming onstream. That's in a county that has been neglected by Dublin longer than I care to remember. Where else are we supposed to get that sort of enterprise and investment? And those dangers associated with the pipe that the protestors've come up with . . . ?' The sergeant rolled his eyes. 'Something and nothing. I've been shown the research. The chance of anything happening when the gas is brought onshore is virtually non-existent. You're more likely to get hit by a falling pylon!'

'If it was running under your house, would you be worried?' Tom asked.

Gallagher squinted at him.

'I've lived here all my life. I've family who live along the proposed pipe route and I've family who are working at the site. If I thought there was a danger from the pipe, I'd be down there with the protestors. There isn't. All that Udforske is bringing to Donegal is energy security and a boost to the local economy. Some people build houses in the countryside and expect to have undisturbed scenery surrounding them – but how are those houses supposed to be heated? Supplied with phone lines and electricity? If the bloody house is going to interrupt the view, the infrastructure to provide for it will too.'

The sergeant sniffed indignantly before continuing.

'And now that Bill is being brought in down in Dublin, Udforske will be paying plenty of money into the State's purse. For the life of me, I can't get my head around what the problem is. But, hi, half of those down there waving their placards aren't even from around here. They're being shipped in by radicals opposed to any kind of gas drilling, no matter how safe. We've had some violent altercations – guards being pelted with rocks and fencing, threatened with worse. It gets nasty at times. My men have to live in this community.'

Tom inclined his head, half in agreement. He wasn't going to get into an argument with the sergeant. He didn't know what was going on at the protests, bar what he'd picked up through the media. He could imagine it was no picnic for the local guards, especially in such a tight-knit community. Back in his uniformed days, he'd policed a couple of protests himself and he knew how quickly they could turn. It didn't matter that you had a uniform and a baton when ten angry blokes were bearing down on you.

He was interested to note, though, that the sergeant knew about Blake's Bill and that he was, as Linda predicted, presuming it to be in the national interest. The government's propaganda was certainly working.

The inspector would have been happy to leave it at that, but the sergeant wasn't finished making his point.

'Er, I believe you're actually here to interview the vice-president of Udforske,' Gallagher continued. 'Mind if I ask what about?'

Tom suppressed the urge to respond that the sergeant could certainly ask but he shouldn't expect an answer. There really was no point putting Gallagher's nose out of joint.

'It has nothing to do with local matters. We're here in relation to a Dublin case.'

The other man picked up a well-chewed biro and placed its lid in his mouth.

The whole force knew Tom's team was in charge of the Leinster House murder inquiry. The inspector had no doubt Gallagher knew that Madsen must have some connection to the investigation.

'May I ask,' Tom continued, 'why you are interested in our wanting to speak to him?'

The sergeant dropped the biro, the muscle in his cheek twitching. God love him, if he played poker.

'Just idle curiosity,' Gallagher said. 'Mr Madsen doesn't come to our peninsula too often, mind, but when he does, he's a welcome visitor. He provides a lot of local employment with his company but he's also a contributor to charities and businesses in the county. He's a very generous man.'

'And?' Now Tom was tiring of the sergeant.

Gallagher looked at him blankly.

'I just mean, he's well liked. So, now you have my take on the man.'

The inspector regarded him coolly.

'That's good to know, but it's irrelevant to our investigation,' Tom responded in a clipped tone. He'd had enough of this stuffed shirt. 'We'd better be off.'

Gallagher stood with them.

'I didn't mean to go upsetting you, now,' he said.

Tom paused at the door.

'Not in the slightest, Sergeant. We're in a hurry, that's all. There's a young widow with a six-month-old baby in Dublin waiting for us to find the person who murdered her husband. It sort of focuses the mind, you know?'

Gallagher bowed his head, momentarily shame-faced, but when he met Tom's eyes again, there was a new glint of defiance.

'To be sure. I'm just making the point that your visit to Donegal will be fleeting, but Mr Madsen will, hopefully, be around for the long haul.'

Tom bit his tongue and left.

They waited outside by the squad car they'd arrived in.

'Well,' Ray said, 'perhaps we should go pick up a bouquet of flowers and some chocolates for Mr Madsen before we make our way over.'

Tom laughed, his anger dissipating.

'I don't know why I'm so irritated,' he said. 'Two Dubliners show up to interview the local bigwig, of course Gallagher's going to want to stick his oar in. I guess I'm not feeling very indulgent.'

'Hmm. Did you pick up on that thing he said about the gas pipeline?'

'What thing?'

'He said he'd seen research to show that there was no danger from the pipe running under people's houses. Who do you think showed him the research?'

'You've such a suspicious mind, Ray,' Tom responded, drily. 'I'm sure independent analysis has been provided by some objective body about the pipe's safety.'

Ray grimaced. 'Or, Udforske has organised public briefings with information provided by its experts and the good sergeant has bought into it hook, line and sinker.'

'Good God, Detective. You're not on the side of those reds under the bed down at the protest, are you? The great unwashed?'

Ray was still devising his stinging retort when Garda Dillon arrived.

'On your own, son?' Tom asked.

The young man flushed red. 'My partner is, eh, busy.'

'Ah, I see. Late lunch? Right, then. You know where Carl Madsen resides?'

Gary scoffed. 'The whole county knows. Is he expecting you?'

'Not at all, but we know he's in situ. We're not going back to Dublin until we speak to him. We haven't risked our lives flying up here for nothing, huh, Ray?'

'Get in the bloody car,' Ray snapped.

*

It took them half an hour to find Udforske's vice-president. They had pulled up at his not insubstantial cliffside house and discovered his car in the drive. After ten minutes of ringing the doorbell to no avail, they decided to check the private beach at the bottom of the cliff, figuring if he was out, he must be in the vicinity.

Sure enough, the man was strolling across the sand, walking two large dogs that could have had starring roles in *The Hound of the Baskervilles*. He called them to heel when he noticed the two detectives approaching.

The inspector called out a greeting and informed Madsen of their identities.

'They're some dogs you have,' Tom observed.

'Rhodesian ridgebacks,' Madsen replied. 'They were bred for hunting lions in southern Africa.'

'And what do they hunt here?' the inspector asked, keeping a wary eye on the animals. He had been bitten by a German shepherd when he was fifteen and still held a healthy fear of canines.

Madsen laughed.

'Not protestors, if that is your concern, Inspector. They keep me company when I visit and a local man takes care of them for me when I'm in Denmark. They're kittens, really. How do you say it – their bark is worse than their bite.'

Madsen's English was almost perfect, the Danish accent barely discernible.

Despite his decree that he not be disturbed at his holiday home, the Udforske vice-president didn't seem overly put out by their sudden arrival. He brought them up to the house and out of the fine rain that had started to sweep in from the sea.

'In other places, they ask, "Is it raining?"' he said, as they entered the cavernous entrance hall. 'In Donegal, they ask, "Is it dry?"'

Tom nodded in agreement.

'Your home is incredible.' Ray, who'd grown up on a working-class estate, had taken in the vast entrance hall wide-eyed, admiring its high ceilings illuminated in daylight by the large glass panels over the door.

'Thank you,' Madsen replied graciously.

He indicated they climb the spiral staircase leading to the open-plan living and dining area.

'I believe the architect who designed the house won awards for his public work. This was his secret project. I enjoy this upper level the most but the rooms downstairs are actually built into the side of the cliff. Very James Bond, no? Let me get you some refreshments. Tea, coffee, perhaps something stronger?'

Sipping his coffee, Tom thought he'd like nothing more than to be relaxing in this huge lounge with its floor-to-ceiling windows, taking in the glorious vista, a glass of deep red Amarone in hand. No doubt downstairs there was a wine cellar, which Tom imagined would be stocked top to bottom with the finest vintages. Madsen, with his thick mane of blonde hair, deep tan and general look of a man used to luxury, would settle for no less.

'So, did you buy this place before your company started drilling offshore, or after?'

Tom turned to face his host, his back to the ocean view.

'I bought this place before the company came here,' Madsen answered, amused. 'What do you think? That I stood where you stand, looking out at the spectacular sea and thought: "I must despoil that view"?'

'Did you?' Tom asked, only half-smiling.

Madsen observed the inspector.

'I knew there was oil and gas off the Irish coast. The research had been done. Very few others were interested at the time and I thought, why not harvest the energy? I have no desire to ruin the landscape. My company is contributing to the Irish economy. Our drilling activities create jobs and make money for Ireland.'

'And for Udforske.'

'Certainly. We are a business.'

'Nothing wrong with that. So long as everything is above board.'

Madsen flashed Tom a shrewd look. He sat back on one of the expensive, bespoke armchairs. Ray perched nervously on a designer sofa, holding his cup with both hands for fear it might spill. He'd never felt more like a fish out of water.

'Are you referring to the pipeline?' Madsen asked. 'I must tell you, whatever you have heard, we have done our homework. There is nothing to fear from running gas to an onshore treatment facility. It is safe and the most cost-efficient way of bringing it inland. It's unfortunate that there are elements so opposed to the latest advances in technology, but I suppose that has always been the way. We must reach out to them, but we can't let them hinder us indefinitely.'

'I don't know anything about the pipeline,' Tom confessed, 'safe or unsafe. I've heard segments on the news about the protests and the company's plans, but I've taken no interest.'

'You must explain what you mean, then, by "above board".'

'The Resources Bill that Minister Aidan Blake is to pass through our parliament shortly. Have you had any influence over whether it will contain a provision that protects your company from future increases in royalty and licence payments?'

Madsen's countenance remained placid and Tom strained to

detect the tiniest hint of discomfort in the Udforske vice-president's voice when he answered.

'I do not understand. The Bill you speak of is much lauded by Irish politicians and public commentators, no? All of the players in the energy game, including those least supportive of drilling, have had their input into its planning. I imagine there are many in my industry who will be unhappy with its provisions.'

'Yes, many future entrants into the market,' Tom said. 'But not existing forces.'

Madsen shrugged.

'If the early explorers are protected a little more, so be it. We were the ones who took the risk and drilled, not knowing what we'd find. We gambled and now everyone is reaping the reward.'

'Yet you said the research had already been undertaken confirming there were natural resources off the Irish coast before you brought your company here.'

There was a flash in Madsen's eyes. The first sign their host was not as laid-back as he appeared. Tom had succeeded in provoking him.

'But that's not why we're here,' the inspector continued. 'Not directly, in any case.'

The indulgent mask settled back on the other man's face.

'Indeed. Why are you here?'

'To question you as a potential witness to a murder, Mr Madsen.'

The other man flinched.

'Excuse me?'

'You visited Leinster House on Friday evening, am I right?'

'Correct. I was there to discuss the very legislation you refer to. It was a final conversation before the minister concludes his . . . how do you say it . . . deliberations. I am hopeful that once the law is introduced, the protests that have hindered my company's work to date will cease. They have been in decline all summer, since the government hinted the legislation was coming. Now that people see how the energy industry will be paying, those so passionately opposed to us will lose popular support. They will have to go home, Inspector. But what does any of that have to do with murder?'

'You met with the minister at 9 p.m. for a half hour and then spent some time with Darragh McNally, after which you were escorted to the Dáil bar, where you were to wait for your driver. Is this correct?'

'Partially,' Madsen replied, his brows knitted. Something had shifted in the atmosphere. Tom sensed the other man was on high alert. 'I wasn't waiting for my driver, as it happens. I was waiting for a taxicab. My usual driver was unwell on Friday evening. The company sent me a new man, who made the mistake of leaving after he dropped me off at Government Buildings for my meeting. They're supposed to stay and wait, you see. I won't be using that firm again. McNally had to call a cab for me and assured me it would be a matter of minutes. It took rather longer.'

'Were you unaccompanied in the bar?'

'Yes.'

The lie detector alarm went off in Tom's head.

'Is that why you didn't stay there for long?'

Madsen was silent.

Tom waited, glancing over at Ray, who had forgotten his surroundings and was now staring at Madsen, his half-empty coffee cup tilted precariously. The rain had picked up and was pummelling the glass windows in great sheets, creating the effect of a wall of water. Outside, the Atlantic crashed against the cliff, causing a vibration so strong the house thrummed. How quickly the balmy day had turned.

'You seem to know a lot about my movements on Friday night,

Inspector, yet I still don't know why they are of such concern. Do I require a solicitor for this conversation? And what is this talk about a murder?'

'You can hold off on the solicitor for now. You really haven't heard what happened in Leinster House? You haven't seen any news or read any papers since yesterday?'

'No. I had several back-to-back meetings yesterday morning and then I retreated here, to the house. As you can see, I like to shut myself off from everything for my stay. I have no television. I read books, not newspapers, over the weekend. I listen to records, not the radio. It is so rare for me to have any peace and quiet that I guard it jealously. No one mentioned anything at our meetings, but then we had a heavy agenda and they would not have known that I had been in Leinster House. I had several missed calls but no intention of returning them until I resume work on Monday.'

'A man was shot dead.'

Madsen paled visibly.

'Impossible.'

'And yet, it happened,' Tom said. 'During your visit. And I have a witness who places you in the main lobby, a few hundred metres away from the dead man, minutes after he was murdered.'

Madsen abruptly sat forward, a move Tom suspected was about as animated as the powerful man got when rattled.

'Clarify something for me, please. Who was this man? Did I know him? I have had dealings with very few individuals in the Irish government. If you suspect my involvement, it must be somebody I know. And you must suspect me in some fashion, if you came all the way up here to question me.'

'It was a man called Ryan Finnegan. He was Minister Blake's political advisor. And I haven't come here to accuse you of anything. Merely to ascertain your movements, as we must do with everybody who was in Leinster House on Friday evening.'

Madsen sat back.

'I have never met this Ryan Finnegan. The name means nothing to me, which means *he* meant nothing to me. I was in the main lobby because I got bored waiting in the bar. It's not something I am used to, waiting. The coffee was foul and the company not much better. I left to use the facilities and to enquire as to whether my transport had arrived. I'm sorry you've made such a long trip but as I have no knowledge of the dead man . . . didn't even know he was deceased, in fact . . . you have wasted your time.'

'Perhaps,' Tom said. Was there a tiny flicker of something in Madsen's eyes? Was the inspector imagining uneasiness there?

'Let me enlighten you as to why we think Mr Finnegan was murdered.'

Madsen shrugged and waved his hand, a gesture implying he was willing to humour Tom. It was like getting the upraised thumb from a Roman emperor.

'Mr Finnegan and Minister Blake go back a long way, as friends and as work colleagues. Unfortunately, their political ideologies appear to have diverged in recent times. Luckily for the minister, Mr Finnegan was absent for most of this year due to an accident. Over the same period, the clauses protecting your company's interests were being written into this new legislation.'

'Not just my company . . .' Madsen interjected.

Tom continued, unperturbed.

'My theory is that Mr Finnegan returned to work this week and discovered the changes. There was something found about his person that has led me to believe he may have decided to blackmail the minister to return the Bill to its original format.'

Madsen raised an eyebrow.

'I can't imagine this Finnegan man would have had anything to blackmail the minister with. Aidan Blake is well respected in political and business circles, no? He has fostered a reputation of being a new type of politician, hasn't he?'

'So, is it pure coincidence that his revised Bill is of such benefit to your company and others?' Tom probed.

Madsen said nothing for a few seconds. Instead, he stared at Tom. His countenance remained relaxed and unreadable and yet the inspector suddenly felt cold. He couldn't describe what it was that was so threatening about the other man. But, in that instant, Tom knew that he would never want to encounter Carl Madsen as a business or any other type of adversary.

'I am offended by what I think you're implying.' The Udforske vice-president broke the silence. 'Our dealings with the Irish government have always been rigorously transparent. I am certain that in drafting this Bill, the minister must have known the difficulties it could cause for existing industry activity off the Irish coast and the impact that would have on jobs and the economy. Hence the clause you speak of.'

Tom held the other man's gaze and his own resolve.

'I'm sorry if I have upset you, but what you're describing does sound like blackmail of a sort, Mr Madsen – an economic threat to a country already on its knees.'

'Perhaps, but that's a debate for another day. What you came to speak to me about has nothing to do with me or my company.' Madsen's voice was icy.

Tom said nothing, allowing the muted strains of the wailing wind outside to fill the silence.

'Surely somebody with your influence could have unearthed details of any sordid past Blake might have? We're men of the world, Mr Madsen. Sometimes business needs a little nudge.'

Madsen opened his mouth to speak, then paused. He pinched the bridge of his thin nose and studied Tom. The inspector sensed the other man was swallowing his anger and forcing himself to be diplomatic.

'You are a sensible man, Inspector. Or I will treat you as such, at least. You are clearly not interested in the interaction of politics and business, other than any relevance it might have to your case. So, I will be straight with you.

'Attempted blackmail of a government minister – that is news to me. Minister Blake, as I said, is seen as untouchable. I have not tried to force his hand on this licence issue. It would seem that the economic arguments that I, and others like me, have made have been sufficient to influence him. Like all industries, of course we try to exert pressure on government. We lobby. To do that, you need access.

'I am speaking anecdotally now, you understand? Good. If I wanted to have the ear of the relevant decision makers, I would go to the man who pulls the strings – there is always such a man. It's useful to have friends, Inspector. Today, my interest is resources. Tomorrow, it might be telecommunications, water services, media. Politicians change, but the men who operate in the background rarely do.'

Tom stared at Madsen, a section of the puzzle falling into place.

'I see,' he said.

'You said "partially".' A splash of Ray's now cold coffee found the floor and he moved his foot to cover it, hoping it wouldn't be noticed.

'Excuse me?'

'When Inspector Reynolds asked you about your movements on Friday night, you said his account was partially correct and that you hadn't been waiting for your driver. Was that all that was inaccurate?'

Madsen hesitated for a moment. Ray's suspicion was confirmed. The other man had deliberately not answered Tom's question fully, instead diverting them with the response about the taxicab.

Downstairs, unsettled by something, the two dogs began to bark and howl.

The Udforske vice-president's calculations were swift.

'No. It was inaccurate to say I met the minister for a half hour.'

'How long did you spend with him?' Ray asked.

'I spent a half hour with Mr McNally. I didn't spend any time with Aidan Blake. I met McNally, alone, until just after 9.30 p.m. on Friday evening. In fact, I've never met Minister Blake in Leinster House.'

CHAPTER 12

'We could drive home.'

Ray peered out the car window at the gloomy low-hanging clouds and ceaseless rain. The unseasonably warm October was behind them, if it had ever reached Donegal.

Gary Dillon had driven them to the airport, where they discovered all flights had been cancelled due to the storm.

'We're not driving,' Tom said. 'You heard Garda Dillon. There's flash flooding at the bottom of the county and it's dark now. We'd be nearly five hours driving from here on a good day. We'll stay over tonight and get the first flight back in the morning, when the weather has settled down.'

'Stay where?' Ray asked, raging. He'd rather paddle back to Dublin than risk going up in that potential death trap again. The prospect of yelling 'I told you so' to his boss as it crashed held little satisfaction.

'In the village,' Tom replied. He was busy typing a text to Louise. It was the most prudent form of communication. If he rang and told her she'd have to drive the Citroën home herself from the Wicklow hotel this evening, he'd get an earful.

He'd called Michael and told him to organise another interview with Blake for tomorrow. If they accepted Madsen's version of events, the minister had lied about the first part of his alibi. They would give him the opportunity to correct his statement. And Tom was especially eager now to talk to McNally. He assumed that he was the man with the strings to whom Madsen had referred.

'I'd offer to put you up, but I'm lodging with a relative at the moment until I find my own place,' Gary said. 'There's a nice hotel down the road from the station. I'll drop you there.'

'What if it's booked out?' Ray asked, hopefully.

Gary shook his head, mournfully.

'The place used to be bursting at the rafters, even outside the tourist season. These days, well, it's barely kept going. They still keep it nice, though.'

'What did you think of Madsen?' Tom asked Ray, to pass the time as they drove.

'I think if we'd explored his home a little more, we'd have found the passage tunnelled into the cliff that leads to his underground nuclear missile bunker. He's just missing a cat to stroke, while he plots world domination in his lair. God knows what those dogs get fed.'

The inspector smiled.

'Such a vivid imagination, Junior. But I reckon we'd be wrong to peg him as some type of comedy foreign villain. That man has an undercurrent I don't like. There's something . . . I can't put my finger on it.'

'I get what you're saying,' Ray agreed. 'Is there any gossip about him in the village?' He directed this to Gary.

'He generally keeps to himself, bar when he needs people to do work up there or mind the dogs,' the young guard replied. 'We haven't had any small children go missing from their beds since he moved to the peninsula, if that's what you're getting at. No virgins turning up bloodied and ravished.'

'He's from Denmark, not Transylvania,' Tom remarked, as Ray and Gary snorted laughing.

The whitewashed Moorhaven Inn was named for the village it graced. Gary left them as close as possible to the door and they dashed in, past the hanging baskets of hardy autumn flowers swinging precariously in the gale.

Inside, by contrast, all was calm. A young woman sat behind the reception counter, the soles of her feet resting against its top, giving her momentum as she rocked back and forth on the chair's hind legs.

She looked up from the book she was reading, mildly amused at their dramatic entrance. A large peat fire blazed in the corner of the old-fashioned lobby and Ray hurried over to it as Tom approached the desk.

'Innkeeper, we'd like your finest rooms,' he said, slapping his hands down on the wood theatrically.

The girl arched an elegant eyebrow.

'Ach, I'm terribly sorry. We only dole them out to dry guests.'

He smiled. 'Whatever you have going, then. Two, please. If I have to share a room with my colleague he'll insist on ghost stories and a midnight feast.'

She glanced over at Ray, still sulking as he warmed his hands at the fire, unaware he was the centre of attention.

'I'll do his bedside story, if he's desperate.'

She gave Tom a cheeky wink and pulled the guest register out from under the counter.

'Just sign here. I assume it's for one night?'

'I'm afraid so. Do you do food?'

'I can organise sandwiches but there's a pub further down the village that does hot fare. We run that too. Tell my dad you're staying here and he'll sort you out.'

Tom finished filling in their details.

She gave them adjoining rooms on the first of the hotel's two upper floors. As promised by Gary, the lodgings were well maintained. Each room was large and comfortable with an impressive view of the bay, albeit interrupted by the very prominent construction site they'd passed earlier, lit up with industrial halogen lamps. The weather might have sent the protestors home for the night but it hadn't halted work.

Tom drew the heavy drapes across the window.

Ray was still out of sorts as they made their way downstairs.

'Ah, look, would you cheer up?' Tom said. 'We're in the middle of a case and we've managed to swing a night off for a nice dinner and a pint. The flight tomorrow will take no time. I'll hold your hand the whole way.'

Ray rolled his eyes. In fact, the plane journey had gone clean out of his head. The reason for his dark humour lay elsewhere. He'd rung Laura after Michael to get an update on the day's work and Eoin Coyle had answered. Ray had hung up hurriedly and didn't answer when Laura rang back. He sent her a text instead, saying they were stuck in Donegal and the reception was bad. They'd talk in the morning.

He was struggling to understand what was going on in his brain. How was it possible that, in the last forty-eight hours, he'd suddenly gone from seeing Laura as a companionable workmate to . . . what exactly was he seeing her as now? A possible girlfriend?

He shook his head. Enough. This was a pathetic carry-on for a grown man.

The girl at the desk held out two raincoats.

'An umbrella would be no use to you in that,' she told them, her tone knowing and wiser than her years.

The pub was only a minute's walk away, but they still needed the protection from the elements. They entered the imaginatively named Moorhaven Public House thinking the family that owned both businesses hadn't exactly put themselves out in their choice of names.

Inside was busy, by Irish country pub standards.

An older man, with a shock of black hair and the same sharp eyes as the girl in the hotel, stood behind the bar polishing glasses with a tea towel. He looked up at the new arrivals, as did the ten or so customers – all men – gathered in little groups at the bar and the low tables.

The room had an inviting interior, even with the eleven sets of eyes trained on the newcomers. Here, again, a generous fire crackled and hissed in the corner, infusing the air with the comforting aroma of burning turf. The tables were made of dark wood and each one was unique, probably carved by a local artisan. The brass-studded chairs looked newly upholstered and the wooden floor was beautifully varnished. The shelves behind the owner were cluttered with standard spirits bottles, but also featured rarer finds and a mish-mash of old curios.

Yes, Tom could enjoy a pint in here. And he had a cigar in his pocket for later.

'Good evening,' the barman said. 'What can I get you two gentlemen?'

Tom and Ray approached the counter, conscious of their audience. There was no television suspended in the corner showing sporting events, no radio churning out news or music. Tonight, the two strangers would be the entertainment.

'Two pints, please,' Tom ordered. 'Your . . . daughter? She said to tell you we're staying in the hotel. We're hoping to get a hot meal, if that's possible.'

'Aye, is that right?'

The barman leaned across the counter to shake their hands.

'Moorhaven,' he said.

'Eh . . . Dublin?' Ray answered, bemused.

The bar erupted into laughter. Ray looked around, startled. The man on the stool beside him, who had long passed his three-score and ten, gripped the detective's elbow with a claw-like hand.

'His name is Mattie Moorhaven,' he cackled toothlessly, pointing at the grinning barman.

Tom smiled. 'I thought you'd struggled to come up with names for your businesses; I didn't realise you'd called them after yourself. Your family must be here a long time, so?'

'The longest,' the barman said. 'Padraig Óg there, his family came along a few decades later, but my clan started up the township itself nigh on two hundred years ago.'

'We had to come to stop the inbreeding, hi,' the man called Padraig Óg remarked, approaching from the table behind Tom, empty pint glass in hand. 'Put another one on for me there, Mattie. Aye, things were getting desperate. All the Moorhaven women were cross-eyed and bearded.'

'Just as well, Padraig. Or your godawful ugly ancestors wouldn't have got a look in.'

The barman strode down to the end of the bar and opened a door.

'Majella! Stick on two dinners. We've company. Use the clean plates.'

Tom and Ray pulled out two counter stools and settled in.

'You up for business or pleasure, folks?' Mattie asked them.

'It was business, now it's pleasure,' Tom said.

'Is that right? You're not reporters up covering the protest, are you?' The man topped off their pints of stout with creamy heads and placed them on beer mats.

Ray shook his head.

'No. We're Gardaí.'

Tom groaned inwardly. He'd meant to remind Ray not to mention the day job and had hoped the weather would prevent news of their arrival spreading. Anyone in the bar could have been involved in the fraught protests down at the Udforske site, where officers were pitched against the locals.

As he feared, it was like a switch had been flicked. The barman's lip curled in distaste and the old man on the chair beside Ray turned his back to him. He couldn't see it, but Tom knew the men behind them were also surveying them with a sudden hostility.

'You might have mentioned that first,' Padraig Óg said, glaring at Tom. The man was gripping the side of the bar counter so fiercely his knuckles had turned white. 'Are you proud of being sent up here to baton women and kids off a public road? Is that what you aspired to do when you grew up?'

'Padraig. That's enough now.' The barman's tone was low, warning.

Tom raised his hands defensively and shook his head.

'We're not policing any protests, *chara*. I'm Detective Inspector Tom Reynolds and my colleague is Detective Sergeant Ray Lennon. We came up to interview a witness in relation to something that happened in Dublin. That's all.'

The man called Padraig continued to stare confrontationally at Tom, as though he didn't believe him.

The bar owner spoke again.

'We've had bad run-ins with your lot these last few months. There's history there, so forgive us for not rolling out the welcome mat.'

The inspector cocked his head to one side.

'I know about the protests and that they've been violent at times, but people can be forgiven for reacting strongly in the heat of the moment, surely? Even the guards? I imagine a lot of the officers down there are local lads, am I right?'

Padraig snorted.

'We're not talking about a bit of heavy-handed policing here. We're talking about the Irish police force being used as a private militia for those Udforske vultures. And if you don't know what your colleagues up here are at, you should get yourself an education.'

*

Their dinners arrived. Tom realised he'd been expecting some kind of roast meat after the bar owner had ordered for them without offering a choice, but the chef, Majella, had confounded them. They were presented with two beautifully decorated plates of Dublin Lawyer lobster, the creamy brandy sauce sending up a mouth-watering aroma.

Tom and Ray had spent the time waiting for their meals convincing the regulars they weren't henchmen for Udforske. Both were curious to hear the locals' perspective on the protests and their impressions of Carl Madsen and his company.

The air of suspicion still lingered but it was fading. Mattie Moorhaven wouldn't let them pay for the meal, so they'd put money behind the bar to buy everyone a drink. As the Guinness and Jameson whiskey flowed, tongues loosened.

'In the beginning, we thought it was to be embraced.' Padraig Óg was clearly the designated spokesman. He reminded Tom of a schoolteacher he'd once had, who in turn had always made him think of the poet W.B. Yeats: a small face with a skinny nose and pince-nez glasses.

Padraig pushed those spectacles up his nose, now. The sweat on the man's face kept causing them to slip. The bar had been cosy when Tom and Ray arrived and it was getting warmer as the evening wore on. The fire was burning solidly and the front door had yet to open again to allow any heat to escape.

'Madsen bought the cliff house a few years ago. He was an irregular visitor but good to the community any time he was here. Shopped local, hired village women to do the cleaning. If he needed a repair job done, he'd always ask a Moorhaven man to come up, that sort of thing. We've been so badly hit by the cuts to the fishing quotas, jobs are few and far between.'

The old man beside Ray, who'd been introduced as Dinny and had swivelled back in their direction, picked up this part of the tale.

'Aye, that's right. You wouldn't think it to look at us now, but Moorhaven was a thriving fishing port once upon a time. Every second family had a boat. Then those traitors sold us out in Europe.'

'What traitors?' Ray asked.

'The government, son. The Common Fisheries Policy in the

'70s. A third of the fleet has been lost across the island since then. Those Dublin boys went over there with the farming lobby breathing down their necks and came home with big quotas for beef and dairy but they sold the fishermen down the Swanee. They have our lads restricted in how many days they can go out, how much and what they can catch. Irish trawler owners are flinging good fish back into the sea. Then they're forced to watch as the Spaniards and Scandis come over in their massive factory ships and harvest our fish to their hearts' content.'

The old man sucked in already hollow cheeks.

'Ruined little villages like this, they did. But sure, we never mattered anyway, away in the West.'

Padraig nodded in agreement.

'Aye. Dinny is from a fishing family. Lost a son and brother at sea, didn't you, *chara*?'

Dinny nodded sadly. Mattie moved seamlessly into what looked like a familiar response, slipping a whiskey chaser in front of the old man.

'*A bad day of fishing is better than a good day at work.*' The bar owner cited the anonymous quote as Dinny downed the spirit, a glint of tears in his eyes caused by the loss and the strong liquor.

'At least they died doing what they loved and still living in their homesteads,' the old man said. 'Unlike those poor souls who've had to emigrate to Britain and beyond.'

Tom nodded in sympathy. Emigration was a spectre once more in Irish homes and the loss was being felt most keenly in the rural West. Most townlands were lucky if they could field a Gaelic football or hurling team, so many young men and women had left for jobs, for college, for a better life.

'All we had left when fishing went was tourism,' Padraig continued. 'That's a short season, as you can imagine. So when Madsen announced he was planning to use the harbour as a base for offshore drilling and would be bringing jobs to the area, well, we could be forgiven for thanking the Lord for the good news. We didn't know what he had planned. It's unprecedented, do you know that? To bring untreated gas that far inland. Normally, it's treated offshore and made safe before it's piped anywhere.'

'What does it mean, untreated?' Tom asked.

'In simple terms, it's high-pressure natural gas that hasn't been refined – that's cleaned and depressurised to you and me. It's far more likely to flare and even cause explosions. Would you want that running under your house, hi?'

'With a great big bloody drilling station plonked in the middle of your sea view and an ugly refinery taking up acres of previously beautiful woodlands,' Mattie added.

'Hence the protests,' Tom said.

'Oh, no, that's not all,' Padraig continued. 'He said he was going to use local lads. But straight away he started shipping in contractors from Europe who offered cheaper labour costs. Only a few villagers work down there and they're the ones saying the right things, with the right connections. Then they tell people on the news that they're bringing energy security to the region, but that's not the case. All that gas is being sold to mainland Europe. Nothing has changed for us. We're not running this village on free Udforske energy.'

'And the real scandal,' Mattie interjected, 'is that it's our bloody resource. Udforske don't own the territory under the Atlantic. The Irish people do. Do you know how much they pay in royalties for what they extract? Nothing. Sweet FA.'

'But this legislation the government has promised – won't that make Udforske pay?' the inspector asked, feigning ignorance.

Mattie snorted.

'I'll believe it when I see it.'

Tom and Ray exchanged a meaningful glance.

'I can see why there's a lot of anger at the protests,' the inspector said. 'But, gentlemen, the guards are just doing their jobs.

Udforske are operating their business legally; they're entitled to have access to their workplace. And I can't imagine it's in anybody's interest for the company to bring gas ashore unsafely. After all, Carl Madsen owns a house a few miles up the road. He clearly loves the place.'

Padraig shook his head.

'Look, our protests were peaceful to begin with, man. That's what you didn't see on the news. We sat on the road. Sang, chanted. Held up placards. The violence started on your side. You ask Sergeant Gallagher,' he spat out the guard's name. 'You ask the good sergeant who it was that landed the first blows. Ask who incited the violence. There were women and young babbies at those protests. Not because they were put there but because it's their homes that are under threat.

'The news claims there are political forces at work. Horse shite. We get people coming in from other counties to stand with us from time to time but we're there every day. Locals. Ask Sergeant Gallagher about the overtime his little gang is getting paid to police those protests. Ask him about his trips to Madsen's house, the fancy dinners, the hampers at Christmas and Easter, his brother getting a job as foreman on the site.'

Padraig Óg paused for breath before resuming his passionate tirade.

'There's no doubt, Inspector, the county was already torn about the merits of Udforske in the area, but the policing of the protests has ripped the heart out of this community. Your lot are meant to be on our side. We're your own. When did it become a crime to show a wee bit of patriotism, to want what's best for your community and country? Madsen will make his money and be off, fancy house or not. We'll be left with the destruction – if we're not blown to kingdom come beforehand.'

Tom considered what he'd heard. He'd seen images of the protest, with irate locals and embattled officers. His natural inclination was to sympathise with the guards, while having an understanding of where the protestors were coming from. He was long enough in the tooth to know there were always two sides to every story. But there was an emotional honesty to this account that there hadn't been in Gallagher's version earlier. There was no doubt the sergeant was satisfied that the Udforske method of bringing gas onshore wasn't dangerous. He said himself, he and his family lived in the community, so it wasn't like he was at a remove from any danger if it existed. But Gallagher may have just bought the line and was now spinning it, whereas the anger in these men stemmed from a genuine sense that they were being treated unjustly.

Given what he'd learned about the forthcoming legislation, Tom was starting to suspect the village and its inhabitants did have the weight of the establishment stacked against them. And he was wondering about the overtime Padraig had mentioned. A moratorium had been placed on additional paid hours for the force since its budget had been slashed last year, so what was happening in Moorhaven? Had overtime been sanctioned by a political system determined to keep companies like Udforske onside? Or was the company providing bribes to some officers?

Of one thing he was sure: it was the right decision to look closely at this Bill Blake was introducing. The drilling controversy clearly incited extreme reactions in people. Who knew where that could lead?

CHAPTER 13

Sunday Night, Dublin

Laura had tried to text Ray back, but the message wouldn't send. Either his phone was off, or the signal in Donegal was poor. The latter was unlikely, though. She'd managed to get hold of Tom via SMS.

She had been irrationally irritated when Eoin had answered her phone. Fair enough, she'd been in the ladies and had left him sitting at her desk, but nobody else in the office would just pick up her mobile like that. Why did he think he was entitled to?

Eoin didn't seem to mind her snapping at him, which annoyed Laura even more.

Would she have cared if he'd answered the phone to anybody else but Ray? No, she thought. Better not dwell on that.

Michael came around to her side of the desk and perched on the edge. They were back in headquarters in the Park, filling each other in on the interviews that had been conducted that day and on the results of the background checks, specifically concerning those on their list who'd had gun training or held firearms certificates.

'There are twenty-four people with previous experience of handling guns – all ten guards, ten of the Leinster House staff, two TDs and two guests who were in the bar,' he summed up. 'And we've no idea about this Carl Madsen, but from what we've researched, he likes his safaris.'

'Hmm. We're flying through all this background work but I'm not sure how much it's helping,' Laura remarked. 'I hope Tom is having some luck with Madsen. The safari thing is kind of interesting, considering Ryan was basically chased down like an animal. Are any of our other persons of interest on that list of yours? Blake? McNally?'

'No. The only one on the list with previous weapons experience of any note is Mr. Morrison. But, you know, I'm not sure if the list means anything. Applying for a gun licence is such a bureaucratic nightmare that we know people dodge the process when they can. Blake doesn't have one. But I Googled images and found a photo of him in a British magazine from a few years back. He was visiting an MP friend of his and they were pheasant shooting. Pheasant, not peasant. The picture actually shows him holding a shotgun.'

'Not very Reform Party, is it, hunting game? Right, let's keep that one in the bag.'

'Did you tell Tom about the tunnel entrance Morrison showed you?'

'Yep, I sent him a text earlier.'

'Oh, Brian and Bridget confirmed that Kathryn Finnegan was home on Friday night,' Michael added. 'The neighbours on either side said the car was parked outside the house all evening and a friend of Kathryn's rang her on her home phone just before the 9 p.m. news. They talked for at least a half hour, she said. That seems to rule the wife out.'

'I'd never really ruled her in,' Laura said.

'What do we do now?' Michael asked.

'Finish up for the evening. Have you organised that interview tomorrow with Blake for the inspector?'

'Yes. And I rang McNally to see when he's back. That was a laugh a minute. His mother is being buried tomorrow. He'll be back on Tuesday, in any case.'

'Sorry about that.' Laura was glad she'd dodged that bullet. 'Oh, did a car call out to Grace Brady's sister's house?'

'It did. There was no answer, though. We'll have them check again in the morning. Most of the CCTV footage from the perimeter has been examined and Grace did leave Government Buildings before everything happened but it's odd we can't get hold of her.'

Laura chewed her lip and picked up the file that Eoin had left for her.

'What's that?' Michael asked. His backside was getting uncomfortable on the hard desk. He wanted to get home to Anne. He'd two missed calls and a message telling him to hurry the hell up and to bring a chicken tikka masala or his life wouldn't be worth living.

'It might be something, it might be nothing. I need to do a bit more background checking.'

'In relation to what?'

'One of the visitors in the bar. Apparently he wasn't entirely upfront in his interview. He might be connected to somebody who was in Leinster House on Friday night and didn't say. Leave it with me for a day or two.'

'What's his name?'

'Damien Reid.'

Laura tapped the file. She'd forgotten to thank Eoin for his work. She'd pick up some food as an apology and head straight for his apartment.

'By the way,' Michael said, moving around to his own desk so he could retrieve his jacket, 'Morrison was on to me about our girl Grace. He sounded relaxed, but I sensed he was a little on edge about us wanting to question her.'

'Really? Why?'

'I don't know. I just got that feeling. He knew we'd been asking about her. One of Grace's colleagues must have mentioned it.

Morrison said he knows her well and asked us to inform him when we found her safe.'

'Maybe he's just concerned,' Laura said. Michael shrugged and nodded.

Laura didn't add anything but the absence of the minister's secretary was starting to worry her. They'd spent two days now trying to get in touch without success. And she still had that feeling that there was something a little off about the chief of security in Leinster House.

Just how well did Morrison know Grace Brady?

Sunday Night, Donegal

The tales about the Udforske protests continued into the night, with no sign of anyone having a home to go to. In the corner, somebody launched into a bittersweet ballad. Tom started to worry that two members of *An Garda Síochána* were going to be discovered in a public house post closing time. He was leaning over to say this to Ray when he noticed that his colleague was looking the worse for wear. Unbeknownst to Tom, who'd been bantering with one of the men about the merits of Donegal's Gaelic footballers versus Dublin's, his deputy had abandoned beer and progressed to whiskey.

'Jesus, Ray, you realise we're going back up in the flying tin can in the morning? Have you lost your reason?'

Ray struggled to open half-closed eyelids, his elbow propped on the bar, hand supporting his head.

'Yep. 'M grand. Can I ask you something? A personal thing?'

'Eh . . . ?'

'Women.'

Tom frowned. 'Women?'

'Yeah. Women.'

'I've heard tell of them. Anything specific you want to know?'

The inspector had a sinking feeling in his stomach. He'd tried to talk to Ray about Ellie Byrne several times over the last year, but each time the younger man had brushed him off, not ready and unwilling to go there. Tom had known he'd want to talk at some point, but this was neither the place nor the time. They were in company, it was late and drink was taken, though Tom suddenly felt stone cold sober. He needed to get Ray back to the hotel and make him a coffee.

'How does it work?'

'Why don't we get some air?'

'No, tell me first. What happens . . . in your brain? How come, one day, a woman is just a woman and then the next, she's a *woman*. Y'know what I mean.'

'Not really.'

'You love Louise.' Ray said it as a statement, not a question.

Tom was reminded of the expletive-filled text he'd received from his beloved earlier in the evening. The 'ducking' car (thankfully her predictive text saved him from the worst of it) had billowed smoke all the ducking way home. Motorists had pulled up alongside her on the M50 ring road trying to warn her the engine might be on fire, while she'd smiled politely and shrugged her shoulders, all the while planning to ducking kill her husband.

'Light of my life,' he responded to his deputy.

'But when did you know?' Ray's face was pained. 'Did you just wake up and fancy her one day, or was it love at first sight, or . . .'

'Is this about Ellie?' Tom asked, tentatively. 'Maybe we should go . . .'

''S'not about Ellie. It's about . . . Ah, never mind.'

Ray stood up, wobbling a little.

Tom rose with him.

'Will ye be down at the protest tomorrow?' Padraig Óg asked, a very drunken gleam in his eye. 'I could make up a banner – *I brought the sheriff. And I even brought his deputy.* What do you think?' He snorted with laughter.

They departed the bar to a chorus of good-natured guffaws, emerging into the crisp air.

The rain had ceased and the heavy clouds had drifted on. A million stars twinkled overhead in a beautifully still night sky.

'Where are we going?' Ray asked, as they turned away from the direction of the hotel.

'A little walk to clear your head. Let's go down and look at the pier.'

There were several boats in the harbour, most of them recreational craft. The few fishing vessels looked jaded, their nets loaded haphazardly and in need of repair.

The sea itself was calm and enticing. It was easy to imagine men pulling anchor here on an early morning, their heads full of the day's potential haul, their hearts longing for the sea but also praying they'd come home safe. Tom looked back up at the village. From here, at this hour, you couldn't see the boarded-up windows or broken signs that they'd passed, forlorn reminders that the community was now a shadow of itself. The view was one of welcoming lights along the road and in the homes spread out across the hills.

'Louise and I were friends first,' he said, turning to Ray, who was sitting on a wall and gulping in the sea air, trying to avoid getting sick. 'I already had a girlfriend when I got to know Louise. I nearly missed my chance. She'd started going out with some lad from her college before I realised I missed having her at our group nights out. She'd been growing on me and I hadn't even noticed. Suddenly, she was the most beautiful girl in the world and she'd been under my nose the whole time.'

Ray perked up.

'But what did you do? If she was with someone else?'

'I broke up with my girlfriend and I waited for Louise. As it turned out, I'd been growing on her, too. Like an itchy rash, she claims.'

He smiled.

Ray looked comforted.

'So, it happens,' he said.

'Yes,' Tom replied. 'But Ray?'

'What?'

'Don't hurt somebody with a rebound. Make sure you're over Ellie before you move on.'

He looked down at his deputy, the puzzle slowly resolving itself. He had known Ray would notice Laura one day, but for the second time that night he found himself questioning the other man's timing. Was it the appearance of a rival on the scene that had turned Ray's head or was he just lonely and looking around for someone close to home?

The inspector strolled over to a stone plaque erected at the bottom of the pier and read its inscription. *Erected in memory of the Moorhaven men who perished at sea. Your chairs may be empty, but your places will always be set. You remain in our hearts.*

Tom touched the stone. A way of life had been extinguished in this village and now it faced further challenges.

For the men in power, Moorhaven was just a casualty of business.

And all the evidence was starting to point to Ryan Finnegan having been another unfortunate victim of men determined to get their own way.

*

'We have a problem.'

Madsen was standing where Tom had positioned himself earlier, in front of the floor-to-ceiling window in his sitting room. The lights behind him were dimmed, allowing him to see out. The full moon was reflected on the sea's surface, its water lapping in gentle waves now, a far cry from today's storm. In the distance and further along the coast, a lighthouse beacon swept from left to right, warning inexperienced sailors of the precarious rocks that lay in wait.

Madsen had picked up the broken glass from the tumbler he'd angrily flung to the floor after the inspector's visit. In doing so, he'd sustained a small but deep cut to his little finger, which stung even now as he gripped the fresh drink in his hand. A dribble of whiskey had solicitously found its way into the wound as he had poured.

There was silence on the other end of the phone he had clasped to his ear.

'Do you hear me, McNally? I said, we have a problem.'

The other man let out a deep sigh.

'I heard you.'

'Where are you?'

'In my mother's house.'

'Your mother's house? What . . . No, it does not matter. I had a visit from the police today.'

'And?'

Was McNally being deliberately obtuse? Madsen's grip on the phone tensed.

'And they came to my house in Donegal,' he snapped. 'Are you with somebody?'

He was used to Darragh McNally being much more responsive. The party chair normally bent over backwards to please Madsen. Something had been amiss these last few days.

The Udforske vice-president had suspected on Friday evening when he had met with McNally that a problem had arisen with the proposed law the Irish government had for the oil and gas industry. He'd sensed it in the other man's demeanour, but it had taken a while to wrangle it out of him. Even then, he hadn't been entirely forthcoming.

'I'm with my mother,' McNally answered.

'Well, leave the room, man.'

Madsen didn't want to lose his temper for a second time but he was struggling to remain calm.

'Don't worry, she's not listening.'

The businessman was startled by the sound of laughter on the other end of the line. Was that McNally – was he actually laughing?

'Have you gone mad?' Madsen snapped. 'Listen to me. The police came to my house today. They were asking questions about Blake and mentioned the possibility of him being blackmailed. I was led to believe he was reliable. You said he would be the man to sell this new law to the public, that the Reform Party would make life easier for my company. Now, everything is falling apart. Have you nothing to say to me?'

There was silence again.

'McNally?' Madsen barked.

'I'm here. Why are you worrying? The guards have nothing on you, do they? What did you tell them?'

'I told them I never met Blake in Leinster House, for a start. They had been led to believe I had. Which would explain all the missed calls on my phone.'

'Well, you didn't meet him. Blake and I screwed up. Don't worry about it. I'll sort things. That's what I do, isn't it?'

Madsen took a sip from his drink. He was rattled and McNally's strange behaviour wasn't helping.

'There's another problem. When you left me in the Dáil bar on Friday evening, something happened . . . I –'

'I really don't care.'

Madsen nearly dropped the phone.

'Pardon?'

'I said I don't care. Do you know what I'm doing right now, Carl?'

Madsen shook his head, even though McNally couldn't see him. He was overcome with an odd feeling. An unfamiliar feeling. Helplessness. Everything about the last couple of days had been off-kilter. He was used to being in control of every situation. But here he was, having yet another bizarre conversation which should have been straightforward.

'I'm sitting beside my dead mother,' McNally said, his voice low and hollow. 'And I have to tell you, Carl, I really don't give a shit what happens next in this sorry little scenario we've found ourselves in.'

He hung up.

Madsen froze, staring at the phone in his hand like it was a foreign object.

A new feeling swept over him, one that he was altogether more comfortable with.

Fury. He had paid a lot of money to get what he wanted. McNally owed him.

Somebody would pay for this.

CHAPTER 14

Monday, Dublin

Tom sent Ray home as soon as they arrived in Dublin the follow-ing morning. He was good for nothing. His hungover deputy had spent the short flight with his head cupped in his hands and emerged from the airport looking like death warmed up.

The inspector returned to his own abode to change shirts. There, he discovered Louise and Maria in whispered conclave.

'What are you two up to?' he asked suspiciously.

'God, Dad. We're not all potential criminals plotting despicable deeds,' Maria retorted, a bit too defensively.

Tom studied the two of them. Both their faces were flushed. They were absolutely up to no good.

'I'm onto you,' he said, grabbing his keys from the counter.

'Well, that's nice, drop in, insult us and go right back out again, is it?' Louise rounded on him. He flinched as she arrived in range.

'Why are you flinching? Do you think I'm going to smack you? You deserve a bloody smack!'

'After the text you sent me last night, I'd be forgiven for worry-ing you might,' Tom ventured.

'You'd better get yourself out of this house and come home tonight better behaved,' his wife grumbled, clamping her lips shut when he tried to kiss her. He stole one anyway, covering her whole mouth with his.

'Eughh,' she moaned, but he could see the smile in her eyes.

He left the house and made his way to headquarters for a briefing with Sean McGuinness, the unusual morning encounter with his family already forgotten. Tom was nervous. He'd spoken to the chief on Saturday night after they'd interviewed Blake but he'd several missed calls from his boss yesterday. It was rare for McGuinness to contact him on a Sunday, even during a case. He had a long-established routine on the holy day – Mass, followed by his grandson's football match, lunch and a couple of hours listening to his favourite music with a glass of fine wine or cognac.

Maybe with June's illness, McGuinness's Sundays weren't so relaxing any more. And no doubt he was looking for an update on the trip to Donegal, checking that Tom hadn't upset the vice-president of Udforske.

The inspector went directly to his boss's office. He'd rung Laura in the car to get an update on the weekend's work and to fill her in on what they'd discovered in Donegal. She told him a squad car had seen movement in Grace Brady's sister's cottage that morning and that she'd be going out herself in the afternoon to see if the woman was there. He instructed her to pick up Ray on the way, which would give his deputy another couple of hours to get over his hangover.

It was only afterwards that Tom realised he'd unintentionally paired Ray and Laura up for the day. Was that a sign of things to come? Having to watch out for awkward situations between two members of his team? God, he hoped not.

McGuinness ushered him into his office, pacing as he spoke urgently on the phone. He signalled to Tom to take a seat. The inspector sat down in the chair facing the window and watched as the trees' leafless branches twisted and bent to the wind outside.

'Is she with you now?' McGuinness said into the receiver. 'Please, June, just ring her and tell her to come back . . . Because I'll be here a while . . . I know that, love. Yes . . . okay. Bye.'

The chief remained stationary for a moment after hanging up, then sighed and returned to his desk.

'She has good days and she has bad days,' he said, eventually. 'Today's a bad day so I asked her sister to drop in. The kids have their jobs; it isn't fair to keep calling on them. June wouldn't answer the door. She was afraid I'd be angry. Most days she ignores me, but today she decides to listen.' He shrugged.

Tom struggled to find something useful to say.

'Can you take some time off?' he asked, knowing before he said it how redundant the notion was.

'For how long?' McGuinness answered. 'Months? Years? Until she gets so bad I can't leave her alone and she has to go into a home?'

The big man looked away for a moment and cleared his throat.

'Anyway, enough of that. Fill me in on what happened in Donegal. Start with why you didn't answer my calls.'

'Shocking reception up there,' Tom lied.

He filled McGuinness in on the interview with Madsen.

'So it wasn't confrontational?'

'Ray had to punch him a couple of times before he'd talk, but he didn't mark him any place it could be seen.'

'Tom.'

'It was all very amiable. I don't think you'll be getting any irate calls from the Danish PM.'

The inspector went on to describe their unpleasant encounter with Sergeant Gallagher and the revealing evening with the Moorhaven locals.

McGuinness sat back in the chair and scrunched up his face as he considered what he'd been told.

'Let me get this straight: a high-ranking local guard informed you that relations are fraught down at these protests and our lot are coming in for a lot of flak from a gang of New Age hippies who'd prefer we were all living in harmony with nature. But then you and Ray went and got stocious drunk with some locals and now you're on the side of the villagers, who you think are the victims of police brutality? And this all within the crucial forty-eight-hour period after a murder, when you should be arresting a suspect?'

Tom raised his eyebrows.

'You sum it up so . . . concisely,' he replied. 'It's great to see you haven't lost your comedic flair. And if you're worried about my lack of arrests so far, I can always go pick up Minister Blake? Or maybe pop back up to Donegal to slap the cuffs on Madsen? But I was under the impression you'd rather I had some actual evidence before I charged somebody.'

'I'm just letting you know how that account would be perceived by some, Tom.'

'Yes, you were as subtle as a brick. But I don't like this blind allegiance to "us" and "them", Sean. Something stinks up in Donegal. Maybe Gallagher's on the payroll for Madsen, or maybe he's not and just believes he's on the right side of the law. It wouldn't be the first time, though, that there's been political policing on the island.'

'I know that. But you're a fool, son, if you think that's all in the past and this is noteworthy. You don't know how lucky we are in this department. We've found our niche, we do our jobs well and we're left to our own devices. I, and others, lobbied long and hard for the establishment of centralised specialist units to tackle major crimes. It removed us from the parochial baggage – the crap, basically – that regional teams have to deal with.

'That doesn't mean we left police corruption in the '80s. Guards are still human and by God, there are plenty of flawed individuals in the force. But unless you're planning on becoming some sort of crusader, Tom, I'd suggest keeping your head down and concentrating on the job in hand. You set enough of an example by being the decent guard that you are.'

Tom fidgeted in his chair, entirely dissatisfied, although he couldn't really understand why. For years he'd been resisting promotions that would lead him down the path of accepting more responsibility for shaping the direction of the force. He had told himself he was happy to focus on murder cases. Sometimes his job was as frustrating as it was harrowing, but when he did solve a case, there was nothing better than that sense of reward. He didn't want to leave all that and have to deal with the 'crap', as McGuinness put it.

But there was something about the men in that pub last night that had struck a chord with him. They were decent folk and grey areas aside, he believed them. He knew in his gut that they had been hit with the shit stick in recent years. Tom felt like their natural ally, yet they saw the police as the enemy.

Their predicament had awoken some sort of youthful idealism he'd long since relinquished.

McGuinness studied his top inspector. He could see a dangerous fire in Tom's eyes. Reynolds was a respected man in the force. He had a higher-than-average solve rate, an exceptionally hardworking and loyal team, and was one of the sharpest detectives McGuinness had ever worked with. Tom followed the rules, knowing that anything less could jeopardise convictions. He was far removed from some of the fast and loose detectives that McGuinness had encountered in his long career.

McGuinness had sheltered Tom from much of the dirty, internal politics of the force. Although rarer these days, there were Sergeant Gallaghers all over the place and plenty of people protecting them. A whole world of trouble would be brought down if that pot was stirred.

'Forget Moorhaven,' McGuinness said, deliberately changing the subject. 'You've got bigger fish to fry this afternoon.'

'What? Blake?'

'No, you can see him later. You, my son, are off to see the Taoiseach.'

*

'You look like hell.'

'Thanks a lot,' Ray moaned as he fought with the passenger seatbelt, eventually shoving it shut angrily.

'I think that's in,' Laura said, turning the key in the ignition. 'This should be fun.'

She had pressed the buzzer for Ray's apartment on and off for five minutes before he answered, yelling at her that he'd be out when he was ready. He was still in a foul mood when he got into the car, slamming the door so forcefully it could have shattered the window.

For a man who smelled of hangover, he was sure making a lot of noise. And she would have to put up with him all the way to Meath.

On the positive side, any creeping feelings of affection she'd had for Ray were certainly being put to bed over the last couple of days. She hadn't seen him so bad-tempered since the period immediately after Ellie Byrne's death. He was doing a sterling job of making himself unattractive, down to the wrinkled shirt and unshaven face.

Eoin had never been more appealing, and he wasn't even aware there was competition.

Ray sat red-faced and annoyed with himself beside her. What a great job he was doing. It transpired that this thing that was wakening in him, this sudden awareness that he might fancy Laura, ran concurrent with him carrying on like he'd had a lobotomy. He was normally relaxed around women, especially the ones he liked. Confident, but not arrogant. Yet, here he was, acting like a first class shit.

'Sorry about your door,' he muttered.

Laura kept her eyes focused on the road.

'That's okay. I was thinking about getting a new one. Liven the car up a bit.'

Ray smiled. If he just stopped behaving like an idiot, he could enjoy this journey. Under the pretext of checking for oncoming traffic as they waited to turn out of the apartment complex, he studied Laura's profile. She had her hair tied up in a ponytail today, long chestnut curls tumbling down her back. Her face was flushed, natural. She rarely wore make-up, he realised. She didn't need it. She was wearing a black skirt suit over a fitted blue pin-stripe blouse. His eyes strayed down to her legs, watching her skirt ride up as she moved her feet on the pedals.

Laura had lovely legs.

I'm screwed, Ray thought.

'Are you sure you're not properly sick?' she asked him. 'You look a bit feverish.'

She passed him some mints from the compartment under the car radio and his fingers brushed against hers as he took them.

'Actually,' he said, 'I'm pretty sure I am coming down with something.'

They filled each other in on their respective weekends as she drove.

Grace Brady's sister lived in a detached cottage in a pretty part of the County Meath countryside. A background check showed that Maire Doran was married with no children.

Laura slowed to a halt alongside the squad car parked beside an immaculately pruned hedgerow across from Maire's home. Ray wound down his window.

'Is Grace Brady in there?' he asked.

The lone officer in the car shook his head.

'Maire is in, for certain. I didn't see the sister. Didn't want to ask in case we spooked her.'

'Good thinking. You can go now, thanks.'

Laura did a three-point turn and parked outside the cottage gate. They got out of the car and made their way up the winding stone path. They were halfway there when the front door opened. A middle-aged woman stood looking at them expectantly.

'I saw you parking. I guess you're after my sister, Grace?'

She posed it as a question, but one she knew the answer to.

Laura nodded. This was Maire, then. Grace's employment photo ID showed a woman with shoulder-length, mousy brown hair, a pale complexion and a thin, downturned mouth. She had a stocky, almost manly, build. This woman's hair was streaked with red, she was tanned and had pleasant dimples in her cheeks. And she was quite petite. There was a tiny familial resemblance around the eyes, but Maire had definitely been blessed with all the looks.

'Is she here?'

'She'll be back shortly. She's out on a run. You'd better come in.'

She ushered the detectives down the hall to a rustic-styled kitchen at the side of the house, offering them tea.

'I need to explain a few things before you see Grace,' Maire said.

'Is she all right?' Laura asked, taking one of the wooden-backed chairs at the pine-coloured table. She didn't know if she was relieved or angry to have found Grace. Ray was hastily typing a text to Tom to tell him they'd located the missing girl.

'When did she arrive?' he added. 'We've been trying to contact her all weekend.'

'She turned up on Saturday,' Maire answered, filling the kettle with water at the white Belfast-style sink.

'We sent a guard here yesterday, but there was no answer,' Laura said.

'Oh. I'm sorry. It must have been when I popped out to the shops. Grace was probably out jogging or she might have just been in one of her humours and refused to open the door.'

Maire carried a jug of milk and three cups over, then the

fresh pot of tea and some small plates. She prised open the lid of a cake tin and offered them fruit scones.

'I made them this morning,' she said.

'Why did your sister come here?' Ray asked. 'You must have seen the news; her office colleague was murdered on Friday night. We were quite worried about Grace.'

'I didn't see the news until late last night,' Maire replied. 'I had a migraine on Saturday and was in bed when she turned up. Impeccable timing, as usual. My husband's on a stag weekend; he's not home until tonight. So, here I was on my own, happy to take my pain medication and lie in a dark room, when Grace hammers down the flipping door. Always with the drama. Not that it would ever occur to her that she was putting me out.' Maire shook her head with all the pent-up frustration of a long-suffering sibling.

'Anyway, as I said, there's something you need to know about Grace. Our parents died years ago and she's always running to me. Never bothers our brother, of course. So I've had the full force of her growing up – or not growing up, as it happens. God, I can't believe I'm saying this out loud. I'm so used to dealing with her, sometimes I think she's normal, do you know what I mean? But this is serious. Obviously. I've two bloody detectives sitting at my kitchen table. I'm absolutely mortified that you've had to come out here at all. The stupid girl. Causing all this fuss. Oh, sugar! I didn't get sugar.'

'Maire,' Laura interrupted. 'We don't need sugar. Why is Grace here? What has she done?'

Maire had pushed out her chair but paused mid-stand.

'Well, according to her, she's responsible for a man's death. But then, that's Grace. She never likes to undersell a story.'

CHAPTER 15

Government Buildings, Dublin

Tom and DS Michael Geoghegan sat waiting in an antechamber to the Taoiseach's office. Michael drummed his fingers on the carved oak arms of his chair. He felt awkward and uncomfortable in his most presentable sweater and pair of trousers. Like a child stuffed into a pageboy suit. The inspector had made him get changed before letting him accompany him to Government Buildings.

'Do you think O'Shea is leaving us out here to show us who's boss?' he asked.

'He doesn't need to show us,' Tom replied. 'He *is* the boss. Besides, he's not even in there.'

'What do you mean?'

Tom pointed at the TV monitor suspended on the wall behind Michael's head. It displayed the live feed from the national broadcaster's twenty-four-hour news channel. The Taoiseach's car had just pulled up at Government Buildings and was making its way through the crowd of reporters that had somehow discovered the hour of his arrival.

A few minutes later, the door to the main office opened and Cormac O'Shea filled its frame.

'Gentlemen, my apologies for the delay. It probably would have been easier for you to come to the house, but God knows how they'd have spun that one. Come in.'

O'Shea reminded Tom of McGuinness in a way, even though he was shorter and more rotund. They both came from families that worked the land and both men were blunt and forceful in their personalities. But the similarities were superficial. The chief was a handsome man, notwithstanding the permanent irascible expression on his face designed to deter timewasters.

The Taoiseach was not remotely attractive. He was far too red-faced, his nose too big, various orifices overrun by wiry dark hairs. His eyes were small and cunning – intelligent, but in a calculating and devious way. That didn't come across on television, but Tom could see it now, face to face.

He pondered who'd be brave enough in the Reform Party to try to oust this man.

O'Shea didn't take the seat behind his desk, instead leading them over to armchairs by the window.

'The carrion birds are circling,' he said, nodding towards the press visible through the window. He sat, shirt buttons straining, a sliver of white vest showing at the belly. 'At least vultures wait for their prey to die before attacking. That lot would have me hanged, drawn and quartered just to fill column inches. It would be really helpful if you could make an arrest. The media seems to hold me personally culpable in the absence of a suspect. The lot of a Taoiseach. Responsible for trying to lead us out of the worst recession in history as well as ensuring nothing untoward, like murder, occurs in Leinster House.'

The inspector nodded politely, thinking this version of O'Shea was a far cry from the man who'd basked in a veritable press love-bombing in the run-up to the last election. But what did he expect from journalists reporting on a murder case?

'Ignore me,' the Taoiseach sighed. 'My gripes aren't important in the scale of things. I keep thinking of that young lad's wife. Kathryn, I'm told her name is. And a wee babby, too. What must she be going through? Her husband goes to work and winds up shot dead. It's not like he was a member of the armed forces. He worked in politics. The biggest risk is a heart attack.'

Or cirrhosis, Tom thought, surveying the other man's blood-shot eyes, the network of tiny, visible capillaries that flushed his cheeks, and the sheen of sweat over his lip.

'What can I do to help you, Inspector? I would have spoken with you in any case, but of course, I was here on Friday night. I suppose I'm on your list of suspects? Something for the Wikipedia entry, eh?'

Tom smiled thinly.

'A career first, no doubt, Taoiseach. I'm afraid I do need you to confirm your whereabouts for the period between 9.30 p.m. and 10 p.m. I know Aidan Blake went looking for you, but he's been coy about where he eventually found you.'

'Ha! Good old Blake. And he's the stalking horse they want to use to topple me. You'd think that would spur him on to drop me in it. You want to know what Aidan was keeping schtum about?'

Tom nodded, wondering if he'd be asked to sign some kind of disclosure form before he left the office.

'I was in the company of a lady who works for the party. There are . . . rumours about our relationship. You know what it's like for politicians. We're supposed to be whiter than white.'

'When you say in the company of a lady . . . ?' Tom asked, astonished.

'Jaysus, man, there's no need to blush. I wasn't mounting her on her desk!' O'Shea slapped his knee and roared laughing. 'I often call down to her office to have a drink or a chat.'

He guffawed again.

'So, she works in this building, then?' Tom asked.

'She does. She's one of our press advisors, as it happens. She'll verify my movements on Friday. I came into the complex through the Leinster House entrance just after 9 and chatted with a few people in the lobby. I made it to Government Buildings some time around 9.30. There were people with me the whole time. Aha!'

'What?' Tom asked.

'I just realised what that clever bastard Blake was up to. There was no need for him not to be straight with you. He could have just told you I was in the press office, you wouldn't have thought anything of it. He was pretending to be a good guy, knowing full well you'd find out without him having to be the gossip.'

O'Shea shook his head in wonder.

'You don't have a good relationship with the minister?' Tom asked.

'Of course I do. I have a good relationship with all my cabinet. Even the ones after my job. Keep your enemies close, Inspector.'

'Hmm. That's interesting. I might be going off-track here a little, Taoiseach, but do you have an opinion on the Resources Bill Minister Blake is bringing forward? Specifically those changes he's recently made concerning existing forces in the energy market?'

'It's my government bringing the Bill forward, Inspector. Blake is just the spokesperson. We've been advised the changes are necessary. Sometimes, you have to be pragmatic in politics. Use the stepping stones. We make this first move, then we can improve the State's terms down the line. Surely that has nothing to do with your case.'

The Taoiseach didn't blink. He maintained his genial body language and smiled as he delivered the last sentence but Tom knew he'd been given a little slap. The inspector couldn't resist a jab in return.

'It might have,' he said, 'if someone had been blackmailing the minister to write something in or out of the Bill.'

O'Shea shifted in his seat and tutted impatiently.

'I think you'll find that people with more brainpower and political savvy than Blake are drafting that particular piece of legislation. I wouldn't leave something so important in his hands – I'm not sure he's up to it. He's just our mouthpiece.'

'Is Darragh McNally up to it?' Tom prompted.

'You have been doing your homework.' The Taoiseach leaned forward, as if he was about to entrust a confidence. 'McNally is a genius, he really is, Inspector. I respect him, but I also fear him. Don't get me wrong, he puts the Reform Party first, but ultimately, the man has his own agenda and he's never felt he has enough control over me. Blake's his stooge. The vain idiot. You know, the only person McNally has ever placed above his own ambitions was his poor, dead mother, God rest her soul. He will be completely lost without her.'

He blessed himself.

'McNally is a powerful nemesis. He has stamina. Blake is wrapped around his ugly little finger and I think he's only starting to realise now what a puppet he is. What none of them get is that I ain't going to roll over easy. You don't get to this position in life without having a few tricks up your sleeve.'

'Such as?'

'That would be telling. Suffice to say, McNally might be a crafty old fox but he's met his match. With me, what you see is what you get. I'm not hiding any secrets. McNally likes the world to think he's in control of everything. But he has his weaknesses. As does Blake. Ask the minister about the club, Inspector.'

'The club?'

O'Shea smiled enigmatically and tipped the side of his nose.

Tom examined the Taoiseach's face. Yes, there was no doubt. If McNally was behind a planned coup against O'Shea, he was going to have his work cut out.

The inspector had been given some food for thought. The party chair's name had been mentioned a number of times and not in a flattering way. And following the visit with Blake they now knew that McNally didn't have an alibi for the time when Ryan Finnegan was killed.

And what was this obscure reference to a 'club'? Some political thing? Perhaps a group plotting O'Shea's overthrow – or was it something more sinister?

'The victim – did you know him?' the inspector continued.

'Not well, I'm afraid. He was Blake's PA and seemed competent. He was a party member and I saw him at political events and so on. But I never had a drink with the man, never got to know him.'

'Taoiseach, one last thing. What time did Aidan and his wife actually find you?'

'What time does Blake say?'

'Taoiseach.'

'Ha! Alright then. I think it was just before 10.30 p.m. In fact, I know it was. I looked up at the clock on the wall moments before and thought I'd better get over to that Silent Voices ball or I'd miss the group photos. Sure, then there'd be no point in being there. Is that any use to you?'

'Yes,' Tom said. 'Plenty.'

He considered what he'd just discovered. Aidan Blake claimed he had made it back to the ball at 10.30 p.m. He'd been adamant. But once again, his timing didn't add up.

Why did the minister keep lying?

Meath

'I decided to visit my sister for the weekend. I can't see that it's a big deal. I didn't see your calls. I was trying to relax and I was out running a good bit. I like to exercise. It's good for my mental health and it keeps me trim.'

Grace Brady looked Laura up and down as she said this, with an expression that implied the detective could benefit from a workout herself.

Laura bit her tongue. Grace had a clipped, rude manner of

speaking and apparently no grasp of social etiquette. She'd already told Laura the homemade scone she was enjoying would make her fat – adding a quiet 'er' at the end of the word – because her sister Maire couldn't control herself when it came to butter in her recipes.

The woman had returned from her jog and made Laura and Ray wait in the kitchen until she'd showered, Maire apologising profusely on her sister's behalf.

What an absolute delight to have around the house, the detective mused. She noted that Grace had yet to insult Ray and actually appeared to be flirting with him, albeit ineptly.

Grace was not a good-looking woman. Her mouth soured at the edges and she had a permanent indignant look that screamed 'the world owes me a favour'. Yet, she seemed to think herself attractive. There was an air of arrogance to her jutting chin as she fired questions at them.

'It *is* a very big deal that we couldn't get hold of you.' Ray spoke sharply and Grace recoiled.

Good on you, Ray, Laura thought.

Undiagnosed on the autism spectrum – that's how Maire had described her sister.

'At least, I hope that's what's wrong with her,' she had said. 'Otherwise, she's just a bitch.'

The two detectives had been amused by this depiction, but after spending a few minutes with Grace, Laura's tolerance levels were already waning.

How the hell did she hold down a job? Maire had said her sister was smart but had got into trouble a few times in work. This, despite Grace's claims that Shane Morrison and Aidan Blake held her in high regard.

'Job for life, that civil service,' Maire said. 'She'd never survive in the private sector. I'd say Blake is just too polite to ask for her to be moved and she does tend to tone it down a little for men, or tone it up, whichever way you look at it. I can't imagine what it was like for Ryan Finnegan sharing an office with her, though. She told me a couple of times that she reckoned he fancied her and was on for leaving his wife. 'Course, she said the same about Blake. That's something else you should be aware of. She has these delusions and mixes them up with real life. I don't know about Ryan, but everybody knows Minister Blake and his wife are loved-up. They're always in the magazines.'

Laura stared at Grace, trying not to let her dislike show. The woman might know something that could be of use to them.

'You were clearly aware that your colleague had been murdered,' Ray continued, unblinking eyes trained on Grace. 'You mentioned as much to your sister. You must have known we would want to talk to those who worked closest with Ryan. Yet you left your apartment and refused to answer your mobile phone. Why?'

Grace's eyes started to water and she sniffed dramatically, glancing dolefully at Ray. What a little actress, Laura marvelled. She sat back in her chair, content to leave this one to her partner. Ray Lennon could have his pick of women. Grace Brady might think she looked all bambi-like and vulnerable when she cried, but she didn't and it wouldn't wash with Ray anyway.

'There was a reason,' the woman whispered. 'I was frightened.'

'Of what?'

'It's obvious, isn't it? That whoever killed Ryan would come after me.'

'Why?' Ray persisted.

'I work with him, don't I? And it's my fault that he died.'

Laura sighed and Grace flashed her a stony look before returning her attention to Ray. This time she tried for beguiling, lowering her eyes and peering coyly from beneath short, wet lashes that looked like little spider legs.

'How is it your fault?' Ray continued, ignoring the antics.

'I let the IT guys take his computer. Then, when he found out this week they'd switched it, he was incandescent. Wouldn't stop whining about it. So I told him to get a grip and just go over and get whatever he needed off the thing. I was really looking forward to him coming back from sick leave, but all he did last week was moan.'

'So, you think you're responsible for his death because you told him to go over to LH2000?'

'Yes.' Grace sniffed for effect. The tears had long dried.

'And that's the only reason you decided to flee Dublin and go into hiding?'

The woman hesitated.

Ray's eyes bored into Grace's.

She looked away first.

'Yes.'

'You're sure?' he asked.

'I said so, didn't I?'

Ray sat back and took a deep breath.

'Grace, making a throwaway remark to Ryan before he died was not the catalyst for his murder. Nor was letting IT take his computer. You have nothing to be frightened of, if you are telling us everything. What time did you leave Leinster House on Friday night?'

'Dunno.'

'Do you drive or use public transport?'

'I walk. I live close enough.'

'Did you encounter anybody on your way home?'

'I don't know. Yes. Probably. I think I called into a garage for milk.'

'The name of the garage?' Ray asked.

Grace glared at him, the lame effort at flirtation abandoned.

'This is ridiculous. I would be the last person to hurt Ryan. Maybe you haven't heard, but he had a thing for me. It was tough being the only girl working in an office with two men. It's such long hours in politics, you get close, you know. If it hadn't been for Ryan's clingy wife, I think we'd have made a go of it. He liked women who take care of their appearance, who live healthy lives. His wife completely let herself go last year. I mean, I know she was pregnant, but I'm pretty sure that doesn't give you a licence to eat everything you see.'

'Are you saying you and Ryan were having an affair?' Laura interrupted. 'An actual relationship? Did you sleep with Ryan?'

The other woman tilted her head back and looked down her nose at Laura.

'No. We didn't sleep together. As I said, his wife was in the way. I won't be any man's mistress. I've made that mistake before. But we both knew what we wanted.'

'Was anything ever said explicitly?' Laura continued. 'Did Ryan actually say to you that he wanted a relationship? Did he even say he liked you?'

Fresh tears welled up in Grace's eyes. She turned to Ray.

'I feel like I'm being interrogated. I just told you I'm scared. And I've lost someone close to me. Why are you asking me so many questions?'

Laura stood up, her irritation getting the better of her.

'We're getting nowhere here. Come on, let's go.'

She stormed out of the kitchen.

Ray followed her out of the cottage a few minutes later.

'I hope you weren't mopping up tears for that silly woman,' Laura barked as he got into the car. 'What an absolute time-waster.'

He angled himself in the seat so he could look at her properly.

'I was getting the name of that garage she says she dropped into. I don't believe her story. I want to check it out. She seems very unstable. We'd better make sure she didn't shoot Ryan in the head because she caught him glancing sideways at another woman.'

Laura snorted.

'Her sister's deluding herself about the autism,' she said, putting the car in gear. 'The only thing wrong with Grace Brady is that she's a bad-mannered bully with a high opinion of herself.'

'I don't know,' Ray said. 'She's certainly lacking in social skills, that's for sure. I do think you missed a beat in there, though.'

'What do you mean?'

'You disliked her, so you dismissed her. She wasn't telling us something and we weren't able to delve any further because you assumed what she was saying about her and Ryan was all in her head. But I think she was also alluding to something with the minister.'

'She's just trying to be the centre of attention,' Laura retorted, defensive. 'I've spent the weekend trying to chase down that bloody woman for no good reason. She'd left the complex before anything happened – we should have been able to cross her off the list on Saturday instead of all this running around.'

Ray shook his head.

'I agree with you, to a point. But just because she's annoying doesn't mean she had no role in what happened on Friday. I think she is genuinely afraid of something.'

Laura stared out the window.

'Maybe. But I had to break the news to Kathryn Finnegan about Ryan. The woman was devastated. She loved her husband and there's nothing to say he didn't love her just as much. That fool back there is tainting his memory.'

'When you went to Kathryn's house, was that your first relative visit where a kid was involved?' Ray asked, gently.

Laura's hands tightened on the wheel.

'Yes.'

Ray paused. He felt awkward, but he wanted to seize the moment.

'Do you want to get some dinner later? We can talk about the case. And Kathryn Finnegan.'

Laura kept her eyes straight ahead.

'Okay,' she said, focused on keeping her voice steady.

It's just dinner with a colleague, she told herself. No harm in that.

CHAPTER 16

Monday Night, Dublin

'Are you sure you won't have something? I'm cooking anyway. You must be starving.'

Sara Blake led Tom and Michael towards the kitchen, her heels beating a staccato rhythm on the hallway's wooden floor. She had seemed distracted and a little upset when she opened the door. Blake must have confessed to her about the photos.

They had come directly from Government Buildings. The minister was at a constituency meeting in North Dublin some-where but had assured them he'd be going straight home afterwards.

Sara bustled around the cooking area, inviting them to sit on stools parked beside the centre island as she prepared the food.

Tom was happy to find her home alone. It gave them time to ascertain if she was still corroborating the latter part of her husband's alibi. He wondered if Sara knew her husband hadn't met with Madsen. The inspector still couldn't get his head around why Blake had lied about the meeting. What a stupid thing to do. He must have realised they'd check.

Unless . . .

Tom quickly typed and sent a text.

'Sorry about that,' he said.

'Not at all. I think I'll help myself to a glass of wine, if you don't mind,' Sara said, moving to the retro Smeg fridge and retrieving a bottle of *Albariño*, condensation running down its sides. 'Tough day at the office.'

'You're the CEO of Silent Voices, aren't you?' Michael asked. 'I read about your charity in a feature in one of the wife's magazines. You really do a great job. It must be tough, though.'

'Well, thank you. Yes, it can be. We were compiling personal stories today for our annual report. I met some girls who live in one of our respite homes. Kids, fourteen, fifteen years of age. They ended up on the streets after running away. Both of them suffered years of abuse at home. One at her father's hands, the other from her mother's boyfriend.'

She frowned as she poured a large measure of wine, the liquid glugging from the bottle and splashing without finesse into the glass.

'I don't know why it got to me so much today. I'm used to dealing with tragedy. It doesn't make it easier but it's like being a social worker. If you want to do your job properly, you can't let it get under your skin. I guess I've other things on my mind.'

'Do you have any kids yourself?' Michael asked.

'No, not yet.' Sara smiled. 'One day. I remember when Ryan told us Kathryn was pregnant. God, he was over the moon. I've always thought I'd make a good parent. Better than what I had, anyway. Sorry. I'm being maudlin!'

The inspector shook his head dismissively. She didn't need to apologise.

He wondered what had stood in the way of the Blakes having a child to date, if she was eager. Sara looked fit and healthy and could only be in her late thirties at most – hardly past it in terms of childbearing years, though pushing towards the thin edge of the wedge. The demands of her and her husband's careers had probably acted as a block to family plans. And that was the second time she'd made a reference to her own upbringing. She'd clearly gone into helping children because her own childhood hadn't been up to much.

Tom sensed that what she witnessed in her job got under her skin far more than she let on.

'Mrs Blake, I want to follow up on a couple of things concerning Friday night, if that's okay?' Tom said.

'Sure.'

'Remind me, what time was it precisely that you arrived over in Government Buildings with your husband?'

'I can't remember to the exact minute, but it was 9-ish.'

'And you parted ways with your husband . . . where?'

'His office.'

'What time did you see him again?'

'About 9.45, in the bar.'

Tom didn't say anything. For a few seconds, the only sound in the kitchen was the gentle hissing of onions frying in the heavy pan on the cooking range.

Sara looked the inspector straight in the eye.

'My husband didn't kill Ryan,' she said, quietly. 'Is that what you think?'

Tom rested his elbows on the countertop and leaned forward.

'Why would I think that?'

'Inspector, you've asked me twice now what time Aidan found me on Friday. You keep checking his alibi.'

'We're checking the alibis of everybody in Leinster House that night,' Tom said.

'Yes, but this is the third time you will have spoken to him and the second time you've visited our home. Can I tell you something?'

Tom nodded.

'I'm sure you hear this all the time, but I know my husband. He has flaws. He can be weak and he can be selfish. He's even a bit reckless at times. But that's about as bad as he gets. If he was harbouring murderous intentions, I'm pretty sure I'd have noticed by now. I've seen a lot of evil people in my life. Aidan is not one of them. I'm not in denial; I'm just stating a fact.'

The inspector bowed his head in a gesture that indicated he'd give what she said due consideration. He'd lost count of the number of times he'd listened to somebody's spouse protest their partner's innocence, even in the face of overwhelming evidence to the contrary.

The minister's wife was staring at him, waiting for a response.

'He couldn't do it, Inspector. He just couldn't.'

'Has he discussed with you what was found with Ryan the night he was murdered?'

She winced as she nodded, the anguish apparent on her face.

'Do you think Ryan was trying to blackmail Aidan?' he asked her.

Sara started to shake her head, but stopped. She sighed resignedly.

'I would never have thought Ryan capable of it, but his having those pictures that night is pretty telling. I am upset about the photos. It's something we have to deal with as a couple, but, then, I'm also conscious that the past is the past. It's the future that matters.'

She tugged at her bottom lip.

'But, Inspector, regardless of Ryan's intentions – which are pretty damn inexplicable – it doesn't mean my husband murdered him.'

'Sara, blackmail is often at the heart of murder. If Ryan was attempting to hurt your husband by exposing him in the worst possible way, haven't you considered at all that Aidan may have reacted to that in a manner that would be out of character?'

Tom was probing, hoping she'd give something away with her body language, if not her words. He could see panic in her eyes, but it was replaced quickly with resolve.

'You're wrong,' she said. 'I know in my heart Aidan couldn't murder anybody.'

Tom observed her silently. She was either utterly convinced or in complete denial. He wasn't able to tell which.

They heard the sound of the front door being opened. At the same time, Tom's phone beeped.

He looked down at the screen. Carl Madsen had just replied to the text he'd sent minutes before. The language he'd used was curt and to the point. Now the inspector had the answer to something that had been bothering him and in addition, he'd learned something about Madsen's relationship with Aidan Blake.

'Good evening,' Aidan Blake said, entering the room. 'Any news?'

He dropped his briefcase on the floor and crossed the room to kiss his wife, studying her face with concern.

'We're just looking to have a quick word, if that's okay?' Tom said.

'Of course. Follow me.'

This time the minister brought them to a sitting room instead of his office. There was nothing like seeing pictures of a man having sex to turn casual acquaintances into old friends.

Tom introduced Michael before they sat down.

'So, have there been any developments?' Blake asked. He was noticeably more nervous in this room, away from his wife.

'I'm a bit concerned, Minister,' Tom said. 'The timeline of your movements on Friday night doesn't add up.'

Blake paled, but said nothing.

'For instance, you told us you were in a meeting with Carl Madsen until 9.30 p.m.' Tom paused. 'But as it transpires, you didn't meet him at all.'

Straight to the point.

Blake stared at the carpet, unspeaking, his wavy fringe flopping onto his forehead.

'I was wondering why you'd lie to us about something that could be so easily checked, but I think I've figured it out. You thought you could get Madsen to lie for you, didn't you? You rang him several times on Saturday, but he didn't answer your calls. He told me he had missed calls earlier that day and he just confirmed for me that most of them were from you. Your wife mentioned to us on Saturday that you'd been on the phone all day. You had no way of knowing that Madsen would be uncontactable for the weekend and you must have assumed that if you couldn't get hold of him, I wouldn't be able to either. But I did. I went to Donegal.'

Blake was fidgeting in his seat now, anxiously crossing and uncrossing his legs.

'So, that leaves us with a problem,' Tom continued. 'I think we need to start again, Minister. What were you doing between 9 p.m. and 9.45 p.m.? And why did Ryan have those pictures the night he was murdered?'

The other man exhaled so loudly his whole body seemed to deflate. He dropped his hands onto his lap, defeated.

'You've caught me out in an untruth, Inspector. Yes, I tried to get hold of Madsen. He wouldn't answer the damn phone. I suspect his nose was out of joint because I didn't meet him on Friday. I'm in trouble now, aren't I? Because how will you believe anything I'm going to say from this point on?'

'Try me,' Tom said.

Blake sucked in his cheeks, then nervously brushed his fringe from his forehead. He folded his arms, almost hugging himself.

'I still can't believe Ryan was capable of following through. But he was certainly doing his best to convince me of it. He came across the photos months back when he opened an email I hadn't been expecting. I'd told my blackmailer to use a private address I'd set up, but when I ignored one of his emails he contacted me at my Oireachtas account, a warning shot. Ryan told me he'd forwarded the pictures to his own account. I was shocked and upset. Ryan had always said that my private life was my own business. He maintained that was still the case but intimated that my secrets could be an issue if I "kept on the path I was on". His words. Our friendship had soured so quickly, I hadn't even noticed.'

Secrets – not secret. Tom noted the plural.

'So, he did threaten you?'

'Yes. I mean, no. I didn't feel threatened. I didn't take him seriously. I was hurt by his actions and I think I shamed him when we had that exchange. I asked him what made him think he was morally superior to me if he was willing to sink to such depths to get his way. That seemed to affect him. He said no more about the pictures and we seemed to be getting on a little better. I suppose he was trying to redeem himself. Then the car crash happened. I visited him in hospital, sent gifts to the house, and so on. I started to hope he wouldn't come back to work, but he turned up on Monday and by Tuesday I knew we had a problem.'

'Because of your Resources Bill?'

Blake nodded.

'Yes. So you know about the changes to the Bill?'

'I've heard tell.'

'I should have known it would be leaked.'

'Did Ryan tell you he'd use the photos unless you withdrew the clause about existing licence holders?' Tom continued.

'Yes.'

Tom studied the minister's face before asking the next question. Blake was right. He had lied, several times. How could they believe anything he said now?

'Did you murder Ryan Finnegan to stop him blackmailing you?'

'No.' Blake shook his head vigorously. 'Please believe me. My only crime is stupidity. I did go looking for Ryan on Friday night. I'd had to leave the office at 8 to help Sara meet and greet at the start of her ball. Ryan and I had words before I left. He'd given me until the end of the week to amend the draft of the Bill. On Friday he claimed that I was forcing him to go to the press with the pictures. I decided to call his bluff. I didn't believe he had it in him. Over at the ball I could think of nothing else.

'When Sara said she had to go over to Leinster House to find the rest of the cabinet, I told her I'd help but that I had to meet Madsen first. That was the original plan but I had already told Darragh McNally what Ryan was threatening and asked him to step in for me. My head wasn't in it, with everything that was going on.

'I went looking for Ryan to continue our conversation. When Darragh rang me and told me about Ryan's murder, I asked him to cover for me and keep to the story that I'd met Madsen as planned. I told him I'd done something stupid but not criminal and would have no alibi. Darragh is a party man. He said he'd help me out if I gave him my word that I'd had nothing to do with Ryan's death. I suppose he was terrified that if I fell under suspicion for the silly reason of not having an alibi then all the work we have done would amount to nothing.

'And that's the truth. I wasn't planning to hurt Ryan. I swear. Jesus, if I had wanted to kill the man, do you think I'd choose Leinster House as the place to do it? You'd have to be cracked. I wanted to talk Ryan round. Appeal to his humanity, his sanity, our friendship . . . I mean, he was going to destroy my life. But I couldn't find him and I knew Sara would be getting worried. I abandoned my search and just left it to fate. I heard nothing more from Ryan so I assumed he'd thought twice and gone home.'

'Why did you lie to us if you had nothing to hide, other than the pictures that we'd discovered anyway?'

'Why do you think? I went looking for Ryan and Ryan was shot. I wasn't thinking straight and I panicked. I'm sorry. I should have told you the truth.'

'Did you see Carl Madsen when you entered the Dáil bar that night?'

'No.'

Tom reflected on what the other man had said. For a man in

charge of a government department, he'd shown incredibly poor judgement. And that was the most benign reading of the situation.

'Why was keeping the Bill intact so important to you that you'd risk being publicly humiliated?' he asked. 'Were you that opposed to Ryan's position? You were once close, am I right? Politically and personally? What changed?'

Blake shrugged.

'I did. Obviously. Holding power means taking responsibility. But I haven't had a complete personality transplant. That legislation is progressive. It's the first step in a longer game and it ensures we don't alienate the energy companies outright.'

'And none of this has anything to do with you letting those companies influence you as minister?' the inspector asked. 'Udforske is a powerful lobbying machine. You haven't by chance received any political donations from it? Is that why you didn't want to, or couldn't, meet Ryan's demands? You were already in a corner?'

Blake held up his hands defensively.

'I have never taken a bribe in my life, Inspector. For God's sake, I've enough to worry about without the risk of being embroiled in a brown envelope scandal. Look, I know what you're thinking. I let myself be blackmailed once, so why didn't I just give Ryan what he wanted? Well, this was different. The scum in Thailand just wanted money, my own money, which I could give him. Ryan was trying to influence government policy. The public put me in office, not him.'

And they put you in office on a promise of reforming oil and gas royalties, Tom considered quietly. It sounded like Linda McCarn had made the correct analysis of Blake's personality when it came to what he would and wouldn't allow himself to be blackmailed into doing.

'Where does Darragh McNally stand in all this?' he continued.

'He's heavily involved in the drafting of this legislation and you sent him to meet with Madsen in your stead. Is it possible that he was open to undue influence?'

'I don't know what McNally is or isn't capable of. You'd have to ask him.'

Tom was surprised the minister didn't even try to defend the party chair.

'Did McNally get on with Ryan?'

'There's no point pretending they were friends. Ryan was jealous of Darragh. The atmosphere was certainly more harmonious over the last few months with Ryan out convalescing.'

'Jealous, you say?' Tom queried. 'Why?'

Blake pursed his lips. 'I suppose he felt that Darragh had too much access to me, that he'd usurped the role Ryan felt was his by right. But then, Darragh is the chair of the party. I was always going to have to pay him more heed once I took ministerial office. He holds seniority.'

'So, their relationship was acrimonious?'

Blake nodded.

'Before Ryan's crash, he and McNally were at serious loggerheads. We were in the planning stages of this piece of legislation that's caused so much bloody bother. McNally insisted that the Bill be drafted to apply to new entrants only, as it is now, and Ryan lost the plot. He believed that everything should be applied retrospectively. The cabinet decision obviously went with McNally. Ryan was always going to lose the argument. Contrary to what some people might believe, I'm not easily led. I hold the same position as Darragh.'

'Would you say their arguing went beyond the normal cut and thrust of a political disagreement?'

'It did, yes. McNally is such a shrewd operator. He's normally able to win people round to his way of thinking without being overt. But on this issue he did seem uncharacteristically desperate to get his way. Ryan stood in his path and McNally went over him like a steamroller.'

'Why didn't you mention this before?' Tom asked.

'I figured McNally would tell you himself. He doesn't normally hide his dislike of people. It's a moot point, though. He got his way with the Bill, in the end.'

'But if Ryan had managed to blackmail you into changing the draft legislation, McNally would have lost, wouldn't he?'

'I guess he might have felt so,' Blake answered. 'Darragh takes things personally. He and Ryan were alike that way. But Darragh can go to very dark places. He suffers on and off with depression. Even when he's not having a bout, he's never really *happy*. He seemed particularly stressed this last year or so and Ryan kept provoking him. McNally wouldn't have had to resort to murder, though. Like I said, I wouldn't be blackmailed into doing something I don't believe in.'

Tom studied the minister and saw a renewed boldness in his eyes and in the set of his jaw.

Blake meant what he said. He was done with being blackmailed. But he was missing the point. McNally wouldn't have been worried about Blake changing the Bill. He could, though, have been worried about losing the man the government needed to sell its flawed legislation, which was precisely what would have happened if Blake's reputation had ended up in tatters. Perhaps the minister was right and Ryan wouldn't have had it in him to go to the press. But that seemed like a very reckless assumption to make.

'And are you absolutely sure you met Sara at 9.45?' he asked. 'If you've told us another lie, Aidan, it's better we clear it up now.'

'No, that's the truth.'

'And you both returned to the ball at . . . what time did you say it was – before 10.30?'

Blake hesitated.

'I can't remember the exact time, if I'm honest. It might have been after 10:30.'

Tom stood up, straightened his tie and adjusted his suit jacket. The minister was adapting his story in the face of what he suspected the inspector now knew. He was caught in a net and wriggling every which way as he tried to get out of it.

The inspector wouldn't trust him as far as he could throw him.

'Oh, one more thing. Are you the member of a club?'

It was simple question, but from the look on Blake's face, Tom could see the man's world had just imploded.

'A club?' he replied, trying and failing to sound casual. 'Oh, lots of them, Inspector. It's a politician thing. You get roped into everything. For example, I'm the treasurer of our local sailing club in Howth.'

'I see.' Tom grimaced. Lie after lie. 'It was just something somebody mentioned – that I should ask you about "the club". Never mind. I'll go back to them.'

He left the room before Blake could respond, leaving him to stew in the web of deceit he'd spun.

CHAPTER 17

Living with another detective had its pitfalls.

Laura had hurried home to get ready for her dinner date with Ray that evening and found Bridget already in situ, takeaway menu and DVD in hand.

'Oh, are you going back out? I was going to order in food and watch a movie. My brain is fried.'

Laura stepped out of her heels, avoiding eye contact with her housemate.

'Sorry. I need to see somebody before I finish. I just came back to freshen up. Long day.'

She spent the next ten minutes worrying her way through her wardrobe, trying to find an outfit casual enough that Bridget wouldn't suspect anything but nice enough to impress Ray.

She settled on a pair of skinny jeans and a tight black V-neck sweater. After a moment's hesitation, she opted for a push-up bra. She let her hair down, spritzing the curls with spray, and was applying lip-gloss when Bridget appeared, leaning against the doorframe.

'See who?' the other woman asked, continuing the conversation as if Laura hadn't left the sitting room.

Laura kept her focus on the mirror, trying to stave off the blush that was threatening to make its way from her neck up to her face. She wasn't sure she had it in her to lie to her best friend. But it was just dinner and she wasn't in the mood for another lecture about Ray. A line had to be drawn.

Laura came from a large family and the whole point of moving out was to get some personal space. But it might have been a mistake to start dating her flatmate's relative. Bridget wouldn't be able to help feeling defensive of Eoin should Laura decide to end things.

Had she really just thought that? Laura glanced guiltily at her phone. She hadn't even texted her boyfriend today and had left his apartment this morning while he slept.

'I have to follow up on something that Grace Brady said,' she replied breezily.

Bridget was still staring at her. 'You look lovely.'

'I might call over to Eoin's after.'

Oh, God, she was a horrible person – to be able to summon up such an appropriate fib.

It worked, though. Bridget smiled conspiratorially and left her to it.

'You're going to hell,' Laura told her reflection.

*

'In all the years we've been working together, we've never had dinner,' Ray said, pulling out a stool for Laura. He'd reserved seats at the bar.

She'd been so glad to see he'd arrived earlier than her. He'd freshened up, too, exchanging his wrinkled shirt for a navy short-sleeve polo over Levis. The navy brought out the dark blue in his eyes; the sleeves were short enough to show the muscles that rippled underneath. He smelled of Lynx and Laura felt just a little dizzy as he helped her up onto the high stool.

'That's not true. We've eaten together lots of times.'

'Yeah, I know. With the others. But the two of us have never gone out alone.'

'That's true, I suppose,' Laura shrugged. 'I hadn't noticed.' She said all this lightly. He had no way of knowing she'd spent the last few years longing to be alone in his company. How many times had she fantasised about the two of them being sent to investigate some case in the middle of nowhere and being forced to share the one last hotel room? Daydreams that always ended up with Ray declaring his unspoken and undying love for her . . .

Sweet Lord. Laura fidgeted in her seat.

'Did you get that message from Tom's wife about Wednesday?' Ray asked. 'It's still on.'

'Yes. I thought she'd cancel, but she's absolutely right. When *would* be a good time to do it? We're always on a case. And she and Maria have already put so much effort into getting us all together.'

'You're right. Do you think Tom knows? I'm his designated minder for the day. I have to find some way of keeping him busy and away from his house.'

Laura shook her head.

'That shouldn't be too hard, with the week that we're in. No, I don't think he suspects anything. Why would he? It's only October. It's absolutely hilarious. We're all in on it and the best detective in the force hasn't noticed anything.'

Ray tutted, but smiled along with her, complicit in the secret plan their boss's wife had devised.

'Is that Elvis?' Laura tilted her head sideways, straining to hear the music.

Ray closed his eyes and listened.

'In a sushi bar, of all places. Are you a fan of the King?'

'Who isn't?'

Laura smiled and watched in amusement as Ray curled his lip and started warbling.

His impromptu rendition ended abruptly with the arrival of their server.

'Oh, I'll have a bento box, please.'

'The same.' Laura picked up one of the complimentary glasses of sake that had been placed on the counter for them. She necked it, eyeing Ray sideways.

'Aren't you drinking?'

'I'm not sure my stomach can handle it. I had too much to drink over the weekend.'

She looked disappointed. He threw caution to the wind.

'I guess I can't leave you drinking on your own. Not after the way you knocked that back. People will think you've a problem.' He smirked, then downed the fiery liquid. Shit. If that didn't cure the last vestiges of his hangover, there was no hope for him.

'What do you think Grace Brady is hiding?' Laura asked, helping herself to a handful of wasabi peas and passing the bowl over to Ray. 'Other than a functioning brain and heart.'

Ray tossed some peas into his mouth. He missed with one and it shot over his shoulder, narrowly missing a fellow diner.

'My apologies,' he said to the woman, earning a dirty look in return. Embarrassed over his lack of hand-eye coordination, he replied, 'Grace? I honestly don't know. Do you mind if we talk about something other than the job? For a change.'

Laura signalled to the barman for a drinks menu. Ray seemed really uncomfortable. She was starting to worry it was because he only had her for company rather than their usual group of colleagues. He'd suggested this dinner. Was he bored? She tried to think of something interesting to say.

Ray filled the silence before her.

'You moved in with Bridget recently, didn't you? You must miss your mam and all that lovely cooking.' Wow. Ray could actually feel his brain seeping out of his ears. Why couldn't he be himself? Then again, being himself hadn't exactly panned out too well. They had worked together for years and she'd never even looked at him.

'I really do miss her and the rest of the gang.' Laura answered the question as earnestly as if he'd asked whether she believed in God, she was so grateful for the conversation. 'I didn't think I would. I wanted space and now I have it. It's great and I really like living with Bridget, but I didn't realise how much I'd miss the banter. Do you know what I mean?'

'I do,' he answered. 'There are loads of us in my family too and we shared a tiny three-bed council house. I never had a bed to myself, let alone a room. It used to drive me nuts. Now, I go over there just for the noise.'

Laura caught the server's attention and ordered a Sakura Martini.

'Oh, sorry, I didn't even show you the menu.' She passed Ray the card, mortified.

'It's fine. I'll have what she's having. You seem to know your way around the list. Have you had that before?'

'No. It was the only thing I felt confident pronouncing.'

Ray laughed. The sake must be working. He was starting to relax.

Their food arrived and she watched, amused, as he started to extract all the seaweed from the salad portion.

'What are you doing?'

'I'm taking the slime out. You can't eat that stuff. We take baths in it after footie games down the club.'

'Is that Dublin wisdom?'

'Yep.'

She smiled.

'It's actually very good for you.'

He mock gagged.

They chatted about something and nothing while they ate. The drinks arrived. Laura tasted hers first and nearly choked.

'Sweet Jesus! We're suicidal ordering these. That is some serious alcoh—' she didn't finish the sentence. Instead, she clapped her hand over her mouth.

'I'm so sorry,' she said, after a moment had passed. 'I didn't mean to say that.'

Ray pushed his remaining food around with the chopsticks.

'That's okay. People can't erase every turn of phrase from their vocabulary for fear of upsetting me. Ellie Byrne killed herself. It's a fact.'

Laura didn't say anything for a moment.

'You still think about her.' She stated it as a fact, not a question.

Ray hesitated. He had been starting to enjoy himself. Did he really want to go down this path? But Laura had been down in Kilcross with him and Ellie. She understood.

'Yes,' he said. 'I do. But it's stupid, because I spent so little time with her. I suppose the only way I can explain it is that I fell fast and hard. In my head, I had it sorted – we'd go back to Dublin, have a few dates, start seeing each other seriously. She was so funny and kind-hearted. And beautiful. She was . . .'

He looked up, the words he was about to say dying on his lips.

Laura was twisting the stem of her glass between her fingers, her expression downcast.

She didn't look like she wanted to hear what he had to say about Ellie.

Ray was confused. She'd asked him if he still thought about her. Hadn't she?

He examined her face and slowly, slowly, it began to dawn on him. A warm feeling began to envelop him that had nothing to do with the alcohol.

'Actually . . .' he started to say. He got no further. Laura's mobile was buzzing on the counter and she picked it up. He could see Eoin Coyle's name flashing on the screen.

'I have to take this,' she said, jumping off her stool and walking over to the window.

He lifted his drink and waited patiently. He knew what he

wanted to say to her. So it was like a bucket of iced water when Laura returned and removed her coat from the back of the stool.

'I'm so sorry,' she said, barely glancing at him. 'I have to dash. Can I leave some money for the food?'

He shook his head, struggling to find words that would make her stay.

He didn't have the time. She was out the door before he could react.

Before he could say, *I barely knew Ellie.*

Before he could say, *But I know you. And I've just realised I want to know you a lot better.*

Tuesday

'My deepest condolences on the death of your mother. I am very sorry we have to do this now.'

Tom sat across from Darragh McNally, unable to prevent the surge of sympathy he felt for the man who appeared bereft, completely shaken.

Shane Morrison had met Tom and Ray just inside Government Buildings. He expressed astonishment that McNally had come back to work, given the state he was in.

'We all know Mr McNally is fanatical about politics,' Morrison had said, his face grave. 'He has a reputation of being the first in here in the morning and the last to leave, so it shouldn't be a massive surprise to see him back today. However, from what I gather, his mother meant the world to him. I don't think he has any other family. I suspect he may still be in shock. Well, you'll see for yourselves.'

And now Tom did see. The party chair, gaunt when they'd met him first on Friday, today looked a mere shadow of himself.

They were sitting in his office. A full-sized elderly grandfather clock graced the corner, ticking soothingly. Bookshelves lined the walls, packed with aged, eclectic texts. Tom wryly noted a copy of Machiavelli's *The Prince* among them.

'She lived to a great age and she'd been ill for some time,' McNally said. 'I should be feeling relief. She was never really happy in that nursing home but there was no choice. I'm in Dublin full time and I have no siblings. I tried to persuade her to move up here but she refused. She had rural Ireland in her blood, hated the city with all its crowds and noise.'

His face crumpled and he let out a long, heartbroken sigh.

'She was so supportive of me. I should have been there for her more.'

'I imagine she was very proud of everything you've achieved,' Tom said.

This seemed to perk the other man up a bit.

'She was, yes. She was pleased to see me do so well. I gave her the best of everything.'

Ray observed his boss, wondering how they were supposed to proceed. He'd spent the early part of the day brooding on last night's dinner with Laura, but this interview was putting his selfish little problems in perspective. McNally was clearly in mourning but they had to question him about his movements on Friday night and possible bribe-taking.

'Again, I apologise for having to conduct this interview now,' the inspector said. 'Unfortunately, the matter is too serious to leave any longer.'

'I understand,' McNally said. 'I was coming back to Dublin last night and I kept thinking about Kathryn Finnegan. Not that I didn't think of her on Friday night; it's just, I suppose I understand her grief now in a way I didn't – I couldn't – before.'

He placed his head in his hands and sighed again. Tom gave him a moment, watching him closely. Was that genuine empathy? Or remorse?

McNally composed himself.

'All right, then,' the inspector said, gently. 'There were a number of people here on Friday night and we're just trying to establish what everybody was doing. We didn't actually discuss with you how you spent the evening. You told us that Minister Blake met with Carl Madsen. Is there anything you would like to clarify about that statement? What time did you meet with Mr Madsen?'

McNally swallowed.

'The whole point of Madsen coming here was to meet Aidan,' he said, his voice bitter. 'Then Aidan cancelled. I'm sorry, I should have told you that on Friday. It was stupid of me.'

'Why did you tell me Aidan had met Madsen when that wasn't the case?'

'The minister asked me not to, is the answer to your last question. I wasn't thinking very logically – still imagining that politics was more important than the investigation into the death of a man. He swore he hadn't hurt Ryan. If I thought he had, I wouldn't have covered for him. You get used to helping politicians deal with all sorts in here; it becomes second nature.'

'But what you're talking about in this instance is obstruction in a murder case.'

McNally bowed his head. Tom sensed if he arrested him right now the man wouldn't care a jot. He seemed to be on the verge of giving up.

'I can't begin to tell you how all over the place I was on Friday. I knew my mother was dying and I had all this drama to deal with. Case in point – I left Madsen alone down in the Dáil bar. I said I was going to check if his taxi was coming but I just wanted to be alone. We didn't have a particularly amicable meeting. He was annoyed at Aidan's no-show and I was generally frustrated at being left to clean everything up. I was also under time pressure to finalise the Bill everybody wants passed and I wanted to get on the road down to Clare. If I'd gone down on Friday night I would have had a little more time with my mother before she died.'

Tom hesitated. McNally was really struggling to keep it together. But the inspector had no choice but to press on.

'So, when you left Madsen, where did you go?'

'Back to my office.'

'Alone?'

'Yes.'

'And you didn't see anybody on the way here? Nobody called in to see you?'

McNally shook his head.

'Only the usher who was arranging the taxi. I looked briefly for Morrison, because I didn't want to leave the organising of Madsen's transport in the hands of just anybody. But I couldn't find him. That was unusual; he's normally on hand when you need him. I didn't see anybody again until I was summoned to the tunnel after one of the ushers found Ryan's body.'

'Let's talk about Ryan and Aidan's relationship. Are you aware that Ryan was trying to blackmail the minister?'

McNally stiffened.

'You know about that, then. I only found out on Wednesday. Aidan just dropped it in my lap. He'd been keeping it secret for months and suddenly, days before this Bill is to be finalised, he drops the bombshell.'

'What did he expect you to do about it?'

'He didn't ask me to do anything, but he assumed I'd sort it out. He claimed he didn't really believe Ryan would follow through but he wanted to have me onside to make sure that was the case. It's not like I could simply fire Ryan. I said I'd talk to him. If I'd known about the problem earlier, it would never have progressed to the point it did. Ryan was a party man, for all his flaws. He wouldn't have risked the wider political fallout over one issue.'

'Are you sure about that?' Tom probed.

McNally's wan face flushed under Tom's searching gaze. He held up his hands and shrugged.

'I'm not sure of anything any more. I planned to talk to Ryan and remind him of his party allegiance. I don't know how it would have gone.'

'Why didn't you advise the minister to go to the police about Ryan's threats?'

McNally rubbed his hands together. He couldn't stop fidgeting.

'Aidan point blank refused to have the police involved. I did suggest it but he was adamant. He feared his personal life would be exposed if things went that far. He likes his privacy.'

'And was your motivation to protect Blake personally or because you need him to ensure this Bill is passed? It is a little disingenuous, isn't it, what has been written into the Bill?'

'Inspector, the legislation is written that way to minimise risk to our economy. The business conducted by the existing exploration companies mightn't generate huge revenue for the State, but those companies record a lot of their profits here and that has a positive effect on GDP. The layman mightn't understand the complexities of the country's finances, but it's the government's job to ensure we don't drive multinationals out with short-sighted populist measures.'

Again, McNally shifted uncomfortably in his chair. He was on edge, impatient for the interview to be over. The words sounded right, but there was no sincerity in the delivery.

'You strike me as an intelligent man,' Tom observed. 'I appreciate you were under pressure on Friday night for a variety of reasons. I understand that you are loyal to the Reform Party and possibly to Minister Blake. But – and correct me if I'm wrong – he seems to have asked an awful lot of you in relation to that night's events – first to talk to Ryan and then to lie for him about his whereabouts. Why didn't you just say no?'

McNally opened and closed his mouth. He made a steeple with

his fingers and shook his head. Whatever reply or defence he'd been about to advance, he'd changed his mind.

'To hell with it. To hell with everything. You're right. To think, that was the thing that consumed me last week. Protecting the party and getting that Bill passed. Covering for Blake. My mother was dying . . .'

His voice broke.

'Excuse me, Inspector. I need a drink.' He stood up and walked to the cabinet at the side of the room, lifted a glass and removed the stopper from a decanter of brandy. He poured a large measure and held the glass up to his nose.

Tom watched, uncomfortable. He was in a bind. They were conducting an interview, so he could ask McNally to wait until they were finished before he helped himself to alcohol. On the other hand, they hadn't brought the man down to the station to do this formally and he was clearly devastated by his loss. Still, there was something not right about the way McNally was caressing the tumbler in his hand, like he'd crossed a desert and arrived at an oasis.

The inspector didn't have much time to think through his dilemma. In a heartbeat, the party chair whispered an inaudible toast, drained the glass, refilled it and returned to his seat.

'I won't offer you one, Inspector. I know you're working. But please, let me honour my mother. She was a great woman. She raised me on her own, you know. There were so few people at her funeral, fewer still who understood what a phenomenal lady she was. It's so sad.'

'You were very close,' Tom remarked.

'She was all I had. My father died when she was seven months pregnant. Just dropped dead from a massive brain haemorrhage. The shock of his death sent her into early labour and I was born premature. Hence, my short stature. I was bullied all the way through school. Too small, too smart.

'But my mother made life worth living. She never stopped telling me how brilliant I was, how much I was loved. There was only ever the two of us. She'd been an only child herself and her parents were dead. She gave me everything and ran a farm on top of it. You can't imagine how hard that was back then. She came under huge pressure from the farmers around her to give up her holding. It was like something from a John B. Keane play. But she had a will of iron.'

He raised the drink again, his face despondent.

'I've always had her drive but I have too many weaknesses. My political ambitions have been like an addiction. I'm fierce good at those, Inspector – addictions. And depression. It's all swings and roundabouts for me.'

McNally stared into the glass with a mixture of desire and contempt that now made sense to Tom.

'How long are you sober?' he asked, sitting up straighter.

'Over five years.'

'I think maybe you should put the drink down,' Tom said, mentally kicking himself for not speaking sooner about the alcohol. He'd pushed the man with his questioning, but then, he suspected McNally had been heading in the direction of breaking his sobriety anyway. They couldn't leave him like this. 'Have you somebody you can call? A sponsor?'

McNally shook his head.

'I never went to AA. I sobered myself up. I discovered a trick. Replace one craving with another. Like I said, I was blinded by power. I even neglected my mother, the only person in the world who'd ever loved me. Fool, fool, fool. The things I've done . . .'

He took another large mouthful. Tom's frown deepened, matched by Ray's.

'Mr McNally, you should go home. Get some rest. You probably haven't slept, have you?'

The other man shook his head. His suit was crumpled. He

probably hadn't showered or changed since attending his mother's funeral yesterday.

'We can resume this tomorrow. Can I call you a car, or get somebody to drop you home?'

McNally shrugged.

'I'll be fine. I'll finish this' – he nodded at the glass but Tom suspected he meant the decanter – 'and go home.'

Tom handed the party chair his card.

'We'll speak again before the week is out. If there's anything you want to discuss with me before then, please ring me on that number. It's my mobile; you'll get through to me direct.'

'I appreciate that.'

'May I ask you one more thing before I go?'

McNally shrugged, permission granted.

'Is there a club that Minister Blake is a member of that I should know about?'

The other man smiled thinly.

'Ha, yes. It's not *a* club you're interested in, Inspector. It's *The* Club. That's what it's called. He's a member all right. Who dobbed him in? I can think of only a handful of people who'd have given you that information, all of them extremely powerful and not likely to mention it to you . . . unless . . .'

He gazed thoughtfully into his drink.

It was Tom's turn to shrug, as though whoever had told him was irrelevant. He wasn't at ease in this political world of game playing.

'How would I go about sourcing contact details for this place?' he asked.

'Are you a fan of crime novels?' McNally seemed to be mildly enjoying himself, momentarily distracted from his previous maudlin ruminations.

'Not particularly. They're a busman's holiday for me. My wife keeps the thriller book industry in business, though.'

'Well, she'll know, then, that in all good plot devices, the best place to hide is in plain sight. The Club is private and its membership list is a secret – but you'll find an address for it on the web. It just won't tell you any more.'

'I'll do that. How do you know about it?'

'I know everything Blake does. Or at least, I thought I did. Up until this week.'

Tom paused at the door as they were leaving and cast a backward glance at the party chair. He was slumped over again, his head back in its depressive state, both hands clasping the glass of alcohol. He was a small man anyway, but right now he was so hunched into himself he was disappearing into the chair.

The inspector felt a shiver go through him, a hint of foreboding. He almost couldn't leave the room, feeling he should stay and say something, although what, he didn't know. He didn't want to leave the man alone and yet he barely knew him. Perhaps the best thing Tom could do was find somebody who did know the party chair and get him help.

If he had known . . . if he had suspected what was to come, the inspector would have stayed. But he didn't.

After a final glance, Tom pulled the door closed behind him.

CHAPTER 18

Morrison met Tom and Ray in the corridor outside McNally's office. He grimaced when he saw their faces.

'I know,' he said, in hushed tones. 'I've never seen him like this. He's shell-shocked, isn't he?'

Tom nodded.

'I think it might be more than that. Allegedly, he suffers from depression. His mother's death may have triggered some sort of episode. No doubt you've considered this anyway, but perhaps you'd be good enough to ensure he gets home safe. He's had a drink and I think he plans to have more.'

'I'll drive him home myself. Sadly, it's true. Mr McNally has battled with depression in the past. It's no secret. The events of the past week have obviously taken him to a bad place.'

'Thank you. I can't imagine you get asked to chauffeur intoxicated employees home too often.'

'Not in this job, but I am a former guard, so I've had plenty of experience dealing with the inebriated. I'll be able to handle Mr McNally.'

'I didn't know you were in the force.' Tom wasn't terribly surprised. Morrison had the bearing of a man who'd worn a security forces uniform all his life.

Tom and Ray walked in the direction of Leinster House. The inspector wanted to see the other entrance to the LH2000 tunnel he'd heard about.

'What do you make of McNally?' he asked Ray.

'He's not well,' his deputy replied. 'I can't decide if it's solely as a result of his mother dying or if there's something else upsetting him. She was elderly, ill for a long time by the sound of it. Her death must have been expected. What did he mean by "I've done things"? Was that a confession of sorts?'

Tom reflected on the conversation.

'I'm not sure. The man's not married, has no siblings, no remaining parent. He has dedicated his life to politics, so all his "friends" are probably colleagues and acquaintances. Who, of those he works with, attended his mother's funeral? Nobody we've dealt with, that's for sure. He lied for Blake on Friday night, but the minister didn't even go down to support him.'

'Blake was dealing with his own drama,' Ray remarked.

The inspector sighed.

'McNally is a middle-aged man with nothing to show for his life bar his career, which he doesn't seem too satisfied with right now. But even with all of that, he seems disproportionately upset. If he finished with Madsen at 9.30 he could have gone straight over to LH2000 and found Ryan. Maybe he did more than lie for Blake. Send somebody around to his house tomorrow and we'll catch up with him again in a day or two. Here, is that the way to the bar?'

'I think so. Fancy a quick one?'

'Hardehar. Let's take a look.'

The Dáil bar was larger than the inspector would have guessed. Striped blue and beige couches lined the walls, facing dark oak tables. In the centre of the deep-pile royal blue carpet were several high tables and stools. On a busy night, with those tables populated, it would be difficult to have a full view of all the patrons.

Today, it was empty of customers, as the majority of Leinster House staff were still prohibited from entering the building. A lone employee stood on the far side of the counter, a pad and pen in hand for her stock-take.

'I'm sorry, we're closed,' she called out.

'Detective Inspector Tom Reynolds, Miss. This is Detective Sergeant Ray Lennon.'

'Oh.' She reached over the bar to shake their hands. She was in her late fifties, with streaked blonde hair tucked into a neat bun and large glasses. The skin on her face was covered by a thick layer of foundation, but the pockmarks of long-gone youthful acne were still apparent.

'Sorry to barge in like this,' Tom continued. 'We're still trying to establish a few facts in the Ryan Finnegan case. Are you the manager?'

'I am,' she said, sweeping a stray hair from her face, obviously pleased he'd correctly identified her position. 'I was working. I've already been interviewed. I didn't see anything, I'm afraid.'

'That's okay. Were you serving on Friday night?'

'I was. We were unusually busy and I didn't have a full complement of staff, so I mucked in.'

'I see.' Tom casually picked up a bar mat and folded it in half, then into quarters. 'Did you happen to see Minister Blake come in that night?'

'Yes. That is, I didn't see him come in, but I saw him when he was here. His wife had come in earlier and was up the back there. He was looking for her. He ordered two sparkling waters and joined her.'

'Do you remember what time that was?'

'I think so. I served him at about 9.50. I remember because a few minutes earlier I'd looked at my watch, wondering when we could start shifting the crowd. They were a bit boisterous.'

'I see. And Sara was up there?' Tom nodded in the direction of steps at the rear of the bar.

'Yes.'

'Thank you,' the inspector said, and he and Ray made their way over to that section.

They passed through open double doors to the lounge exten-
sion. A large marble fireplace dominated the top of the room.

Ray flopped down on one of the seats.

'That's five minutes later than Blake claimed,' he said. 'But he
could have been in here for a few minutes before he went to the
counter. You look lovely, by the way.'

Tom was staring at an almost floor-to-ceiling mirror in between
the couches facing Ray.

'What?' he answered his deputy, distracted. 'Listen, head over
to that tunnel. I'll be along in a minute.'

Ray lifted himself wearily from the chair and departed. Tom
returned to the bar manager.

'That emergency exit up there,' he said, referring to the mir-
rored door he'd been examining. 'Is it alarmed?'

The woman looked puzzled.

'Of course. Why?'

'If somebody came into the bar through that door, what would
happen?'

'All hell would break loose. People know not to use that door,'
she answered. 'The alarm on it is like nothing you've ever heard.'

'Who else was up in that section on Friday, do you recall?'

'It was packed. I'm afraid I couldn't remember all of them. Even
the chief of security called in at one point. It felt like most of
Leinster House was here on Friday. It may as well have been
Budget night.'

*

Tom rejoined his deputy at the tunnel entrance.

'What was that about? Ray asked.

Tom shrugged. 'I had a hunch but it turned out to be nothing.
Come on, let's walk through.'

Forensics had removed the last of the crime scene equipment
from the far end of the tunnel and the floor and statue where

Ryan had been discovered were scrubbed clean of his blood. A large wreath had been left at the foot of the sculpture and the ushers had roped off the immediate area.

'Those ministers Sara was looking for on Friday night,' Tom said. 'Did we follow up with them? They were with her when Blake says he arrived in the bar.'

'Michael interviewed three of them. The others she was with are based outside Dublin but will be back up tomorrow, so we can set up meetings. Anyway, of the ones he talked to, two of them met Sara outside the Dáil chamber shortly after 9 p.m. Several others have confirmed she arrived in the bar at about 9.15 and stayed there. The other minister we spoke to entered the bar at 9.55 p.m. and tried to buy her a glass of wine but he said she was fuming with him and wouldn't let him purchase any drink at all, just made him leave and go over to the ball.'

'Did he mention her husband being with her?'

'No. He told Michael she was alone. But Blake may have been up the back or something and the bar manager said herself she served him at 9.50.'

'Hmm. Okay. There's something else I want to you to check. Find out what Darragh McNally earns. He's worked for the Reform Party all his life. There isn't a lot of money swashing about when a party is in opposition and this is their first time in power in a long time. He's a government appointee but there's a cap on civil service wages under the Troika agreement. I'd guess he's earning, what, one hundred grand a year? Max? Find out about that home his mother was in. He would have put her up in the best and paid for private health care all the way. I'd like to see if the sums add up. If he was an alcoholic up to five years ago, I doubt he was saving vast amounts of money, but maybe there was money in the family.'

'I got the distinct feeling when we were talking with Madsen that his "man with the strings" was on the payroll,' Ray said.

'Maybe that's what McNally was referring to when he said he'd done things.'

Tom nodded. 'McNally might seem like a shell of a man now, but let's say on Friday night he was faced with a crisis. He was taking bribes from Madsen – maybe he didn't know that his mother would be dead within hours. She's been ill a while; she might have stayed ill for a while longer. Ryan Finnegan was threatening to bring the whole house of cards down – make Blake change the Bill or expose him; either way, whatever McNally had promised Madsen wouldn't be delivered. So, he's a desperate man, forced to do a desperate thing. And now he's wondering about the point of it all.'

'Here's the problem,' Tom continued. 'If McNally killed Ryan and is now regretting it, is his next step a confession? Or is it to punish Blake because he was forced to protect him? Because if there's one thing I know, it's that a man with nothing to lose is capable of anything.'

'We'll keep an eye on him,' Ray said.

'Another thing,' Tom remarked, his forehead creased in concentration. 'He said his mother ran a farm.'

'And?'

'If he grew up on a farm, McNally knows how to handle a firearm.'

Wednesday

Tom had thought he was tired, but Kathryn Finnegan gave new meaning to the word. Barely five days had passed since her husband's murder and she looked to have aged years. Her eyes were bloodshot and ringed with dark circles; her skin was deathly pale. She'd pulled the top half of her unwashed hair back into a small ponytail. The young mother stood in the centre of the sitting room, Beth straddling her hip, and looked as if she was close to collapsing under the weight of the small baby.

Her brother's wife noticed it too and came to her aid.

'Kathryn, let me take Beth. You talk to the inspector.'

The widow barely heard her sister-in-law and was startled to find herself suddenly relieved of the baby.

'Oh. Thank you. Um, can I get you something, Inspector? You look as exhausted as I feel.'

Tom shook his head. His lack of sleep paled in this situation, though it was certainly taking a toll on his home life.

Louise had arrived back on Sunday night and, as predicted, immediately challenged Maria's new routine for Cáit. Despite his daughter's apparent success (a one-off, according to Louise), his wife had insisted they continue to put the baby into her cot in her own room at 8 p.m.

'It will work eventually,' she said, ignoring the dubious and mutinous looks from Tom and Maria respectively.

'Please, sit down, Kathryn. How are you managing?'

She perched nervously on the edge of a chair, picking at the fabric on the armrest.

'I can't stop thinking about it. I bring Beth into bed with me and I lie awake staring at her, imagining Ryan lying on the other side. She'll never have that now, will she? What if I'm not enough?'

'Of course you are enough,' Tom reassured her.

Kathryn shook her head.

'I'm just meant to go on,' she continued. 'They tell me I have to be strong. For Beth's sake. I have to keep going. But it feels like the world has stopped turning. Sometimes I forget and I walk into a room expecting Ryan to be there . . . His smell, his . . . energy, it's still all over the house. Then I realise and it's like a punch in the stomach, every time. How do people do this? How do you keep living?'

Tom swallowed. The woman's grief was unbearable.

'I can't say I understand what you're going through,' he replied honestly. 'I've never lost anybody so close. But I have seen this many times and I do know that it gets easier. You take one day at a time. And eventually, a long way from now, it won't feel this bad.'

'Do you know what happened yet?' The question sparked some life in Kathryn.

Tom shook his head.

'We're following some strong lines of inquiry but no, we haven't arrested anybody. That's why I'm here. I'd like to look through Ryan's belongings, if that's okay with you. Get a better picture of him.'

'Your officers went through his things on Saturday.'

'I want to go over everything again. You only have the one shared computer, am I right?'

'Yes.'

'Have you gone through his possessions yourself? Diaries? Books and so on?'

'He didn't keep a diary. He had a calendar for work events on his phone. His books are all mixed in with mine. We shared the same tastes, even the political biographies. I . . . I haven't been through his clothes.'

'No,' Tom said gently. 'There's time enough for that. If it's not too much of an intrusion, may I look upstairs?'

She nodded, distracted.

He left her with Ray and climbed the stairs to the couple's bedroom, taking in the family pictures hanging along the wall. Ryan and Kathryn, arms wrapped around each other, the waves of an anonymous beach lapping behind them. Their wedding day, him gazing at her adoringly while she looked shyly at the camera. Her hair longer and wavy, him sporting a beard and wearing glasses. Ryan, nose to nose with his new baby in a hospital ward, unaware the photo was being taken. Enraptured.

Photo after photo of a young man in the throes of life.

Tom paused on the last step and took a deep, sorrowful breath.

Dealing with such loss, even somebody else's, always affected him and these pictures felt particularly poignant.

The bedroom was a mess of discarded baby clothes and crumpled nightwear. Downstairs was being kept in order by the extended family, but Kathryn probably refused to let anybody past the door of this room. It was her sanctuary, the only private space she had left for her and Beth. Somewhere she could hide and cry amongst the most intimate memories of her husband, away from well-meaning sympathisers.

Tom rummaged through the clothes hanging in the wardrobe, searching the pockets. He checked the drawers on Ryan's side of the bed. He knelt on the floor and looked under the bed, then under the mattress. He delved into the shoeboxes stacked on top of the wardrobe and found old bills, cards and pictures.

He scanned some cutouts of political articles with Ryan's name on the byline. At a glance, they appeared to be well-written, compelling and admirable pieces. Picking through the fragments of the other man's life, Tom felt like Ryan Finnegan was someone he would have liked.

The inspector sat with his head in his hands, frustration welling. This was the house of an ordinary man who, despite his high-profile job, seemed to be living a fairly ordinary life. Until he decided to blackmail his boss to make him change a piece of legislation that Ryan believed went against the national interest.

But who'd shot him because of it? Blake? McNally? Madsen? Had they missed or overlooked somebody who didn't have an alibi? They didn't have a complete list of everybody who was in the parliament complex that night. They were examining CCTV footage to see if the ushers had missed anybody. Tom knew that kind of painstaking manual evidence-gathering left room for human error.

Back downstairs, Tom found Ray playing with Beth on the floor. Kathryn wasn't exactly smiling at their antics, but she didn't look quite as forlorn as she had when they'd arrived.

'Are your family looking after you well?' the inspector asked. Something was nagging him, but he couldn't quite put his finger on it.

She turned to him.

'Yes. Too well. They won't go home. I went out for a walk with Beth this morning, down to the church on the Strand where Ryan and I got married. It's the first time since everything happened that I felt some peace. I need space and everybody keeps fussing over me. I know I should be grateful, but I just want my house back.'

Tom nodded, distracted. He knew now what had been niggling at him.

'Kathryn, the car crash Ryan was in. What caused it?'

'Someone came out of a side street and rammed into him when he was stopped at traffic lights then drove away from the scene. Why?'

Tom's eyebrows furrowed.

Her jaw dropped.

'You don't think somebody tried to kill him that time?'

'I don't know. Nobody mentioned it was a hit-and-run before now. If I find anything out at all, I'll let you know, okay? Ray.'

His deputy stood up from the baby, smiling ruefully.

'She is very beautiful, Mrs Finnegan,' he said.

Kathryn was still staring at Tom, her head spinning at this new possibility, but she acknowledged Ray's compliment.

'Thank you. She has Ryan's eyes. Do you know when my husband's body will be released? My brother is the only family member to have seen him since he died. When do I get to bury him? I just want to see him one more time.'

*

'That's the group shot there. Jesus, the effort it took to get everyone together for that. What's the saying? "Don't work with children or animals." Well, they should add government minis-ters. Particularly drunken ones. Prima donnas, one and all.'

Laura and Michael were sitting with Hugh Masterson, the vice-CEO of Silent Voices, Sara Blake's charity. Masterson had suggested meeting in the Grand Hotel, where the ball had been held on Fri-day night. On arrival, the detectives were escorted to one of the tables in the first-floor dining room overlooking Merrion Square. Hugh joined them minutes later.

'You'll spot me easy enough,' he'd told Laura on the phone. 'I'm a six-foot-four bearded hippie with a penchant for colourful shirts.'

He hadn't lied. He strode into the high-class restaurant wearing ripped denims and a garish Hawaiian T-shirt. In the group photo they were now studying, Masterson was squeezed into a tux and looked distinctly uncomfortable.

Sara Blake stood beside him, tiny in comparison. She wore a tight-fitting, floor-length navy dress that covered her lithe body like a glove. Her general style was unremarkable compared to the other women in the frame, as though she were a minor guest and not the person running the show.

Laura was squinting at the faces in the various rows when Michael's phone beeped. The text was from Tom, relaying the news that Ryan's car crash had been a hit-and-run and requesting that Michael pull up the incident report. He showed the text to his colleague.

Laura nodded, immediately aware of the significance. If an ear-lier attempt had been made on Ryan's life, maybe something had been overlooked at the time that might now give them a clue to his murderer's identity.

'How did Aidan Blake seem on the night of the ball?' Laura asked Masterson. 'Did you notice what time he left for Leinster House with his wife?'

'Yes. They both left just before 9. The first course was being served, so nobody really noticed. Sara was hopping mad because she knew, and she was right, that our late guests were going to arrive still expecting to be fed. It wasn't the type of food you reheat in the microwave. And the press wanted their group shot as soon as dinner was finished and before the speeches.

'Anyway, I offered to go over with her, but Aidan was adamant. We were all surprised by that. He rarely helps her out with anything. Shane Morrison had been due to attend but didn't make it – he would have assisted her normally. He's good like that. But he was busy in the early part of the evening and then I guess they found Ryan and he couldn't come over. Tea?'

Laura nodded and Masterson poured the hot liquid into the dainty china cups.

'It was a great night,' he continued, helping himself to three lumps of sugar. 'Sara is a fantastic organiser. We've worked together for years and she's never lost her passion for what she does. This sort of job usually has an attrition rate – people can't handle the horror we see routinely. But she sucks it up. It's never about her; it's always about the kids.'

He smiled fondly. Laura glanced discreetly at the man's wedding band finger. Empty. Well, if Blake ended up going to prison for murder, it looked like Sara wouldn't be stuck for suitors.

'The minister – did he seem . . . relaxed? Nervous? Did you notice anything out of the ordinary?'

Laura peered at the picture again. Aidan Blake was in the front row. He was grinning but – and she wasn't sure if she was just imagining this – the smile didn't seem to have reached his eyes. He looked a little distressed.

Masterson stroked his beard.

'He seemed frazzled, if I'm honest. Especially when they returned from Leinster House. At one point I saw him snap at Sara. He grabbed her arm too. She was upset with him but she just got on with doing her job. I put it down to Blake having no interest in being there. As I said, he never shows her much support but expects her to be there for him at every political event he attends. He could have brought those ministers over with him in the first place, but he just rocked up at 8 in a mood.'

'Did anybody else seem out of sorts?' Michael asked. 'Any of the ministers who came over later?'

The other man shook his head.

'No. People were enjoying themselves. Of course, nobody knew then what had happened in Leinster House,' he said, his voice grave. 'To be honest, though, most of them probably wouldn't have given a damn, bar revelling in the drama of it. They don't even care about the charity. They're happy to be seen donating to a worthy cause but when you think of the power they have to make the country a better place to begin with . . . I'm sad to say we had a fairly superficial bunch here on Friday night. It's such a shame about Ryan because Sara had mentioned him as somebody who could help us with lobbying. She liked him.'

Laura noted a change in Masterson's voice on the last sentence. Had he been jealous of Ryan?

'Carl Madsen, the vice-president of Udforske, was due to meet Aidan Blake in Leinster House on Friday evening,' she said. 'I believe he's a philanthropist of sorts. Did you consider inviting him to the ball?'

'Well, funny you should mention that because Sara raised that very thing with Aidan a few days before the ball. She told me when we were setting up the room that Mr Madsen was meant to be in Dublin and she'd asked her husband to extend an invite. It would have been great for the charity.'

'And?'

'And Aidan said no because Madsen had other business to attend to. I imagine it was more to do with his ego. Like I said, Aidan likes to shine. It's hard to be the most important person in the room when the likes of Carl Madsen are there with you.'

Laura nodded and thanked Hugh. His description of Blake's behaviour on the night raised a few questions. Chief among them was why the minister had refused to ask Madsen to attend his wife's ball. The detective couldn't imagine it was only because Blake didn't want Madsen stealing his thunder.

Was it because he knew if the Udforske president were there at his invitation, he'd be stuck entertaining him? And how could Blake do that if he had planned to kill Ryan Finnegan on the same night?

Even more importantly, if Masterson was to be believed, there'd been discord between Aidan and his wife at the ball.

They knew already Sara had had a good relationship with Ryan Finnegan. If her husband had murdered his PA and Sara knew . . .

Laura had no doubt that the minister's wife could end up being his Achilles heel.

CHAPTER 19

Tom and Ray left Kathryn Finnegan's house, both privately relieved to be temporarily escaping the young widow's desolation. The wind was biting, but at least it was dry. The inspector could smell burning in the air – the whiff of residents incinerating fallen leaves in their back gardens.

Ray was quiet, staring off into the distance.

'You seem preoccupied,' Tom remarked, buttoning up his overcoat as they walked back to the car. They'd parked up the road from Kathryn's. Half her family seemed to be visiting today – their cars were lined up the length of the street. No wonder she felt she had to get out of her own house. 'Do you need to be somewhere?'

His deputy looked down at his phone.

'Not right now. What's the plan?'

'Why do you keep looking at that thing? And while I'm thinking of it – who spoke to McNally today?'

'I sent Bridget and Brian out to his house. He didn't turn up to work but he answered the door when they knocked. Brian said he looked the worse for wear.'

The inspector cursed.

'I'm not feeling as sympathetic as I was yesterday. I know the man has suffered a loss, but his mother was elderly and dying. Kathryn Finnegan just lost a husband in the prime of his life. We're interviewing McNally again tomorrow if we have to turn up on his doorstep with a vat of coffee and stick him in a cold shower. And if we get anything on potential bribes, I'm bringing him in to the station. We've been lenient enough. Let's go back to HQ and pull together a quick team meeting for updates. I want to get home early tonight – I'm shattered.'

'Don't do that!'

Tom ground to a halt on the pavement, astonished at being shouted at.

'Don't do what?'

'Eh, go home,' Ray said. 'I assumed we were working late.'

'Working all hours won't change anything, Junior, I've told you that before. Sometimes you need to take a step back. A quick trip to headquarters and I'm done for the day.'

'But we've made no progress,' Ray argued. 'The man was murdered last Friday. It's Wednesday already.'

'It's like the world has turned on its axis. Isn't that my line? Okay then, let's go sit on Emmet McDonagh and see if forensics have turned up anything. If they could provide an exact time of death, it might make things easier. I refuse to believe they can't narrow it down to less than a fifteen-minute window in this day and age.'

'No. Not that.'

Now Ray was starting to sweat. Tom raised his eyebrows.

'What's going on?'

'What? Nothing.'

His deputy was frantically avoiding eye contact, desperately searching his brain for a plan.

'Actually, I'm starving. Let's go for dinner. My treat. Maybe on the way we can check out that 'Club' place that keeps cropping up.' Ray began walking again, mentally reprimanding the inspector's wife for putting him in charge of keeping Tom out for the day. She understood better than any of them how contrary her husband could be. Most days he worked well into the night but of course he would pick today to want to knock off early. It was like he knew something was going on.

Ray had thought he had the day's events well organised. They'd been due to meet the rest of the ministers who'd been present on Friday night, but the Taoiseach had called a special cabinet meeting and the interviews had been postponed. Whatever happened, he couldn't let his boss return to headquarters. There was no way the inspector wouldn't notice his entire team had upped sticks so they could rendezvous with Louise Reynolds.

'Look, Ray, I'm sorry we've breached your arbitrary five-day rule for solving a murder but that's out of my control. I want it cracked yesterday, if for no other reason than to give Kathryn Finnegan some peace. I'll look up an address for this Club, we'll call in there, and then grab a quick dinner on the way back to the office. Then I'm calling it a day.'

'Okay. Actually, I just need to phone somebody. You go ahead, get the car warmed up.'

Ray tossed him the keys, his phone already to his ear. Tom caught them, sighing to himself. What was he letting himself in for?

*

'Is this it?'

Ray pulled the car into the fortuitously vacant spot facing one of the old Georgian buildings on Fitzwilliam Square on the south side of the city.

'It's the right number,' the inspector said, looking from the image of the three-storey house on his iPhone Google map to the building in front of him.

'I'm going to pay for parking,' his deputy said, hopping out of the car.

Tom opened the passenger door and hurriedly shut it again as a passing cyclist narrowly avoided clipping it.

'Idiot!' the un-helmeted green warrior yelled.

'Stay on the cycle path!' Tom roared back, getting out of the car. 'Kamikazes,' he grumbled when Ray returned with the meter ticket.

'What?'

'Cyclists in Dublin city centre. All the rights, none of the responsibilities.'

'Jesus. You are getting old. Come on.'

A plaque was affixed to the small railings at the front of the building they'd parked beside. Ray had to lift the ivy from its gold-plated front to see the inscription.

Founded in 1879 –The Club

'You must remember this being established, huh?' he jibed to his boss.

Tom ignored him and approached the black-painted door between two white stone pillars, sitting under an elegant fanlight window. He looked for a bell, but seeing none, lifted the ornate brass knocker and dropped it twice.

'What's that?' Ray asked, pointing at an iron piece set into the ground.

'A boot-scraper,' Tom answered, as the door opened. 'So the wealthy resident of yesteryear could remove the horse manure his shoes had picked up walking through the streets.'

'You know your Georgian architecture.' The man standing in the open doorway was tall and thin. He was in his late fifties and dressed head to toe in black. His polo neck and creased trousers were sharp and his leather shoes polished until they shone. His face was a mass of lines and crevices – a lived-in face, as some would say. He furrowed bushy eyebrows as he beheld the two visitors on the doorstep.

'Oh, hello,' Tom said. 'Are you the owner of this building?'

'I'm the proprietor. We're actually closed at the moment, gentlemen. May I ask who you are and what your business is?'

'Absolutely.' Tom introduced them both and extended his hand. 'We would like to discuss the Club with you. And you are?'

The website for 'The Club' had provided a picture of the house and address against a dark background. Nothing else. No number, no names, no description of what activities went on there.

The other man took the inspector's hand in a limp handshake.

'My name is Isaac Arnold.'

He hesitated for a moment before inviting them across the threshold. It was too cold to leave the door open – perhaps if it had been milder, he'd have left them standing there, trying to make themselves heard over the din of the passing road traffic.

The entrance hall was high ceilinged; a decorative ceiling rose surrounded the impressive chandelier that hung above their heads. To their right was a set of oak stairs, a red-plush carpet runner pinned to the middle of each step with brass studs, the bannisters wrought iron. There were doors along the length of the hallway. The space was dull once the front door was shut behind them, the light from the window above the front door insufficient to dispel the shadows.

The man seemed to be uncertain as to where to bring them, eventually determining on a room further down the hall, past the stairs.

It was a windowless sitting room, opulently decorated with assorted chairs and chaises longues. The cushions and pillows were a mixed variety of reds and golds, some with tassels, some embroidered with silk threads and diamante sparkles.

In fact, Tom thought, the penny dropping, it was more of a boudoir than a living room.

Arnold indicated they should take a seat.

The inspector chose one of the hard-backed black velvet upholstered chairs.

Ray gave his boss a conspiratorial glance before taking his own seat.

From the outside, you'd never guess, but once inside . . .

'So,' Tom began. 'What we really want to know is, what kind of club is this? Your website is a little . . . vague.'

Their host raised his eyebrows, his expression sardonic.

'We don't actively seek out clients. Our membership is a very elite group. Generally, people only hear about us through word of mouth. Actually, how – ?'

'How did we hear about you? Through word of mouth, like you say. Can we speed things up a little, Mr Arnold? I'm presuming this building isn't for Bridge soirées. Are you running some kind of private gentleman's club?'

Arnold tugged at his bottom lip with his finger and thumb.

'Yes,' he replied.

'And what do the gentlemen come here for?'

'I can't speak to that.'

Tom sighed. He looked around the room again. A Napoleon mantel clock ticked peacefully over the unlit fireplace. Parisian bistro tables were dotted amongst the seating arrangements, places where drinks could be placed when men's hands were busy elsewhere.

His gaze returned to Arnold, who was sitting calmly, fingers laced across his stomach.

'If I were to mention the name Aidan Blake to you, what would you say?'

Arnold inclined his head.

'You've said the name and I say nothing in return. The reputation of this institution is built on absolute discretion and privacy. Always has been. I can't disclose the members' list.'

'You do realise it's 2011?' Tom remarked, his tone dismissive. 'This is not a Freemasons venue. You're running a high-class brothel, am I right?'

Arnold blanched. Previously soft-spoken; his voice, when he replied, was coarse with anger.

'I am beyond insulted. How dare you. To come in here and make an accusation like that – you've no idea the type of men who frequent this place, men who could – '

Tom held up his hand.

'What? Men who could get me fired? Come on.' The inspector laughed. 'I'll repeat what I said already. You may have been founded in 1879 but times have changed. Aren't you at all curious how we found out about this place? Which of your illustrious guests led us to you?'

Arnold said nothing, but considered the inspector. Tom could tell it was this question that was troubling him far more than his having figured out what The Club was for.

He threw their host a lifeline.

'Look, Mr Arnold. Let's start again. I'm willing to ignore the threat I suspect you were carelessly about to make. I'm even happy to turn a blind eye to what goes on here, the fact the place exists. I need some information purely because it may help with a murder investigation I'm conducting. It may shine some light on the character of one of those involved in my case. That's all. Tell me what I want to know and I will leave here and you are unlikely to hear from or see me again. I'll leave it in your hands to source your leak – I'll even give you a clue as to where it might have originated.'

Arnold rubbed his hands together. Tom allowed him a few moments to ponder his options.

'If it were to be discovered that you had been here asking about members and activities, the damage to my business would be considerable, Inspector. But, then, I suspect if I don't give you what you want, I may lose my club anyway. You have the power to cause me a lot of discomfort.'

'You're a smart man,' Tom replied.

Arnold smiled, red lips pulled back to reveal a dreadfully crooked set of teeth.

'So, I find myself between a rock and a hard place. This is very vexing indeed.'

'Indeed.' The inspector waited. The clock ticked some more. Ray cleared his throat. And wondered how much it cost to be a member of a place like this.

'We cater for a very niche market, Inspector,' Arnold began. 'Powerful men who have discerning desires but ultimately require total confidentiality. These aren't men who could risk driving through some of the more colourful Dublin streets after hours or sourcing companionship from one of the more popular sites on the internet.'

'I understand,' Tom said, though in reality, he didn't. Never once in his life had he entertained or even considered paying for sex. He couldn't understand the desperation that had to accompany such an act and he'd worked too long in law enforcement to be blind to the sheer misery of the young men and women involved in the flesh trade.

'So, your clientele hear about this place through the grapevine?' Ray asked.

'Yes. They're men who move in certain circles and there is an element of trust built in. Nobody would recommend this place unless they'd been here themselves.'

Tom wondered. He just could not imagine Cormac O'Shea needing to visit such a place. That man had been pretty upfront about his affair with the government press secretary. McNally said he always knew what Blake was up to – but was that because Blake told him, or had he had him followed? And who, then, had told O'Shea? One of the members must have broken the code of silence.

'What circles do they move in?' Ray asked.

'Politics. Finance. Big business. The professional classes. No celebrities. They attract too much attention.'

'And what sort of services do they seek out here?' Tom took up the questioning.

Arnold shifted nervously.

'They make the acquaintance of men and women and . . . have relations.'

Tom nodded. It didn't sound quite as reputable or upmarket when The Club's owner had to say it aloud.

'And so, Mr Arnold. We're back to my original question. Aidan Blake.'

The other man lowered his eyes. His nod was almost imperceptible.

'He is a member, then,' Tom said.

'Yes.'

'Does he attend regularly?'

'Yes.'

'To spend time with both men and women?'

Another slight nod.

'And your . . . employees? Are they young, old? Irish, non-national?'

'They're all adults, I assure you. But they aren't Irish. That would be too dangerous for the men who come here. Ireland is too small. They're mainly of Latin American origin, or African.'

And possibly working illegally, the inspector thought, which made it all the more unlikely they'd ever reveal who frequented The Club.

The inspector had what he needed.

Tom stood, followed by Ray and a mightily relieved-looking Arnold.

'Is that all?' he asked, looking from one to the other.

'For now,' the inspector agreed.

'You said you'd give me a clue as to who'd mentioned this place to you?' Arnold was anxious to resolve that mystery.

'I did, didn't I?' Tom mused on his answer for a moment. He shrugged.

'To be honest, Mr Arnold, half the populace seems to know

about this place. It would be easier for me to list who hadn't mentioned The Club during this investigation.'

And with that, he and Ray departed. Tom didn't feel an ounce of remorse about the man left in their wake. The building made his skin crawl.

And he was starting to get the measure of Aidan Blake.

*

'You want to talk about Laura? Did we not have this little chat on Sunday night on Moorhaven pier?'

The inspector stacked the various components of his burger into position, wondering how he'd manage a bite of the whole lot in one go. He'd suddenly regained the appetite he'd thought he'd lost after visiting The Club.

'I didn't tell you it was Laura,' Ray said, frowning as he poked chips around his plate.

'I thought you were hungry. You're destroying that grub. A symptom of being lovesick, is it? And I guessed it was her.'

Ray looked up.

'Is that all you have to say? Doesn't it worry you, considering we're both on your team?'

Tom wanted to say something but risked choking if he tried. The burger was delicious. It was also far too unwieldy.

'I don't know how it happened,' Ray continued, taking his boss's silence as a signal to keep talking. 'We've worked together for years and I've never looked at her like that. I always thought she was pretty. Smart. Funny. Just not girlfriend material.'

Ray loosened his tie and unbuttoned the top of his shirt. He didn't know if it was unusually hot in the restaurant or if he was burning up with embarrassment at having this conversation with his boss. It was a different matter when you were sober.

Tom put his food down. He'd have to deconstruct it and start again.

'Pretty, smart, funny,' he counted out on his fingers. 'Yes, I can see how she never crossed your radar. What is your criterion for a girlfriend? Remind me. A deity of some sort? I suppose that explains why you've been single for so long.'

Ray clicked his tongue dismissively.

'You know what I mean. You don't look at your teammates like that. Bridget is an attractive girl too, but I don't feel anything for her.'

'Are you sure? Maybe they could share you.'

'Very funny. And now she's with that Eoin fella.'

'Dum, dum, dum.' Tom sang the three words like a comedy villain had just been introduced.

Ray flushed red.

'Sorry,' his boss said. 'I'll be serious. Isn't it a bit unfair to suddenly decide you fancy her now, especially when she has a boyfriend?'

'You said that's what happened with you and Louise.'

'Well, yes, but it sort of happened at the same time for us. She hadn't been after me for years and then given up and begun a relationship with someone else.'

'Back up. What do you mean, "after you for years"?'

Tom mentally kicked himself.

'Are you saying Laura has liked me for a while? And you knew? For how long?'

'I might have noticed she had a thing for you last year,' the inspector said, feeling like he was betraying a secret that he hadn't even been entrusted with.

Ray stared at his plate, mulling it over.

'Ah, forget about it,' he said, deciding he didn't want to dwell on his dilemma any more. Maybe if he just ignored it, it would resolve itself. 'I still can't get over that club. To think, Blake is lining up to be the next Taoiseach!'

Tom nodded. 'What astonishes me, and I know it shouldn't, is that a politician can still behave in that way and not be found out. I know we've had characters like that in the past but that was when a politician's private life was considered out of bounds. He's very clever, though, the minister. All his little forays have been very discreet. Well, they were, until the people around him started dropping him in it.'

'Yeah, on that – why do you think the Taoiseach mentioned it to you? And how come he and McNally know about it?'

Tom frowned.

'Well, we know why they ratted him out. He's getting notions above his station. O'Shea is happy for Blake to be out selling the government's agenda, but he's not happy with the notion of the man stealing his job. And McNally realises Blake's boat is heading up shit creek.

'I can't picture O'Shea as a member. But he is wily enough to find out that sort of information about an enemy and store it. Somebody has been loose-lipped. I can't decide whether Blake confided in McNally or if his old pal was keeping close tabs on him. I suppose if you're positioning somebody to be the leader of the country and your puppet, you're going to want to know their dirty laundry. Honestly, though. Who knew our Dáil was a den of reprobates!'

Tom was only half jesting.

'I'd love to get a gander at that members' list,' Ray said wistfully.

'You want to perve on the perves?' Tom retorted.

Ray was about to reply when his phone buzzed.

'You're getting a lot of mysterious texts,' his boss observed.

'It's an email from Michael. The Thai police have tracked down the blokes in the photos with Blake.'

'And?'

'They all had records. Drugs, soliciting and – surprise, surprise – extortion.'

'Records that started before or after they turned eighteen?'

'After. They're approaching their forties now, which means they were of age when Blake was with them. Their youthful appearance might have been a selling point in the game they're in, but they were consenting adults. Also, the man Blake claims was blackmailing him is deceased and his death isn't considered suspicious. Overdose.'

'Hmm. That's that, then.'

Tom picked up the now slightly less macho-looking burger for another go.

Ray's phone went again.

'More from Michael?'

'Eh, no.' The detective pushed his chair away from the table and crossed to the bar. Tom watched, wondering what Ray was up to now. His detective sergeant returned and grabbed his coat.

'I've paid. Let's go.'

The inspector frowned.

'I haven't finished. You've hardly touched yours.'

'I have to be somewhere, so unless you're getting a taxi . . .'

'You're behaving very oddly today, Ray. There had better be a good explanation for it. Let me get the damn dinner to go, then.'

Tom followed his deputy to the door, muttering all the way.

His deputy drove at speed back to the north side of the city, adding to his litany of bizarre acts. Ray normally liked to keep the car to a crawl. Tom checked his phone as they were passing through an orange – just about red – traffic light. It had been oddly quiet all afternoon. Nobody had rung, not even Sean McGuinness.

Ray kept his eyes focused on the road in front of him. He was starting to wonder if Louise's decision to proceed with this evening's plans had been a good idea. He'd never been so stressed in his life.

The detective sergeant pulled up outside his boss's garden gate, nearly crashing into the kerb. Tom glared at him, exasperated. He made to open the passenger door but found it locked.

'Ray, open the door.'

His deputy was tapping away on the phone again.

'Ray!' Tom roared.

'Sorry. Hang on . . . Okay, sent. What? You want to get out? There you go.'

'Have you been bodysnatched? Listen, get whatever the hell that's turned you into a raving lunatic out of your system and come into work tomorrow as the old Ray. No acting weird on the phone, no obsessing about Laura, no out-of-character dining and driving experiences. Got it?'

'Got it. Out you go.'

The inspector slammed the car door and stomped up the garden path, still shaking his head.

The house was in pitch darkness. Tom closed the front door with a lot more finesse than he had Ray's passenger door, just in case Maria had got Cáit down early and they were both sleeping upstairs. He had no idea where Louise was; she'd left the house this morning before he'd even got up.

He slipped off his shoes and was just kicking them out of the way when he heard a noise. He froze, all of his senses alert. It had come from the kitchen, which was also blanketed in darkness.

Tom put his hand to his side before he remembered he wasn't carrying his weapon. He squinted in the dark for some sort of blunt instrument. His daughter and grandchild could be upstairs. If some bastard had broken into their home, he wouldn't be getting past Tom.

The inspector's eyes adjusted to the dark and he spotted his golf clubs. He'd taken them out with the intention of playing a round while they were away in Wicklow. Louise had clocked them before he could smuggle them into the car and berated him for even thinking about golf on their short break.

He selected a five-iron and crept towards the kitchen.

Taking a deep breath, Tom flung open the door, brandishing the club.

He heard a switch flick and was suddenly hit by a splash of light and a cacophony of noise. His jaw dropped.

'Surprise!'

A gang of people stood there, fronted by Louise and Maria. Their mouths fell open when they saw what he was wielding.

'Really, Tom,' his wife said dryly. 'Are you that determined to golf that you've taken to playing it indoors now?'

*

'No wonder you haven't arrested anybody yet. The killer probably has a big neon sign emblazoned on his head and you haven't spotted it.'

Maria's jibe was met with howls of laughter from around the table. Tom scowled at her then directed his peeved glare at his wife.

'I didn't suspect you were planning a surprise fiftieth birthday party for me because it's October and my birthday isn't until the twenty-sixth of December.'

Louise tutted. She looked breathtakingly beautiful this evening, brown eyes sparkling, her long dark hair plaited and wrapped around her head in the Greek style. She was wearing a simple black dress, the picture of elegance.

'We never would have caught you out if we'd had it on the actual day. Anyway, aren't you the one who's always whining about how rubbish it is to have your birthday at Christmas? You're an awfully hard man to please.'

She stuck her tongue out at him as she placed his favourite meal on the table in front of him – lamb tagine, the delicious aromas of saffron and harissa filling his nostrils. He groaned. That idiot Ray had played the role of decoy to perfection, except the part where he decided to stall Tom by going for dinner.

Ray had knocked on the front door, shamefaced, just as the inspector's heartbeat was returning to normal. He was seated now on one side of Laura, Eoin Coyle on the other. The poor girl was blushing furiously.

Sean and June McGuinness were seated next. His boss had grabbed Tom before they sat down, expressing his relief that June was having a good day. 'Otherwise, I couldn't have come and I'd have felt terrible missing your fiftieth.'

'I'm not fifty,' Tom protested.

June was regaling Anne, Michael's wife, with an unintentionally hilarious tale. The younger woman sat across from the older one, an untouched glass of champagne in front of her. Louise had insisted she have one but as the designated driver for several guards, Anne was taking no risks.

Brian, Bridget and Ian Kelly were present, as was Willie Callaghan, who was attending to his wife Therese's every need. It was obvious to everybody around the table that the man worshipped the small blonde woman, despite his great act of throwing his eyes to heaven as though he'd brought her along under sufferance.

If the guest list had ended there, it would have been fine. Louise had told him before dinner that this was a small party with his friends (and as he worked all the time, that meant people from work). A bigger celebration for their extended circle was planned for December.

With two parties in the offing, Tom couldn't understand why she'd thought it was a good idea to invite Emmet McDonagh and Linda McCarn to the same one. Was it pure mischief on the part of his wife? Louise knew Linda outside of Tom's work – the criminal psychologist had been one of her lecturers when his wife was studying law. And she knew full well about the animosity between Linda and the forensic scientist.

Emmet was wearing his best suit and a glower that would

curdle milk. Linda was wearing a headache-inducing sparkling silver evening gown and seemed deliriously happy.

She sat to one side of Tom's chair at the top of the table, Emmet to the other. The inspector was afraid to make eye contact with either. He felt like a minnow trying to keep the peace between two sharks.

Not that they were paying him any attention. They were busy competing with each other to prove who could be the most entertaining and outgoing dinner guest, their jokes and stories gaining more forced gusto and frivolity as the meal progressed.

Linda grabbed his arm.

'You must eat, darling. Your wife put so much effort into this meal. There's no point watching your figure at your age. Life begins at fifty – enjoy yourself.'

'I'm not fifty,' Tom repeated wearily. 'But, yes, thank you, Louise. It's a beautiful meal. You need to chastise your lackey there for getting me something to eat beforehand.'

Everyone booed while Ray murmured an apology.

'In my defence, the old fart wanted to go home to bed at half four,' he argued.

'This is how it starts,' Emmet tutted. 'In bed by 6 p.m. and the only thing he'll want to warm him is a cup of tea and a hot water bottle. You poor thing, Louise.'

'Oh, he's been like that for years,' Louise quipped. Everybody laughed. Tom was starting to wonder if this was a birthday party or a good old-fashioned roast.

'Where is *your* wife, by the way?' Linda asked, eyeballing Emmet. She smiled, but there was ice behind it.

'Where's your husband?' Emmet snapped.

'You look lovely tonight, Linda,' Tom interjected, to prevent a spat. 'Very . . . elegant.'

He'd felt the usual astonishment when he'd seen her get-up for the evening. The sequined, shoulder-padded silver dress wouldn't have been out of place in an '80s American soap opera. She'd paired the disco-ball gown with blinged-up Adidas runners and looked a little like a background dancer in a Run-D.M.C. music video. Her hair was unadorned – not that the wild brown cork-screw curls needed any decoration.

'I'm like a swan, darling. Gliding on top, but ready to work it underneath. With my height, stilettos are simply too intimidating for men. Isn't that right, Emmet?'

'What?'

'You're intimidated by women, aren't you?'

'Linda, I meant to ask you something.' Tom spoke before Emmet could retaliate.

'Oh darling, it happens to all men over a certain age. Your man over there will tell you.'

'What? Jesus, Linda. I want to talk to you about the case.'

'It's your birthday, you shouldn't be working.' She feigned indignation.

'Well, my fake birthday has fallen in the middle of a real murder investigation. You said you didn't like Aidan for his politics. Fair enough. But I got the feeling when we met him that he doesn't like you back. What's that about?'

'Well, his life's work is maintaining the perfect persona he's created – the handsome, strong minister; beautiful wife; impressive home; amazing career. He's a master of spin and I see through that crap. He's just a power-hungry little pup.'

'What's his relationship like with his wife?'

'Honestly, Tom, I wasn't joking. I know Sara better than I know Blake, so I can't speak authoritatively on this.'

That was interesting. Linda, who knew most people's secrets, was admitting she didn't know Blake's.

'They don't have any children but I got the impression she'd like some,' the inspector pushed. 'Do you think everything is okay in the bedroom department, or is he taking it elsewhere?'

'Heavens, Tom.' Linda guffawed. 'You're making me blush. I don't know. I haven't got cameras set up over their bed. I'm sure Sara does want children. She's devoted her life to them. I did hear a rumour, actually, that they can't have any. That they've tried. But I can't verify that. It could have just been nasty gossip because the Blakes seem to have everything else. To be honest, it's probably no bad thing. Sara could do better. She's a decent skin. I'm not sure I could say the same for Aidan. I imagine she got on quite well with that Finnegan chap, especially if he was putting it up to her husband.'

'How would Aidan feel if she had an affair – if his perfect image was being threatened?'

Linda puckered her lips and raised an eyebrow.

'Oh, murderous, I'd say.'

'Do you think their relationship is strong enough to withstand the worst – would she provide him with an alibi if he'd done something wrong?'

'Like actually murder somebody?'

Tom shrugged.

'I'm not sure, is the answer.' Linda inclined her head as she thought. 'They're married, with all of the complicated emotions that brings. If he asked her to lie for him in the heat of the moment, she may have felt she had to. And having done that, she might feel like she has no choice but to keep lying. She would be thinking about her job and the ramifications.'

Tom paused for a moment before he asked the next question. It was one of many outlandish possibilities that had been playing on his mind.

'Linda, do you think Sara Blake would kill somebody for her husband?'

CHAPTER 20

Darragh McNally's head felt fuzzy. It was like a blanket had been wrapped around his brain, muffling the sounds of the world and blurring his vision.

It wasn't an uncomfortable feeling. Years ago, if he had drunk this much, the desensitising effects of the alcohol would have been countered by the weight of his guilt. There was no need to feel remorse now. It didn't matter if he drank. There was nobody left to worry about him and nobody in this world he cared about.

Anyhow, he had a plan and he needed the alcohol to give him the courage to carry it out.

Darragh swayed slightly as he stood to fetch a fresh bottle from the cabinet in the corner of his living room. He'd bought the half-litres of whiskey yesterday in three different shops – a hangover (ha!) from his drinking days, when he had tried to hide his habit by buying little and often. He refilled his glass then returned to lying on the couch. He was drinking it neat. No ice, no mixer. He could almost hear his liver screaming for mercy. The doctors had told him just before he stopped drinking that he had been tipping into cirrhosis territory. Darragh had already guessed. The skin on his palms had begun to yellow. His mother had asked how many cigarettes he smoked before suggesting that maybe he was drinking too much.

Darragh had felt so ashamed.

No. Enough of that.

He couldn't be mawkish tonight, even if that was where the booze wanted him to go. He needed a degree of clear-headedness.

A noise announced itself – muted, as though from a long way down a tunnel. He raised his head from the couch and felt the room spin.

There it was again. Rapping on a door. His door.

Who would be calling at this hour?

Darragh stood up slowly, finding his balance. It was amazing, really, his tolerance for alcohol. Even now, after so many years dry. He could drink enough to float a small boat and still function – partially, anyway.

He stumbled into the hall, driven by curiosity. Maybe this was the distraction he needed to prevent him acting on his intentions. A chance at redemption.

It was only as he was lifting his hand to turn the latch that he noticed the outline of the man through the stained glass window. A familiar figure. He suddenly felt a sense of danger.

It was too late. His hand had worked automatically, his brain not sending the signal to stop the action fast enough.

McNally clutched the open door and stared at the man, knowing this wouldn't end well.

'You,' he slurred, suppressing a hiccup. 'What the hell do you want?'

*

'Do I think Sara Blake would murder somebody for Aidan?'

The psychologist repeated Tom's question, paused, then shook her head adamantly.

'No, I don't. Being willing to lie for a man is a far cry from being willing to kill for him. Sara is no fool. She's a shrewd, capable, and compassionate woman. She might be a supportive wife but she's her own person and has her own career and dreams. We live in different times – her future does not depend on her being happily married and her husband being a paragon of virtue.

'If Aidan Blake got himself involved in something desperate, she could just extricate herself. She'd survive it. But you might be onto something with your earlier point. If Blake had asked her to give him a false alibi, maybe she was panicked into a bad move or maybe she even believed him. Maybe he told her something serious enough to be convincing, like he was with another woman or something. Perhaps she's in denial that the man she shares a life with could be capable of anything worse than that. I'd keep checking in with her if I were you, because if he did it, and she suspects, she'll crack. She was fond of that Ryan fellow and she won't jeopardise her charity for Blake. Not once she's had time to think.'

Tom was conscious they'd been monopolising each other's company. Everybody at the table was eating contentedly, but as the main man, he'd have to re-engage soon. He had needed to voice the Sara theory aloud, even though her alibi had been verified by several people. He agreed with Linda, though. He had seen enough of the minister's wife to sense she wouldn't kill somebody for her husband.

'You know Darragh McNally's mother just died?' he said, moving on. 'They seem to have been very close.'

'I heard. I'd say she was the only person in his life he was ever close to. He's been too busy mowing people down in his quest to get to the top to give a damn about anybody else.'

'He has depression, apparently.'

'So would I, if I were him.'

Linda, blunt as ever.

'Shane Morrison had to drive him home yesterday. He was in a bad state.'

'That's Morrison. He loves a victim.'

'You know him, too? What do you mean by that?'

'Of course I know him. He's been around Leinster House for aeons. The man loves being in charge. He's at his happiest when he's the knight in shining armour. Especially for the ladies, mind. He's not married, you know. It would have ruined his fun.'

'His fun?' Tom repeated. 'Actually, have you heard of a place called The – '

'I've never had erectile dysfunction in my life,' Emmet belatedly interjected, banging on the table and casting the psychologist a foul look. He'd just realised her earlier comment about it 'happening to all men over a certain age' was directed at him.

'Aren't there any presents at this party?' Tom practically shouted, attempting to forestall an argument about penile deficiency.

'Oh, but it's not your actual birthday,' Louise remarked caustically.

'Anyone who doesn't have a gift can leave now,' Tom declared.

Emmet was the first to stump up. The inspector unwrapped a pack of Diplomaticos cigars, Cuba's finest.

'Perfect!' Tom enthused. 'They must have cost you a pretty penny. Thanks, Emmet.'

McDonagh waved his hand dismissively.

'You might share one with me later. I think I'll need it after tonight.'

Generous with the Diplomaticos, not so good with the diplomacy, Tom thought.

He received his remaining gifts graciously, nearly falling off the chair when Louise handed him a card with a brochure for Cuba inside.

'I thought next summer,' she said. 'You can stock up on cigars in person.'

Tom grabbed her around the waist and kissed her, to the cheers of the table.

'A toast!' Maria cried, raising her glass unsteadily. 'To my dad. Half a century old.'

'Not yet,' Tom rebuked, but joined in the celebratory drink. He could do with skipping dessert and having a coffee. As could his neighbour. Linda was pouring drink down her throat like it was the elixir of life.

'You won't find happiness at the bottom of that glass, hag,' Emmet muttered.

'No, but I will find blurred vision,' Linda retorted, her hearing perfect. 'And you are sat across from me, you old codger.'

'You'd never think you two had been an item.'

June's interjection with the unmentionable was met with stunned silence.

'Good God, who gave you champagne?' McGuinness moved to take the half-empty glass from his wife's hand.

'I think that was mine,' Anne said, embarrassed.

'You shouldn't be drinking. Not on your medication.' McGuinness stretched for the flute but June held it away from him.

'Fiddle-cock.'

'What?' McGuinness spluttered.

'Oh, you know what I mean. Fiddlesticks, poppycock. Whatever. Don't worry, I wasn't being rude. Who's the dotty one here?'

The chief flushed red to the roots of his grey hair.

'Louise!' Tom yelled, desperate to create a diversion. This was the hardest he'd ever worked at a birthday party. 'I think we need coffees.'

'And some cake,' Louise said, leaving the room with Maria.

'She started it,' Emmet muttered in Linda's direction.

'*She* has a name, and you started it with your puerile insults. Hag, indeed! You used to have another name for me, need I remind you?' Linda retorted.

'Bitch?' Emmet snarled.

'Okay, that's enough,' Tom snapped. 'You two, give it a rest.'

'See what you did?' Linda hissed. 'You've ruined his birthday.'

'When the lights came on and he saw you, the evening was already tainted.'

'Stop!' Tom pleaded.

Thankfully, he didn't have to say any more, as Louise and Maria returned holding a cake lit up by the brilliant glow of fifty candles and leading the chorus of 'Happy Birthday'. The inspector almost expired with relief. He waited for the rounds of 'For he's a jolly good fellow' to finish and leaned forward to blow out the candles.

The clapping died down. Louise was about to ask who wanted a slice when a further interruption from June silenced her. The older woman had turned to her husband, a puzzled expression on her face.

'Is it someone's birthday? Did we bring a present?'

*

'I'd no idea things were that bad. God love Sean. Is he still working full-time?' Louise finished applying lavender-scented cream to her face and neck and lay down beside her husband, fluffing the pillows and wriggling down the bed until she was comfortable.

'Yep. It's a bad time to ask for leave.'

Tom turned over on his side and studied his wife's profile. Louise's eyes were fixed on the ceiling, her brow creased with concern.

'I should go over more.'

'We both should. Sean won't ask for help but he needs it.'

'I couldn't bear it.' Louise turned to him. 'I saw it with my granddad. When he died, my gran said it would have been better if he'd been hit by a bus or had a massive heart attack. She spent years providing round-the-clock care for a man she'd loved all her life and he didn't even know who she was.'

Tom stroked his wife's cheek.

Louise exhaled loudly and kissed his palm.

'Did you enjoy tonight?'

'As much as any man who's been unwillingly aged could.'

'Oh, get over it.'

'Why in God's name did you invite both Emmet and Linda? Don't you know I spend most of my working life trying to make sure they're never in the same room?'

Louise giggled.

'I'm serious. You weren't stuck sitting between them. I knew you were up to mischief. You're really fond of Linda, aren't you? I mean, I like her alright, but half the time I think she's bloody nuts.'

'She isn't.'

'Really? You should have seen the outfit she almost wasn't wearing when we were in her house on Sunday. Poor Ray didn't know where to look.'

Louise shook her head.

'You really don't get it, do you?'

'What?'

'She plays mind games. That's her thing. She's eccentric – I'll give you that. But she's not some wanton woman, overcome with lust every time she sees a man. Tell Ray he's safe.'

'She plays the part very well.'

'That's exactly what she's doing. Acting. She zones in on what disturbs a person, what makes them uncomfortable, and she adopts that characteristic. If you're unsettled, she's in control of the interaction. She obviously has you and Ray pegged as two frigid prudes.'

Tom blinked. Was that what the psychologist was doing? Prodding his subconscious like he was a specimen in a lab?

'Well, whatever. I really thought those two were going to kill each other tonight, though. I'd love to find out what the hell happened between them.'

Louise turned to face him.

'Don't you know?'

Tom leaned up on his elbow.

'No. Nobody at the station does.'

'Hmm.'

'Hold on a minute. That's a very loaded "hmm". Do you know something? You do, don't you? How on earth . . . ?'

'I just asked. At one of your work Christmas parties as it happens, a couple of years ago.'

'I've asked and I was told to keep my nose out. You've known for two years? Bloody hell, Louise. You're good at keeping secrets, aren't you?'

'Huh.' His wife bit her bottom lip.

'Don't you dare not tell me. I've considered investing team resources to figure this one out. We're not leaving this room until I get a confession.'

Louise took a deep breath.

'I'll kill you if you breathe a word of this. It's obviously more hush-hush than I thought. You know they had the affair, then?'

'That's common knowledge. Their poor spouses.'

'Well, they were madly in love. I mean, crazy, passionate, fiery, red-hot . . .'

'Enough! You're searing images onto my brain.'

'I think Linda has you down pat, Mr Puritanical. All right then, they were *very* attached to each other. But Linda comes from a certain type of family.'

'The strange type?'

'You missed your vocation as a comedian, do you know that? Linda's family has money and they also have very set opinions. When her father entered politics, it was Linda's mother's job to be his faithful rock. She raised their family and supported him at every turn. Not so unusual for the day, but they also believed their daughters should follow suit. Linda was indulged when she decided to study psychology. That she specialised in criminality upset them, but they presumed when she got married she'd settle down and leave all that grubby police work behind.' Louise smiled as Tom flashed her an indignant look.

'Anyway, she met Geoff and he wasn't short of a few bob, but she was adamant about continuing with her career. Geoff stood with her in defying her family's expectation that she become a stay-at-home mommy and society belle.'

Tom chuckled at the idea of a domesticated Linda. An image filled his head of her vacuuming while drinking a Long Island Iced Tea, a cigarette hanging out of the corner of her lips and tots hanging onto her rake-thin legs.

'But they couldn't have been that shocked,' he interjected. 'Anybody who knows Linda can see she's not cut out for day-time TV and pram-pushing. And this must have been – when? The early '80s? Women were entering the work force in their droves.'

'Are you listening to me at all? Not from Linda's class, not women of her background. Don't make assumptions based on your experience of the world, Tom.'

'Fair enough. She has a set of balls on her. What has that got to do with her having an affair with Emmet, though?'

'Oh, pet. The only thing Linda's family would consider worse than her not fulfilling her marital duties was a failed marriage. She fell in love with Emmet and told her parents she was going to leave Geoff. She was informed in no uncertain terms that she would be utterly ostracised by her family if she did. And, while Linda loves her mother, she utterly adored her father.'

'I'd gathered that. I thought he was a progressive man. Hardly somebody to sever ties with his daughter for the sake of what the neighbours might think.'

Louise tutted.

'Progressive politically, maybe. Not in his personal life.'

'Okay, so threatened with being cast from the bosom of her family, what did Linda do?'

'She forged ahead with the plan. She and Emmet agreed to come clean to their respective spouses.'

'And what happened?'

'Linda told her husband and packed a bag. Went through all the recriminations, the tears and screaming rows. She broke Geoff's heart in two, the man who had taken her hand when she stood up to her family the first time. And then Emmet welched on the deal.'

'What do you mean?'

'He refused to leave his wife. Said he couldn't do it to her.'

Tom gawped at Louise. Emmet was his friend. He'd known him for years but he hadn't known this. There must have been a good reason for his change of heart.

'What happened then?' he asked, enthralled and aghast in equal measure.

'Linda was heartbroken. Her husband – and the man is a saint – forgave her and begged her to come back. She agreed. But her parents didn't talk to her for five years.'

'Jesus. She's never said anything. Hold on – isn't her father dead?'

'Yes. He died without seeing her and she had to beg to be allowed to attend the funeral. They only permitted it because there would have been talk if she'd been missing. Age, and probably the absence of the father, has mellowed her mother. They have a relationship now but it's never been the same.'

Tom was speechless. He had never felt anything for Linda other than a grudging professional respect and irritation at her amateur dramatics. Now, he felt overcome with sympathy for the woman. She'd talked so fondly of her father when they'd met in her house recently.

'I don't understand one thing,' he said finally. 'Linda and Emmet are as bad as each other when they're together. Why is Emmet not filled with remorse for what he did to her? Why does he pick at her? If he's completely in the wrong, why is he so offensive?'

'He has cause. After a couple of months, the combination of the heartbreak and being cut off from her family made Linda bitter. She told me she drank a half litre of vodka one night, then got a cab to his house. She banged down the door until his wife came out. Linda told her loud enough for all the neighbours to hear that she'd been screwing her husband, he'd been about to leave her, what a cowardly shit he was, etc., etc.'

'I can imagine that wasn't very pleasant for Emmet but what did he expect? That she'd just slink off into the night?'

'He was an arsehole but, it seems, not a total one,' Louise continued. 'He'd decided to stay with his wife for good reason but hadn't the bloody cop-on to tell Linda what that was. Maybe he was in shock, maybe his wife didn't want anybody knowing, or maybe he just likes drama. Anyway, his wife had breast cancer. And when Linda went around shouting the odds, she'd just finished a bout of chemo.'

'Oh.'

'Yes. I don't think he and his wife have really ever got over it. I'm pretty sure he's there out of guilt and I think she makes him stay to punish him. Everybody knows he still has little flings, though nothing as serious as what he had with Linda. So, there you have it. Emmet and Linda have inflicted so much heartache on one another that they can't help themselves when they meet. But they need to put the past behind them. They're two lovely people and circumstances conspired to ruin something that might have been very special. They need to be angry at that, not at each other.'

It all made sense to Tom now. The cutting jibes, the nasty remarks. What a tragedy. And at least Emmet had some redeeming part in the story. Tom had been really worried his friend had slipped irrevocably in his esteem.

'You've a good heart, Louise,' he said. 'But I don't think even you can fix this one.'

'It's worth a try.'

His wife snuggled into his chest and Tom inhaled the scents of her soft hair – coconut shampoo and hairspray.

'There is something that bothers me about Linda's story, though,' Louise said.

'Hmm?'

'I'm not sure she told me everything.'

'What makes you say that?'

'I don't know. It's just, I feel there's something else to it. I don't know what the catalyst was for her wanting to leave her husband. She's Catholic to the brainwashed core and she had the family pressure – why not quietly maintain the affair? Why bring everything out in the open?'

'She's Linda, isn't she? She doesn't do things without theatrics. And maybe Geoff isn't the saint you think he is.'

'Hmm.' His wife sounded unconvinced.

Tom's eyelids were growing heavy. Louise would have to solve her Linda riddle herself, if there was anything more to it. He was drifting off to sleep when a little part of his brain started to niggle. Somebody had said something during dinner that had jogged his memory about the case. Or was it that someone had done something? What was it?

He was still wracking his brains long after Louise had started gently snoring.

He had missed some clue to do with Ryan Finnegan's murder. But he couldn't for the life of him work out what it was.

CHAPTER 21

Thursday

'What do we have?' Tom addressed his team, then took a gulp of water to wash down the headache tablets.

A dinner party in the middle of an investigation. What had his wife been thinking? What had his boss and colleagues been thinking?

The team was already gathered in the incident room when the inspector arrived. To a man and woman they seemed full of the joys and especially eager this morning. The racket as several detectives clamoured to speak at once nearly sent him over the edge.

'One at a time, for the love of God! Laura.'

'We've had a development. We did a background check on one of the Dáil bar patrons on Friday night – Damien Reid. Wait until you hear this: it turns out he worked for Udforske. Not in Ireland, but when he lived in Denmark, ten years ago. He worked as a safety officer on board one of their offshore drill stations. He was quite sketchy about his background in his interview. He was asked how long he'd been operating his own company and he wouldn't give an exact date.'

'Who interviewed him?' Tom asked. 'It seems a bit above and beyond, going ten years back because he was vague about his work history.'

'Eoin Coyle,' Laura said. 'He just had a suspicion there was something off about the guy.'

'Coyle – ace lover by night, super sleuth by day,' Michael quipped, winking at Laura.

She blushed furiously.

'Udforske is a multinational company with thousands of employees,' Ray interrupted quickly. 'We probably all know somebody who has worked for them. And didn't the TDs vouch that all their guests stayed in the bar?'

Laura barely looked at him as she replied.

'On your first point, yes, Udforske has thousands of employees, but not all of them were awarded merit plaques for bravery from Madsen himself. Damien Reid was one of a small team who helped to prevent a fire taking hold on the Ulysses oil rig off the coast of Denmark in 1998. He helped save hundreds of lives and the company gave him a special award. Madsen and the CEO presented the plaques themselves and brought the safety crew out for a special thank-you dinner.'

Tom frowned.

'This guy was in the bar? Madsen never said anything. I knew there was something he wasn't telling us when we interviewed him . . . I got the feeling he hadn't been entirely alone that night.'

'Reid was with a delegation from Galway,' Laura said. 'They were making a presentation about marine entrepreneurships at the invite of their local Reform Party TD, Jarlath O'Keefe. He brought them to the bar afterwards. The TD is already wavering on his story. Bridget spoke to one of the barmen who told her O'Keefe was drunk as a skunk on Friday night. She questioned the man himself this morning and he admitted he hadn't been keeping tabs on everybody as closely as he'd originally claimed.

'And here's the thing.' Laura paused. 'Damien Reid has a gun licence.'

Tom felt a shiver of excitement. Could this be the development they were waiting for?

'Well, let's talk to Reid. He sounds like an unlikely assassin, but that's too big a coincidence to ignore. Okay. Next. Ray?'

'You're not going to like this bit as much. Grace Brady lied. And our lads checking the CCTV footage cocked up. Don't worry, I've already had words. Grace did leave the complex at 8 on Friday. But she returned at 8.55 p.m. One of the uniforms checking the footage noted her departure. A different guard spotted her re-entering – but, and here's the clanger – he assumed the first guy had caught it. It was only when a third officer went over the information that had been compiled that we spotted Grace had left and gone back in, contrary to her statement.'

'Ah, for crying out loud! That is taking the biscuit. How did none of the ushers at the entrance spot her coming back in?'

'Shift change.'

'Typical. There's always something. Right. I want to take this Reid fellow. I have a bad feeling about Madsen and want to follow up. Laura, go back and scare the bejaysus out of Grace Brady. What time did she actually leave the complex?'

'10 p.m.'

Tom groaned. What a nest of liars they'd stumbled upon.

'Jesus. Arrest her for lying during an investigation or something. And if she has no alibi, bang her in a cell. Is she capable of having done this?'

Laura shrugged. 'As capable as a government minister or a vice-president of a multinational company.'

'God, let it be Damien Reid, the paid assassin. I want to get out of this rabbit hole. Next. Michael?'

'I was following up on Ryan's car crash. The investigation team at the time had no luck finding the other driver and vehicle, even though the accident report suggested the second car would have been quite banged up. A witness said she saw a dark blue saloon speeding down the side street that intersected the junction where Ryan's car was stopped at lights. It's a residential street and she noticed the car because the area is used as a bit of a rat run. Local homeowners – she is one – want the council to install speed ramps to stop cars racing down the road.'

'How could the driver have known Ryan would be sitting at the lights at that junction?'

'We have a theory. The lights are at a crossing between a school and a church. Apparently, they're very pedestrian friendly – they give road crossers plenty of time. There are a number of streets off that main road and they interlink. If someone had been following Ryan and was familiar with the area, they just had to see him stop at the red light, turn up one side street and come down the other. He'd have been still sitting there. Ryan told the investigating officer that this was his usual route to work and that he always left home at 6.30 a.m., before the traffic got too busy. If somebody was determined to kill him and make it look like an accident, they only had to follow him for a few mornings until they got lucky.'

Tom massaged his temples. The headache tablets were kicking in. He could feel the pain receding.

'It seems a reckless way to attempt murder, especially if you want to get away with it. Wouldn't the killer be at risk of injuring himself or being identified?'

Michael shrugged.

'That's less likely to happen if you're controlling the impact of the collision and I suppose they could have claimed it was an accident, their brakes went or something like that. Or maybe our murderer is suicidal.'

There were a couple of titters around the room until Tom barked for order.

'We really are having a morning of breakthroughs. It certainly looks like Ryan could have been previously targeted. Ian, get whatever CCTV footage you can dig up from around the scene of the accident. Have somebody help you – actually, get the two officers who made a balls-up of the Leinster House tapes. They'll be bursting to prove themselves now. The original investigating team probably sought out footage from where the other driver fled the scene but check along Ryan's entire route for that day and in the days preceding. If he was being followed and we're really lucky, we might catch a licence plate. Anything else?'

'We saved the best until last,' Ray said. 'I checked out the care home that Darragh McNally had his mother in. It's a five-star set-up, privately run, attended by top clinicians. It has beauty therapists, a masseuse, etc., etc. It's only lacking its own Michelin-star chef. Have a guess at the cost.'

'No idea. A grand a month?'

'Two thousand euro per week.'

'You're kidding.' Tom was astonished.

Ray shook his head.

'Top end of the market, like you said. That's what they charge. His mother was in that nursing home for four years. She did run a farm, but it was leased and she gave it up fifteen years ago. She had a little cottage, which McNally sold for €150,000 when she went into the home – boom-time prices. The cost of his mother's care over the last four years ran in excess of €400,000. Up to the election, his salary was sixty thousand annually. We've applied for a warrant for his bank records.'

'Good work. While we're waiting for the warrant, let's question him again and put what we've discovered to him. McNally might just be in a place where he'll admit to taking bribes from somebody like Carl Madsen, which would put him in the frame to want Ryan Finnegan out of the way.'

Tom assigned the follow-up work and watched as his team members, all except Ray, left to pursue their tasks. That was an excellent morning's work, by any standards. Maybe he could take up full-time drinking and hangovers after all.

'This Reid fella who worked for Udforske?' Tom asked.

'He's in Dublin for the week,' his deputy responded.

'Good. Get him in. We'll leave Darragh McNally until later. I'm in a terrible mood and you've all performed too well today to take it out on you. Mr Reid can bear the brunt. I'm bringing in Linda McCarn for this interview. She's really growing on me.'

Ray raised a surprised eyebrow, but knew enough to make no remarks.

There was always logic to his boss's decisions.

Usually, anyway.

*

Damien Reid looked an unlikely hitman. Bespectacled and with a neat beard, he was dressed in chinos and a corduroy jacket. The inspector would have tagged him as a college professor, educated and affable. Indeed, after a short time in his company, Tom found himself rather liking the man.

It was the similarities in interests that did it. Reid had arrived for the interview with a paper bag from the inspector's favourite cigar shop off Grafton Street and explained that he was stocking up before he returned to Galway. They spent a few minutes talking about the brands they both liked, Reid impressing Tom with his extensive knowledge of tobacco.

After a few minutes of this enjoyable small talk, Linda passed the inspector a note.

'I hate to interrupt the bromance but can you wrap up so we can start the interview? I thought I was your new friend. You're making me jealous.'

The inspector smiled.

'Sorry, my colleague is just reminding me we need to speed things up. I know you will have been over much of this with my officers at the weekend, Mr Reid, so bear with me if the questions seem repetitive.'

'Not a problem. It's sort of thrilling to be involved in such a sensational case. I hope that doesn't make me sound insensitive.'

'That's a fairly normal reaction. Remind me, what were you and your group doing in Leinster House?'

'We were there to make a presentation to a couple of TDs on our business. We harvest seaweed and convert it to high-grade fertiliser. We've started to export and there's demand for our product. We want to franchise the business throughout the island. Try to create environmentally friendly jobs.'

'Sounds fascinating. It's a change in career for you, am I right?'

'Of a sort.' Reid smiled. 'I guess you've done your background checks on everyone. I started life in science and technology and specialised in energy resources. Seaweed is actually a biomass; it can be used as a sustainable fuel. Not our forte, though, yet. We are also looking at branching out into the specialist food market.'

Linda cleared her throat, indicating she wanted to speak. Tom motioned her to proceed.

'The sector of the energy game you were involved with before wasn't as sustainable, Mr Reid.'

'Ain't that the truth. Oil and gas are dying entities – thankfully, for the planet's sake. I knew that then and it's even truer now. My job was always in the safety end of things, ensuring that drilling was at acceptable environmental levels, that the technological equipment in use was the best industry standard and up to date, that sort of thing.'

'Thank heavens we have men like you.'

Reid blushed at Linda's remark, taking it at face value. He was unfamiliar with the psychologist's own brand of sarcasm.

Tom took up the questioning again.

'So, can you tell us about your time working for Udforske?'

'It's so long ago now,' Reid said. 'But what do you want to know?'

'You received a merit award for what you did on the Ulysses, didn't you?'

The other man bowed his head, embarrassed.

'Yes. Making sure I didn't die and saving a few other people as a by-product. How gallant of me. I don't like to brag about it.'

'Most heroes are accidental, but finding courage in that moment of crisis is what sets them apart,' Tom said. 'We noticed Carl Madsen himself presented you with your award.'

'He did, along with the president of the company. One of those rare occasions when the boss men paid a visit to us lowly employees.'

'They brought you out for a celebration dinner also, didn't they?' Linda commented.

'The president hosted the dinner. Madsen didn't go. He's notoriously strict about keeping work and pleasure separate. He'll only entertain you if there's something in it for him. An evening with employees doesn't fit that world view. A good propaganda photo does.'

'So, you only met Madsen that once, for a short period?' Tom asked.

'Yes.'

The inspector frowned.

'And you didn't notice him in the Dáil bar on Friday night?'

'The bar? Are you kidding? Madsen wouldn't be caught dead in a public bar. What would he even be doing in Leinster House?'

The other man's expression was inscrutable. There was no telltale tic, no sheen of sweat or flicker of the eyes.

And yet Tom knew the man had just lied.

'He was there,' Linda remarked, her tone implying she'd made the same assumption. 'Was the bar crowded?'

'Yes. And we were all more than a little inebriated. It had been a good presentation and we were toasting the future.'

'Did you leave the bar at any point?' the inspector continued.

'I went to the gents.'

'Tell me,' the inspector said. 'You know your stuff about natural resources. What do you think of this legislation that Minister Aidan Blake is introducing, the Bill that increases licence fees for exploration companies and royalties from their drilling? Do you know Minister Blake at all?'

'I'm afraid I don't and I don't know much about the Bill. I gave up my interest in oil and gas when I stopped working for Udforske.'

Again, Tom struggled to believe the man. He could feel Linda bristling beside him. How could Reid not have an opinion on a Bill so relevant to his field of expertise?

'When did you leave Udforske?'

'2001.'

'Was it a happy parting?'

The other man hesitated.

'To be honest, at that stage I'd become quite disillusioned with the industry and wanted to start my own business. But I didn't resign in a fit of pique or anything like that.'

Tom leaned forward, hands clasped.

'You have a firearms licence for a pistol, Mr Reid. What type of handgun do you own? And can you tell me why you applied for the licence?'

'It's nothing sinister, Inspector. I'm a member at a target shooting range. I own a Ruger Mark .22. In case you're wondering, it's in a safe in my gun club this week. I don't like leaving it in the house when I'm away for any period of time.'

'Is that the only weapon you own?'

'Yes.'

Tom held the other man's gaze, but Reid didn't even blink.

Ryan had been shot with a Glock. But it was interesting that the other man was a target-shooting enthusiast.

'I think that's everything for now, Mr Reid. Unless you've anything to add?'

Reid shook his head.

'Not that I can think of, Inspector. I plan to return to Galway tomorrow, but if I think of anything, I will let you know.'

'Please do,' Tom said.

After Reid had been escorted from the interview room, the inspector turned to Linda.

'That friendship was short-lived,' she commented. 'Do you want to talk about it?'

'Ha. The man's a consummate liar.'

'What's your theory?'

'You show me yours.'

Linda smiled.

'This is like one of those flash analysis exams we used to do for fun in college. Okay, I'm thinking on my feet here, and I don't know as much as you about this Udforske gang, so go easy, darling, but here's my guess: this fellow Reid's head is raised above the parapet in Udforske after he becomes a Ulysses hero. He stays in the company for a while, continues to do well, but is moving on to other pastures. Maybe he's telling the truth and he wanted to start his own business, harvesting seaweed. But there's not as much money in a start-up, especially not in recession-hit Ireland. And according to the file you gave me, he did wait until the recession to begin his business, oddly. He has a few lost years after he left Udforske. Didn't work in 2002, 2003, 2004, 2005. We'll call them his tobacco research years. He only started with this thing in 2006 and it wasn't listed as a company until 2007.

'So, perhaps he encountered money problems. And perhaps he contacted his former employer, Mr Madsen, who doesn't need a safety officer but does require someone for a clean-up job. Reid knows how to handle a gun, he's loyal to Udforske and willing to take on any job to pay for his new business. Including shooting a man dead. How am I doing?'

'Okay,' Tom said. 'You've a flair for this. But did you notice any blemishes on Reid's record, Sherlock?'

'No. There was nothing there to indicate he's capable of any kind of violence. In his file anyway.'

'Kind of blows a hole in your hypothesis. Hero turns killer for cash. Hardly plausible. Close, but no cigar, Columbo.'

'Good Lord, Tom, can't you name a female detective? Ever heard of Miss Marple?'

Tom contemplated the file in his hand, the background material they'd managed to pull together on Reid.

'Yet he was in that bar on Friday night and so was Madsen. Ray's on to the Danish police at the moment. Reid lived there for a few years before working on that rig. His record's clean in Ireland, but there's something he's not telling us.'

'I would agree.'

Tom thought of something. He opened the file in front of him and scanned the contents again, as he had done shortly before Reid's arrival.

There it was.

'You look all animated. What is it?' Linda asked.

'Reid said they were all inebriated on Friday night.'

'He did.'

'That merit award he got. There's an article in here about it. There was a party on the Ulysses that night for the crew and that's how things nearly got out of hand. The drilling operation wasn't fully manned when everything went pear-shaped. But a couple of safety officers and one or two crew members managed to get everything under control before the Ulysses could light up the night sky.'

'And?'

'And Reid was at the party. But luckily, he was sober.'

Linda paused for a moment.

'Ahhhh,' she said, the light dawning. 'I saw the article. Damien Reid is a recovered alcoholic. The piece was all about his triumph over adversity.'

'Yes. He got on the wagon in 1990. The company had all that on his record because he barely passed the necessary criteria to be a safety officer. One of the things they look for is a clean bill of health – physical and mental. His dedication to sobriety won over in the end. So, it would be a bit odd if he was downing pints last Friday, don't you think?'

Linda nodded.

'Yes. Very odd indeed.'

*

'We know for a fact you re-entered Government Buildings on Friday evening. You lied to the police, Ms Brady, which is a criminal offence in itself. I strongly suggest you tell us the truth now.'

Laura kept her tone even. She was attempting to go in easy, sensing if they went too hard at Grace Brady she'd clam up out of spite. But it was difficult.

Grace glared at her inquisitor, her eyes narrowed in dislike. She turned to Michael, ignoring Laura.

'I remember now. I had left my bag in my office and ran back in to get it. Silly me.'

'No,' Laura sighed. 'You didn't. The CCTV footage captured you going back in with your bag on your arm. Grace, this is serious. Now, I'll ask you again, what time did you leave the complex?'

The woman raised an eyebrow and continued to pick at the skin around her nails. They were in her apartment, a one-bed poky affair near Fairview Park. Grace was on extended sick leave from her job, allegedly because of the stress caused by the events of Friday evening. Laura had noted the gym bag dumped in the hall and Grace was in workout gear. She was clearly exercising through her anxiety.

'This is harassment. It's six days since he was murdered and you still haven't arrested anyone. Yet, you're here annoying me, and I'm on sick leave. I'm going to complain to your boss. And to Shane Morrison. He won't be happy to know you're upsetting me.'

'We are on the verge of arresting someone,' Michael said.

'Yeah? Who?'

'You. If you don't amend your statement and give us a truthful account of your movements on Friday night, we will arrest you for obstructing the course of justice.'

'You wouldn't dare.'

'As you rightly point out, everyone is waiting for us to bring someone in and our boss gave us clear instructions to charge you. My colleague and I are affording you as much leeway as you can hope for, but if you can't give us a rational explanation for your behaviour, you are in a lot of trouble.'

Grace's eyes started to water.

'I want to talk to the other detective, the one *she* brought with her to my sister's house.'

Laura coolly examined her own fingernails. How predictable. Ray hadn't been any kinder to Grace, but he was better looking than Michael.

'Sure. We can bring you down to the station. Detective Lennon will be busy until later, but I'm sure you won't mind waiting in the custody suite. He should be free before the evening is out.'

Grace's eyes flicked between the two detectives before settling on Laura, the lesser of two evils in this instance.

'Fine,' she said. 'Fine, fine, fine.'

Laura leaned forward, all ears.

'I went back in to warn Ryan.'

'Warn him about what?'

'I knew he was up to something. He and Aidan had a falling out and Ryan was planning something. I heard them shouting in Aidan's office. I couldn't hear exactly what they were saying but I heard Ryan say he would do something to hurt Aidan. I don't know what.

'He'd been away for a few months; Ryan didn't realise that Minister Blake was no longer his pal. He's no one's pal. The only thing he cares about is his career. He uses people, then discards them when he's finished. I wanted to tell Ryan to think carefully about his actions.'

'And did you?'

'No. He was gone by the time I got back to the office.'

'Why didn't you just ring him?' Michael said. 'You'd left the building at that stage. Why the sense of urgency?'

Grace twitched.

'I don't know. Maybe I had a premonition or something.'

'Did you speak to anybody?'

There was a tiny hesitation before Grace's answer.

'No.'

'And what time did you leave?'

'Just before 10 p.m. I didn't go out through Government Buildings. I took the Kildare Street exit from Leinster House so I could pick up dinner in Marks and Sparks.'

'You didn't leave until 10? What were you doing until then?'

'Nothing. Just . . . sitting in the office.'

Laura studied the other woman, her mind spinning with possibilities. Not having an alibi was insufficient cause to charge her with Ryan's murder, regardless of Tom's angry throwaway remark earlier.

Ray had been right, though. Grace Brady was still hiding something from them.

The question was, what?

CHAPTER 22

Tom had tried to get hold of Carl Madsen several times, first on his mobile, then through his company headquarters. In the end he left a curt message with the man's secretary demanding the vice-president ring him immediately.

Having failed to make contact, the inspector instead summoned the Galway TD Jarlath O'Keefe to headquarters. The man, inadvertently or not, had given all his guests in Leinster House an alibi for Friday night, among them the less than truthful Damien Reid.

O'Keefe was waiting for him in the interview room, his foot tapping nervously on the floor. Tom recognised him instantly, not from any previous encounter, but because of the younger man's larger than life moustache. It was such an unusual feature, trimmed as it was in a bizarre handlebar fashion.

It was a clever way, Tom thought, for the backbench government TD to stand out. Throw in his dapper pinstripe suit and the man cut quite a striking figure. The downside was it was difficult to take him seriously.

'You know why I asked you to come in,' Tom said. The inspector was alone. He'd offered Linda the opportunity to sit in on the meeting with O'Keefe but she'd declined with a rather half-baked excuse. He had thought it odd, but didn't press her.

O'Keefe gave an embarrassed grin. Underneath the moustache, he was a handsome man, with amiable, open features.

'I have an idea why,' the TD answered. 'I think you may have had a word with one of the bartenders from Friday night and he might have told you about the state I was in. When your guys interviewed me I said I'd been keeping a close eye on all my guests that evening, when clearly I was not in an entirely professional state. My PA tells me I sang the entirety of "The Fields of Athenry" with my eyes squeezed shut, so that's a fair few minutes at least when I wasn't watching the group.'

Tom raised an eyebrow. The other man seemed to think this was all a big joke.

O'Keefe waited for Tom to say something, then, realising the charm offensive wasn't going to work, changed tack.

He adopted a solemn demeanour.

'I am sorry, Inspector, that I wasn't more forthcoming in my first interview. I'm afraid the reality and gravity of what had happened didn't dawn on me immediately. It seemed so utterly ludicrous. My instinct was not, "How can I best help with this investigation?" It was, "Oh crap. I was responsible for seven people last night. Seven potential witnesses and I was as pissed as a fart." I know it sounds awful, but I was putting my reputation above the important work you have to do.'

'I appreciate you saying that, Deputy,' the inspector said. 'And I can understand you were embarrassed to admit you were drunk in charge. Now all the cards are on the table, let's start at the beginning, shall we? This group you brought to the Dáil. Why were they there?'

O'Keefe relaxed his shoulders.

'They're from my constituency in Galway,' he said. 'They've got this great company, converting seaweed to fertiliser. I invited them to make a cross-party presentation in the audio-visual room on the sustainable and economic benefits of the business. Fascinating stuff.'

'So you invited them? Nobody approached you and requested you bring them to the Dáil?'

The TD screwed up his eyes in concentration as he tried to recall the exact circumstances of the invite being extended.

'I had met a couple of the fellows before, when we were canvassing during the election. They asked if I could organise a trip to Leinster House. I said I would bring them up when the new government was formed. I determined the date. I wasn't contacted about any specific time or even month. Last Friday suited my calendar commitments. It wasn't ideal. Most of my colleagues go home on a Thursday evening, but as it happened there were enough people around that day for me to fill a room for a half hour. Probably because of that charity event. I arranged a tour of the House that afternoon and then brought the group to the bar.'

'Had you met Damien Reid before?'

'Yes.'

'Do you know him well?'

'Only in a business capacity and I wouldn't say well. He seems a likeable chap.'

Yes, Tom thought. That had been his initial impression, too.

'Was he drinking on Friday night?'

O'Keefe shook his head.

'I can categorically say that he wasn't. I paid for all the drinks. All Damien had was orange juice.'

'You seem very certain of that.'

'I'm positive. When I know someone in my company is stone cold sober, it tempers me somewhat. Does that make sense?'

'It does, yes. But you've told us already that you might have lapsed in your . . . eh, hosting skills.' That was a delicate way of putting it. 'Could any of your guests have been absent for a period without you realising?'

O'Keefe stroked the edges of his moustache.

'I've given this a lot of thought since the weekend, Inspector. Yes, I'd consumed a large quantity of alcohol on Friday, but I can hold my liquor. I would never get so drunk that I would do or say anything that would jeopardise my position. I might have been economical with the truth in terms of how closely I was watching everybody, but I genuinely don't think anybody from my group went missing for any length of time.'

The inspector changed tack.

'Did you know the man who was killed, Deputy?'

O'Keefe shrugged.

'Enough to make polite small talk with him. He gave a couple of policy briefings at party meetings. He seemed intelligent, very passionate.'

'You don't move in the same circles as Aidan Blake, then?'

The TD smiled.

'I'm just a lowly backbencher, Inspector. Aidan Blake has a halo and glides on water. He condescends to give me a polite word and a handshake when he's passing, but that's the extent of it.'

'Are you in the O'Shea camp, then?' Tom continued. 'You're not aligned with those who would like to see Minister Blake become the next Taoiseach?'

O'Keefe shifted uncomfortably, as if he feared there might be a camera in the room recording his answer.

'You can speak freely,' Tom said. 'I'm only latterly aware of your party's inner workings; I haven't taken a side yet.' He smiled, to show he intended the exchange to be informal.

The twinkle was back in O'Keefe's eye.

'Cormac O'Shea gets a hard time in the media and sometimes for good reason,' he said. 'But he didn't get where he is without knowing how to foster loyalty among the rank and file. He's done an excellent job of building the party and leading us to where we are now. But he's not Taoiseach material. He's a parish-pump politician, not a statesman. There are a number of us, myself included, who acknowledge that public opinion will necessitate a heave at some point, because Cormac won't go willingly.

'The difference is, my group doesn't believe party apparatchiks like our chair, Darragh McNally, should dictate who the next leader will be. It should happen organically, from the grass roots. Designating Blake as Taoiseach-in-waiting has done him no favours. He might be popular with the red tops and Ireland's housewives, but he carries little weight with the party membership. He doesn't travel to see them or go out of his way to engage with them. Blake is the sort who asks you how you are but looks over your shoulder as you reply, seeking the next person to impress. He's an empty vessel.'

Tom tried to hide his surprise. In the space of a few minutes, O'Keefe had risen in his estimation from a genial, publicity-seeking politician of the average kind to an astute, insightful and potentially cunning operator.

Impressive.

'Would you have reservations, then, about the direction the party would take with Blake at the helm? What about this legislation he's producing to do with the energy sector?' he asked.

O'Keefe scoffed.

'My cosying up to the environmental sector is not just about winning votes, Inspector. I have very definite opinions on that Bill. But I know damn well it has senior figures in the party behind it. Blake is just their organ grinder. Not that he sees himself in that role.'

Tom hesitated, an idea forming.

'Has the Bill been presented to the Reform Party backbenchers by the cabinet yet?' he asked.

O'Keefe pursed his lips.

'No. It hasn't. Apparently it's receiving the final flourishes and we will be briefed on it imminently. Then we'll be instructed to toe the party line and vote accordingly.'

'How have you formed such a fixed opinion, then,' Tom asked, 'if you haven't seen it yet?'

'I didn't say I hadn't seen it, Inspector. Just that it hasn't been presented to us yet.'

'Hmm.' Tom observed the man. 'By any chance do you know Linda McCarn? The criminal psychologist?'

O'Keefe grinned.

'Everybody knows Linda. A wonderfully engaging woman, don't you think? I'm a big fan.'

Tom smiled. He suspected he now knew the source of Linda's leaked information. Always keep in with the little people, she was fond of saying. Fate had led him to meet with Jarlath O'Keefe. And that was why Linda had avoided this interview, so she wouldn't give anything away. Well, he'd got there anyway.

Tom stood up to signal the interview was over and thanked O'Keefe for his time.

The house of cards really was collapsing for Aidan Blake.

*

They should have demanded Skype. In the absence of an inter-view room format, the inspector would have settled for a video link so he could observe Madsen as the man answered questions. Over the phone, Tom had no way of judging whether or not the man was telling the truth. It was like playing cards with your eyes closed.

'You could plan another jaunt, this time to Denmark.' Sean McGuinness had been remarkably unsympathetic.

'It's a bloody murder inquiry. I know that man has lied to us and I'm conducting his second interview over the phone,' Tom griped.

'If you discover he did it, you'll be tied up in extradition red tape for the foreseeable,' his boss retorted. 'The format of how you speak to him will be the least of your worries.'

'You aren't coming back to Ireland any time soon, are you?' Tom asked Madsen, after the initial small talk.

'Next month, yes. But I'm sure I can answer any questions you have for me now.'

'I guess we'll have to do it this way, then. Do you remember a former employee of yours, Damien Reid?'

There was a pause. Madsen's voice was clipped when he replied.

'Yes. I remember him.'

'He worked for your company in the late '90s, early noughties, am I correct?'

'I believe so.'

'Tall guy. Bearded. Glasses. He was presented with a bravery award for his role in preventing disaster on the Ulysses.'

'I recall him, Inspector.'

'That's amazing. Out of so many thousands of employees. Did you remember him on Friday night, when you bumped into him in the Dáil bar?'

Silence filled the line.

'It's strange,' Tom continued. 'When you told me about leaving the bar that night you made a comment about the company being foul. To whom were you referring? Surely you'd have been thrilled to bump into Mr Reid – a man you held in such high regard that you paid him the highest tribute when he worked for you. A man . . .'

'I do not hold Damien Reid in high regard, Inspector, and I have no intention of playing this game. Have you spoken to Mr Reid?'

'Yes. Would you care to elaborate on that first sentence?'

'Did he inform you about the circumstances of his leaving our company?'

'He said he wanted to start his own business.'

'He had to. He was never going to get a character reference from us for another employer.'

'Excuse me?'

'I left the bar because I wanted to use the facilities and enquire about my transport, as I said. I can assure you it was pure coincidence that I happened to be there on the same evening as Mr Reid. I personally dismissed that man from our employ and had no desire to see him again.'

'How did Damien Reid sink so low in your esteem, Mr Madsen?' the inspector asked through clenched teeth. The lack of face-to-face was infuriating.

'Mr Reid was one of a handful of people we trusted with the safe and successful operation of the Ulysses oil rig. His line manager had initially been reticent about hiring the man – he is a recovering alcoholic. But Reid came highly recommended by a previous employer and was eminently qualified.

'He appeared to be a model employee. He received the bravery award for actions that we believed helped to prevent a very near catastrophe. However, it subsequently turned out that the man had not acted honourably. He may have helped save the men on the rig while he was saving his own skin, but were it not for him, there would have been no incident in the first place. Reid attempted to sabotage the Ulysses.'

'He did what?'

'The man is a fanatic,' Madsen snapped. 'An eco-terrorist. He had boarded the Ulysses with a ridiculous plan to make a point about our industry. He interfered with the on-deck equipment in an imbecilic attempt to show that Udforske oil rigs were not of the required international safety standards. Mr Reid thought he could cause a small but significant accident and leak the news to unfriendly forces.

'Of course, he is ultimately a stupid man, academic achievements aside. His inept efforts almost caused an oil spill that would have affected Danish marine life to this day.'

'When did you discover this?' Tom asked, incredulous. 'Why was it not made public? There's nothing about this in Mr Reid's file.'

'Our internal investigation unearthed the facts shortly after he was awarded his bravery medal – which he accepted without a murmur. We kept it quiet because it would have brought our company adverse media coverage, something we do not court willingly.

'We rigorously vet all our employees, especially our safety officers. We had discovered Reid's history of addiction, but we clearly failed to uncover his subversive leanings. Our rig employees are doing a job that has the potential to be extremely dangerous. If they suspected men like Damien Reid could infiltrate their place of work, they would be uneasy. We agreed not to press charges against him on the strict condition that he kept quiet about the incident and did not try to seek employment in the industry again. There was a degree of embarrassment on our part, as you can imagine.'

Tom exhaled. What a tale. They'd have to verify it, but it certainly didn't sound like Madsen had invented the story.

'Did he try to talk to you on Friday night?' the inspector asked.

'Yes, as it happens. He followed me from the bar. The man had the temerity to suggest I invest in his business, if that is what you could call it. I harvest oil and gas from the sea. Liquid gold. He scavenges for weeds. I dismissed him. I have no time for these so-called men of principle, Inspector. Not when their principles are selective.'

'Why didn't you tell us this when we met you?'

'I didn't see the point, Inspector. Reid tried to speak to me. I shut him down and continued on my way. The incident was immaterial to our interview.'

'And you're sure you didn't see Aidan Blake? He entered the bar at 9.45, apparently.'

'No,' Madsen snapped. 'Now, if that is all, Inspector, I really must go. I am a busy man.'

Tom was left with the dial tone as Ray entered the room.

'I have something interesting on Reid from the Danish police,' he said, plopping onto the chair in front of Tom's desk.

The inspector slammed down the phone, muttering about Interpol and international arrest warrants.

'What?' his deputy asked, bemused.

'Nothing. I have something interesting too. You go first.'

'I was lucky. Got through to someone efficient. Or maybe they're all like that in Denmark and we could learn something. They came back with a small file on Reid. It seems that after he left Udforske, before he came back to Ireland, our guy was involved in a number of anti-establishment protests, mainly to do with environmental issues. All legal, of course, but at one of the demonstrations there was a scuffle and he was arrested for assaulting a police officer. He was charged and did their equivalent of community service. I also discovered that he moved to Germany for a couple of years. I talked to our colleagues there and it turns out he was on the fringes of an environmental terror group that Kripo was monitoring. He never got in too deep, so they only had a small file on him.

'He told you he'd had an ideological parting of the ways with Udforske but it still seems strange that he'd go from working for the industry to engaging in violence at protests.'

'Not strange at all,' Tom said and filled Ray in on the conversation with Madsen.

The detective whistled when his boss had finished.

'He kept that quiet, didn't he?'

'He sure did.'

'I suppose that rules him out as Madsen's hired gun. It sounds like our Great Dane ran away from Reid when he saw him.'

'That's what he says. But let's not drop Mr Reid just yet.'

'Why?' Ray asked. 'It's open and shut, surely? Just a coincidence he was in the bar. He'd hardly be willing to murder someone for the man who had fired him.'

'Willingly, maybe not. But what if it was unwilling? Why did he lie and say he hadn't seen Madsen? What if his former boss threatened to expose the man's past unless he carried out a task? That seems more likely to me than him being prepared to shoot some-body for money. Reid is at the helm of an expanding business. The last thing he needs is his past being raked over.'

Ray mulled it over.

'It's unlikely, though,' Tom conceded.

'Bloody hell, you had me pondering that. Why are you striking it out now?'

'Neither of them had any way of knowing Ryan would be in Leinster House on Friday evening. And Madsen could have denied seeing Reid and we couldn't have proved either of them was lying.'

'They would have a way of knowing where Ryan was – if Aidan Blake or Darragh McNally had told them.'

Tom raised his eyebrows.

'So you think there's potentially four of them in the planning now, with Reid instructed to do the dirty deed?'

'Well, you keep telling me that the truth is always stranger than anything you can make up,' Ray argued.

'True. But a minister, a top-level civil servant and the vice-chair of a multinational company colluding in the assassination of an ordinary PA? That's a conspiracy to rival the Moon landing, JFK and Roswell.'

Tom's mobile rang and he answered it without looking to see who was calling.

The first thing he heard was the muted sounds of a woman screaming in the background. The inspector shot up from his seat, adrenaline racing. For one horrible second, he thought it was Louise or Maria, but then a man's voice came on the line.

'Inspector Reynolds? Can you hear me? It's Aidan Blake.'

'What's going on?' Tom was still agitated.

'Please, can you come out to our home? It's an emergency. I was going to dial 999 but thought it might be better to phone you.'

'I'm on the way,' Tom said, grabbing his coat and pulling it on awkwardly with one hand as Ray looked at him questioningly. The inspector gestured for his deputy to start moving. 'Just tell me what's happened.'

'It's Kathryn Finnegan. She's banging down our front door. She's threatening to kill me.'

CHAPTER 23

The electric gates to the Blakes' home were open. They'd used the siren the entire way, Tom trying Kathryn's number all the while. As Willie brought the car around the bend in the driveway, they were greeted by the sight of the young widow slumped on the step outside the front door, head in hands.

Tom jumped out of the car as soon as it came to a stop.

'Kathryn,' he said gently, kneeling down beside the woman. She looked up. Her eyes were bloodshot from crying, her nose red and running. She had no coat, just a thin red cardigan, despite the cold. Tom noticed her fists, still clenched at either side of her head, raw and bloodied at the sides.

'What have you done?' He pulled out a handkerchief and dabbed at her hands.

Behind them, the door opened and Kathryn leapt up so force-fully, Tom toppled onto his backside.

'You murderer!' she screamed, as Aidan Blake appeared on the porch step.

She flew at him. He raised his arms defensively as Willie and Ray pulled Kathryn off. She struggled against them, trying to free herself from their firm grip, swearing at Blake as he stood there, shaking with shock.

'You killed him!' she shrieked. 'You bastard! I know what you've done. You murdered him because he was going to expose you and your dirty little secrets. I know everything. You took my husband.

You stole my baby's father from her. You should be dead, not him. I'll kill you!'

Kathryn howled, a sound so raw and full of anguish it was heart-wrenching.

She collapsed, sobbing uncontrollably.

'Ray, Willie, get her in the car,' Tom said. 'Kathryn. Kathryn? Look at me. Go with my officers. They'll bring you home. Detective Lennon will stay with you until I come. Do you understand?'

She barely acknowledged him, but let herself be bundled into the car.

'I'll come back out for you,' Willie said, before shutting the driver's door.

Tom watched as the vehicle drove off, then he turned to Blake. The minister had covered his mouth, too stunned to speak.

'Let's go inside,' the inspector said. 'You can tell me what happened.'

Blake looked at Tom as if he was only now noticing his presence. He dropped his hands.

'Of course,' he said. 'Yes, of course. Please, come in. Thank you for getting here so promptly.'

As Tom passed the light-coloured wooden front door, he noticed the bloody marks where Kathryn had pounded it with her fists.

What had driven her to turn up here and lose it like that?

Sara Blake was standing in the kitchen. She was trembling, her arms wrapped around her body.

'Is she gone?' she choked, her voice thick with emotion.

Blake nodded and went to hold his wife. Tom could see that she stiffened when he touched her. What did that mean? Was she angry with Kathryn for turning up and making accusations against her husband? Or did she believe the young woman?

'What happened?' Tom asked.

'I'll . . . I'll make tea,' Sara said, shrugging free of her husband's embrace and moving to the kitchen counter.

Blake let her go but remained standing where she'd left him. He was looking at his wife like she was a fragile piece of china, Tom noted. Probably fearing she might crack and give away his secrets.

The minister regained some composure and indicated they sit at the table.

'She just turned up at the gate,' he began. 'I buzzed her in, because I could see on the monitor that she was crying and she was on foot and not dressed for the weather. I was going to offer to drive her home. I thought she wanted to talk about Ryan. I was finishing a call so I didn't go straight to the front door. I was just about to when she started going mad.'

'You should have let her in,' Sara said, so quietly that Tom almost didn't hear.

Blake spun round in the chair and glared furiously at the back of his wife's head. The inspector was taken aback. The look on the minister's face was vicious. It was the first time Tom had seen the other man show such anger.

'For what?' he hissed. 'So she could attack me and upset you?'

'You should have talked to her,' Sara retorted. 'Not left her screaming out there on the step while you called the police. What were you thinking?'

Tom intervened.

'I don't think there would have been any talking to her. The woman is overcome with grief. But why did she turn up here now and why is she blaming you?'

'I've no idea,' Blake replied. 'She's clearly not thinking straight. Like you say.'

'No,' Tom insisted. 'She was very specifically referring to what her husband had planned. She wasn't just ranting.'

'Well, have you shown her those photos? Because I certainly haven't.'

'Obviously not.'

Blake banged the table angrily.

'Then she couldn't have any reason for thinking I was responsible.'

'Unless her husband had told her something,' Tom said. He wondered privately why Kathryn hadn't said anything before now, if that was the case.

Blake grimaced.

Tom glanced at Sara. Her expression was a mixture of shock and disbelief. She looked . . . frightened.

Blake collected himself quickly.

'I apologise, Inspector. I'm distressed. I've known Kathryn a long time. I've never seen her so . . .' He shook his head. 'This has hit her so hard.'

'Of course it has,' Tom said. 'She loved her husband. They just had a baby – a child that will never know her father. We can't even imagine Kathryn's suffering.'

Out of the corner of his eye, he saw Sara wipe tears from her eyes and turn her back on her husband.

'I'll go speak to her,' the inspector added. 'Try to calm her down and ask her why she came out here and said those things. There must be a reason.'

Blake looked worried.

'While I'm waiting for my driver, I've been meaning to ask you about Grace Brady, your secretary. What was her relationship with Ryan like?'

The minister glanced nervously at the back of his wife's head.

'Grace? I don't think they had much of a relationship. She's a . . . strange woman.'

'Strange?' Sara spun on her heel, her voice acidic. 'Grace Brady is a nut job. She made a pass at Aidan, Inspector. Seemed to think he was flirting with her and was quite rude to me any time I visited the office. She's obsessed with him. I've no doubt she had designs on Ryan, too. I ended up having words with her.'

'What did you say?' Tom asked.

'I told her that if she didn't conduct herself properly, I wouldn't just stop at making sure my husband had her moved out of the office. I've known Shane Morrison a long time and he in turn has the ear of the Captain of Leinster House – the man who oversees the hiring and firing. They'd be in charge of where she was sent next. I'm sorry if that makes me sound petty, but I have no tolerance for her type.'

'There's no harm in her,' Blake said. He seemed particularly flustered. 'She's peculiar, that's all. I think she got on okay with Ryan, in answer to your question. And Morrison likes Grace, you know that, Sara.'

'Well, Shane can be a silly bugger for women but Ryan had no time for her,' Sara snapped. 'He'd have been delighted to see her moved from the office. Stupid, vain creature. Ryan would never have looked at another woman. Kathryn was everything to him.'

Why was Blake defending Grace, Tom wondered?

Sara gave her husband one last glare and stomped from the room.

'By the way,' the inspector added quietly, taking the opportunity of her leaving. 'I found out what I needed to about The Club, Aidan. I don't understand why you continue to believe you can keep things from me in this investigation. Is it yourself you're trying to delude? You do realise your secrets are starting to worm their way out from under the rock, don't you? I didn't stumble upon that place by accident.'

Blake made a fist with his hands and clenched his jaw.

'You've no right to judge me,' he snapped, his voice little more than a whisper. 'You don't know anything about me. Do you think I want to do what I do? Do you think I have a choice?'

'What do you mean – a choice? Who's forcing you to have sex with prostitutes? You have so much to lose. Why risk it all?'

'I don't want to!' Blake shouted, then caught himself. 'I can't help it. I . . .'

Sara had returned to the kitchen. Tom thought she must have been alerted by her husband's sudden roar, but she had just come to tell him Willie was at the gate.

Blake put his head in his hands, unable or unwilling to say anything more.

The inspector stood up and followed Sara to the front door.

'He's falling apart,' she choked, as Tom waited on the front step for Willie to come up the drive. 'It's all this pressure. He didn't kill Ryan, Inspector. I keep telling you. Please, don't push him any further.'

Tom felt sorry for this woman, clearly devastated by what was happening around her. But what could he say to make her feel better?

'I just want everything back to normal,' she added, her face a picture of torment and anguish.

So does Kathryn Finnegan, the inspector thought sadly. So does she.

*

'You gave me the idea. When you were here and you wanted to go through Ryan's things again. I knew you hadn't found anything so I decided to look in some of our old hiding places.'

Kathryn Finnegan was wild-eyed, desperate.

'Was it amongst his clothes?' Tom asked. He was holding the letter she had given him, scanning its contents again.

'No, mine. You see, I have this coat. Well . . . there's a story. We'd only started dating, you see. I was leaving Ryan's house to go home when it started lashing rain. I only had a light jacket so his mother gave me a loan of this old-fashioned, hideous raincoat.' Kathryn laughed, her whole face aglow with the memory.

'She was being kind, but I was young and fashionable and I'd have rather got soaked to the skin than let Ryan see me in that get-up. I had to put it on to please her and she started clapping her hands, saying it was gorgeous on me and I was to have it. So then I was in trouble, because I had to let her see me wearing it.

'Ryan knew I was making a sacrifice for his mother. I mean, I can't describe how awful this coat is – poo-brown with yellow stripes. Anyway, I was leaving his house in it one time and he slipped a little note in the pocket, telling me how much he loved me for wearing the coat. I found it when I got home. He did that every time I wore it. I was like Pavlov's dog; I started to enjoy wearing the raincoat. Eventually, he talked his mother into buying me a new one for Christmas and he helped pick it out. Win-win. The old one is in the back of my wardrobe and every now and again he sticks a note in there for me. I mean . . . he used to.'

'I understand. And that's where he'd put the letter.'

'Yes. In the pocket.' A fresh wave of despair crossed her features, the realisation that this was the final note she would find there.

Tom looked at the single page in his hand. It was most definitely unlike the usual love notes Ryan would have hidden for his wife. It read:

Kathryn, my love,

I cannot believe I'm writing this. It's absurd, like something from a film. Because if you are reading these words, it means I never got a chance to rip this letter up.

This week I told Aidan Blake that I would be forced to reveal secrets about him to the press, unless he rights a terrible wrong. We made a promise to the people of Ireland before the last election about taxing oil and gas finds. Aidan has reneged on that promise but is still trying to present what he's doing as the right course. This is just one in a long line of broken commitments but I think it's the worst.

I should have known he would do this. There are others pushing it, but he has the power to stop it. Aidan is not as perfect as he would have people believe, Kat. I have material to destroy him – photos of him at an orgy, drinking and taking drugs. And his indiscretions aren't just in the past.

I've given him until tonight to do what I ask.

I'm sorry I haven't told you about what has been going on, sweetheart. I couldn't because I knew what you would say. You would have told me to stop and walk away. But I can't.

When our beautiful little girl was born, I saw the world properly for the first time. I've always been passionate, Kat, you know that, but I have never felt so strongly that it's my job to help ensure a better future for our child and for others like her. If I don't, then why have I dedicated my life to politics?

I'm not pleased with myself. I wish I had better leverage over Aidan. But I know his head has been turned by the oil and gas industry and by men in the party with bad intentions, so I have to fight dirty. It's the only language they understand. And I have to use the images. Nobody would believe me otherwise. Who doesn't trust Aidan Blake, the good guy of Irish politics?

I'm playing a high-stakes game, my darling. The men Aidan moves with don't let anybody stand in their way. I feel in my gut that I may be in danger. I don't know if Aidan is capable of harming me himself. I don't know what he's capable of. I don't know him at all, any more.

Kat, I love you and Beth more than life. Please understand why I have to do this and forgive me. I hope you never read this and when I hold you tight in bed later, you'll be none the wiser. But if you do see this letter, something has happened to me and you need to go to the guards and show it to them. Don't let the Party leadership get away with what they're doing.

All my love,
Your Ryan.

'Why?' Kathryn sobbed, as Tom read the letter for a third time. 'Why was he so stupid? I don't forgive him. I'm furious with him. He could have just left it alone. If he thought what he was doing was dangerous enough to leave me a letter like that, if he thought that Beth risked losing her daddy, why didn't he just stay clear of it all? It was just politics!'

Tom didn't know what to say to her. He knew that when the woman calmed down and reflected, she, who knew her husband better than anyone, would understand why he acted the way he did. Maybe Ryan did think it was about making the world a better place for his child. Maybe, despite having written the letter, he didn't fully understand the danger he was in.

'Don't you see?' Kathryn beseeched, her voice rising. 'Aidan Blake must have had him killed. Or killed him himself. That's what Ryan says in the letter. That's why I went to his house. I wanted to see it in his eyes. I've known that man for years; let him look me in the face and lie to me. He wouldn't even open the door. That says something, doesn't it? He's guilty.'

'Kathryn, you need to calm yourself,' Tom said, his tone firm and reassuring. 'We're looking at every possible motive for Ryan's murder and the fact he planned to blackmail Aidan Blake is already at the forefront of our investigation.'

Kathryn nodded.

'Good. That's good. Will you arrest him, then? Now you have this note?'

'No, I can't do that on the basis of a letter. Kathryn, you need to understand, there are other people involved who may have had cause to kill Ryan for wanting to blackmail Aidan. We're looking at all of them. This letter just confirms for us what we already suspected.'

The woman looked like she intended to argue with him, but she couldn't summon the energy to say anything else. She sank, deflated, back into her chair.

Tom sat there with her, quietly. He'd seen this in family members of murder victims before. They so desperately needed their loved ones' killers to be found and brought to justice. And it was true, a certain measure of solace could be gleaned from that. But it changed nothing. The hunt for the murderer, the arrest, the trial – they all brought their own distractions, but none of it brought people back from the dead.

'Kathryn, you can't go to the Blake house like that again. Aidan's wife was in the house when you called and was very distressed. He hasn't been arrested for anything. You need to let me do my job.'

Her eyes flickered to the letter. Tom caught the glance.

'And don't do what Ryan planned, Kathryn. Don't broadcast Aidan Blake's secrets to the world. You know it's not the way to achieve anything.'

She lowered her eyes.

'I know,' she said, her voice a whimper. 'I think that's what makes me so mad. How could Ryan stoop so low?'

Tom sighed.

'I'm sure he didn't want to expose Blake at all. He was just using whatever method he could to persuade him to do the right thing.'

But in his head, he cursed Ryan Finnegan for his stupidity.

CHAPTER 24

Thursday Night, Denmark

Calle Lund was a man who got things done.

He wasn't unlike the Irish man, Darragh McNally, in that regard. Or at least, that's what Carl Madsen had thought. It transpired that ultimately, McNally really wasn't that effective.

Madsen wasn't a novice. He hadn't relied solely on the party chair; he had made other contacts with the Irish government early on. Being the middle child had taught him some valuable lessons. The lessons he had learned in playing his siblings off against one another meant he generally got his way.

Except, in this instance, the people he'd chosen had all failed him.

Lund studied the notes in front of him, leaning over them like an examining doctor would a patient. His hair was thinning and one of the arms of his glasses was stuck on with Sellotape. He wore woollen-type brown trousers and a grandfatherly waistcoat, though he was only in his forties. Lund was generally an inoffensive looking man, yet Madsen knew his stratospheric IQ made him a formidable ally.

And he was Madsen's man.

'I don't see how they can link these payments to you,' Lund whispered huskily, looking up from the page briefly, then back down. He wasn't good at eye contact. Even with people he knew well, like Madsen. Lund preferred to work on computers or through letters, not face to face. He'd suffered from recurrent bronchitis as a child and his vocal cords had never recovered. 'What about the other man you have over there – have people seen you with him?'

Madsen considered carefully. They were meeting in his home office in his penthouse apartment in Ørestad. The Udforske vice-president didn't want people to see Lund anywhere near company headquarters in Copenhagen.

The building they were in overlooked the canal in the centre of the modern development. It was a stunning city vista, one he could appreciate after the solitude of Donegal. Yet the Irish county seemed to have got under his skin. He longed for it.

'Only at public events,' he answered the other man's question. 'And I know I was careful with these payments. But I want to see McNally implicated in wrongdoing of some sort. The imbecile took our money and failed to deliver. It's imploding over there.'

'If they learn he was receiving bribes, he will tell them from where. You won't be able to stay out of it. Udforske's reputation will be tarnished and that's what you want to avoid.'

Madsen sighed. It was so unlike him to make a mistake like this. Both the Irish men had seemed so . . . solid. He should have done better research. If he'd brought Calle Lund in from the start, this wouldn't have happened. He wouldn't have got embroiled with two such . . . disappointments.

'There is only one thing you can do,' Lund croaked.

Madsen sat up, eager to hear what the other man had. Were it not sufficient, he would have to resort to other means, to deal with McNally at least. It wasn't a path Madsen wanted to take, but he'd already set the train in motion.

'There is no paper trail connecting you to McNally. The police in Dublin will discover these payments and he will claim they are from you. You will deny it.'

Madsen shook his head, half amused, half annoyed.

'Where will that get me? They mightn't be able to prove it, but my name will have been dragged in and the company involved. Worse, Holm will get involved.'

Bernd Holm, the president of Udforske. Nowadays, he was more or less retired, happy to leave the running of the business in Madsen's hands. But the old man valued his legacy and if he suspected his company was under threat because of Madsen's screw-up, he'd come riding into the boardroom like John Wayne, all guns blazing. The only thing Holm was loyal to was money.

'Your name is going to be dragged into this sorry affair no matter what you do, unless you want to discuss other options . . . more final options. You haven't gone down that road yet, have you?'

Madsen said nothing. Lund looked up from the page momentarily and just as quickly looked down. There were some things he didn't get involved in. He liked the slow, steady, sure approach to solving a problem. He'd never been comfortable with his boss's volatile temperament.

'In any case, I haven't finished,' he resumed. 'Udforske is not the only company that will benefit from the law due to be processed through the Irish parliament. Name a company. One of your rivals.'

Madsen rubbed his jaw, staring at Lund, whose head was still bowed.

'Karlstad oil,' he said, throwing out the name of one of the Swedish energy giants.

'What if there was a paper trail linking Karlstad to McNally's payments?' Lund said.

'But he would just deny it, as would they. They would bring in their lawyers . . . Ah.'

Madsen had got it.

McNally's word would mean nothing. And it didn't matter what the guards thought. Ireland's record on challenging corporate misdoings was diabolical. They still hadn't investigated properly the State's massive banking scandal from four years ago. Nobody in the State's law enforcement agencies would have the gumption to take on Udforske for bribery, even if they knew for certain it had happened. What mattered was public opinion and maintaining the relationships with the Irish establishment that the company had nurtured.

And they didn't have to prove Karlstad were guilty. Karlstad had to prove they were innocent – a task which would be made much more difficult once Lund's specialist had finished with his false trail. And while everybody was discussing the Karlstad scandal . . .

'You can call in the favours owed to you in Ireland,' Lund said, completing Madsen's thought. 'You've done enough in your philanthrophic role. It's time you drew on your currency. This will be a blip for Udforske. Nothing more.'

His boss nodded appreciatively. He would have to make a phone call. It seemed the other course of action he'd been considering wouldn't be required after all. Hopefully, he wasn't too late to stall it.

Good old Lund. Saving the day, as always.

Friday, Dublin

'What is it?'

Tom looked up from his desk as Ray entered the office. He'd made the cardinal error of buying a newspaper on the way into work and was halfway through a devastatingly accurate article bemoaning the lack of progress by the guards in the Finnegan case.

Half of him was protesting that it had only been a week but the more analytical side knew they should have made a breakthrough by this stage if they were to have a hope of catching the killer. The colder the case got, the less likely it was they'd solve it. They hadn't a shred of evidence against anybody they suspected – Blake, McNally, Madsen or Reid.

'Darragh McNally's bank account details. He received payments from an offshore bank account four times in the last year. Large sums. They started last September. I've a limited attention span when it comes to politics, but I'm pretty sure that's when the last government imploded and the Reform Party soared in the polls.'

'It was,' Tom said. 'The Troika was coming to town. It was obvious the Reform Party was headed for government. So, someone started buying McNally's influence early. No guesses as to who.'

'The offshore account belongs to a small bank in St Lucia.'

'Can we link Carl Madsen to the payments?'

'No. We'll have to interview McNally and ask him.'

'Let's get him in. We should have done this yesterday; it went out of my head with everything else going on. He has a history of altercations with Ryan. He may have had debts and we know he was in receipt of money from somebody for something. If those funds were from Madsen to ensure the passage of this damned Bill, then McNally needed to make it happen. Send a squad car to pick him up.'

'I already put the call through. They should be pulling up at his door any minute now. Aren't we supposed to be interviewing those remaining cabinet ministers later?'

'Postpone them. I want to see McNally first.'

*

Tom had just finished reading the paper when his door burst open.

Ray's face was thunderous.

If McNally had made a run for it . . .

Tom could feel his pulse quicken as he pushed the chair out from the desk.

'Have they got him?' he asked.

'They've got him all right. We're not going to be asking him any questions, though.'

'Solicitor?' Tom asked, but he already knew it was something far more serious.

'Dead,' his deputy replied. 'They got no answer and his garage door was ajar so they opened it to see if his car was there. He was hanging from one of the beams.'

*

'Death by hanging,' Emmet sighed, shaking his head sadly. He'd opened the forensic seal on the garage and they were in the process of lowering the body.

'Did somebody do it to him?' Tom asked. 'Or was it suicide?' He'd taken a long look at the corpse and turned away, the sight too upsetting to stare at for any length of time.

Tom felt a pang of guilt at the thought that McNally had killed himself. He had seen that the man was on the edge. Was there something he could have said or done? But no – the inspector knew that if McNally was intent on suicide, there was little anybody could have done to stop him, short of attempting to have him sectioned.

'You heard the pathologist: he seems fairly positive it was self-inflicted,' Emmet replied. 'He's dead at least thirty-six hours, which would make the estimated time of death sometime during the early hours of Thursday morning. Our friend has all the signs of asphyxia and venous congestion. The rope is sufficiently thick and long and matches the ligature marks on his body. I made a preliminary examination and didn't detect any other injuries. The pathologist has verified that. You can smell alcohol on his clothes, by the way. Unless somebody talked him into hanging himself . . .'

'The garage door was partially open,' Tom remarked.

'He probably did that himself so somebody would find him,' Emmet replied. 'In any case, he left you a note.'

'Do you mean a suicide note for anybody who found him? Or a letter to me personally?'

'For you personally. One of your team bagged it. The envelope was propped up on the bench over there.'

'This is the second post-mortem letter connected to this case that I've been presented with in two days.'

'A man of letters.'

McNally had been lifted onto a wheeled stretcher and was about to be zipped into a body bag. The inspector took one last look at the man's swollen face before it was covered. Death always took Tom by surprise, regardless of how often he saw it or the many guises it took. To be alive one day and dead the next. How could it be anything other than overwhelming?

'By the way, does he have family?' Emmet enquired.

'Not that I know of. A man he worked with is on his way over. We'll get him to call by the morgue to formally identify the body if there truly is no family to be reached.'

In the driveway, Ray and Laura stood beside the waiting ambulance. Laura hadn't spoken a word to her colleague since her arrival.

Ray seized the moment of their being more or less alone. Now he knew she had feelings for him, he felt more confident. Not cocky, though. The way things had gone so far, he wasn't counting any chickens.

'The other night,' he started, but trailed off. She was staring at him with a bored expression, a look that said she had no interest in anything he had to say.

In her head and in her heart, Laura had written Ray off once and for all. She wasn't going to entertain any more silly fantasies. It had been different when she was single but now Eoin was starting to wonder about Ray. He'd asked her on the drive over to McNally's house if they'd ever dated.

'No,' she had replied. 'Why do you ask?' She had felt a shiver of excitement that anybody would imagine that she and Ray had been an item. He didn't even seem to realise she was female.

'You never talk about him,' Eoin had said, careful not to take his eyes off the road.

'Wouldn't that indicate that we hadn't dated?' Laura had responded casually, her eyes also fixed to the front.

'You talk about everybody else,' he had said with annoying insightfulness.

Laura knew she was being unfair to Eoin. But Ray Lennon certainly didn't deserve any more of her time.

Ray, oblivious to this new resolution, was undeterred. The wind whipped a stray curl from her ponytail onto her face. He wished he could reach over and tuck it behind her ear.

'I want to apologise,' he said, a lump in his throat. 'I shouldn't have mentioned Ellie. I shouldn't have been thinking about her at all. And I don't really, truth be told. I barely knew the girl. Her death affected me, but that wasn't the time or the place to talk about it. I was really enjoying being out with you.'

Laura felt the familiar treacherous flutter in the pit of her stomach. It began to make its way up to her supposedly closed heart, which was beating a little faster.

'It was just a drink,' she said abruptly, angry with herself. 'I wasn't bothered. Anyway, *this* is hardly the time or place to be talking about our social lives.'

Laura turned to talk to one of the paramedics. Ray flushed. He waited for a moment or two, then walked towards the garage.

Laura watched him go, her head muddled. Damn him. What had he meant by that? She glanced guiltily at the house where her boyfriend was on duty. Eoin deserved better. She would have to do something.

*

Ray grimaced when he saw the body bag in the garage.

'Is it definitely suicide?' he asked his boss.

Tom shrugged.

'I know you don't mean to sound disappointed, Ray, but yes, it looks like it.'

He'd just been given the envelope McNally had left addressed to him, now enclosed in a plastic evidence bag.

'Do you think it's a confession?' Ray asked.

'That would certainly wrap things up nicely.'

They left the garage through an internal door and entered Darragh McNally's home. The sitting room revealed that they were indeed in the lair of a single man. His love of politics and literature was again evident in the multitude of bookshelves, heaving under the weight of many tomes. McNally's affection for his mother was even more apparent. The dresser beside the fireplace was adorned with several framed photos of the woman with her son.

The table in the centre of the room was cluttered with empty bottles. McNally had even taken a glass out to the garage with him. Maybe he had needed one last drink for courage before placing the rope around his neck and climbing onto the stool they'd found kicked over beneath his body.

'I can never understand how people go through with it,' Ray said. 'Even if McNally was guilty, why didn't he just try to make a run for it? What goes through your mind when you decide to kill yourself?'

'The man suffered with depression. There's nothing to say he had any direct involvement with Ryan's death. But let's find out.'

The inspector withdrew the envelope from the bag with gloved hands and opened it to reveal the letter within. The penmanship on the pages sloped precariously, the untidy script of a drunk.

'We'll need to verify this is his handwriting,' Tom said. 'It's so messy, it could have been forged.'

He placed the letter on the table and they read together.

Inspector,

By the time you read this, I will be gone from this world. Don't pity me. I am free at last.

I cannot face down the black dog this time. I have nothing left to fight for. My darling mother was my only family. My career will soon be over. That was all I had in my life. I suspect I seem very clichéd and one-dimensional to you – the ugly little man with only his mammy to love him. There is more to me, but what's the point in even trying to explain to you the hopes and dreams I once nurtured?

I have battled with depression for more years than I care to remember. I started drinking because I was depressed and I became more depressed because I drank. Ironic, isn't it? I can articulate all of this so well. But just because I know what's wrong with me doesn't mean I can fix it. That's why I must end the pain.

I want to take my good name, what's left of it, to the grave. I want to protect my mother's memory. I know you believe I murdered Ryan Finnegan. No doubt you plan to arrest me. The prospect of a trial and a prison sentence is the last straw. What chance would I have? I have no alibi, I had motive and I disliked the man intensely.

I did not murder him, though. I have made bad decisions but I'm not a killer.

You probably know that I took bribes for the past year to influence government decisions. I'm certain that I was being played. I don't think the man who paid me even needed my influence. He has a finger in every pie. He just wanted to make sure I was bought.

I was a fool, but I took the money for the right reasons. I couldn't see my mother live out the remainder of her life with anything less than the dignity she deserved. I sacrificed everything for the sake of the Party, so I took what was rightfully mine.

Ryan Finnegan is one of those who looked down his nose at me. If there is one thing I have learned with age, it's that if you scratch hard enough, nobody is good all the way through. Given the right, or wrong, circumstances, most people are capable of bad deeds. Even goody-two-shoes Ryan was quite happy to resort to blackmail to get what he wanted.

I've garnered a reputation for being ferocious in my career, but people always knew what they were getting. I am surrounded by people who go to extremes to get what they want. All the while, they pretend to have honour and integrity.

I know I'm being thrown to the lions to protect those people and I won't allow it. I had planned to try to expose them but I know, as your prime suspect, that my accusations would now seem like the desperate untruths of a condemned man. Who would believe me against them?

So I leave you with this. The word of a dead man with no reason to lie. I am not the one you seek.

I am at peace now, something I have desired for so long. I am with my family.

And after all, isn't family the most important thing?

Darragh.

'Is that it?' Ray said, turning the sheets of paper over.

'What are you looking for? A postscript that tells us who shot Ryan?'

Ray raised his eyebrows.

'It's a bit cryptic, isn't it?'

'That's an understatement,' Tom replied. He felt like he'd been hit in the head with a hammer. 'Why the hell was he so convinced we already had him down as guilty and convicted? He hardly got that impression from our interview with him the other day. What did the lads say to him when they knocked on his door yesterday?'

'Nothing that would imply he'd spend the next thirty years rotting in jail, that's for sure.'

The inspector shook his head. He was shocked at what had been going on in McNally's head. He was going over his own actions to analyse whether he'd gone too hard on the man and forced him to take such a desperate course. McNally had been a person of interest but he wasn't their only suspect. Had his depression made him paranoid? Was the notion that the guards were moving in on him the straw that broke the camel's back?

Tom had no idea, but he was filled with regret for leaving the man alone after his interview the other day.

'He didn't name Madsen,' Ray said. 'Why?'

The inspector shook his head. McNally hadn't named anybody. Perhaps, despite the bribe-taking, he really was the better man.

The door opened and Garda Eoin Coyle appeared.

'The chief of security from Leinster House has just pulled up.'

The inspector nodded. 'Send him in, Eoin.'

Shane Morrison was rattled. He chose to stand rather than sit. The shock of two sudden deaths in less than a week was taking its toll.

'Thank you for coming,' Tom said. 'I'm very sorry to have had to request your presence, but we can't establish any family contacts for Mr McNally. I know his party colleagues will be informed but I'm not sure if he had any close friends among them. You seem to know a lot about the goings-on in Leinster House and you were aware of Darragh's . . . troubles, when we met with him in Government Buildings.'

Morrison nodded.

'I understand. It's no bother at all. I know Darragh the guts of twenty-five years. That's how long he's worked in Leinster House. I'm sad to say that while we may have been cordial acquaintances all that time, we weren't friends. But I drove him home the other day. I should have stayed. I was driving home on Wednesday – I actually live not too far away – and considered calling in. But it was late and I worried he might be drinking and . . . not fit for company. I'm ashamed to say I drove on by his house.'

'What time was that? Did you notice anything unusual?'

'It was around 10 p.m. I thought I saw a car pull up at the house as I was driving around the corner further on, but I couldn't be certain. It could have been parking in front of any of the houses along here. I wish I'd called in. Maybe I could have helped him.'

Tom reassured Morrison that there was probably nothing he could have done, using the same logic he'd tried to use to absolve himself earlier.

'How was Darragh perceived in Leinster House? Was he well liked? Respected?'

Morrison blinked. 'Hold on. He hasn't been murdered as well, has he? I thought it was suicide.'

Tom shook his head. 'That's how it appears. But the events of the last week do seem to have contributed to his decision to take his own life.'

'Well, I always found Darragh to be polite and pleasant. But then, I wasn't a political opponent. I know he could be tough at times. He was ambitious for his party, some might say for himself. He wasn't the worst I've seen in that regard. With some people what you see is what you get – that was Darragh. Others are a lot more devious about getting their way.'

'Are you talking about anyone specifically?' Ray asked.

Morrison fidgeted uncomfortably. 'My role is to assist in the smooth operation of Leinster House, Detective. I would never hold political or personal bias against anyone who works there. My job forbids it.'

'How well do you know Minister Blake?' Tom asked.

'Better than I knew Darragh. I've known both the Blakes a long time. I'd consider Aidan a friend. He's going places and I'm pleased to see it. I introduced him to Sara, in fact. I've known her since she was a child, even helped get her into her first job. I attended their wedding. They really are like family to me.'

'But you didn't know Ryan that well, even though he worked with Aidan?' Tom asked.

'No.'

The inspector was surprised at the abrupt, almost sharp reply.

'So, you didn't know there was discord between the pair of them?'

Morrison hesitated this time.

'I had heard something. There was some gossip in Leinster House earlier in the year. I asked Sara about it. She didn't seem overly bothered. She said that Aidan and Ryan were clashing on policy matters. Sara thought Aidan should pay his PA more heed. I disagreed. A PA is a staff member, like any other. Aidan is a future Taoiseach. Ryan clearly had notions about himself.'

Tom studied Morrison thoughtfully.

'There seem to have been a few problems in the minister's office. Are you familiar with Grace Brady, the minister's secretary?'

Morrison hesitated.

'Yes. I know Grace can be a little . . . difficult. But she's had a hard life. She lost both her parents when she was younger. I'm fond of her.'

'Fond of her? What do you mean?'

'I don't mean anything improper. Grace is a troubled girl but she's a hard worker. She's been employed in various civil service capacities in Leinster House over the years, that's how I know her. We may be a large workforce, but you get to know the ones who are around a while.'

'Hmm. Did Mr McNally say anything when you dropped him home?'

'He barely spoke at all, Inspector. He said thank you when I dropped him off. Just that.'

'I see. Would you be kind enough to inform his former colleagues of his passing?'

'Certainly. Is there anything I should do with the effects in his office?'

'Leave it until we've had a chance to look through everything. One more thing – have you ever heard rumours in Leinster House about any high-ranking politicians being members of a certain . . . Club?'

Morrison blinked once. It was the only thing that gave it away.

'I'm not sure what you mean. They're all in clubs of some sort.'

'Oh, never mind. It doesn't matter.'

When the chief of security had left, Ray turned to Tom.

'Another member?'

'Possibly,' Tom agreed. 'And if he's that good a friend of Blake's, maybe he introduced him to it.'

'He is a fan, isn't he, despite his so-called objectivity.'

'I noticed.'

'You know what else?'

'What?'

'He keeps popping up, doesn't he?'

*

On the journey back to headquarters, Tom pondered what Ray had said. Shane Morrison knew all the players in this investigation. He had full knowledge of and the ability to move freely around the Leinster House complex. By his own admission, he'd been at McNally's house the night he died, even if he claimed he hadn't called in.

Back in the office, the inspector sought out Laura.

'Laura – Morrison's interview. What was he doing throughout Friday evening?'

'The chief of security?' she said, looking confused. Then her neck started to colour, the red spreading up to her cheeks.

'What is it?' Tom asked, with a sense of foreboding.

'Sorry. I was just going through the interview lists in my head. It's just . . . I think we slipped up.'

The inspector closed his eyes. He had a notion of what was coming.

Laura took a deep breath.

'I don't think we interviewed him.'

CHAPTER 25

Tom did have a lot on his mind that evening, but that wasn't why the row started. The argument with his wife over Maria and Cáit had been brewing. But he could have done without it that night.

The inspector hadn't lost his temper with Laura. He was just as culpable. The possibility of Shane Morrison being a suspect had seemed as improbable to his team as it had to him. The man was responsible for security in Leinster House and had helped the detectives set up the interviews. It hadn't occurred to anyone to question Morrison himself.

Laura and Michael would interview him in the morning. As unlikely as it seemed, if it turned out he had no alibi, Tom would have to give serious consideration to whether or not the man had motive to murder Ryan.

When he opened his front door to the sound of his wife and daughter bickering, with Cáit's pitched wail upstairs acting as a backdrop, part of him considered turning on his heel and sleeping in headquarters.

His foul humour made him impetuous though, and he threw open the kitchen door and roared at the two of them, inserting himself slap bang into the middle of their melee.

'What the hell is going on?'

'Ask her,' Louise snapped, then clamped her lips shut in a petulant pout.

His daughter was barely out of her teens. His wife had no such excuse. Louise was standing with her hands on her hips; her cheeks were red and she looked like she was about to stamp her foot.

'I've had enough,' Maria shouted. 'I'm moving out and I'll rear *my* daughter the way *I* want to.'

'And who's funding this little adventure?' Louise flung back. 'Are you packing in college and getting a job? Where? In a shop? A bar? How will you pay for childcare or is that where I'm supposed to step in?'

'Louise!' Tom roared over the din. 'Get your coat.'

His wife froze.

'Excuse me?'

'I said get your coat. Maria, walk that baby or feed her. Do something. She's going to burst a blood vessel.'

'That's exactly what I wanted to do. See, Mam, I'm going upstairs and picking her up. Oooooh, a break in the routine! Expect the sky to have fallen in when you return.'

Louise glared at her before stomping out of the kitchen, followed by Tom.

'Where are we going?' she barked at him.

'We're going for a walk. You need some air.'

'I don't need air,' she muttered as she pounded away from the house in the direction of Castleknock village. Tom nearly had to run to keep up with her. 'I need a bloody punchbag. I'm so frustrated with that girl. She's too immature. She hasn't a clue what she's doing but thinks she knows everything. She wants to be a mother, a student, and earn money all at the same time, and she thinks she can do that without the child having any kind of structure. Why won't she just listen?'

'Like you listened to your mother when Maria was born?' Tom replied.

Louise ground to a halt, throwing her scarf back around her neck.

'That is not the same thing and well you know it. You and I were older and more than capable.'

'Have you been working out or something?' He took the opportunity to catch his breath. His wife hadn't even broken into a sweat.

'I power-walk with the buggy in the mornings, when Maria's enjoying her lie-in. How's that going to work out for her when she moves? I'm not driving across town every morning to collect my grandchild from some dingy bedsit so her mammy can go back to sleep. How can she even consider moving Cáit out of her home? We have the space. She has everything she needs. And it's hard enough now when she's just got medical theory to study. What happens when she's interning in a hospital, working fifteen hours a day? How will she make it work then?'

'She can't make it all work but if you keep pushing her, she will move,' Tom retorted. 'And it will do her no harm to have a dose of reality. You can't stop her being independent. Do you remember when my parents offered to let us live with them after Maria was born? So we could save on rent and build up a deposit to buy our own place? You nearly had a fit.'

'Again, our situation was entirely different,' his wife fumed. 'There were two of us, for heaven's sake. I could choose to become a full-time mother. There's no comparison.'

'It doesn't matter if the situations aren't identical; I'm making the point that Maria is her mother's daughter. She wants to make her own decisions for her baby. She doesn't need to move into a bedsit: we have the resources to support her in a nicer place. We don't need to abandon our daughter and grandchild if they move out. And maybe it would be good for us too. We could get our lives back.'

'Is that what you think?' Louise shouted, causing a passing dog-walker to stumble off the kerb in shock. Tom cast the elderly man an apologetic glance, but his wife forged on. 'You think I'd abandon her? I would never do that. I only want what's best for her. And how dare you talk about us getting our lives back. Seriously?

The life where you move from case to case and I wait patiently for one to be closed before another one opens, without ever complaining or throwing it in your face that we barely bloody see each other? What will I do all day if I don't have the baby to mind? I finish my English studies, what then? All you're concerned with is getting sleep because you're a – a – you're a big lazy oaf!'

Tom was alarmed to see tears in his wife's eyes.

'Louise,' he said softly, and tried to pull her to him. She shook him off angrily. They stood there, at an impasse, while Tom rewound the conversation in his head and tried to think of what to say next.

'What are you more upset about?' he asked, treading carefully. 'Maria not taking advice about parenting or the possibility of her and Cáit moving out?'

She sniffed and rubbed her eyes.

'I don't want Maria to move out, let alone Cáit. Oh Tom, I'd miss them so much, rattling around the house on my own. I'm not ready for an empty nest. I've barely got my head around Maria not being a child any more.'

This time, she let her husband take her hand.

He caressed her fingers with his, feeling her soft skin, knowing every line on her palm.

'If that's the case,' he said, 'then you need her to know that if she stays with us, you'll let her make her own choices about the baby. You raised her well; let her show you what a good job you did. Stop breathing down her neck and reminding her you would do it better, because she already knows what an amazing mother you are.

'But, love, she will move out one day. I'm not best pleased about it either. But I had my moment of realisation when she told me she was pregnant. She's not a child any more. And as for my job, I didn't realise it was taking such a toll on you. You manage it so well, I just assumed . . . well, it doesn't matter what I assumed. We can fix it. I'm not going to work forever, you know that.'

Now Louise was sobbing. Tom panicked. What had he said? What could he do?

'Why didn't we have more children?' his wife wailed. 'I wanted more. I still want more and now I'm a dried-up old prune and I can't have any.'

Tom nearly laughed. Red-eyed, snotty-nosed and bathed only in the harsh light of a street lamp, she was still the most beautiful woman he'd ever laid eyes on.

'Are you kidding me?' he said. 'An old prune? Look who you're talking to. I just turned fifty, apparently.'

'But I can't ever have another child,' she sobbed plaintively.

Tom said nothing. Her eyes were so full of pain. He couldn't remedy this one with humour.

He put his arms around her and held her close.

'I'm sorry, Louise,' he said. 'I had no idea that you felt this way. I . . .' He was lost for words. She was right, of course, and there was nothing he could say that would make it better. Being a grandparent was lovely, but it was a pale imitation. Their one little girl had grown up. Why hadn't they had this conversation a decade ago?

He knew why, really. His job was all-consuming and Louise's days had been full with Maria. Neither of them could have imagined how they would feel at this point in their lives.

Tom must have looked upset because this time Louise took his hand in hers.

'It's okay, pet. I'm just . . . blowing things out of proportion. I'm tired and I've been feeling a bit low lately. You seem to always be busy. I wouldn't swap our life together for anything but sometimes I wish I had a bit more of you. If Maria and Cáit go, I'm worried I'll be left climbing the walls.'

'How can I make this better now?' he asked. 'Are you sure it's too late for us to try again?'

She snorted. 'Oh my God, yes. That ship has sailed. If for no other reason than Maria would be absolutely mortified if she found out we were trying to give Cáit an aunt younger than her.'

Tom smiled weakly.

'Should I take time off work? When this case is put to bed, if it ever is – we could just go away, the two of us.'

'In addition to Cuba? Do you think we're made of money?'

'I'm serious.'

She smiled sadly. 'I know you are, love. It means the world to me that you are. But I feel better already for getting this off my chest. I do. You know what would make me happy right now?'

'Name it.'

'A bag of chips. I'm starving. I need something dripping in grease and smothered in salt and vinegar.'

'You're a cheap date.' He kissed her forehead.

'Not that cheap,' she said. 'I might require a burger as well. Come on.'

They strolled, hand in hand, Tom stealing occasional glances at his wife's face.

He knew, deep down, that he neglected her at times. They had an unspoken arrangement that seemed to work for their marriage – she allowed him to focus on his cases and he made it up to her when work was quiet. Many of his peers had failed to establish a similar understanding and he'd seen plenty of marriages fail because of it. The birthday party in the middle of an investigation had been a surprise and a break from the norm. She had been putting her foot down, reminding him that she wouldn't always bend to what his job demanded. The last year had been unusually hectic. Had he been pushing it?

Louise squeezed his hand.

'Don't worry about it until after you've wrapped up this case,' she said, reading his mind. 'You have until Hallowe'en.'

He smiled. If only it were that easy.

They went to bed early, exhausted and full of starchy food. As they lay in the darkness, Tom brought her up to speed on the case, talking until he felt her head grow heavy on his chest and the rise and fall of her breathing become steady and deep.

He was just on the cusp of sleep when it came to him. His eyes shot open and he sat bolt upright in the bed. Louise muttered crossly and turned over, plumping the pillow beneath her head.

Tom considered shaking her awake but knew she wouldn't thank him for it. He wanted to talk through his theory with somebody, but he also needed more information.

He'd been looking at the Ryan Finnegan case all wrong. The pointers had been there; he just hadn't seen them. He had allowed himself to be distracted and missed what was under his nose.

Tom lay back on the pillow, making a mental list of all the things he would have to find out tomorrow. And if all of that clicked into place, then he might just have it.

He would know who'd murdered Ryan Finnegan.

Saturday

'You're here early for a Saturday,' Michael observed. He'd entered his boss's office to drop off some paperwork and was surprised to find Tom already at his desk. They were all used to working weekends during an investigation, but there was no team meeting scheduled for today.

'Michael – good. Where is everybody else? Never mind. Who was tracking down the CCTV footage around the vicinity of Ryan's hit-and-run?'

'Ian Kelly, but I was giving him a hand. We haven't found anything. There's some footage near Ryan's house, but the last clip we have is from a garage where he stopped for petrol and a coffee.'

'You've read the accident report, then?'

'Yep.'

'Does it say anything in there about Ryan's condition at the scene of the accident? Was he conscious or unconscious? What was in his statement when he came round?'

'He was barely conscious when they got to him, but was able to nod and say a couple of words to one of the paramedics while they were taking him from the car. When he came to, all he could remember was leaving the house that morning. The doctors said that level of memory loss wasn't unusual for the trauma he'd sustained.'

'He spoke to a paramedic? What did he say?'

'He didn't raise a pointed finger and name the person who drove into him, if that's what you're getting at. The report says he asked for help but was struggling to make sense and stay awake.'

Tom massaged his jaw, deep in thought.

'Find that paramedic, Michael. Is it a man or a woman?'

'A man.'

'See if you can get him in. I take it he's named?'

'Sure. I'll round him up this morning.'

'Tell him it's urgent.'

Tom glanced at the clock on the wall as Michael left. Was it too early to start ringing people? He'd struggled to fall asleep last night, as his theory floated around his head. No matter what angle he came at it from, he kept arriving at the same conclusion. It was all so obvious now, but that bloody Resources Bill had completely distracted him.

The inspector looked at his list. He couldn't wait any longer. He had to start dialling.

By the time the other members of his team began to arrive, Tom had almost completed the calls.

Ray walked in as the inspector was finishing a conversation with Shane Morrison. He took a chair in front of the desk and waited, his forehead creased in puzzlement as Tom asked his final question.

'What's all that about?' he asked, when the call was finished. 'Was that Morrison? Isn't he being interviewed today?'

'Ah! Decided to turn up, did you? That's good of you. I thought you lot lived in work and it transpires you were just getting in five minutes before me. Yes, it was Morrison. I couldn't wait for his interview. And he's given me what I need. Now, I want you to do a job for me.'

'What?'

Tom pushed the notepad he'd been scribbling on across the table.

'What's that got to do with anything?' Ray asked, startled, as he read the question his boss had written alongside a list of names.

'You'll see. Don't tell any of them why you're asking.'

'That's hardly likely, considering I haven't a clue myself.'

'I have an idea. I don't want to go into detail yet because it's left field, but I feel in my gut it's right.'

'Are you moving on somebody today? If I get you the answer you want from this, how does that help?'

'I'll fill you in when you find out that information for me. I'll tell you one thing, though. You and Linda were right when you said at the start that it was unlikely Ryan was killed over a piece of legislation. You were dead right.'

Ray was confused.

'What about the interviews with the ministers?' he asked. 'I've moved them twice now.'

'Don't worry about that. I've spoken to everybody.'

His deputy raised his eyebrows.

Michael popped his head around the door.

'That paramedic is en route, boss. He was just coming off a shift in the Mater Hospital up the road.'

'Excellent. Right, I'll be there shortly. Michael, while you're here, organise a squad car to go out and keep an eye on Kathryn Finnegan's house, will you?'

Michael looked questioningly at Ray, who shrugged to show he was equally in the dark.

'Where's Laura?' Tom asked.

'Why, is she the main suspect now?' Ray jibed.

'Funny. Get her in here. Don't delay her with your witty repartee.'

While Tom waited for Laura he entertained himself by drawing circles around the list of names he'd called already.

The detective arrived minutes later, looking flustered.

'Sorry, boss, I didn't realise you were in. If it's about Morrison, I'll be doing the interview myself.'

'Don't worry about it; I've already spoken to him. I'm ahead of everyone this morning. Hopefully.'

Laura cocked her head, wondering what was going on.

'Tell me again about the two interviews you did with Grace Brady,' he said.

'I gave you the reports.'

'I know. I've read them. I wish I'd spoken to her myself, but it's too late now. Go through them with me again, in any case.'

Laura took a deep breath and relayed, as best she could, the exact exchanges over the course of both her encounters with Grace.

Tom leaned back in his chair, listening intently and nodding.

'And she mentioned Morrison, too?' he asked, when she'd finished.

'Yes,' Laura confirmed.

'Hmm. He was everywhere, just like Ray said. I'm surprised we missed it.'

'Sorry?'

'Nothing. Family matters, indeed.'

'You've lost me.' Laura shook her head.

'Something that Darragh McNally said in his suicide note.'

Tom pushed the phone across the desk.

'I want you to ring Grace and ask her something. Go gentle on her. Be apologetic, even sympathetic. Let her talk. And find out where she is. Discreetly. Don't scare her.'

He flipped to another page in his pad, where he'd written yet another question that had occurred to him last night.

Laura viewed her boss quizzically but didn't comment. Instead, she picked up the phone and dialled the woman's number.

The conversation lasted a number of minutes, most of them involving Grace being rude and uncooperative. Laura kept her cool and managed eventually to coax the woman into answering the inspector's question.

'Well?' Tom asked, when she had replaced the phone receiver.

Laura looked even more baffled.

'She says she slept with Blake. Boss, I don't understand what that has to do with anything. Why would we give any credit to what Grace Brady has to say?'

Tom sat forward, his elbows resting on the desk.

'Exactly. Who would believe anything Grace Brady has to say? That's why he slept with her. It's why Ryan Finnegan was willing to resort to using the photographs to change Aidan's mind. He knew how he'd be painted if he just came out publicly against the minister. An embittered PA, claiming Blake was manipulative, untrustworthy, and had a sordid past. Who'd believe him?'

'So, he went against his own principles.'

'Yes. But there was something far bigger going on than that Bill. Something that we overlooked and Ryan hadn't even considered. But I'm getting ahead of myself. Come and talk to this paramedic with me.'

They left Tom's office and made their way to the interview room, where a very tired man awaited them. The inspector took one look at Simon Kelleher and apologised profusely for having to bring him in. To his credit, despite having just worked a twelve-hour shift in a tough job, the young man was eager to help.

'Whatever you need, Inspector, though I'm not sure I can be much help. That said, you're lucky you're not relying on my partner, Eddie. He struggles to remember what day of the week it is, let alone the details of an incident six months ago.'

'You do remember the accident then?' Tom said.

'Yes. When I saw on the news that the same man had been murdered it brought it all back. I held his hand while my colleagues from the fire service cut the car roof off. It's awful to think he came through that only to die so tragically months later.'

The inspector agreed.

'It says in the report that he was semi-conscious when you arrived at the scene and managed a few words. Do you recall exactly what he said?'

'I do, as it happens. He only said one word though. Over and over. I don't think it will be much use to you. He just wanted us to help him.'

'Is that what he said?' Tom asked. 'Did he say "help"?'

'No.' Simon shook his head. 'He said "aid". Repeated it a few times. He needed first aid. I told him we'd treat him as soon as we had him out of the car, that he was in good hands.'

'Nothing else?'

'No. I visited him in the hospital a couple of weeks later. I do that sometimes, pop up to the ward and see how they're doing. He didn't remember me, but he was effusive in his thanks.'

'You deserved it. Thank you, Simon. You've been a great help. I'll get someone to see you out.'

'Really?' Simon looked bewildered. 'That's all you need?'

'That's all.'

Outside the room, Tom turned to Laura.

'What do you think?'

Laura blinked. Her boss had obviously pulled several strands of his hunch together, but she was still trying to grasp their meaning.

'I have an idea where you're going. But I'm struggling.' Laura was hoping her boss would keep going and not expect her to fill in the blanks.

'Let's start with the piece of information we just heard,' Tom continued. 'Simon is a paramedic, so when he hears the word "aid" he immediately thinks of "first aid". But that's not what Ryan was saying at all.'

'No,' Laura shook her head. 'He was identifying the man who'd crashed into him. Aid for Aidan. You have him, don't you?'

'Yes. When Ryan wrote that letter for Kathryn, he said he had a feeling he was in danger. Those weren't paranoid thoughts. His subconscious was telling him something. Aidan Blake had already tried to kill him once.'

CHAPTER 26

'This is becoming quite a habit, Inspector. I'm loath to invite the legal profession into our little conversations, but I feel I may have to if our tête-a-têtes are to continue.'

On the other end of the phone, Tom stiffened.

He'd been unable to get hold of Madsen that morning but had managed to reach him while they waited for a warrant for the search and arrest they were about to make.

'I just wanted to keep you up to date on developments, Mr Madsen. And also to let you know that I know.'

'Do you always speak in riddles or is that something reserved solely for me? What is it you know?'

'I know you've been lying to me about your relationship with Minister Aidan Blake. And I know that contrary to what you said when we chatted last Sunday, you are predisposed to blackmail, of the financial kind at least.'

There was silence on the phone, filled only by the slow breathing of the Danish man.

'That's a very grave allegation, Inspector,' Madsen replied coolly. 'I hope you have proof to back up your accusation.'

'No. I've no proof as yet. But let me fill you in on what I suspect. I'm not recording this phone call, Mr Madsen. We can do this properly at a later stage.'

Madsen sighed, a casual sound, but Tom knew the man was on his guard. He also thought he'd heard a little click, the sound of another line being activated, somebody listening in on the conversation at Madsen's end.

His advisor, no doubt.

'Proceed, Inspector. I don't have all day.'

'I understand. Let's start with this. When we met in your home, you told us you'd never met Aidan Blake in Government Buildings. That didn't translate to you never having met the minister at all.'

'I never implied that it did. I've seen the minister at many events.'

'Oh, your relationship is closer than that. During my first encounter with Blake, he referenced your holiday home in Donegal. He said it was built into the cliff, that it was palatial and like something from a James Bond movie. I saw that for myself. The thing is, most of the house's architectural delights aren't visible from the outside. Aidan Blake visited you at home. It's the only way he could have described it in that manner.'

'You visited my home.' Madsen laughed thinly. 'It's not surrounded by a moat. People are allowed entry.'

'Not many, though. You've stressed that you like your privacy.'

'That is true. But I'm very much in the dark as to why my relationship with Blake is relevant at all. I imagine you're going to enlighten me.'

Tom smiled bitterly. He sounded calmer than he was, while inside he was churning with anger. He despised men like Madsen, who believed they could control every situation – who had the money and power to evade the normal laws governing society. Madsen would get away with what he'd done somehow. But the inspector wanted him to know he had his cards marked.

'Do you know that Darragh McNally killed himself?' he asked.

'No. I was unaware of that. What a terrible tragedy. I'll have flowers sent to the family.'

'There is no family, Mr Madsen. McNally said in his suicide note that he'd been played by somebody. I believe that person was you. I suspect you bought him off as much for Aidan Blake's benefit as for Udforske's.'

Madsen made an effort at indignation, but Tom cut him off.

'McNally wanted to manipulate the minister and Blake is too ambitious to be controlled for long. The party chair might have thought he had his protégé where he wanted him, but it was a ruse on Blake's part. He said himself, contrary to what other people think, he's not easily led. We just didn't believe him. I kept buying the "he's only the spokesperson" line.'

'I haven't the least idea what you're talking about.'

'I apologise. I'm racing ahead. When you confirmed for me that Blake had been trying to ring you on the Saturday, you also said you hadn't taken his calls. Now, there are two items to note there. First, that Blake thought you would provide him with an alibi. Second, that even when your phone was on, you decided to ignore the minister. You were putting him in his place. You were only willing to help Blake so long as it benefited you. You weren't going to stand by the man in all circumstances.'

'Or perhaps I was just ignoring my phone as I usually do when I'm off, Inspector? Have you considered that during your wild speculations?'

'I have,' Tom answered. 'I also considered how you made it explicit that you generally deal with the man who "pulls the strings". But I don't believe you were being truthful. You said that Blake had fostered a reputation as untouchable, which doesn't mean he actually was. Blake having that sort of myth about him, however, would actually be quite useful to someone who had successfully won his influence. You also said that you hadn't pressed Blake on *this* issue.'

'Where are you going with this?' Madsen asked.

'Well, I think you're a very clever man. Blake's star was rising and you were backing him all along. McNally was just small fry. You're not the sort to stop at buying civil servants. You buy governments.'

'If only,' Madsen chortled affably. 'But if I had, what would be in this for Blake?'

'Good question. I know McNally needed money, but I suspect Blake wanted a powerful ally. He could promise you anything – the contract for a national broadcasting licence, State building contracts, anything Udforske wanted to expand into – if you committed to creating jobs and photo opportunities, and to support Blake in his campaign to become Taoiseach. You know how to play that game, don't you? You've spent a lot of time in Africa, as we discovered. You're probably used to buying influence in small nations everywhere, especially in countries that are basically bankrupt, like ours. The sad thing is that in the end, Darragh McNally realised what had been going on. I think somebody told him. He was planning to kill himself anyway, but I have a feeling he was helped along the way.'

'What you are implying, Inspector, is entirely incredible. Have you any actual evidence to support your claims? Are you expecting me to crack under the weight of your stunning exposition and make a confession of some sort? To what – running a business effectively?'

'No,' Tom said, unable to disguise the defeat in his voice. 'I don't expect you to confess to anything. Like I said, you're an extremely astute man and I'm sure you have a plan in operation to limit your company's exposure to the fallout from this. Because you should know, there will be fallout. We will trace those payments you made to McNally back to Udforske. Bribing a government official – I'm not sure what that sentence carries or if we can even indict you in Ireland – but I know it will look bad for your company. And I imagine that Bill that was going to help Udforske continue to make millions from Irish resources is dead in the water.'

Madsen sucked in air and exhaled slowly.

Tom waited.

'I'll leave you to chase your fantasies in your own time, Inspector,' the Danish man said, his tone icy. 'You won't trace anything back to Udforske because there is nothing to trace back. And you have wasted my time with some of the most ludicrous and unfounded charges I have ever had the misfortune to listen to. Other than some personal vendetta you must have against my company, I am still at a loss to understand why any of this is relevant to me.'

'You may be right,' Tom conceded. 'Maybe we will struggle to trace anything back. But I want you to know something. I want you to understand what you contributed to in Ireland this week – the collateral damage you and Aidan Blake have left in your wake. Two men are dead, Mr Madsen. One man was murdered because he wanted to stand up to the type of business you like to see done. Another man is dead by his own hand because of the predicament he allowed himself to become entangled in – with you.

'You show no feelings for either of these men. Perhaps the only thing you understand is money. But I have a theory about you. I believe you move in circles with men such as yourself. Men equally unsympathetic to other people's cock-ups. And you really messed up when you became involved with Darragh McNally and Aidan Blake. I think your peers – maybe the board members of Udforske, maybe the president of the company – will come after you.

'And I think you know that.'

For the second time on a call with Madsen, Tom was left listening to the dial tone. The other man had hung up. His anger had got the better of him.

And the inspector knew he'd landed his blow.

*

'Sorry about that. It's tax-filing week, the bane of my life. Silent Voices is one of the most transparent charitable bodies on the island, what with Sara being married to a minister and everything. But there's always something the auditor asks for that we're not expecting. What is it you need from me anyway?'

Ray was sitting in Hugh Masterson's office. He'd made his way directly to the headquarters of Silent Voices on Dame Street, near Trinity College in Dublin's city centre. His visit wasn't expected and Masterson had been in a meeting, which he'd cut short to accommodate the detective. Ray was grateful, but he hadn't minded the brief delay. It had given him some time to ponder how he'd ask Tom's question without putting Masterson on his guard. The detective had decided to start with him, as opposed to somebody from the Blakes' extended family, who would be more likely to clam up and ring the couple as soon as the detective had gone.

'I apologise for just landing on top of you like this,' he said, trying to ignore Masterson's shirt – a luminous pink affair that wouldn't have been unusual in a surf bar but was certainly out of place on a cold October morning in Dublin. Masterson was sitting with one leg resting across his knee, the rips in his jeans exposing dark-skinned hairy knees. 'We're just revisiting all the statements we took from people concerning events on Friday night. I know when you met with my colleagues you confirmed the timeline Aidan Blake gave us for leaving and returning to the charity ball with his wife.'

'That's right. I haven't remembered anything else, I'm afraid.'

'That's fine. You also mentioned that he seemed very cool with Sara when they returned – that she was upset.'

Masterson frowned, a look of puzzlement on his face.

'Yes. She did seem distressed. Why is that relevant, Detective? Sara's okay, isn't she? Her husband hasn't done anything, has he?'

The confused expression was transforming to one of concern.

Ray realised his route to asking the right question would be easier than he'd thought. Masterson was desperately fond of Sara and not happy about the idea of anybody hurting her.

'She's fine,' he replied. 'I'm afraid I can't really discuss her husband at this point, but do you mind if I ask you a couple of general questions about the Blakes' relationship?'

'Sure – whatever you need.'

'Does . . . Has Sara ever said anything to you about being afraid of Aidan?'

'Afraid?' Masterson was now fully upright in his chair, his features contorted in panic.

'Yes. Has she mentioned any problems they've had, any issues with his fidelity or stuff like that?'

The other man was shaking his head adamantly.

'No. No. If Sara had been afraid of Blake, I'd have known about it. I'd have intervened. I would never leave her in any danger. He upset her the night of the ball, but he's never been violent with her. And Sara wouldn't put up with that. She had a very difficult relationship with her father. He was a bit of a shit, by all accounts. Prone to giving her mother the odd slap. He never laid a hand on Sara, just ignored her, but she wouldn't stand for any abuse from Aidan like that. Her upbringing is why she's so protective of children now.'

'I see.' Ray rubbed his jaw. 'Is he unfaithful to her though?'

Masterson hesitated. His eyes flickered to a picture on the wall. Ray followed his gaze. The framed photograph showed Sara and Masterson at the front of a group of children, their arms around each other's shoulders and the small children to either side. They were both beaming for the camera, a happy couple.

'She's never said anything,' he said, turning back to Ray. 'But I have my suspicions. I think Sara is one of the most beautiful people I've ever known, inside and out. I've no doubt Aidan loves her, but he doesn't appreciate her the way she should be appreciated. He's too self-involved. I thought, for a little while, that their marriage wouldn't last, but they seem determined to make it work. And I think that's down to the fact she's so forgiving. No matter what he does, she stands by him.'

'How do you know he's trying to make it work?' Ray probed. He sensed they were getting close to what he needed.

'Well, they're going to have a child together.'

'Really?' Ray asked casually, but his heart was thumping. 'Is Sara pregnant?'

'No.' Masterson shook his head. 'She can't have children. Tragic, isn't it? A woman so brilliant with children, so caring. You would think she was destined to be a mother. But, sure, if it doesn't happen naturally, there are always other ways, aren't there, Detective?'

Ray looked at the other man, his face thoughtful. So Tom had been right. Jesus, his boss's brain worked in unusual ways.

'Yes,' he answered Masterson. 'There are indeed.'

*

The Blakes' house in Howth was quiet as the two cars rolled up the drive. Somebody was in – the gates had opened electronically when they pulled up. Aidan Blake wasn't answering his phone but Tom knew he was home.

The sky was darkening overhead. Bronze-coloured clouds had rolled in from the horizon and the air smelled of rain to come. Red, gold and brown leaves swirled in the breeze, their colours intensified by the surreal light.

The inspector had just spoken to the Taoiseach. After he'd filled Sean McGuinness in, the chief had told him to ring Cormac O'Shea immediately.

Tom outlined his theory for the Taoiseach, stressing that he was still gathering evidence but was moving to make an arrest on the basis of what he'd already established. The other man listened quietly. Belying his boorish reputation, he made an intelligent and considered contribution when Tom had finished.

'I thought I'd take more pleasure in the downfall of the people who would take my job,' he said. 'And I never thought I'd say this, but it sounds like Darragh McNally deserves justice. It seems I have more compassion than my enemies give me credit for. But I think the ending of a career in such ignominious circumstances for this individual will be a greater punishment than everything else that lies ahead.'

Laura parked the car, but the inspector didn't get out immediately. Ray's number flashed on the screen of his mobile. This was the last piece of information Tom needed. He answered the call.

'Well? Did you find out what I asked?'

'You were right. I just spoke to Huge Masterson. It wasn't a secret, but nobody thought the Blakes' family matters were relevant. Care to fill me in now?'

The inspector told him where they were and outlined the idea that had sprung into his head last night and what he'd done so far this morning to verify it.

'The motive was wrong,' Tom said. 'That's what threw me. I just had to look at it from other perspectives and take everything we'd been told into account. It wasn't the Bill we should have been focusing on. It was Blake's indiscretions. All that matters is family, as McNally said.'

Ray said nothing and Tom could sense he was flummoxed.

'It makes sense, now you say it,' he said. 'But I'm not sure it would have occurred to me. Have you enough to make an arrest?'

'I secured the warrant to seize Blake's car this morning,' Tom replied. 'He's ferried everywhere in a ministerial vehicle, but there's a garage behind his house. I've only ever seen one car parked out front, presumably Sara's, so his is probably sitting in there. I imagine he's had it fixed but it shouldn't be too hard to link it to the hit-and-run. Either way, I actually think he'll cave when I go in here. He's hardly a criminal mastermind. He could have killed himself in that crash.'

'Clearly. It's pure luck he got away with it at the time. He said himself he had a reckless side. We should have listened.'

'Get over here. We need to search the house and grounds for the weapon.'

'I'm on the way.'

The inspector rapped on the front door, waited a minute, then knocked harder.

'He wouldn't have fled . . .' Laura started, but stopped as the door opened. A haggard-looking Aidan Blake filled its frame. It was remarkable, Tom thought. In the space of a week, the man had deteriorated from a handsome, picture-perfect politician to a crumbling wreck.

'I knew you'd come,' he said. He smelt of alcohol and cigarette smoke. His shirt was stained with whatever liquid he'd been drinking but also with spots of what looked, alarmingly, like blood.

'Where's your wife?' Tom asked, nervously. 'Where's Sara, Aidan?'

Blake shrugged and stumbled into the hallway.

'Come in,' he slurred.

'My colleague will be joining me, as well as these two officers.' Tom indicated the accompanying guards. 'We have a search warrant for your property.'

Blake just raised his eyebrows.

'Coffee,' he said, leading the way unsteadily to the kitchen. 'I'll make coffee.'

Tom took a deep breath and followed the man down the hall. He pointed the two guards in the direction of the other rooms and gave them their orders. Laura stayed with her superior, ready to bear witness to what they hoped would be a confession.

They were armed and wore bulletproof vests, a necessary precaution given that Ryan Finnegan had been shot. It had been a while since Tom had visited the firing range, but he felt confident. And Laura went every other week, so he was safe with her as his wingwoman.

The kitchen, so homely and welcoming when Tom had first visited, was now a confusion of debris. It was evident there'd been an altercation. Fragments of broken cups and other crockery were scattered across the floor. A chair lay upturned in the centre of the room.

Blake fumbled at the counter tops, cursing because he couldn't find whatever he was looking for. Was Sara Blake injured somewhere in the house? Was that where the blood had come from, or had the minister hurt himself?

Blake slumped against the counter, running his hands through his hair, his expression one of despair.

'Where would she hide the damn coffee?' he moaned, as if that was the sole source of his misery.

'Aidan, I want to talk to you about the car accident Ryan was in six months ago,' the inspector said. There was no need for small talk. Tom knew, instinctively, that Blake wouldn't deny what he'd done. The minister was a desperate man who had been swept up in the events of the last few months. He wouldn't be able to maintain the lies, especially in this state. The inspector didn't know when the man had finally cracked, but he sensed it was after witnessing Kathryn Finnegan's grief on Thursday.

'Why?' Blake spat petulantly. 'You must know everything. That's why you're here, isn't it? I presume McNally left some sort of note. I thought, for a short time, that he'd be the one you'd stick it on. But he's not the sort to go off gently into the night. Oh no, not McNally. What diatribe did he spout for his final farewell? I should have stayed until he'd done himself in – made sure he didn't write anything down. I knew when I asked him to lie about me meeting Madsen I'd made a mistake. I never trusted the man. He'd have stabbed me in the back at any stage, but I thought I had enough dirt on him with the bribes he was taking. Why aren't you saying anything?'

Tom waited. Blake stared at him, drunken eyes shifting in and out of focus but still managing to look exasperated.

'Well, I drove into Ryan, didn't I?' he roared. 'He deserved it. Saint Ryan. It was all going so perfectly, until that shit from Thailand turned up with the photographs. My life plan. My goals. I've done stupid things in my life, but to be caught out like that, on bloody camera. How Ryan lorded it over me. All that hand-wringing crap. *You know I don't want to do this, Aidan. This is not my style.*' Blake mimicked the dead man's voice, chilling Tom and Laura. 'Turns out it was his style. Wasn't so much better than me after all, was he? But there was no way he was going to ruin everything I'd worked for.'

Blake banged the counter hard, then looked at his hands like they belonged to someone else. His countenance morphed from anger to despair.

'But . . . Kathryn. I hadn't given her a second's consideration until I saw her in the hospital after the crash. She had that tiny baby and she was so grateful Ryan was alive. She was so appreciative that I was there. I was ashamed. I'd only gone to see if Ryan remembered anything. He'd looked straight at me when I drove into him. He saw me, I know he did. But I was saved by memory loss, of all things. It's a pity he couldn't forget about those damned pictures.'

Blake started crying, tears of self-pity streaming down his face.

'Where's Sara?' Tom asked again.

'I don't know. I don't care. This was all for her, you know. She wanted the perfect marriage. I tried to give her everything. I can't help it that I have needs. I love her, I do. I'm just . . . weak. I need sex like a drug. I'm so ashamed.' Blake slid down the cabinet to the floor and pulled his knees into a foetal position. The inspector observed him coolly as he wrapped his arms defensively around his body and rocked back and forth.

'You couldn't give Sara everything though, could you?' Tom

said. 'You married her, never telling her about your sex addiction, pretending you had everything under control. Then there was the ultimate injury. You couldn't give her a child, the one quid pro quo she demanded.'

Blake looked up, his features furious.

'I was going to,' he snarled. 'It was all going to work out for us, until that interfering bastard Ryan stuck his nose in.'

One of the uniformed guards opened the kitchen door.

'Sir, you should see this.'

'Get up,' Tom said to Blake, and when the politician didn't move: 'I said get up or I swear, I will drag you up.'

Blake sniffed and pulled himself into an unsteady standing position.

They left the kitchen, the minister stumbling between Tom and Laura as they followed the guard to a room at the rear of the house.

Tom stood in the door frame, taking in the sight before them. The space was decorated beautifully, a show-house version of a child's nursery. It was obvious that each piece in it, from the ivory-coloured cot and wardrobe to the cream sash curtains and Winnie the Pooh clock, had cost a small fortune. No expense had been spared for the baby the Blakes were expecting.

The inspector turned to Blake.

'You let her down so badly, Aidan,' he said. 'Now, I'm going to ask you one more time. Where is your wife?'

*

While Laura practically poured coffee down Blake's throat in a vain attempt to sober him up, Tom phoned Michael.

'Is everything okay with Kathryn?' he asked when he got through.

'She'd gone out with the baby to meet a friend,' Michael said. 'Her brother's in the house – he let us know. The guards we sent out rang her and she told them she was fine and would be back soon.'

'Okay. Let me know if anything changes.'

They'd found Sara's passport and her wardrobe appeared intact. The minister had told them he and his wife had fought the night before but she was unharmed. He'd sustained some superficial cuts and bruises from various kitchen items she had thrown at him.

'What did you say to McNally when you visited him at home that night?' Tom asked.

Blake's face contorted.

'I used to respect that man, but Jesus, he really screwed up this last year. Carl let it slip that McNally wouldn't be a problem for me in the future, that he had him on a leash. In the end, that came in very handy. Taking bribes made it look like he had a motive for killing Ryan. I told McNally he was on his own. He was an absolute shambles by that stage. Slobbering and slurring his words.'

Tom beheld the drunk in front of him and let the irony of the moment pass.

'Anyway, I left McNally believing he was ruined – that you knew about the payments and his ongoing disputes with Ryan. It was my finest speech to date, Inspector. He was trying to drink himself to death anyway, but I planted enough seeds to push him to do something more drastic. I said he was going to end up in prison and he'd be remembered in the Party as a disgrace. That his mother's memory would be destroyed. He was sobbing like a baby when I left.'

Laura looked away in disgust.

'Where did the gun come from?' Tom snapped, determined to get what he needed from Blake. He couldn't let himself be riled by the man's callousness, not when he still had pressing questions. The inspector had more or less figured out the source of the weapon, after his earlier conversation with Morrison, but the man in front of him could confirm it.

'Sara's dad was in your line of work,' Blake answered. 'A detective. He arrested some paramilitary in the '70s and found the gun stashed in a barn. He kept it as a trophy. That's not the story he told her, of course. The version she got involved heroic tales of shoot-outs and her father disarming the guy before he arrested him. I got my hands on his service record. It certainly didn't happen like that. They arrested that lad in bed at five in the morning.

'I think she figured it out as she got older but she never let him know. It's ironic – Sara's father had no time for her and all she ever wanted was to please him. She's never been able to get beyond that rejection. He left her the gun and it was one of her most prized possessions. I picked up a silencer for it when I was abroad. It's one of the handy things about being a minister – no one checks your bag when you come through the airport.'

Over the minister's shoulder, Tom spotted Ray passing the back door and gave him a nod. His deputy would take charge of the search. Rain had started to fall outside. The lack of light would make the task more difficult. They still didn't know where Sara was. Could Blake be lying? Might he have lost it completely and taken it out on her? The inspector was getting anxious.

Blake prattled on but Tom found his thoughts drifting back to the conversation he'd just had with Michael.

A worrying thought started to crystallise, followed by a feeling like a cold hand on the back of his neck.

No. Surely not. Not now, when it was all falling apart anyway. What would be the point?

But then, were any of the choices made in the last week rational?

How long had Kathryn been out? Who was this friend she was with?

'Sir?' Laura queried. She could see the faraway look in her boss's eyes.

The penny dropped.

'Shit!' Tom pulled out his phone and redialled as fast as his fingers allowed.

His detective answered immediately.

'Michael. This is urgent. Who did Kathryn go to meet?'

There was silence.

'I don't know – let me check.'

He rang off.

Blake eyed Tom.

'What is it?' he asked, in a tone that said he wasn't sure he wanted to know.

Tom didn't respond. The phone rang again and he grabbed it.

'Kathyrn didn't tell her brother who she was meeting,' Michael informed him. 'But she mentioned she'd done something rash yesterday and needed to apologise to somebody. I think . . .'

'Christ almighty! I'm on my way.'

'What?' Blake choked, as the inspector shot up, his chair scraping noisily on the floor.

'Your wife!' Tom roared, his heart racing. 'What did she say to you when I left on Thursday – after Kathryn's visit? What did you fight about last night?'

The minister's face had taken on a greenish hue.

'She . . . she was furious that Kathryn knew about the photos. She said . . . but no, she wouldn't. I said no. I told her I'd kill her if she harmed a hair on that woman's head. We've done enough. Tell me Sara hasn't done anything. Tell me!'

'You should never have let her out of your sight,' Tom answered, his voice thick with raw anger. 'I think she's with Kathryn. If she hurts her, by God, I hope you can live with that.'

Tom yanked open the back door and yelled Ray's name. As his deputy came running, the inspector barked urgent instructions at Laura. He and Ray rushed from the house – while the man who'd set the tragic events of the last week in motion buckled and fell to the floor behind them.

*

'There was no sign of the gun at the house,' Ray said quietly, as the car raced towards Raheny.

Tom kept his eyes fixed on the road.

Blake's story about the gun had tallied with what Morrison had told him that morning. The inspector had toyed with the notion that the chief of security, evidently fond of Sara, had been some-how involved in Ryan's killing. However, the man had a solid alibi. Once that was cleared up, Tom had asked him to explain how he'd known Sara so long. It transpired that he and her father had worked together as gardaí.

'You said you got Sara her first job,' Tom asked. 'What as?'

'She started as a parliamentary assistant in Leinster House. I've always liked Sara. She was such a smart wee thing as a child. She hero-worshipped her dad but he had little time for children.'

'So, she was working in Leinster House when she met Blake?' Tom asked, another piece of the jigsaw slotting into place. Sara Blake knew the layout of the complex intimately and probably had her old swipe card, if she hadn't used her husband's, to get through any doors that would have been locked.

'Yes,' Morrison confirmed. 'She was working with a Reform Party TD and Aidan was the man's constituency organiser at the time. They hit it off immediately.'

'One more thing,' Tom said. 'You told us that the military police had been moved from their office in the tunnel because of upgrad-ing work. Is there maintenance work going on in any other part of the building?'

'Yes. We're modernising the electric systems in the bar and res-taurant area.'

And then he'd confirmed the remainder of Tom's theory.

'Did anybody else know that the fire alarms were turned off in those parts of the building?' the inspector asked.

The chief of security was quiet. Then:

'Only a few people knew. What does this have to do with anything?'

'Did Sara Blake know?' Tom persisted.

'Yes. We were having coffee last week and I told her.'

The man had been in shock by the time the phone call concluded.

The car skidded to a halt outside the Finnegan house. Tom jumped out first and sprinted up the drive.

Kathryn's brother and his wife were in the sitting room, anxiously awaiting his arrival. They and the two guards sent to keep watch had been trying Kathryn's mobile repeatedly and had then tried her friends' contact numbers. There was still no word of the young mother.

Her brother stood up when the inspector burst into the room.

'Did she say anything at all about where she was going?' Tom snapped. There was no time for niceties.

Her brother shook his head, distressed.

'She just said she had to meet a friend. I don't understand. What's all this about? She has Beth with her; she took the pram – are they in danger?'

'Think,' Tom insisted urgently. 'Where would she go? Did she mention anywhere this morning? Wait – you said she took the pram?'

He'd seen the car parked in the drive when they'd arrived. That meant she'd walked.

'Yes,' her brother nodded. 'So she can't be far. Unless she got a bus, but there'd be no need for her to do that – if she was going any distance, she would've driven.'

'Where would she walk to?' Tom continued.

'I've been trying to think. She's only been out of the house a couple of times since it happened. She said she needed air.'

'Does she have a favourite café? Does she like walking in the park? Does . . .'

Tom stopped abruptly and spun round to face Ray, who'd come in behind him. He had the car keys in his hand and was awaiting instructions.

'What is it?' he asked his boss.

Tom moved to the door, signalling to the uniformed guards to stay with Kathryn's family.

'I've got it. I know where Kathryn went.'

CHAPTER 27

Tom could not get the image of little baby Beth out of his head. Was Sara Blake capable of harming a child? He prayed that she wasn't. She was a woman who had dedicated her life to helping children, who herself wanted a baby so badly she had been willing to stay with a man she no longer loved to get one.

Of course, it was the threat to that plan that had driven her to the direst of extremes already.

The church was situated at Dollymount Strand, overlooking Dublin Bay. The wind had whipped up and the waves were breaking heavily on the shore. Rain pelted down, turning the white pebbledash of the church walls a dirty grey. The storm was winter-calibre and it was loud – violent enough that it would mask the sound of a gunshot.

Tom and Ray stood outside the back door to the old building, rivulets of rain streaming down their faces and the backs of their collars. The detectives hadn't rushed directly to the church. Instead, they had called into the adjacent priest's house. He'd confirmed that Kathryn had arrived earlier and said he had also greeted another woman, who was entering the building as he was leaving to get lunch.

'I hope Kathryn's okay,' he said. 'I spoke to her a couple of times this week and tried to offer some solace. I married the Finnegans and baptised young Beth for them. They were a beautiful couple. It will be such a tragedy to have to preside over the funeral of a man so young and so loved.'

The priest had given them a set of keys and told them they could enter via the vestry and from there, access the rear of the altar.

'We often leave the front door open for worshippers,' he said. 'But the vestry contains the valuables so it's locked unless one of us is in there. The doors have been oiled recently so they shouldn't make too much noise as you enter.'

Tom withdrew the keys from his pocket now. His hands were wet and the metal slippery. He inserted the key in the lock and turned it as gently as he could.

Silently the two men moved into the vestry, swiftly shutting the door behind them to block out the sound of the heavy downpour.

They heard it immediately: two raised voices and a baby crying. Tom couldn't discern what was being said, but immediately picked up from the tones that one voice was threatening and the other was pleading.

He crossed the room to the next door, smoothly sliding the second key into its lock. He held his breath as it turned, but it barely made a sound. Thank God the priest was on top of the church's maintenance.

Tom opened the door a fraction and peered through.

A marble pillar yards away from the altar obstructed his view of the two women beyond it.

He turned to Ray.

'They're in there,' he whispered. 'I have to go in. Stay here and keep the door ajar. If you hear anything out of the ordinary, come in behind me.'

'Shouldn't we wait for the Emergency Response Unit?' his deputy hissed back.

On cue, the baby screamed.

'Do you hear that?' Tom hissed. 'We can't wait.'

The inspector opened the door just enough to slip through. He was still invisible to anybody on the other side of the pillar but he ducked anyway as he crept towards the altar. He crouched behind the alabaster slab for a moment, then crawled to its edge to see around it.

From here, he had a view of what was happening in the mahogany pews below.

Kathryn Finnegan stood facing him. Beth was in her arms, thrashing angrily against her mother's firm grip. The young woman's face was pale, her eyes wide with terror and anguish as she tried to physically envelop the squirming baby to protect her.

Sara Blake was facing Kathryn, arms stretched in front of her.

Tom strained to try to see around Sara.

In that moment, his worst fears were confirmed.

Sara was holding her father's gun, the illegal Glock.

And she was pointing it at Kathryn and the baby.

'I said, put her down!'

Tom didn't recognise Sara's voice. It was loud and harsh, a world away from her usual soft-spoken timbre.

'I can't,' Kathryn wept. 'Please. I'm begging you. I'm all she's got. Don't do this. You're scaring her. Let us go.'

Neither woman was aware of the inspector's presence. Tom's heart raced. If he rushed Sara, would he startle her into firing the gun? He weighed up his chances of getting close enough to stun her with the butt of his weapon or wrestle her to the ground.

He didn't even know if she had the weapon primed. Would she take that risk, while it was pointed at a baby? He knew Sara was a proficient shot. They'd found no evidence of shooting lessons, but she'd picked up the skill somewhere. In these circumstances, however, with emotions charged and her hands shaking as they were, was she fully in control of the gun?

If he were to draw his own weapon, should he chance firing

at her and hope her reaction wasn't to pull the trigger? Could he scare her with his gun or would that exacerbate the situation?

One thing was certain – if she spun round and he did shoot her, it would have to be fatal or he risked her firing at Kathryn.

Tom only had one option. He didn't want to have to kill this woman. He just wanted to make sure she didn't harm anybody else before he arrested her for Ryan Finnegan's murder.

He had to get her to point the gun at him and then try to talk her down. Despite his Kevlar vest, he was aware that he was about to take a massive gamble. The presence of the baby and the fact Sara hadn't fired yet meant it was a calculated one, but a risk nonetheless.

Tom drew a deep breath, stood up and spoke her name softly.

'Sara.'

*

How the hell did he find us? Had Kathryn somehow managed to ring for help? But, no, the other woman's hands haven't moved from the baby. I'd have seen if she'd taken out her phone.

I don't shoot him. He's holding his hands up to show me that they are empty. That wouldn't stop me. If I wanted him dead I'd fire straight at his stupid, calm head without hesitation. All that's preventing me from firing is the unexpectedness of the situation. I hadn't factored him into the equation and now I'm not sure what to do.

'What are you doing here?' I say.

'I'm sorry if I scared you,' he replies.

He's trying to look non-threatening, when his very presence is alarming.

I know I look a state. I tried to smooth down my hair before I approached Kathryn, wipe away the smudged mascara. Still, she looked at me with eyes full of concern, just like he's looking at me now. He doesn't give a shit about me though. Not really. All his thoughts are for Kathryn and her baby.

'How did you know we were here?' I demand.

'This is where Kathryn and Ryan got married, Sara. She mentioned it to me the other day. She said that this was the only place she had been able to find peace. I imagine she had planned to come here today and then you rang.'

He's correct. We'd agreed to meet here but I didn't know she'd have the baby with her. Why did she bring the baby?

He's still talking.

'When she was at your house it was obvious she knew about the pictures of Aidan. You were worried she'd go to the media. I know everything, Sara.'

I laugh.

'What do you mean, everything?'

'I know what happened with Ryan. I want you to talk to me. But let Kathryn and the baby go. I'm pleading with you, Sara. Look at the child. She's terrified. She's tired and upset and probably hungry. Let Kathryn take Beth outside.'

'I don't want to hurt the baby,' I shout in Kathryn's direction. 'Put her down.'

'She can't,' the inspector pleads. 'Kathryn is all Beth has left. Would you really take away both that baby's parents?'

I lower the gun a little. I know he's deliberately focusing on the baby, repeating her name to me. It's a tactic and it's working. He knows I'd never hurt a child.

But her mother . . .

'I have to do this!' The scream that comes out of my mouth takes even me by surprise. He doesn't get it. 'You don't understand. Everything I've done – it will have been for nothing. She'll expose Aidan and everything will be ruined. She won't let it go.'

'What will be ruined? Sara, look at me. Talk to me.'

'I'm sorry,' I say, unable to drag my eyes from Kathryn. 'All I ever wanted is what you have. A child.'

She's standing there, dumbstruck. She looks paralysed, unable to comprehend what's happening. The baby, exhausted from crying, is now mewling quietly, relenting to her mother's strength and letting her body collapse against Kathryn's.

I can't bear to look at it. I crave that intimacy. I hunger for what they have.

'You say you know everything.' I turn to Tom. 'You can't. I loved Aidan Blake.'

And I did. When we were married, I didn't think I could be happier. He was my world. At last – I had a man who cared for me as much as I cared for him. It was only a matter of weeks after our wedding that I started to notice things weren't right. He had told me he'd been a bit wild when he was younger, that he'd slept around. He assured me that part of his life was over. But he tricked me.

Aidan is a sex addict. My husband. He wanted me to pity him and I did in the beginning when I didn't know what it was. When I thought I could help him. Before he gave me my first STD.

What a fool I was. I should have left him but I felt so trapped. Everyone expected us to work. How could the inspector understand that? I don't even understand the shame I felt. Like it was my fault I wasn't enough for Aidan. Like there was something wrong with me that he had to seek out sex with others.

'I know you loved him,' Tom says. He keeps talking. Why won't he shut up so I can think? 'But you were only prepared to stay if he gave you something in return.'

He isn't asking me. He's telling me.

'Yes,' I agree. 'A baby. That's all I want.'

It sounds so simple when I say it aloud. It's just a little word – baby.

If it had been Aidan's fault that I couldn't get pregnant, I'd have left him. I know that much. But I'm the one who can't have children.

'We're adopting,' I say and summon up the image of the gorgeous baby boy that I've only held once but feel like I've known forever. I have everything ready for him. It's almost finalised after years of waiting, an eternity of paperwork. Even with Aidan's job and what I do, there have been so many layers of bureaucracy. It's so damned difficult to adopt in this country.

'Did Aidan want to adopt from abroad?' the inspector asks, like he's reading my mind. 'With the help of Carl Madsen?'

I nod. Yes, my darling husband thought the whole thing could be that easy. I had put my foot down. I know what goes on in Third World countries. Kids bought and sold. It's inhuman. I could wait for a baby in Ireland. I was willing to do that. And then Aidan messed everything up.

'You had everything planned but you didn't know your husband was being blackmailed,' the inspector says.

The rage inside me when I remember finding out is so strong I want to pull the hair from my head. I want to howl. If I'd known, maybe I'd have gone with the Madsen idea. We could have moved somewhere. But Aidan kept everything from me until he was forced to come clean.

I stare at the inspector, wondering how much he knows. Does he know that I tracked down the Thai blackmailer and spoke to him? It took me all of five minutes to realise he was no professional. He was blackmailing Aidan to get money to buy drugs. So I paid him a bonus and the following weekend he was dead. An overdose. Anyone could have seen it coming.

Then there was just Ryan to sort out.

There was no way the adoption authorities would let us complete the process if those images of my husband were splashed all over the tabloids. And it would have just been the start. I'd told Aidan when I found out about his habit that he was to keep it to men and women who wouldn't be believed if they made claims. That silly bitch in his office, prostitutes – whatever. But if there was photographic proof out there, they would have started to come forward and they'd be believed. Our adoption plan would be in tatters and I couldn't let my little boy down like that.

'What Ryan planned to do was wrong.' Tom says it like it's a fact. For a moment, I feel like he's on my side.

'Yes!' I exclaim. 'Why would you ruin someone's life over some stupid piece of legislation? And Aidan had told Ryan that we were planning to adopt. What he was threatening to do would hurt me the most.'

Oh God, how quickly I went from being Ryan's champion to hating him with a passion.

Not that my husband was blameless. I will never forgive him for not agreeing to what Ryan wanted. Aidan's real problem was that he didn't think Ryan was capable of betrayal. He figured he was in the big league and Ryan wouldn't be able to take him on. I wasn't willing to take that chance.

'Did you talk Aidan into driving into him?'

I shake my head.

'I would never have suggested anything so utterly stupid. I told him to get rid of Ryan, not try to kill himself in the process.'

Aidan lost the plot when I told him he had to take Ryan out. He thought we should pay somebody to do it, until I pointed out that we'd have no way of ensuring that person wouldn't reveal our secret, or blackmail us later, keeping the whole cycle going.

'So, he failed once and you couldn't risk him failing again.' The inspector is trying to move closer, but I point the gun more firmly at him. My arms are quivering from holding it up so long and I know that this too is part of the strategy. Keep me talking until reinforcements arrive. What can I do, though? It's like my brain has ceased to function. I'm trying to think of a way out and I can't.

I answer honestly.

'I took the gun from Aidan in anger and went back to Leinster House. He came over with me, said he'd help me find Ryan. We split up. My husband went to the media rooms to check if Ryan had gone there and I went directly to his office. He'd left his emails open and I had what I needed.'

'Grace Brady saw you checking the emails, didn't she?'

I nod. I'd got such a shock when that ugly woman barged into the office and found me at Ryan's computer. But I turned the situation on its head. The idiot was labouring under the delusion Aidan loved her. I told her I knew everything. I left her in no doubt as to how her life would pan out once I'd finished destroying her reputation. She was sobbing and snotting all over her desk when I left.

The inspector is staring at me. He pities me, but he can't figure out if I'm calculating or just unhinged.

It doesn't matter, because now I know what I have to do.

And I don't mind talking for a few more minutes before I act.

*

'For God's sake, won't you tell me what's happening?'

Laura ignored Aidan Blake's question and crossed over to the back door. They'd take him in soon. Tom had asked her to stay at the house in case Sara returned but Ray had sent a text minutes ago saying they'd figured out where the minister's wife was and were en route.

The rain made a tremendous din as it battered the decking outside. Michael pulled the sliding door shut fast behind him as he stepped in from the downpour.

'Shit, I'm soaked through,' he said. 'Any idea what's happening?'

'Tom reckons they're at the church the Finnegans got married in. Will I stick on the kettle and make you a hot drink so you can warm up? There's no point in continuing your search in that weather. I guarantee we aren't going to find the Glock out there.'

'I need to go to the toilet,' Aidan Blake interrupted.

Laura sighed.

'Will you take him to the bathroom?' she called out to the guard stationed in the hallway.

'I really hoped we'd find that gun,' Michael said.

'I know.' None of them could bear to think of Sara loose with the weapon. 'But even if she has disposed of it, I doubt she'd choose the woods behind her house. We're looking for a needle in a haystack. Come on, we'll call it a day here. Let's bring Blake in and leave some officers behind just in case.'

'I'll round up the lads. Go on, throw on the kettle; we'll get everybody a cup of coffee first. Half the squad will be down with pneumonia at this rate.'

A yell from somewhere in the house startled them both.

The two detectives rushed across the kitchen and out to the hall.

'Where did it come from?' Michael asked frantically.

'Down here,' Laura answered, moving quickly towards an open door at the end of the corridor. She held her breath. Had Tom and Ray got it wrong and Sara was back at the house?

They burst into an empty bedroom. The door to the ensuite was open and through it Laura could see the blue-trousered legs of somebody half in, half out of the window.

'What the hell?' she cursed as she rounded the bed.

'He pulled the window down on my back when I leaned out,' the guard groaned in agony. 'I didn't hear him open it, but when he didn't answer me I looked in and he was escaping.'

'Jesus Christ!'

Laura turned and sped with Michael back through the house towards the front door, shouting to another guard to help their colleague. What a bloody amateur error. She'd assumed Blake was still drunk and useless. They'd never live this one down.

There was a loud bang outside. Michael threw open the front door just as a car flew around the side of the house, two officers running after it in futile pursuit.

'He drove through the garage doors,' one of them roared.

'Shit! Shit! Shit!' Laura felt like crying. Now they had a proper crisis on their hands. 'Call for backup – a 2010 dark blue Volkswagen Passat speeding down the Hill of Howth, most likely heading towards the Coast Road in the direction of Raheny. Tell them we're giving chase.'

She and Michael dashed through the rain to her car.

'What the hell is his game?' Michael was incredulous. 'Tom is going to kill us.'

'Let's worry about that later,' said Laura, as she swung the car around, spraying the house with gravel. 'I suspect Blake is gone to try to stop his wife from harming Kathryn. Maybe he thinks that will save him on Judgement Day. Anyway, buckle up. We're going to catch this dickhead before he causes any more damage.'

*

Tom was afraid to move an inch. He sensed Sara wanted to talk, but he wasn't sure if she wanted to get it off her chest or if, like him, she was stalling for time. He'd underestimated her before and didn't want to repeat the mistake.

It had started when he accepted her alibi too easily. Over the course of the last week it was apparent that people had come and gone from the busy Dáil bar on Friday night without being noticed – Damien Reid slipping out without Jarlath O'Keefe seeing, Madsen not noticing Blake had come in.

The fire exit had got him thinking. It led out to another Leinster House corridor. Tom had established it was never locked but discounted it because the fire alarm hadn't gone off that night. But Sara had known the alarm wasn't working and that's how she'd slipped in and out of the bar unnoticed. She'd made sure to keep circulating so she wasn't part of any specific group and wouldn't be missed. The woman was so small and plain that she was less than conspicuous to begin with. Then, when Aidan had entered the bar at 9.45 p.m., he helped with the smoke and mirrors effect, telling people he was up the back with Sara, even buying her a mineral water.

And Tom had made silly assumptions. The killer had chased Ryan Finnegan down flights of stairs. In Tom's old-fashioned mind, Sara Blake had come over to Leinster House from a ball and was probably wearing a dress and high heels. Linda pairing her gown with a pair of running shoes at his birthday party had triggered something in his brain. Laura had told him this morning that in the group photo of the ball, Sara was wearing a floor-length gown. It would have been easy for her to have worn trainers and nobody would have noticed.

'How did I do it?' Sara's voice seemed calm now. Her eyes, too. She looked less frantic. It was like she'd made a decision.

Rather than put him at ease, this new demeanour put Tom on full alert.

'I'm guessing you left the bar just before 9.30 and hurried over to LH2000,' he replied. 'You were fortunate you didn't bump into anybody in the corridor but you had to take your chances. You nipped into the lesser-used tunnel entrance so you wouldn't be seen going through the lobby. I'm guessing, if it was around the same time the Taoiseach entered the building, all eyes were directed at him anyway.'

Sara nodded encouragingly. 'There were a few people in the reception area with him; nobody was looking in my direction.'

'The whole thing took you under a half hour; so fast, you didn't have time to delete the images of your husband on Ryan's old computer.'

She hung her head before looking up again. 'Jesus, that damned computer. I couldn't get into the thing when I went back up to the office. I thought about smashing it but knew that would draw your attention. If I hadn't missed that picture of Aidan beneath Ryan, you'd never have gone looking for the photos.'

'That's probably correct,' Tom agreed. 'But we'd have got there eventually. I'm guessing you arrived back at the bar just before 9:55 p.m. Luckily for you, the last minister you had to find turned up around the same time. All along I thought you were lying for Aidan, but he was actually lying for you too.'

'Clever, huh?' Sara smiled thinly. 'It would have been easier if Aidan and I had just stayed together, then we would have been each other's alibi the whole time. But we split up to find Ryan. I knew what I was doing in the bar, but Aidan made the mistake of thinking Madsen would cover for him.'

'Were you planning to just threaten Ryan, or did you know you were going to shoot him?' Tom asked.

'I don't know,' Sara said, her eyes flicking to Kathryn. 'Maybe, in my heart, I thought I could appeal to him. But when I found him he slammed a door into me and ran off. It was like something took over. I chased him. I took the gun from my bag and when he didn't stop, I pulled the trigger.'

The inspector was conscious of Kathryn a few pews beyond, green with nausea as her husband's final moments were relayed.

He imagined that Sara had had to calm Aidan down after telling him what happened, and go over their alibi, which explained why it had taken them another half hour before they saw the Taoiseach and returned to the ball. He had thought they'd spent an unnecessarily long time in Government Buildings but assumed it was because Aidan was talking Sara round.

Tom's ears were tuned for any sounds out of the ordinary and he thought he could hear the hum of vehicles over the storm. He prayed it was the Emergency Response Unit.

'How did you know we were adopting?' she demanded. 'We never told you.'

'Hugh Masterson told us. He wasn't aware it was a secret. He hadn't said anything before because he didn't think it was relevant.

'I had begun to suspect that there was a more fundamental motive for Ryan's murder, something more important than the Resources Bill. At first, I thought Aidan was afraid he'd lose you and couldn't take the risk that Ryan would tell you about the photos, even if he rewrote the legislation. But when he allegedly revealed all about the pictures, you stayed with him. I had to figure out why.'

'I thought McNally would be your main suspect.' Sara sounded resigned. She had lowered the gun, defeat written all over her face. Tom didn't trust it.

'But then Kathryn came to the house and I knew it wasn't over.' Sara turned to the young woman.

'I didn't want to have to hurt you, Kathryn, but I want my baby. I was going to drive you somewhere nobody would find you. It would look like you'd gone mad with grief and fled.'

Kathryn looked like she wanted to vomit. She buried her face in Beth's hair, unable to look at Sara.

'McNally left a note when he committed suicide,' Tom said, drawing Sara's attention again. 'He swore he hadn't killed Ryan. He made a reference to the importance of family. I only realised later what he meant – you wanted children.'

'I suppose. When Aidan asked for his help dealing with Ryan he told him what the blackmail could do to our chances. McNally agreed to help but not for our sakes. It was to protect his relationship with Madsen. McNally never liked me. He thought I had got ahead of myself. He was my boss when I started working in Leinster House but then I married the man who became his boss.'

Tom said nothing. Something jarred with the sad tale.

In that instant, it came to him.

'You left the tunnel doors open,' he said.

Sara looked flummoxed.

'What?'

'You said you weren't sure what you were going to do when you saw Ryan, but you'd made sure if he did try to flee that he would head in the direction of the empty tunnel. If he'd tried to leave via the main entrance to LH2000, somebody might have seen what was happening through the lobby's glass frontage.'

A shadow fell across her face.

Tom didn't have time to wonder what her reaction meant. Something wasn't right. There was shouting outside.

Sara looked towards the bottom of the church. Kathryn did too, her eyes wide with renewed fear. She'd had the good sense to stay quiet for the last few minutes of the other woman's exposition, probably scared witless that if she spoke the baby would wake from her fragile slumber and the situation would explode again.

Sara noticed Kathryn's movement. Tom saw a range of emotions pass across her face as she looked at the young mother. Hate. Jealousy, because of the sleeping infant pressed to her chest. Confusion. Resolve. And then her gaze focused on Beth and Tom could see the slow, agonising realisation in Sara's eyes.

'I'm so sorry for what I've put you through,' she said, her voice despairing. Tom knew she was speaking to the baby, not to the mother. 'I never meant to hurt you. I didn't even consider you.'

Sara looked up at Kathryn.

'Aidan met you after he tried to kill Ryan in the car and he said it affected him deeply. You'd just had Beth. But I told him that that was all I wanted too . . . that your husband would try to deny me what you had. It was our husbands who did this, do you understand? Not you or me.'

Kathryn stared at Sara as Tom held his breath. She maintained her silence, but her eyes were animated, burning with injustice.

The church door burst open.

CHAPTER 28

'Don't touch her, you stupid bitch!'

Aidan Blake ran up the centre aisle of the church.

Sara spun round with the gun.

'What are you doing?' she cried, torn between shock and fury.

Out of the corner of his eye, Tom saw Ray come through the vestry door behind him and approach silently. A black shadow appeared in the frame of the front door Aidan had stormed through, its owner slipping into the back of the church. More followed. The Emergency Response Unit. They must have been taking up their positions when Blake arrived at the church. But how on earth had he ended up here?

'I'm warning you, Sara!' Aidan Blake roared. 'If you hurt that woman, you had better shoot me next. If you don't, I will put my hands around your neck and wring it. This has to stop, do you understand? It ends here.'

Sara stared at her husband, her eyes full of venom.

'What makes you think I wouldn't shoot you, you spineless piece of shit? If you'd done the job properly six months ago, we wouldn't be here. If you'd kept your trousers on, we wouldn't be here. There is a baby all alone out there waiting for me to become its mother. My little boy. How dare you . . .' She stopped, unable to put into words the loathing she felt for her husband.

Ray took the opportunity of Sara being distracted to creep towards the pillar. He caught Kathryn's attention and signalled to her to duck down and follow him behind the marble.

When they were safely behind the pillar, Tom positioned himself so he was in line with Aidan.

'Sara,' he said. 'Listen to me.'

Her gaze left her husband and travelled to Tom. She was so consumed with rage at Aidan that she hadn't even noticed the inspector moving. Realising she'd lost focus, she swore and looked behind her.

'Where – ?' she started to say.

'Sara,' Tom said more urgently. 'Stop. There are trained marksmen in position all around the church. At any moment, one of them could fire at you. You need to put down the weapon. Do you really want to lose your life? Should anybody else die for this?'

Sara looked at Aidan. Tom could see she was seriously considering shooting her husband. If she did, she'd be shot herself.

'Please, Sara,' Aidan said. He reached out his hand. 'Put the gun down. I'm so sorry it came to this. I don't want to die and I don't want you to die. You loved me once and I've never stopped loving you. This is all my fault. Please, don't let it end like this.'

Sara stared at his outstretched hand, her expression agonised. Tom almost felt sorry for her.

'I always thought that when I grew up I would be the adult that I'd needed as a child,' she said quietly. 'I wanted to do it for my own baby, not just other people's. I wanted that unconditional love. I've been so lonely for so long. I can't bear it any more.'

Time froze. The inspector didn't know what was going to happen next when Sara abruptly jerked her arm. Whether bullets were going to rain down on her. Whether she was going to fire at him or her husband.

Tom counted the next moments in heartbeats.

Sara raised the gun. In that instant, he knew where she planned to aim it, why she'd been happy to talk to him.

In one swift movement he crossed the space between them, just as she made to put the weapon in her mouth.

He dived at her, forcing her arms up and behind as she fell to the floor. Sara issued a blood-curdling scream as she fired the gun. The bullet hit the church ceiling, causing plaster to fall to the ground.

There was a moment of absolute silence after the bang, then a shocked cry from Kathryn that woke Beth.

This was followed by frenetic movement in the church as the Emergency Response Unit and Ray sprang into action, the former moving to secure the minister and his wife, the latter almost carrying Kathryn and Beth out the back of the church.

Sara strained against the inspector as he held her.

'Let go of me,' she howled. 'Let. Me. Go.'

She was surprisingly strong, but Tom had pinned her chest and arms down with his knees and prised the gun from her hands, sending it sliding across the floor to one of his officers.

He leaned down to her ear as she tried to claw and spit at him.

'Kathryn has to live without her husband for the rest of her life. That child will never know her father. You can live with that. I'm not letting you take the easy way out.'

Sara looked at him with absolute malice in her eyes and then he knew for certain. Her actions hadn't been those of a desperate, sad woman. She had known exactly what she was doing. She didn't care who she had to hurt to get what she wanted.

But it was over now.

CHAPTER 29

December

Sean McGuinness had been fiercer than usual when giving Tom his dressing down. He'd waited for a couple of weeks to pass – there had been too much happening immediately after for him to get stuck into Tom properly. He had been furious at his inspector's decision to enter the church that day before the ERU arrived on the scene.

His displeasure was kept private, of course. The media had been fed a line about how the heroic, quick-thinking actions of a senior inspector had saved the lives of a young widow and her child.

'You could have died. Kathryn Finnegan and that baby could have died,' McGuinness had bawled. 'What the hell were you thinking? It wasn't heroic, Tom, and don't you bloody well think it for a second. What you did was stupid and reckless and . . . stupid! And what the hell was Ray Lennon doing in that vestry the whole time? Singing hymns and drinking the communion wine?'

Tom took the bollocking. He had tried to explain to McGuinness that he had wanted to protect Kathryn and Beth and didn't think he had time to follow procedure but his boss was having none of it. So the inspector kept his head down and his mouth shut and waited for McGuinness's fury to expend itself.

'Don't assume there's room to operate outside the lines, Tom,' the chief said when he was done. 'Don't ever assume that. You came into my office a few days ago and complained about cops in

Donegal you thought were receiving backhanders from business-men. You moaned about political policing. Where's the line? If you don't work by the book, it doesn't matter how you justify it, you're breaking the rules. If you start making rash decisions like that now, thinking you know better, you won't be able to control where you end up. Am I making myself clear?'

Tom had nodded, taken aback by his boss's final remarks. He hadn't considered his actions in that light. Not for a second. He felt indignant, but at the same time knew he would give careful consideration to what McGuinness had said. He had too much respect for the man to do otherwise, even if a part of him felt that his boss was angry for reasons that went far beyond the job.

Tom mentally dissected that recent exchange again as he and Ray stood to one side of the graveyard. They'd driven Kathryn out with Beth to visit Ryan's grave. She could have taken her own car, of course, but the inspector knew she was still trying to come to terms with everything that had happened and needed the com-pany. He would continue to check in with her from time to time, to make sure she was coping.

'You never really said – when did it all click in your head?' Ray asked, breaking the silence. 'I know all the details, but when did it all come together? What was the lightbulb moment?'

Tom didn't mind telling him. He'd kept the members of his team in the dark that morning as he'd waited for proof of his hypothesis. Ray was still learning and needed to know how his boss's brain ticked. It was no use if Tom just announced the mur-derer's name like they were playing a game of Cluedo, without rationalising how he had arrived at his conclusion.

'I had a row with Louise on the night we found McNally,' he said.

'You two argue?' Ray feigned horror.

'The secret to any successful marriage,' Tom retorted. 'Bicker often and never be afraid to have an all-out stomper. It clears the air. Just remember to always make up and no matter what she's done or said, you say sorry first. Trust me. Women love the s-word.'

'What was it about?'

'It was about . . . personal stuff. But I suppose I have to tell you for this to make sense. It concerned children. Maria is thinking of moving out and Louise realised we're facing an empty nest. She had been given what felt like a second go at motherhood and suddenly it was being snatched away.

'It occurred to me − my wife is a good woman, through and through, but the desire for children can make people desperate. We only had Maria but wanted more kids. It just never happened. The Blakes were desperate for a child. When you think of the money and time people devote to IVF, to adopting from abroad, even resorting to buying children . . .

'Obviously, not very many people would be willing to murder to acquire one, but babies provoke very powerful, basic emotions. Aidan was always on our suspect list, but I'd overlooked Sara because I couldn't see her motive for murdering Ryan.'

'You did wonder about her, though,' Ray said.

'Fleetingly. I asked Linda if she thought Sara could have killed a man for her husband. Linda discounted the notion of her protecting Aidan for his own sake. She knew Sara didn't love Aidan enough to kill for him. But, ultimately, she would kill if her husband's ruination would affect something she wanted.'

'You know she's trying to plead insanity?'

'Hmm. Figured as much. It won't work. The level of planning involved proves premeditation.'

'How long do you think Blake will get?'

Tom shrugged.

'He's claiming Sara forced him to make that first attempt on Ryan, trying to apportion all the blame to her and make out he was manipulated. It's a weak defence. We've nothing on him when it comes to McNally, though. The man committed suicide. It doesn't matter how much poison Aidan dripped in his ear.'

Ray's phone beeped. Tom knew from the look on his face who had texted.

'Laura?' he said.

'Hmm. She's asked us to drop by the station. We think that man murdered in Wexford last night might have been done by the same gang who killed that chap in Dublin last July. The stabbing incident.'

'We'll bring Kathryn home shortly then shoot over. How's Laura's boyfriend keeping?' he asked. It was like being a minor character in *Romeo and Juliet*.

'Not great, would be my guess,' Ray smirked. 'She called it a day.'

Tom observed his deputy closely. 'I hope you know what you're doing,' he said, at last.

Ray nodded, his face serious.

'Yeah. I do, actually. Anyway, what's the story with your love life? Will you and Louise be trying for another little one?'

Tom cocked an eyebrow at the younger man, ignoring him and turning back to look at Kathryn.

He'd read somewhere once that the secret to happiness wasn't getting what you wished for but being grateful for what you already had. He and Louise had each other. They had their family and friends and their lives were complete.

Sara Blake had seemed to have it all but, beneath the surface, she was an unhappy woman, full of loneliness and bitterness.

Aidan Blake was a man with the world at his feet. And yet he had set himself on a path of self-destruction and paid the ultimate price.

Then there were those closer to home. Sean and June, so content for so long and now facing the biggest battle of their lives.

And here they were with Kathryn and Beth, a young family robbed of a man they held dear, their future torn asunder.

Tom had been complacent with Louise, not paying enough attention to his marriage and her needs. He'd had a little reminder of what was important during this case. He knew he would keep doing his job to the best of his ability. He also knew that, as soon as he was able, he would retire and spend more happy years with his wife and family.

That would be his happy ending.

*

Beth kicked against her mother's stomach then pulled her knees up and pushed her arms out, making it impossible to hold her. The ground was probably too cold to put her down but Kathryn relinquished her anyway.

'Just for a moment,' she said, in her sternest voice. The baby looked up at her with big eyes and a round, open mouth. She turned to her father's grave, picking up the white gravel stones and shoving a handful in her mouth.

'For heaven's sake,' Kathryn said, and sank to her knees. She extricated the now spotless stones and gave Beth a baby biscuit from her pocket, then plonked the child back down against the corner stone of the grave's surround.

'Do you see what I have to put up with?' Kathryn spoke in the direction of her husband's headstone. 'She's a little despot. She's started crawling and has everything pulled asunder in the house and me driven demented. Don't you, you naughty girl?'

The baby placed her hands on her mother's knees and raised her mouth for a crumby kiss.

'Mmm, chewed-up bikkie. How nice.'

Kathryn wiped her lips as the baby fumbled at her pockets for more treats.

'Tom drove me here,' she said, addressing the headstone. 'He and Ray are very good. They've called out to the house a few times.'

Her voice started to quiver but she steadied it as she stroked the stone plaque. *Beloved son, brother, husband and father. Always missed.*

Beth watched her mother and leaned over to touch the stone in imitation, leaving a sticky handprint on the smooth granite.

'There, she's marked you, Ryan. Like everything at home.'

Kathryn touched their daughter's cheek, flushed red with the cold. The baby didn't mind the temperature but they'd have to go soon.

The grief was still raw. It was so hard to believe her beautiful husband was lying beneath the frigid soil, barely six feet from her and yet an eternity away.

'Dad. Dad-dad.'

Kathryn flinched.

Everybody had told her Beth's first word would be 'dad'. Not because she was calling for her father, but because it was the easiest sound for a baby to make. And she made it as often as she could. When she first said it a couple of weeks ago, Kathryn had almost had a heart attack. She didn't mind it now. In fact, she liked to think that Beth was actually saying 'dad' for Ryan. That she remembered him.

'Yes. This is where Daddy sleeps,' she said, picking up the baby. 'And he watches over us all the time, doesn't he? Because he loves us soooo much.'

It was time to go.

'Let's go back to the nice guards, shall we?' she said, standing up.

Kathryn heaved herself into a standing position, struggling with the weight of the growing infant in her arms. The sooner Beth started walking, the better.

She turned to face the grave one more time.

'I'm still angry with you, Ryan,' she said, 'for leaving us. But I know you didn't want to. I'd give anything to have you back. I can't accept that you're gone.'

She rubbed her eyes with the sleeve of the brown and yellow

striped raincoat. It hadn't improved with age. The garment was still as hideous as it was the day Ryan's mother had given it to her. Tom had laughed with her when he saw it for the first time, then given her a big hug. Now she wore it every time she came to the grave. She didn't know why. Perhaps she hoped one day she'd find another letter in the pocket.

She reached in, knowing she'd only find a handful of biscuits and her phone.

But there was something else in there. Pebbles.

'Are you putting stones in Mama's pocket, you divil?' she said to Beth. Kathryn looked down at them, then smiled and put them back in her pocket, her heart still sore but filled with love for her baby girl.

She couldn't come here every day, but the little white pebbles would be her reminder of Ryan.

EPILOGUE

He'd won them round. They'd been sceptical at first. The moustache was often his least off-putting characteristic. Being a politician was nearly worse than being a cop in these parts.

Some people were amazed that Jarlath O'Keefe wasn't known by one and all, as if unusual facial hair and dapper dress should make him a household name.

He knew better. In Galway, he was a rising star. But most people were only ever aware of their local politicians, if that. The general public was at a remove from the whole democratic process and its players.

Sure, weren't all politicians the same?

That's what made party leaders stand out. They ventured beyond the boundaries of their narrow home constituencies. They made the effort to attend fundraisers and benefit nights, canvasses and candidate selection conventions in places where there were no personal votes to be garnered. Many people wanted the glory of being the leader of the country, but very few were prepared to put in the Herculean effort required to get there.

Jarlath had charmed the establishment's owner, Mattie Moorhaven, first. The old fellow propping up the bar had been the next to warm to him. But the real coup de grâce was the younger man, Padraig Óg. He was the opinion former in the village, Jarlath could tell.

He'd used the lines that had become second nature to him over the last couple of weeks. 'There are no votes for me here. I've nothing to gain from travelling to see you. In fact, I have every-thing to lose, considering I'm probably missing an event in my hometown as we speak, not to mention upsetting the party man-darins in Dublin. But I want to hear what you have to say.'

It worked every time.

They told him the same tale he'd been hearing the length and breadth of the west of Ireland. Local economies decimated by the centralisation of public services. Post offices closed. Rural transport cut. Garda stations unmanned. Fishing a dying art. Multinationals pillaging the coastline and giving nothing back. Politicians promis-ing the sun, moon and stars but leaving their loyalties on the train when they arrived in Dublin. A government perceived as aloof and at a remove from its citizens.

The Taoiseach was gripped in a crisis of such magnitude it threatened to topple him. It didn't matter that the actions of Blake and his wife had nothing to do with O'Shea. People wanted to know how the Taoiseach could have appointed such an unstable man to high office.

O'Shea was facing the storm head on, but no matter how much others in the party might support him privately, public endorse-ment was not an option. Not for anybody who cared a jot about the party's survival. The full details of the Finnegan case were still undisclosed. Once the story about the Resources Bill got out, O'Shea would be done for anyway. If the Reform Party didn't change its leader, the public would force it from government, egged on by headlines and editorials.

Why not me?

Jarlath had asked himself that question many times. He was young. He was smart. He'd topped the poll in his Galway constitu-ency and he was willing to put in the hard yards around the country. He'd no hidden skeletons. He'd no family commit-ments.

One more scandal would see out O'Shea.

Jarlath selected the number on his hands-free car phone, admiring the picture postcard Donegal landscape as he drove.

A female voice, smooth and professional, filled the car.

'Jarlath, as I live and breathe. I thought you'd be afraid to ever waste my time again. To what do I owe the displeasure?'

Emily Heaslip had attended the University of Galway around the same time as Jarlath. He'd taken the political route, she the journalism road. Which was just as well. If she'd gone into his line of work, she'd already be Taoiseach and he wouldn't stand a chance against her. Emily was like a dog with a bone. Once she got it in her head to do something, it would be done. It made her an excellent journalist and a real thorn in the establishment's side. Which, in a small state like Ireland, could leave her very isolated.

'I just wanted to hear your dulcet tones, Emily my lovely. Are you still keeping a flame burning for me?'

She snorted.

'Yes. A flame and a canister of flammable liquid. The tip you gave me a few months ago about your pal in Leinster House and his dodgy tax affairs – do you have any idea the research hours I put into that? You said it was an exclusive and the bloody *Times* broke the story a week before I was ready to move. Thanks a bunch, *chara*.'

'I swear, that had nothing to do with me. I never spoke to the *Times*; I was just happy to give them a quote when they rang. What else could I do, Emily, pet? They asked me my position on a colleague failing to meet his revenue requirements. I could hardly say "no comment". I tried to tell you all this at the time. I offered to, over a bottle of Bordeaux, remember? Someone else must have known what he was up to and given them the scoop. You know I only have eyes for your work.'

'You're taking up more minutes of my life, Jarlath. What do you want?'

'I have a peace offering.'

'I'm not having dinner with you.'

'Control yourself, temptress. You playing hard to get like this is really doing it for me.'

'Ugh. I just got sick in my mouth.'

Jarlath laughed.

'Do you want this or not?'

'It really depends on what *this* is.' Her voice had softened. Just a little.

'Oh, it's big, baby. Very big.'

'Now I know you're talking about a story. You couldn't possibly be describing anything else, you sexist twat.'

'Hush, now. I want to meet. I've something to show you.' His tone grew serious. He was enjoying the banter, but this was no laughing matter.

'Okay. More innuendo but let's assume you're not BS-ing me. What have you got?'

Jarlath glanced at the photocopied pages on the passenger seat beside him. The draft legislation lay open at the appendix where he had highlighted the one short, innocuous-looking paragraph.

The opposition would have seized on it anyway, he'd reasoned, before deciding to call Emily. But then they would have got all the coverage for exposing the Resources Bill's fatal flaw and he, Jarlath, would have been rolled out along with his colleagues to defend the damned thing. And what was the point in having sources if you didn't put the information they gave you to use?

Leaking it would put him ahead of the curve. Emily would run the article and he'd be the heroic whistleblower, horrified at the discovery of further duplicity by Aidan Blake and Darragh McNally. Other cabinet members would be implicated including, importantly, the Taoiseach. Jarlath was sure of it. He would be the one doing the implicating.

And when the dust settled, people would remember that he

had stood up for Reform Party principles and done what was right, not what he was told to do. It was a risk, but a calculated one. The previous government still had too much work to do before they would be forgiven for their multitude of sins. People wanted to believe in the Reform Party. They just needed to see some of that accountability they'd been promised.

His plan was a thing of beauty. And it had the added benefit of delivering one in the eye to Carl Madsen and all those cunning bastards in the exploration and drilling game who thought they were getting another free pass from the Irish State.

'You know that piece of legislation Aidan Blake was working on – the one on natural resources?' Jarlath said.

He could sense the crackle of static energy on the phone line. The mere mention of Blake's name was enough to send journalists into a tizzy these days. Other party members were engaged in damage limitation and rising above speculation about the former minister, using the 'legal due process' line. Jarlath was about to give Emily the Holy Grail.

'I know of it,' she said, unable to keep the excitement from her voice. 'I've even heard a rumour or two about it, but I've yet to see a hard copy of anything. Why?'

'I think you'd better pucker up those juicy lips of yours and get ready to give me a big kiss, because I'm about to give you an early birthday present. I have the Bill and I'm en route to Dublin to give it to you.'

There was silence, then Emily whooped.

'You know what?' she said, when she had calmed down. 'That little double entendre is about the nicest thing I've ever heard. Name the time and the place.'

He did and ended the call.

Jarlath smiled.

He'd remember Emily when he was Taoiseach. She'd earned her stripes. He'd get her a nice little number in the government press office, if she'd take it. Nothing like a poacher turned game-keeper on your side.

And Tom Reynolds. That was the inspector's name.

Someone that clever couldn't stay a detective inspector forever. He'd pull a few strings and make sure Reynolds was promoted.

The man would love him for it.

He'd also call in to see Kathryn Finnegan when he got to Dublin. He'd met her at Ryan's funeral and called out to the house to offer condolences a few weeks after. There was something about her. She was clearly devastated by the death of her husband but she had an inner strength – you could see it in her eyes. She would survive. He felt humble when he was around her, like he should be a better person. If she would let him, he'd like to be a friend to her small family.

Jarlath stroked his moustache with his free hand.

He'd buy a razor in Dublin. If he wanted people to start taking him seriously, the facial hair would have to go.

ACKNOWLEDGEMENTS

I have four little people who make everything in my life, even being an author, feel that bit more special. Thank you, my beautiful children.

My extremely patient husband – I might want to kill you when you're helping me edit these books, but I think our marriage is stronger for it. I think! I love you, Martin Spain.

To all my early draft readers – I feel so sorry you never get the polished version, always the rough, unwieldy Word documents to fight your way through. But you know you make it better, Fern, Pearse and Roisín.

Aengus, you opened up a whole world of history and architecture for me for this book. Go raibh maith agat, a chara.

To my wonderful editor Stefanie Bierwerth; to Kathryn and Hannah and all the fantastic teams at Quercus and Hachette, thank you. Sometimes it's the little words of encouragement, sometimes it's the gigantic flashing arrow pointing me in the right direction – all of it is gratefully received.

And to all the family and friends who offer me love, support, encouragement and lashings of praise – oh, where would I be without the praise! I'd be lost without you.